GALACTIC EMPIRES

GALACTIC EMPIRES

EDITED BY
Gardner Dozois

SFBC
SCIENCE
FICTION

First Science Fiction Book Club printing February 2008

Published by Science Fiction Book Club, 401 Franklin Avenue, Garden City, New York 11530.

Visit the Science Fiction Book Club online at www.sfbc.com

ISBN: 978-1-58288-291-8

Printed in the United States of America

For Andy Wheeler and Ellen Asher

Contents

Preface

Ever since the specific *science fiction* adventure story began to precipitate out from the larger and older tradition of the generalized pulp adventure story, the form that slowly emerged as being most specific to science fiction was the *space* adventure story. It was thus differentiated from the kind of Lost World/Lost Race adventure that went all the way back into the middle of the nineteenth century. It was usually different in tone as well from the more solemn, slower-paced, Visit to a Future Society story popular with Hugo Gernsback and other editors, which, especially after Wells, tended toward Utopian polemic and ran to guided tours of the Great Steam Grommet Works.

The paper spaceships of science fiction have been flying through the entire twentieth century now and on into the twenty-first, since the first proto-space operas like Garrett P. Serviss's *Edison's Conquest of Mars* and Robert W. Cole's *The Struggle for Empire* were published in 1898 and 1900, respectively. At first, writers tended to stay in the solar system, which, in their hands, was as crowded and chummy as an Elks' picnic, chockablock with dozens of alien races, featuring a habitable Mars and Venus, even a habitable Mercury (even occasionally depicting gas giants like Saturn and Jupiter as fit abodes for humanoid–and usually sword-wielding–races). E. E. "Doc" Smith may have been one of the first to venture into deeper stellar waters beyond the solar system in 1928's *The Skylark of Space,* but it wasn't long before writers such as Edmond Hamilton, Ray Cummings, Raymond Z. Gallun, and, somewhat later, John W. Campbell, Jr., Clifford D. Simak, and Jack Williamson were launching paper armadas of their own into the gulfs of interstellar space, issuing in the so-called Superscience era of the '20s and '30s—and the first stories depicting Galactic Empires as well.

By the '40s and '50s, the stage upon which the science-fiction adventure story could be played had been greatly widened, with the rest of the Galaxy—and, indeed, the rest of the universe—becoming the playground in which the imaginations of SF writers were allowed to freely roam; the permissible scope for an adventure and the size of the stakes at risk had also been greatly increased; it was not for nothing that Edmond Hamilton, for instance, was sometimes referred to as "World-Wrecker" or "Planet-Buster" Hamilton, and the space fleets of immense mile-long space-dreadnoughts armed with awesome world-shattering super-scientific weapons that were launched in those days have continued to prowl through deep space throughout all of the subsequent history of science fiction, and, thanks to films such as *Star Wars* and TV series such as *Star Trek,* right on out of the print media and onto television and movie screens, and even onto computer monitors in the form of space-adventure computer games.

Against this busy background, Galactic Empires became a commonplace. The most sophisticated early treatment of the theme of a galaxy-spanning empire, and the one taken the most seriously as mature science fiction rather than "just" adventure writing, were the Foundation stories of Isaac Asimov (which borrowed the rise-and-fall dynamics of the Roman Empire, via historian Arnold Toynbee), but there were a lot of other competing Galactic Empires out there in SF's fictive space, including those featured in James H. Schmitz's Agent of Vega stories, Jack Vance's tales of the Gaean Reach, Poul Anderson's stories of the Polesotechnic League and his stories, set later in the same Future History, depicting government agent Dominic Flandry's doomed attempts to keep the Long Night from falling on the Terran Empire, A. E. Van Vogt's stories of the War Against the Rull and the Empire of the Atom, Cordwainer Smith's ornate descriptions of the far-future empire of the Instrumentality, L. Sprague de Camp's tales of the *Viagens Interplanetarias,* A. Bertram Chandler's adventures among the Rim Worlds, and many others. Toward the end of this period, which can clearly be seen in retrospect as the Second Great Age of the Space Opera, we got Frank Herbert's *Dune,* which dealt with the clash of empires and worlds on a scale that surpassed even what most of the Star-Smashers of the Superscience era had been up to. (And at about the same time, the early '60s, we also got a few novels such as Ursula K. Le Guin's *Rocannon's World* and Samuel R. Delany's *Empire Star,* almost totally unnoticed and unremarked when they first appeared, that would nevertheless foreshadow many of the aesthetic transformations of the space adventure tale that would take place in the '80s and '90s. Delany's 1968 novel *Nova* can thus be seen as either the last important space opera novel of the '60s or one of the precursors of the New Space Opera of the '80s, depending on how you squint at it.)

However, by the late '60s and early '70s, perhaps because of the prominence of the New Wave revolution in SF, which concentrated both on introspective, stylistically experimental work and work with more immediate sociological and political relevance to the tempestuous social scene of the day (critics like Brian W. Aldiss would call for more stories dealing with the Vietnam War, the "youth movement," the ecology, the sexual revolution, the psychedelic scene, and so forth, while, in England, Michael Moorcock would utter his famous demand for work with "real drugs, real sex, really shocking ideas about society"), perhaps because of scientific proof that the other planets of the solar system were not likely abodes for life of *any* sort, let alone oxygen-breathing humanoid natives that you could have swordfights with and/or fall in love with, perhaps because the now more-widely-understood limitations of Einsteinian relativity had come to make the idea of far-flung Galactic Empires seem improbable at best, flat-out impossible at worst (there were those, even SF writers, who said that the whole idea of interstellar flight *itself* was wishful nonsense, never mind Galactic Empires!), science fiction as a genre was tending to turn away from the Space Adventure tale—and the idea of Galactic Empires now seemed outdated and obsolete, something from a dead future that had already become the past without ever coming near the present.

Although a few stalwarts such as Poul Anderson and Jack Vance and Larry Niven continued to soldier on, there would be less Space Adventure stuff written in the following ten years or so than in any other comparable period in SF history. The generation of new writers who would come to prominence in the late '60s and early '70s would write almost none of it, for instance. By far the majority of work published during this period would be set on Earth, often in the near future. Once the space probes of the late '60s and early '70s had "proved" that the solar system was nothing but an "uninteresting" collection of balls of rock and ice with no available abodes for life, dull as a supermarket parking lot, even the solar system was largely deserted as a setting for stories, let alone the distant stars.

But by the late '70s, writers such as John Varley, George R. R. Martin, Bruce Sterling, Michael Swanwick, Gregory Benford, and others came along who began to take interest in venturing into space again, away from the near-future Earth, writers who (even before the later *Mariner* probes to the Jupiter and Saturn system had demonstrated that the solar system was a lot more surprising, complex, and even paradoxical a place than people had thought it was), seemed to find the solar system lushly romantic *just as it was*, lifeless balls of rock and all.

By the '80s, writers such as Iain Banks and M. John Harrison in Britain and C. J. Cherryh, Dan Simmons, and Greg Bear in the United States would be launching paper spaceships out into the interstellar void again, armed with new workarounds for transcending Einsteinian relativity that, even if they were scientific doubletalk, at least *sounded* plausible, and made an attempt to draw upon the latest cutting-edge up-to-date scientific thinking. By the '90s, fueled by authors such as Paul McAuley, Stephen Baxter, Peter F. Hamilton, Vernor Vinge, Greg Egan, John Barnes, Gwyneth Jones, Walter Jon Williams, Ian McDonald, Lois McMaster Bujold, and Stephen R. Donaldson, SF writers had spread out through the Galaxy again, and as the twentieth century gave way to the first decade of the twenty-first, a flood of like-minded writers such as Alastair Reynolds, Charles Stross, Robert Reed, Ken MacLeod, Tony Daniel, John C. Wright, Sean Williams, Karl Schroeder, Justina Robson, Neal Asher, John Meaney, Elizabeth Bear, Scott Westerfeld, and many others left little doubt that the third great Age of Space Opera was under way.

Suddenly Galactic Empires were back in style again, bigger, more intricate, and considerably *stranger* than ever before. In this anthology, we've asked six of the very best science fiction writers in the business today—Peter F. Hamilton, Neal Asher, Robert Reed, Alastair Reynolds, Stephen Baxter, and Ian McDonald—to reenvision the Galactic Empire story for the twenty-first century, and I think its safe to say that the results are not only more surprising and more imaginative than we could have hoped for, they're more *entertaining* as well, generating that quintessential Sense of Wonder kick, based on vistas of almost unimaginable scope and scale, that is not only one of the things that science fiction does best, but which can be delivered *by* science fiction perhaps more effectively than by any other kind of writing. Stories that are gorgeously colored, fast-paced, richly detailed, lushly imaginative, widescreen. Exciting, colorful, and fun.

In other words, the kind of thing that started us all reading science fiction in the first place.

Enjoy!

—Gardner Dozois

GALACTIC EMPIRES

THE DEMON TRAP

Peter F. Hamilton

Prolific British writer Peter F. Hamilton has sold to Interzone, In Dreams, New Worlds, Fears, *and elsewhere. He sold his first novel,* Mindstar Rising, *in 1993, and quickly followed it up with two sequels,* A Quantum Murder *and* The Nano Flower. *Hamilton's first three books didn't attract a great deal of attention on this side of the Atlantic, at least, but that changed dramatically with the publication of his next novel,* The Reality Dysfunction, *a huge modern Space Opera (it needed to be divided into two volumes for publication in the United States) that was itself only the start of a projected trilogy of staggering size and scope, the Night's Dawn trilogy, with the first volume followed by others of equal heft and ambition (and also raced up genre best-seller lists),* The Neutronium Alchemist *and* The Naked God. *The Night's Dawn trilogy put Hamilton on the map as one of the major players in the expanding subgenre of the New Space Opera, along with writers such as Iain Banks, Dan Simmons, Paul McAuley, Gregory Benford, Alastair Reynolds, and others; it was successful enough that a regular SF publisher later issued Hamilton's reference guide to the complex universe of the trilogy,* The Confederation Handbook, *the kind of thing that's usually done as a small-press title, if it's done at all. Hamilton's other books include the novels* Misspent Youth, Fallen Dragon, Pandora's Star; *a collection,* A Second Chance at Eden; *and a novella chapbook,* Watching Trees Grow. *His most recent book is a new novel,* Judas Unchained. *Coming up is a new collection,* The Dreaming Void.*

Here he takes us to the fabulous Confederation universe, to a place where you can take a commuter train *to the stars, for a tense investigation of an act of terrorism whose ultimate implications turn out to be very far-reaching indeed.*

WHAT HAPPENED

Nova Zealand was the world chosen for the massacre for exactly the same reason that the party of youthful Dynasty members had chosen it as their funtime holiday destination. It barely qualified as H-congruous, capable of supporting human habitation; but that bad geophysics gave it some astonishing scenery that simply begged to be exploited by extreme sports enthusiasts. There was a small population without any real industrial base; its commerce was the leisure industry. Yet in case of a genuine emergency, the Intersolar Commonwealth with all its fabulous medical and technical resources was only a single fast train ride away.

The trains came in at Compression Space Transport's planetary station on the north side of the capital, Ridgeview (population 43,000). They arrived through a wormhole that provided a direct link back to EdenBurg, an industrial planet, owned by the Halgarth Dynasty, and one of the major junctions in CST's interstellar transport monopoly. None of the trains went any farther than the station; Nova Zealand didn't have the kind of road and rail network common to most Commonwealth worlds. All medium- and long-distance travel was by plane.

It was midmorning when the train from Hifornia pulled in at the station. The first three carriages were for passengers, while the last two were vehicle carriers. Once it drew to a halt, large malmetal doors on the vehicle carriages retracted and ramps extended out from the platform. The sound of highly tuned engines firing up was unusual enough to turn the heads of the ordinary passengers as they disembarked. Five customized cars growled their way out onto the ramp. The first was a glowing orange Jaguar roadster, with faint blue flames stuttering out of its exhaust pipes as the engine revved. With a final roar of power, it sped off the bottom of the ramp with a showy wheel spin. Second was a silver Cadillac that was half bonnet, with front scimitar fins and a rear variable-camber spoiler; then came an eight-wheeled stretch limo; followed by a hundred-year-old V-class Mercedes; and finally, a brutish Lexus AT PowerSport, hydroskis retracted against its burnished gold sides.

The convoy raced off out of the station, a show of casual affluence and arrogance that brought grimaces of contempt from those watching. After a discrete minute, the rest of the party's vehicles slid quietly out of the carriage; seven long luxury vans that carried the necessary domestic staff and assistants, along with luggage and sports equipment. The Dynasty members never traveled without their home comforts close by.

Ridgeview's airport was five miles from the planetary station, a disappointingly short journey for the owners of the custom cars, hardly far enough for them to jostle and race along the road. They drove over to the waiting Siddeley-Lockheed CP-450, a subsonic cargo/passenger combi plane operated by a local tour company. Inside the vast cargo hold, electromuscle clamps curved out of the floor to secure the fancy cars. Doors opened, and the brash young things sauntered out, filling the air with overloud taunts and calls to each other. Their girlfriends accompanied them, tall slender beauties, terribly young to be dressed in such sensual couture. Stewardesses smiled impassively at the braying sexual harassment they were casually subjected to, and showed their haughty passengers to the upper deck's Imperial Cabin.

The vans purred smoothly into the plane. Staff found their seats in the mid-deck lounge. Within ten minutes, the big rear doors swung shut and the plane taxied onto the runway.

Ridgeview air traffic control cleared them for takeoff to Nova Zealand's arctic continent. It was a nine-hour flight that would take them to the notorious Fire Plain, a hundred-kilometer circle of wet swamps just short of the pole itself, whose abnormal climate was created by a ring wall of active volcanoes. Visitors to the resort could watch glowing lava flowing into the constricting cliff of the polar glacier, spurting out phenomenal jets of super-heated steam all the way up to the ionosphere, while down in the weird wetlands of giant ferns, huge dangerous creatures left over from an earlier geological era wallowed in the mud and ate anything that moved.

The Siddeley-Lockheed CP-450 rose into the air, folding its undercarriage away neatly. It curved toward the north through a clear azure sky, bright blue-white sunlight shining on its green fuselage. Below it, the harsh scrub desert fell away to the sea in long rumpled folds and sharp ravines.

Five minutes after takeoff, the plane was climbing through ten thousand feet as the pilot watched the flight management array throttle the duct fans back to cruise power, at which point one of the Dynasty heirs decided it was time to renew his membership of the mile-high club. It wasn't in his nature to retire discreetly to the washroom. The rest of the party gathered round his reclining couch to cheer as his obedient girlfriend stripped off. Scandalized stewardesses peeked from the galley, trying not to giggle.

A red star alert flared in the pilot's virtual vision. The plane's array was issuing a proximity alarm. It took the pilot a shocked couple of seconds to analyze the data that the radar was presenting him with. An object barely a meter long was streaking toward them at mach five. Disbelief froze him for another second as he struggled to admit that he was seeing a missile. He managed to yell: "Mayday!" into the open channel as he slammed his hands down onto the manual control pads. For someone who hadn't physically flown a plane for over two decades, he managed his evasion maneuver remarkably well, ramming on the power and initiating a steep dive. It delayed impact by a good three seconds, long enough for everyone on board to realize that something was disastrously wrong.

The missile struck the fuselage just below the port wing root. Not even modern superstrength materials could withstand the blast. The wing was ripped off, sending the fuselage into a fast spin. It began to disintegrate immediately, scattering fragments and bodies as it plummeted out of the sky.

Before the first pieces even hit the ground, a shotgun message entered the unisphere, attempting to infiltrate the address stores of every person who had an access code—about ninety-five percent of the human race. The carrier format was new enough to avoid the majority of commercial sentinels, though the unisphere's node management programs soon adapted to the intruder and blocked its progress. Before that happened, it managed to reach several billion people who were annoyed to find the small file slipping into their stores. Most were unisphere-savvy enough to have their e-butlers delete the pest. Those that did open it were shown a simple text.

> The Free Merioneth Forces announce the eradication of more Dynasty parasites. Our team on Nova Zealand have today successfully struck against our oppressors. Until our planet is liberated from the financial bonds that the Dynasty leaders have shackled it with, our campaign will continue.
>
> We urge all Dynasty members to exert your influence and compel your leaders negotiate with our government. Failure to comply with our requests for freedom and dignity will result in the further elimination of your worthless kind. We will no longer tolerate our taxes being spent to uphold your decadent lifestyle.

Senior investigator Paula Myo's e-butler deleted the shotgun as soon as it reached her unisphere interface; it was the newest adaptive version with a real-time update facility to the Serious Crimes Directorate RI, so it knew what it was dealing with. At the time, she was trying to be polite with the decorator who was gazing around the lounge of her new apartment, shaking his head as if he'd been confronted with restoring the Sistine Chapel.

"Next month?" he suggested with a typical Gallic shrug.

Paula was only surprised that he wasn't wearing a beret and

smoking a cigarette; he'd certainly polished the rest of the Parisian indifference routine to stereotype perfection. "That's fine." She'd been in the apartment a week, and even she acknowledged it needed sprucing up. It wasn't much: bathroom, bedroom, and a lounge with a tiny kitchen alcove. The building was a typical Paris block, centuries-old, with a pleasant central courtyard. She really didn't care about the aesthetics. All that counted was its proximity to the office.

"What color scheme?" he inquired.

"Oh . . . whatever: white."

"White?" From his blatant dismay she must have deliberately insulted his French ancestry all the way back to the royal era.

"Yes." A priority communication icon popped up into her virtual vision. She touched it with a virtual hand she'd customized to a red skeletal outline; her physical fingers twitched in mimicry as parallel nerve impulses ran along the organic circuitry tattoos on her wrist.

"Grade one case coming in," Christabel Agatha Halgarth said. "The Director wants us on it immediately."

"On my way in," Paula replied.

"No, don't. I'm going for a car now; I'll pick you up. Three minutes."

"All right, transfer the case files over." Paula dismissed the decorator. Perhaps it was because of her carefully controlled mix of Filipino and European genes, which had given her such a delightful face that he assumed he could bluster and intimidate as he usually did with single female clients. The stare she gave him froze the protest after just a couple of words. He nodded compliance and retreated, counting himself lucky she hadn't actually said anything.

Paula pulled on a gray suit jacket and picked up her small shoulder bag, moving instinctively as the files from the Directorate slipped into her virtual vision. She read the scant details on the plane crash as she hurried down the worn stone stairs to the courtyard below.

One of the Directorate's dark sedans pulled up outside the block's main entrance. The gull wing door pivoted forward, and Paula got in. Christabel was sitting on the rear bench, a brunette with an Asian ancestry a lot stronger than Paula's clinic-manufactured heritage. She was Paula's deputy; they'd known each other since their training academy days.

"Wow, you look great," Christabel enthused. "Positively jailbait. I'd forgotten how pretty you are when you're young. You shouldn't wait so long between rejuvenations."

"I can't spare the time," Paula said automatically. Her hand went up to sweep her raven hair away from her face. With rejuvenation returning her biological age to late adolescence, her hair had grown very thick again. Every time, she was tempted to have it trimmed to a shorter style. But this fitted her, along with the simple-cut business suit and plain black shoes she always wore to work, defining what she was. It was as much her identity as her modified genes.

"Welcome back," Christabel said with a knowing smile. "How are your inserts settling in?"

Paula held up a hand, flexing the fingers. The OCtattoos were invisible against her skin. It was still a relatively new technology, with development houses finding new applications each year. The ones she'd had before rejuvenation were a lot cruder; they'd been eradicated by her treatment, so the last week had been spent at a Directorate facility augmenting her body with the new generation of insert gadgets.

"A couple of glitches left. I'm due a final formatting session on Saturday. Things have come a long way since I had my last installation."

Christabel held up her own hand. Threads of intense blue light appeared, pulsing along her fingers. "You didn't fancy the latest versions then? Function and fashion combined. Not bad, huh? I paid for the customization myself. I can get you a good deal if you like. I've still got contacts in my Dynasty."

Paula gave the glowing strands a curt look. "No thank you."

Christabel laughed.

"We don't seem to have much on the Free Merioneth Forces," Paula said as she continued to open case files.

"No. They're relatively new. Emerged while you were in rejuvenation. This is their fourth strike in five months. Very effective. We haven't arrested anyone yet."

The Directorate sedan drove across Paris to the huge CST station, where it boarded a trans-Earth loop train, taking it through a series of wormholes linking the old world's major cities. From Paris, the loop led to Madrid, then London, before crossing the Atlantic to New York; four more stops, and twenty minutes later, the train pulled in at the massive LA galactic station, where they drove over to the Intersolar terminal and onto a direct train to EdenBurg.

Eighty minutes after Paula got into the sedan, it was driving off a vehicle carriage at the same platform that the Dynasty party had used less than three hours earlier. The car's array took them around the Ridgeview ring road, and out across the scrub desert to the north. Paula watched in surprise as a group of wild camels sauntered across the hard-packed sands. They'd been gene-modified to digest the local cacti-equivalent vegetation, but even so it was a harsh environment. After five miles, the track vanished, and the suspension rose up to cope with the rocky ground.

"Hope you brought a hat," Christabel said. She was squinting out the window at the blazing noon sun. Ridgeview was about as far south as the planet's climate would allow. After another couple of hundred miles the scrub desert gave way to true desolation. Nova Zealand's entire equatorial zone was bare rock, baked by the intense blue-white star; the heat even repelled clouds, leaving the land in a permanent shadowless summer where the daily air temperature rose far above boiling point.

The crash site perimeter was still being established by the local police. Wreckage had so far been spotted over seven square miles. The Directorate car delivered them to a cluster of police vehicles parked together above a wide sandy gully. Helicopters droned slowly through the clear sky above.

Paula reluctantly dug a wide-brimmed hat from her little bag. The door opened, and she immediately held her breath as oppressively hot air swept in.

"Hellfire," Christabel groaned. "Literally."

They climbed out. Paula put on a pair of sunglasses that opaqued up to their highest level. Then she took her jacket off, feeling sweat prickle her bare arms. The arid desert air was burning its way down her throat, drying her sinuses.

"Wouldn't do that if I was you," a man told them. He was dressed in a loose Arabic-style robe with a deep white hood. "Detective Captain Aidan Winkal," he said as he offered his hand.

"Paula Myo."

"I've heard of you, Investigator. But seriously, if you haven't put on screening membrane, five minutes' exposure in this sunlight will burn your skin down to the bone."

"Okay." She put the jacket back on.

"Come on, I've got our mobile situation office set up."

It was a big old van with the Ridgeview police logo emblazoned on the side. Five tall heat-dump fins sprouted out of the roof, glowing a faint rose-pink. Inside, the air was thankfully cool. A bench table down one side was cluttered with various desktop arrays operated by Winkal's colleagues. Screens and small holographic portals relayed various images from the helicopters and jeeps covering the site.

"What procedures are you following?" Paula asked.

Aidan Winkal had pulled his hood back to reveal a weathered face with silver-fox hair cut short. He appeared hesitant. "Look, we're not exactly used to this kind of thing, you know."

"We're not here to criticize," Paula assured him. "We both want the same thing, to catch the people responsible. The Directorate will assume responsibility for tracking down the group that did this. But site control and recovery is all yours. Now tell me what you're doing, and we'll be happy to provide advice."

"Okay, thanks. We're trying to map the debris area. The larger sections of fuselage are easy enough to find, and so far we've picked up thirty-seven personal emergency beacons. My squads are escorting medical teams out to them. The bodies we've located so far . . . they're not intact, you know."

"I understand. However, their memorycells should be able to survive the impact. They're designed to withstand a lot worse than this."

"Sure."

"We have a Directorate forensic team en route. Some of their sensor systems will be able to help your search. I'll assign them as soon as we've identified and recovered the missile. Have you located the launch site yet?"

"No. I'm concentrating on the crash, finding those poor people. We're still trying to build a full passenger list."

"Fair enough. Christabel and I will work out where it was fired from. I'll need complete access to the plane's memory. Have you found it yet?"

"Yes. It never lost contact with the unisphere. We know where it is, but we haven't actually collected it yet. I encrypted the channel and restricted access."

"Good. I'd also like to see the CST station closed to both inbound and outbound trains. We can do without the reporters who are undoubtedly on their way. Secondly, there's a chance the team that fired the missile is still on the planet. If so, I'd like them confined here."

"I, er, don't really have that authority. I don't even think our prime minister does."

"I'll contact my chief right away. But you'll need to post some officers at the station. It might turn ugly once the trains stop running."

"Okay."

Paula and Christabel claimed a couple of fold-out chairs at the rear of the van, and got Aidan to open the restricted channel to the plane's memory. Using the radar data to backtrack the missile's trajectory was easy enough; it had come from a point approximately a quarter mile from the coast, five miles outside Ridgeview.

"Wouldn't take long to get to the city ring road from there," Christabel exclaimed as she reviewed a local map in her virtual vision.

"Pull Ridgeview's traffic management records," Paula told her. "Find out what vehicles if any joined the road from outside this morning. I'll also want the air traffic records scrutinizing. They might have flown out."

"Right away."

"What kind of orbital surveillance have you got here?" Paula asked Aidan.

"Eight low orbit satellites for geophysical observation," he told her. "The resolution isn't good. You could see the Siddeley-Lockheed, and most houses; but a car would be hard to make out, and individual people are too small."

"Okay. We'll see what kind of images the Directorate RI can pull out of the raw data. Right now, we need to get out to the launch site. This sun is degrading our evidence by the minute. Can you give me a helicopter, please?"

The Directorate forensic team arrived in time to join them on the helicopter. Aidan Winkal also elected to come with them. As the coast slipped into view through the cabin window, he shook his head in bemusement. "I just got word from the station," he called above the rotor noise. "CST has suspended the train service to EdenBurg. Your Directorate has a lot of clout."

"Three of the holiday party were Sheldon Dynasty members," Paula said. "That'll speed things up a little."

Aidan nodded in understanding.

Christabel leaned in close to Paula. "I give it ten minutes before *someone's* here to help."

Paula gazed down at the coastline. "You think it will be that long?"

"I've already had two calls from the Halgarth security office. Any assistance we need–"

They circled the zone Paula had identified, seeing nothing but shingle and rock. A scan from the helicopter's radar didn't add anything. Paula's optical inserts were giving her an infrared picture. Every surface was radiant with heat as it basked in the fierce sunlight. "Anything?" she asked Nalcol, the forensics officer who was with them. He was sitting next to the open side door, aiming a specialist array at the ground.

"A spectral of an unusual airborne carbon residual. Could be the launch booster. Don't know for sure. But we'll need to land clear. I don't want the downwash to screw up evidence."

The pilot put them down three hundred yards away.

Paula, Christabel, and Aidan followed Nalcol and his assistant toward the area where the carbon residue had spread. The forensic people were sweeping their arrays at everything as they went. A little pack of bots crawled along beside them, like foot-long caterpillars with thin antenna strands stroking the ground as they went.

"No sign of any vehicle tracks," Christabel said.

"Tough to see on this terrain," Paula said. Her toe nudged some of the flat shingle. "If Nalcol confirms this as the launch point, we'll seal it off and bring in the rest of the team."

"This is going to be a tough one," Christabel said, shielding her eyes as she scanned the gray-blue sea. The land sloped down toward it like a giant beach. "They didn't leave much for us."

"Actually, this isolation helps us a great deal," Paula said. "When we get back to Paris, I want you to put together a team to track down who knew the Dynasty members had booked their holiday here. Get a profile on everyone from the Fire Plain resort staff through the tour company they use, and, most important, the entourage. I want to know if any of them have left recently. Then there's the girlfriends, one-night stands, other friends–their families, connections. It'll be a big list, but finite. Cross-reference for any connection to Merioneth."

Christabel let out a soft whistle. "I'll assign Basker to lead it. He's good at data analysis."

"Fine." A sound made Paula look up, pushing back her wide hat. "Oh, hello."

A small black helicopter was approaching the launch zone, flying low and fast.

"That's not one of ours," Aidan said in annoyance. "How did it get flight clearance? This is a designated restricted zone."

Paula held back on her smile. The poor police captain sounded quite indignant. "A word of advice, Captain," she said as the new helicopter landed beside theirs. "This is where you get to play with the big boys. If you haven't done this before, don't try to claim jurisdiction on any aspect of this investigation. You really do have to work with them."

"Uh huh," Aiden spat onto the stones. "And if I don't?"

"Your career is over. It's not blatant, but it is effective. If you *really* annoy them, then you won't have much of a life after your next few rejuvenations either."

"And you just let them walk all over your investigations, do you?"

"No," Paula said. "There are boundaries, and, with me, they know where they stand. But I've spent decades building that political coverage. You haven't."

A man climbed down out of the helicopter as the blades slowed. He was dressed in a robe similar to the one Aiden wore, except he was like the captain's younger, smarter, richer brother.

"Nelson Sheldon," Christabel muttered. "Impressive. Third generation down from Nigel himself."

Paula nodded appreciatively. Nelson was one of the five deputy managers of the Sheldon Dynasty security service, heading up the external threat division. She'd met him on three Directorate cases when their respective interests overlapped; each time, he'd been the total professional, and very diplomatic. Rumor had it that he'd be chief within fifty years.

"Captain," Nelson said politely, and offered his hand to Aidan. "I apologize for the interruption, but as you can imagine, my family is deeply distressed by this appalling attack on our members. I'm here to offer whatever support you need, practical or political."

There was a moment of hesitation. Then Aiden shook the proffered hand. "Understood," he said. "All of it."

"Ah," Nelson smiled. "The ladies have been telling tales about me. Christabel, nice to see you again. Paula, you look amazing. You'll have to tell me which clinic you use to rejuve in."

"Sorry about your people," Paula said.

"Thank you." Nelson's expression hardened. "They'll be relifed, of course. Everyone on the plane will be, no matter what their insurance status. We owe them that much."

"We'd appreciate a complete list of passengers," Aidan said. "I need to know the full makeup of the entourage to help recovery."

"You've got it. I'll liaise with the other Dynasties for you."

The four of them stood together, watching the methodical movements of the forensic duo and the pack of specialist bots.

"So what's the story with your three?" Paula asked. "Anyone special?"

"Hell no," Nelson said. "They're fifth and sixth generation. Standard-issue brats who were busy pissing away their trust funds. Never done a day's work in their lives. Honestly, the new generations are a real disaster area. As far as I know, it was the same for the Brandt boy and the Mandela. There was nothing important about them other than that they're Dynasty and goddamn easy targets."

"They were important in terms of propaganda for Free Merioneth," Christabel said.

"Yeah. All this crap about their taxes paying for little tits like our useless descendants is hitting a nerve. You know how financially integrated the Commonwealth planets are. It costs a frigging fortune just to begin settlement these days, and as for building up a decent technoindustrial infrastructure, well . . . Any planet starting up today is looking to be paying off those costs for the next two and a half centuries—minimum."

"And the Dynasties control the finance houses," Paula observed.

"Along with Earth's Grand Families," Nelson said in a defensive tone. "They haven't been targeted, please note. Not yet, anyway."

"So the start-up costs go back to you, along with interest payments."

"That's the way the universe works, Investigator."

"I can see the emotive force behind targeting the young Dynasty members. We've all seen their antics, or accessed unisphere reports on it. There's not a lot of sympathy out there for them."

"The rich never have any sympathy," Nelson said. "I can live with that. But it doesn't mean you can go around slaughtering them—us!—to advance your political goal. In any case, there were only five Dynasty members on that plane, out of a hundred and thirty people."

"I wasn't agreeing with them," Paula said. "I'm just trying to understand the motivation."

"I'd have said it was justification, not motivation," Aidan said. They all turned to look at him. He shrugged. "Everyone knows they're not going to win, right? Government does not negotiate with terrorists. That's been public policy number one since before people ever left Earth. It's not going to change now. So this is just an excuse to give your psychosis full head. Serial killing taken to the next level."

"Could be," Paula said cautiously. Something about the case was bothering her. As Aidan said, the motivation wasn't quite right. But as to the result of Free Merioneth's actions, there was no mistake. Their criminality was her primary concern. Her motivation. Which was unbreakable. Her mind-set was aligned through psychoneural profiling, a genetic science comprehensively banned throughout the Commonwealth. The resolution of justice was built into her genes, along with a few other little traits like obsessive-compulsive behavior, which people were extremely uncomfortable with. Paula wasn't. She'd always been perfectly content with what she was. She also quite enjoyed the irony of being a senior Commonwealth law enforcement officer, while technically being illegal on every planet except one—her birthworld, Huxley's Haven, or as the rest of the Commonwealth called it: the Hive.

"Found something," Nalcol called. He was kneeling beside a tough-looking wizened bush cactus, touching the ground with peripheral sensors on his array. Three of the bots were stationary next to the plant's stem, probing its leathery skin. "Could be a urine patch," he said as they gathered around. "Someone from the missile team probably relieved themselves." He pushed a long transparent probe deeper, collecting samples in its spoon-shaped tip.

"Are you certain?" Paula couldn't see any hint of moisture in the crumbly ocher soil. *But then, why send a human out here when a bot is perfectly capable of firing a missile?*

"This goddamned sun," Nalcol complained. "It's evaporating the fluid rapidly, which is how we detected it. The effervescence cloud is distinct to our sensors. But it doesn't leave much to work with." Various graphic displays danced across the array's little screen. "Yep, here we go. Viable DNA. I can get you a positive fingerprint from this."

"Thanks," Christabel said. "What about the missile exhaust?"

"Definite. It's an oxidized carbon trace, with aluminium and several other accelerant compounds."

"What type?"

"All I can tell you is: very crude. No one reported seeing a chemical exhaust, not at altitude, so I'm guessing it incorporated a basic hyperram: an intake nozzle that compresses air, which is then heated with electron injection or high-frequency induction before squirting that hot air out the back like a rocket exhaust. But you need a booster to get it up to operational speed to start with. Solid chemicals are a primitive but effective method of initial acceleration. Nobody builds that kind of thing anymore. At least, not the commercial armament companies."

"You mean it was homemade?" Nelson asked.

"Probably. Most of the components you'd need are widely available. It just needs a bit of skill to put them together."

"That would take some organization."

"Fanatics do that well," Paula said. "But surely a beam weapon would be more effective, and completely untraceable? Every planet in the Commonwealth produces them."

Nalcol stared up into the hot sky. "Not for this range. That kind of power rating is more specialist. Easier to trace."

"What did the earlier attacks use?" Aidan asked.

"The first two were booby-trapped cars, with standard augmented explosives," Nelson said. "The third was arson in a block of flats in Leithpool, with the fire escapes sabotaged. That killed twenty-three—and only three were Dynasty."

"Two of whom were Halgarths," Christabel said. "The Merioneth team have moved up a level with this."

"This wasn't a team," Paula said. She was looking downslope to the small waves washing ashore. "You only need one person to launch a missile like this. That gives minimum exposure to the rest of the organization. It's also easier for one person to get out. Aidan, how far are we from Ridgeview by sea?"

He gestured at a distant headland. "About seven miles to the docks. There are some marinas closer, though."

"The terrain between here and the ring road is bad," Paula said. "Even if you were on a dirt bike it would take too long, and there's too much that could go wrong. Fall off, puncture, whatever. Let's pull up the satellite imagery and check for a boat."

The helicopters took them back to the police situation van. Paula sent Nalcol on to Ridgeview. "If we find a boat, I want samples from it," she told him.

Christabel sat down in front of a spare desktop array as soon as they were back inside the van and started to call up the satellite images. Paula stood at the back, watching her.

"She's good at this," she told Nelson as she pulled her hat off and dabbed at the sweat on her brow. Her hair was hanging limp against her brow and cheeks. Nelson handed her a cup of water from the cooler tower. They both sipped eagerly as Christabel began flicking through images, muttering instructions to the Directorate's RI. "Thank you for shutting down the station," Paula said quietly.

"The least we could do."

"I do require the suspect to stand trial. That means no unfortunate accidents. I will not permit that."

Nelson was watching one of the screens showing two medics leaning over a bloody chunk of gore, inserting surgical tools. "The Sheldon Dynasty has every confidence in you, Paula. That's official. But the perpetrators must be removed from society. The Dynasty will not have its members picked off in this fashion; ideologues must be made to understand that."

"It will happen. However, I will only be going after the team responsible for the actual attacks. Unless we discover complicity or a funding link with their political wing, the rest of the movement will remain untouched by the Directorate. They have a right to free speech no matter how unpleasant their views."

"I am aware of article one in the constitution, thank you. Nigel helped draft it. Leave the politicians to us."

"I still don't understand the point of it," Paula said. "Merioneth is barely self-sufficient. They need continuing investment. They must know that."

"Ideologues aren't rational people."

"A convenient label for us. But—"

"Got a boat!" Christabel shouted out. Everyone in the van

craned for a look at her screens. The satellite image wasn't good. It showed the coast next to the launch site, land and sea dividing the screen in half. A small clump of gray pixels formed a blob in the center. "Time code checks," Christabel said. "This is fifteen minutes prior to the crash." The image changed as the satellite slid along its orbit, showing the coastline further to the east. There was little overlap; the boat was right on the edge of the screen.

"We're going to lose it," Nelson said. "This satellite is moving too quickly. It won't be overhead after the launch. When's the next pass?"

Christable consulted a display. "There's another satellite coming up in forty-two minutes. So we've got no coverage during the launch. I guess they worked that out, too."

"I don't need to see them fire the missile," Paula said. "I just needed confirmation it was a boat. Aidan, get me access to every camera in every marina in Ridgeview. I want the image files from fifteen minutes before the launch to now. Find me a boat coming in. If they took a direct route it'll be about twenty minutes after the attack. Christabel, start there."

Aidan slipped into the seat next to Christabel and used his police authorization to establish links into the city's marinas.

"How many trains left between then and now?" Paula asked Nelson.

"Seven."

"Get the station camera records ready for access."

"Way ahead of you," he grinned. "I'm pulling up passenger carriage camera files as well."

It took Christabel another eight minutes to find a boat mooring at the Larsie marina. A man in a yellow shirt stepped off. "Here we go," she said with a trill of excitement as the camera observed him walk along the wooden quay used by Danney's Boat Hire. She froze an image as he was just short of the camera, revealing the round face of a man in his late forties, with flesh starting to build up under his cheeks and around his chin. Dark skin, with stubble. Thinning gray-brown hair dangled out of his blue cap. His yellow shirt was open at the neck, revealing a dark necklace cord.

"Nalcol, get over to the Larsie marina," Paula said. "We've found the boat. Captain, call up the hire company office; tell them it's impounded. It must not be cleaned."

"You got it," Aidan said.

"Nelson, transfer the station files to our RI. It'll run visual recognition on that face. Christabel, get into the hire company's records. Who paid for the boat?"

"Yes, boss."

The Directorate RI took ninety seconds to review every camera record from the station, running each face through a recognition program to identify the man on the marina.

"There he is," Paula exclaimed contentedly as the largest screen in the situation van showed their suspect strolling down the main platform to a waiting train, still wearing his yellow shirt. The timeline was thirty-seven minutes after the attack. They watched the RI follow him through the cameras until he was sitting in a carriage on an express train heading for Earth. The train moved out of the station.

"Let's go," Paula said.

The three of them took Nelson's helicopter back to the station. There was a train already waiting to leave, packed full of passengers angry at the delay. Paula, Christabel, and Nelson hurried into the first-class cabin and it left immediately, trundling along the track to the big wormhole generator half a mile beyond the marshaling yard. Once it was through, it made an unscheduled stop at a small service platform in EdenBurg's vast terminal. They transferred over to an express heading for Earth.

Nalcol called as they reached the platform. "DNA match confirmed," he told Paula. "The man on the boat was the one who took a leak at the launch site."

"Send the file back to Paris," she told him. "Find his profile."

"He bought his train ticket with a onetime account," Nelson told them. "Untraceable. But we've followed him through LA galactic. He caught a trans-Earth loop and got off at Sydney an hour ago. Caught a taxi."

"Leave that to us," Paula said. "The Directorate can track him."

They sat back as the express accelerated out of EdenBurg. Five minutes later it was pulling into LA galactic.

"Basker just called," Christabel said. "We've got a positive identification; visual corresponding to DNA. Dimitros Fiech. Address in Sydney. Works for Colliac Fak, a software development company. He's a sales rep, so he travels around a lot. Oh, get this, Colliac's Leisure Division supplies software to the travel industry, including the resort at Fire Plain."

They left the express and started to run through the vast terminal to the platforms serving the trans-Earth loop. "Mine his background," Paula told Christabel, then put a call in to the Directorate's Sydney office. "I want a tactical team armored up and ready when we arrive. Have a helicopter pick us up at the station."

"Yes, ma'am," the duty officer replied. "The suspect's taxi dropped him at the Wilkinson Tower off Penfold. We have two officers there now. As far as we know, he's still inside."

"Good work. We'll be there in fifteen minutes."

"I'd like to observe, please," Nelson said.

"Yes," Paula said. "But that's all."

"I know."

The loop train took them to Mexico City, followed by Rio, down to Buenos Aires, and then over the ocean to Sydney. A Directorate helicopter was sitting on the station security division pad, rotors spinning idly.

Paula and Christabel started putting on their armor as it lifted into the dark sky cloaking the city. Nelson watched enviously.

"If you do need back up–" he said.

"Then the city police will be happy to provide it," Paula said.

He sighed and gave up.

The ancient harbor bridge was illuminated in orange and blue holographic outlines as they flew in parallel to it. A wall of skyscrapers punctured the cityscape behind Circular Quay, their surface illuminations throwing cold monochrome light down onto the deserted nighttime streets below. They landed on the roof of the fifty-story Wilkinson Tower. Five of the Directorate's tactical team were waiting for them.

"Stay here," Paula ordered Nelson as she hopped down onto the roof.

Dimitros Fiech's apartment was on the thirteenth floor, looking inland. The Directorate team was evacuating the residents above and below.

"Fiech is a legend," Christabel said as the elevator opened on the thirteenth floor. Three tactical team members were waiting for them, dressed in black armor and holding big ion pistols.

"Basker validates an eighteen-month employment record with Colliac Fak. Fiech's CV and general background are false. It'll withstand a standard employment agency search, but our RI burned right through it. Records were inserted, referees are false. He's a genuine undercover agent for someone, all right."

"Thanks," Paula said. Her red virtual finger touched a communication icon, opening a secure link to the tactical team. "Be aware, we confirm target is hostile. He has access to weapons and does not hesitate to open fire. Civilians are not safe. Squad sergeant?"

"Yes, ma'am."

"Can you immobilize him?"

"We've got a nerve jangler drone, but we'll have to blow the door open to get it in there. We don't know if it's reinforced."

"Has he rigged the approach?"

"No sensors detected in the corridor."

"All right, let's go. Be careful." Paula called up feeds from the cameras on the suits of the entry team, seeing jerky images of the corridor as they hurried along. The wooden door to Fiech's apartment was painted a dull green. They gathered around it and quickly rolled an explosive tape along the edges. One camera showed the drone being held ready, a small triangle of gray plastic.

"Go!" the squad sergeant ordered.

The explosive tape detonated, shattering the wooden door. The remnants crashed inward. Suit sensors went active, cutting through the smoke and dust, producing a sharp black-and-white image. The drone streaked in. Icons blinked green and amber, showing that the nerve jangler field was active. Theoretically, it would stun Fiech's nervous system, giving the team time to get in and cover him before he could go for any weapons. Unless he was ready and protected.

The icons turned blue and the entry team charged in. Fiech was sprawled on a couch in the living room, still wearing the yellow shirt Paula had seen through so many camera images. His head was flung back, hanging over the edge of the cushions as his limbs shook from the aftermath of the jangle. Drool leaked out of his gaping mouth.

Paula was running down the corridor, turning the corner. The wreckage of the door was in front of her. Four more team members were charging through it into the apartment. She followed them in. Fiech was still spread out across the couch. One of the suited figures was pressing an ion pistol to his temple. The second was providing cover. The remainder spread out through the apartment, guns held ready, sensors on full power, scanning ahead.

"Clear," the squad sergeant called.

Fiech was given a full deep scan. His body had a few inserts and a couple of OCtattoos, simple unisphere interfaces, and a standard memorycell, none of them combat grade. They turned him over and secured his wrists. Two ion pistols remained trained on him. He was white and shaking now, on the verge of vomiting.

Paula removed her helmet, shaking out her hair. Fiech gave her a terrified stare.

"It's going to be rough on you," Paula said. "Even if you co-operate, memory reading is never pleasant. But if you give us the names and structure of your movement, we can keep it to a minimum. We'll just verify your information. Trust me, it's worth it."

Fiech started sobbing, tears tricking down his cheeks. "What the fuck is happening?" he wailed. "What is going on?"

Paula gave him a contemptuous look. She'd expected more professionalism. "Take him down to the office. Prep him for a memory read. I'll run it myself."

A whimpering Fiech was dragged past her. Christabel came into the apartment, taking her helmet off to look round. "I'll get forensics in, rip this place apart."

"Sure." A formality, Paula knew. The apartment was part of his cover, it'd be clean.

"Hell of a first day back, boss. What are you going to do to-morrow?"

WHAT I KNOW HAPPENED

I was up early that morning, just like bloody always these days. Damn company is squeezing its staff to husks, always raising our performance targets. You can't keep doing that year after year, people can only do so much.

Anyway . . . the first wave of commuters was buzzing about on the streets when I left the tower lobby. Poor bastards. Just like me. Squeezed on all sides. You can see it in their null ex-pressions. All that effort and angst etched into their faces, and it was only five past seven.

I walked down O'Connal Street to the underground metro station. It's steep ground just behind Sydney harbor, and the skyscrapers are so high you don't see sunlight that time of the morning. Some of my fellow sufferers were gulping down Bean There coffee from plastic cups. I hate that. Food on the run gives me really bad indigestion.

The metro station has a direct line to the CST station on the south side of the city. It took eleven minutes. Three longer than usual. Every bugger is conspiring to make my life worse.

I missed the first train to Wessex. Typical. So I waited on the big platform, with its white wing roof. Me and two hundred others. Time was, I used to be excited just being in CST's Sydney station. Think of it. Out there past the end of the platform there's eighteen wormhole generators, each one with tracks leading to a different phase one world. One line goes to Wessex, the junction to phase two space, with another twelve worlds beyond that. They're going to open five more in the next three years. All that opportunity, the potential out there, and what does my life amount to? Bugger all. Corporate drone, that's me. Worlds aren't new starts and fresh hope, all that crap in the brochures. I've been to all of them. They're just more developments that I've got to flog Colliac Fak's bloody software to. We're covering every H-congruous planet in the galaxy with concrete; building little nests with a window we can look at the neighboring squalid skyscraper with. Yeah, we're a really progressive species, us humans.

So I got the next train to Wessex. Standard class coach, and I just managed to grab a seat next to a window. Beat some woman to it, who looked real pissed at me when I slipped in ahead of her. *Gotta learn, lady. Survival of the fittest on this route. Every route, every day.*

The Wessex station made its Sydney cousin look small. Three big passenger terminals with gold and scarlet roofs curving high over twenty platforms apiece; you could probably fit my apartment skyscraper inside one of them. And a marshaling yard that sprawled over fifteen square miles, a giant zoo of cybernetic machines and warehouses.

I had to switch terminals for the train out to Ormal—that's a five-minute trip on a pedwalk—then I had to find the right platform. The insert that provides my virtual vision has interface problems now, so the guidance icons I was picking up from the station management array were blurred. Nearly misread the damn thing. Finished up on platform 11B waiting with a big crowd for the train. These people weren't so stressed and desperate as the ones back in Sydney. More prosperous types, with suits a lot more expensive than mine. They had neat little leather designer arrays edged in gold or platinum tucked into the top pockets. You could see their fingers flicking about minutely as they shunted icons around their high-rez virtual vision. I even saw a few of those new OCtattoos, the ones that light up, tracing colorful lines across their skin. One woman had green and blue spirals on her cheeks.

The carriage wasn't so crowded, so I got a seat by a window again. I guess most of my fellow travelers were up in first class. Trip to Ormal was a simple eight minutes. We rolled out from the end of the platform and across the marshaling yard. I could see the row of wormhole generators up ahead like a metallic cliff, bloody huge great rectangular buildings side by side with a wormhole gateway at the end, like the mouth of an old-fashioned train tunnel. Only these had light shining out of them: alien suns spreading a multitude of subtle shades across the rusting jumble of the marshaling yard.

Our train headed straight for a pink-tinged hole, and I felt the tingle of the pressure curtain across my skin as we passed through. Then we were rolling along a couple of miles of track surrounded by open countryside with strange bulbous gray and white trees before we reached the CST planetary station.

Harwood's Hill, the capital, was small, barely half a million people. But it was beautiful, one of those places that had banned combustion engines. It was spread across a big slope that rose up out of a freshwater sea, with green spaces outnumbering buildings five to one. If I could afford it, I'd probably move there. You knew this world was making an effort to get things *right*. But it cost to grab a chunk of a dormitory planet for the upper middle classes. For Christ's sake, real estate here was more expensive than back on Earth.

My train had arrived late evening. I took a taxi out to the airport, using the company card. Even the taxi cost more than the return train fare. I watched the yachts out on the lake, trying not to be all sour and envious. There must have been hundreds coming into port, their sails all lit up by the sinking sun. Didn't anyone in this city work?

The flight to Essendyne was another three hours. At the other end, the airport was little more than a flat patch of grass with a strip of enzyme-bonded concrete down the middle, like it was left over from an experimental road building project.

Essendyne itself was a little town of stylish houses at the end of a valley. The surrounding mountains were impressive, too. In winter, they have over a meter of snow. It is perfect for skiers.

I took another taxi out to the resort, a forty-minute ride. The place was only half-finished, with the main building a mass of scaffolding crawling with construction bots. Some of the cabins had roofs, but the insides weren't fitted. I got that shitty sinking feeling as soon as we arrived. The office had told me the whole thing was in its final stage of completion, with the staff busy getting ready for guests. All that was left to do was a bit of landscaping. Complete crap.

The taxi dropped me outside the site manager's office. She wasn't available, some crisis out there among the scaffolding with a malfunctioning bot. Her assistant had the grace to look embarrassed as he explained that the handover date had been put back three months. It was difficult to get the materials out to Essendyne from the nearest train station, a two hours' drive away along a narrow road. No one from the resort company was even on site, let alone available to meet me.

Fucking pricks! Nobody back in Sydney had even bothered to check. Bastard scum! So I'd wasted an entire day on a trip to a client that didn't even exist yet. I wanted to bill the dicks back home for the commission I'd lost and the expenses I'd built up.

The taxi took me back to the airport. And, of course, the plane back to Harwood's Hill didn't leave for another five hours. I hit the bar in the concourse—a grand way to describe a hut with a glass wall. After an hour, when the anger was really peaking, I called Sydney and told the dick of an office manager what I thought of him. I didn't wait for him to say anything back. I cut the channel and got my e-butler to block all incoming calls. There was a seafood bistro next to the bar. I went in and tried some of the local food. Not bad. Waitress was kind of pretty, too. Then I went back to the bar.

I remember one of the stewardesses helping me onto the plane. Great-looking chick with flaming red hair and a cute smile. I told her so, too. Then we took off and I was poorly. She helped clean it up. I slept the rest of the flight.

Harwood's Hill was a grind. Strange city, small hours of the morning, with a mother monster hangover. Took a taxi to the CST station. Managed to find a little store that was still open and bought some cleaner tabs. I don't take them often—they're worse than the hangover if you ask me—but they do only last an hour before your body stabilizes. I was back in Sydney by then. Cold, depressed, with bones that ached. Couldn't eat, and felt really hungry thanks to the cleaners. And absolutely fuck all to show for my time.

I went home. Bugger the expense, I took a taxi. I was kind of surprised my company card was still working by then. You know I thought that was my low point. Then the bloody next thing I know, the police are blowing up my door. I don't know what they hit me with when they stormed in, but it was like my whole body was on fire. I just wanted to die. I mean, how could the universe *do* this to me?

WHAT THE COURT DECIDED

It was the biggest case ever to be heard in a Nova Zealand court; in fact, it was the biggest anything to happen on Nova Zealand, period. Reporters from every unisphere news show flooded into Ridgeview, with their companies block-booking entire hotels. Those unable to snag a room had to park their mobile homes on the ring road, where they were jostled by curious camels brought to the planet by Bedouins eager to re-create their ancient culture out in the freedom of the vast deserts. While in town, the narrow streets with their broad white canvas awnings rapidly became clogged by giant mobile studio trucks.

Paula was given a room in the city Attorney's office. It was cramped, with desks shoved against the wall and a noisy water tower, but better than trying to catch a train in each day.

When the case was opened in front of Judge Jeroen, Paula was surprised when the defense lawyer, Ms. Toi, entered a plea of not guilty.

"Is she going for some kind of technicality?" Paula whispered to Stephan Dorge, the Directorate's prosecutor.

"I don't see how," he whispered back. "They didn't ask for a deal."

"What about the memory deposition?"

"Nah, we can prove it's an implant."

When Paula looked at Ms. Toi, she thought the lawyer seemed uncomfortable.

Prosecution opened with the forensic evidence from the launch site. There was the DNA match between Dimitros Fiech and the urine sample. Skin analysis taken at the Directorate's Sydney office immediately after the arrest revealed traces of the missile's chemical rocket booster exhaust on his arms and face; there were also plume traces on his yellow shirt. The jury was shown camera pictures from the Larsie marina and Ridgeview's CST station. Additional corroboration was skin-cell DNA taken from the boat.

"The evidence that places Dimitros Fiech at the launch site is incontrovertible," Stephan Dorge concluded. "He fired the missile that killed a hundred and thirty-eight people. And for what? To push his perverted ideological platform."

In the docks, Dimitros Fiech shook his head in disbelief.

Defense called Paula Myo. "I'd like to concentrate on the deposition of Dimitros Fiech's memory on the day concerned," Ms. Toi said. "You ran the memory read yourself, did you not?"

"I did," Paula said. "They contained no recollection of the missile launch. We believe false memories of his day on Ormal were inserted at the same time his true memory of the attack was erased."

"False memories? You mean someone created them in a studio like a Full Sensory drama?"

"No. An accomplice went to Ormal in his place to provide an alibi. That experience was recorded, then loaded into Fiech's brain."

"You believe someone like the defendant went to Ormal. How do you know it wasn't him?"

"Because he was on Nova Zealand firing the missile."

"But the person, the *personality,* sitting here in this court-room today did not fire the missile, did he?"

Paula gave the defense lawyer a small smile. "Nice try. The defendant's personality arranged for the current memory to be implanted; therefore he is what he wants to be."

"But what he is now is not the original personality?"

"Who knows? There is no test that I'm aware of for identify-ing personality; in any case, as any first-year psychology student will tell you, personality is fluid. It changes as you age. Some say it matures. Just because you don't remember committing a crime doesn't mean you're innocent of it. That precedent was estab-lished when the first memory erasure techniques were devel-oped. The Justice Directorate suspension chambers are full of criminals who removed inconvenient incriminating memories. I'd point out that Fiech has erased his entire life prior to joining the Colliac Fak company, which has very neatly blocked our in-vestigation into the Free Merioneth movement, and we all know what that's led to in the last six months. To me such behavior is the personality trait of a real fanatic."

"Objection," Ms. Toi exclaimed. "Speculation. I want that struck from the record."

"You asked for my opinion on his personality," Paula countered.

"I'll allow it to stand for the moment," Judge Jeroen said. "It was a legitimate answer to your line of questioning, defense."

"Your Honor." Ms. Toi bowed to the judge. "Investigator, you said that memory erasure is common when a crime has been committed."

"That is correct."

"Have you ever known alternative memory for the time of the crime to be implanted?"

"I haven't come across it before, although the technique is relatively straightforward. You just need a colleague like the one Fiech had to record his day."

"So if I implanted the memory of firing the missile into your brain, would that make you guilty?"

"No. Because I didn't *do* it. The rest of the physical evidence would support that."

"So, in fact, Investigator, this boils down to two sets of opposing evidence. Both equally valid."

"Valid but not of equal credibility. That is correct."

"Please describe to the court the efforts that you undertook to establish that the person on Ormal was not Dimitros Fiech."

"I retraced the route myself, and interviewed everyone he remembered encountering. Security camera images were recovered and analyzed."

"What did they show?"

"A man with similar facial features to Dimitros Fiech traveled to Ormal. We assumed he underwent a cellular reprofiling treatment."

"But you can't prove it. The man sitting here in the dock could have been the one on Ormal, and his made-up doppelgänger could have fired the missile on Nova Zealand. Am I right?"

"No. Under my instruction, a Directorate forensic officer analyzed the seat cover on the plane that flew from Essendyne back to Harwood's Hill. It had been cleaned, but we found large traces of vomit containing DNA. It did not correspond to Dimitros Fiech's DNA, yet it was the seat he remembers using and being sick on. It wasn't him on Ormal."

Ms. Toi gave Paula a startled look. "I see. Thank you, Investigator."

"No!" Dimitros Fiech yelled. "No, you can't believe that. I didn't do it! Damn you, I didn't!" He turned to the jury and gave them a wild stare. "It wasn't me. I wasn't there. I *know* I wasn't!"

Judge Jeroen banged his gavel. "Be seated, Mr. Fiech."

"I'm being framed!" He turned to Ms. Toi. "Do something!" She winced.

Paula quietly left the witness stand as Fiech continued his tirade. Two large court officers moved forward into the dock as the judge banged his gavel repeatedly.

After another day and a half of evidence, the jury retired. They took an hour to reach their verdict of guilty. Judge Jeroen sentenced Dimitros Fiech to two thousand seven hundred and sixty years' life suspension, twenty years for each of the people who suffered bodyloss in the crash.

Paula was packing her bag when Aidan Winkal rapped his knuckles on the office door. "Hello," she said.

He grinned. "I just came to say good-bye."

"That's very kind of you, Aidan. You've handled yourself well while we were putting this case together, and I know this hasn't been easy. I expect your Chief will be promoting you."

"Probably. I gather Christabel got her promotion."

"Yes. Chief investigator at last. I'll miss her. There'll be a party in Paris tonight when we get back. You're welcome to join us."

He scratched at his short hair. "Go to Paris just for a party. That's a real city-dweller thing. An Earth city."

"Come on, you're not such a small-town boy. I'd dance with you."

"I can't believe how thorough you were. I really thought the defense was going to nail you with that question about evidence from Ormal. I guess she didn't realize how methodical you are."

Paula shrugged and dropped her spare jacket into the bag. "It's what I do. I have to be certain for myself. And Ms. Toi should have known, I'm notorious enough for my diligence. He was badly represented."

"So you're convinced he did it?"

"The Dimitros Fiech sitting in the dock this morning was the physical person who launched the missile. I have no doubt of that."

"Now there you go, see: a real lawyer's answer."

"I concede defense did have a point about what constitutes a whole person. Body and memory are the two halves of being human."

"But Fiech's memory of the attack has been wiped. It's over. We got what we could of him."

She smiled reassuringly. "Yes, we did. And he got the sentence he deserved."

Christabel and Nelson appeared behind Aidan. Neither looked as jubilant as they should have done. Aidan gave Paula an uncomfortable smile. "I'll leave you guys to it."

"Try and get there tonight," Paula told him. "I meant it about that dance."

A sheepish Aidan shuffled out past Christabel, who did her best not to laugh at his schoolboyish delight.

"Is he really your type?" Christabel asked.

"I don't have a type," Paula said. "But he is an honest policeman. I value that."

Nelson looked at Christabel, then Paula. Took a breath. "Anyway . . . I'm also here to deliver my Dynasty's thanks. We appreciate the effort involved in securing the verdict."

"You're welcome," Paula said. "It's a shame we couldn't use

Fiech to uncover his coconspirators, but that memory wipe was very efficient. There is nothing left of his life prior to his arrival in Sydney for that job. Until we finally arrest the entire Free Merioneth Forces, we're not going to find out who he is."

"Was," Christabel corrected.

Nelson's expression turned bitter. He made a show of closing the door. "That's unlikely to happen. Not now."

"What do you mean?" Christabel asked.

"Confidentially: my Dynasty, along with several others, has agreed that Merioneth will become an Isolated world."

Paula let out a hiss of exasperation. She'd suspected something like this would happen. The last few months, while they'd assembled the case against Dimitros Fiech, had seen the Free Merioneth campaign expand to alarming proportions. After the Nova Zealand plane, the movement had been steadily refining their operations, developing into more sophisticated assassins. The results were dramatic. Their targets were now dispatched with cool efficiency, and the number of collateral casualties was significantly reduced. In the last twelve attacks, thirty-nine Dynasty members had suffered complete bodyloss. The new generations were now running very scared, with few of them leaving their mansions on the private family worlds. "You gave in," she said in frustration.

"We couldn't afford it," Nelson said with equal chagrin. "The cost of providing upgraded security for every member of every Dynasty was completely unrealistic. Far beyond writing off the investment costs in Merioneth."

"There's more at stake here than money," an annoyed Christabel snapped.

"I know that," Nelson said. "Of course, it won't appear to be any kind of climb down. We wouldn't allow that. We negotiated the terms of Isolation with the new Nationalist Party that sprung up on Merioneth. The terrorists stop their attacks, and in a couple of years we close the wormhole. They'll be on their own. Forever."

"It'll come back to bite you," Paula said. "You've shown

your opponents a weakness. It can be used every time someone wants a concession out of a Dynasty."

"That was one of the reasons we agreed," Nelson said.

"I don't understand."

"We don't have other opponents, not in this category. The Intersolar Commonwealth is a relatively civilized place. Sure, we can all disagree with each other; politicians on half of the planets we've got aren't speaking to the other half; but there's only a tiny minority who want to leave, and an even smaller number who resort to violence to obtain their ends. This whole succession notion is ridiculous. An Isolated planet will never benefit from the advances the rest of us make. Their social and economic development will be stunted; hell, Merioneth will probably regress. When we announce that the wormhole is to be closed, we're expecting a lot of Merioneth's ordinary residents will rush back to the Commonwealth before Isolation begins. Our analysts have reviewed this; they're not sure Merioneth will even be able to maintain basic rejuvenation technology levels, not in the short-to-medium term. I sure as hell wouldn't want to live there. Body-loss will become death again."

"And the Dynasties consider that a big plus point," Christabel reasoned. "Anyone who doesn't like the Dynasties and what they represent will be free to emigrate to Merioneth."

"Then we slam the door shut behind them," Nelson said. "It'll be a bolt hole for malcontents the Commonwealth over. Everyone is better off afterward."

"An old-fashioned pressure valve for hotheads," Paula muttered.

"So the Dynasty leaders decided," he admitted. "It still galls me that the real culprits behind the attacks won't be brought to justice. But that's a political price, and it gets set far above our heads."

The club was underneath a twenty-second-century retro-Napoleonic building on the Left Bank. It was chic enough, though there were far more expensive places in Paris, but aside from Christabel herself, no one from the Serious Crimes Directorate office could afford an evening partying with the truly wealthy Grand Family members who colonized such establishments—and Christabel never pushed her heritage on anyone. Until tonight.

It was dark inside the annular vault, a gloom punctured by holographic blobs oscillating with naughty subliminal vibrations. Paula flinched as she walked down the stairs to the floor; the sound system was like a derated sonic weapon. Glass galleries enlivened by violet light ran around the high stone walls at two levels, linked by curving glass stairs. People thronged along them, Paris's eternal clique of bohemians, wearing clothes of semi-organic fabric embossed with elaborate patterns that merged seamlessly into the vivid OCtattoos on their skin. It was hard to tell what was fabric and what was flesh. Feathers were the current merging trend, curving fronds longer than ostrich quills that sprouted from the spine. Six months ago, it had been membrane petals. Several men displayed their plumage as Paula walked by, having it fan out on either side of their shoulders like wings. One was pure angel white, with a divine body to match. She smiled modestly and walked on, immune to such raffish peacocks.

Christabel was close to the bar inside the central circle of pillars, knocking back a tall glass of Ritz Pimms. Her lips were microlayered gold. Whenever a hologram floated across her, they sparkled dazzlingly.

"You made it!" she shouted at Paula.

Paula snagged a glass from a waitress. "Cheers!"

"Is he here?"

Paula shrugged, pretending not to understand. But there was a specific reason she was wearing a traditional little black dress with a semi-organic hem that swirled about of its own volition. In her newly youthful body, it made her look hot, and she knew it. Several junior investigators were staring in a way they'd never dare back at the office. "Congratulations," Paula said. "Traitor."

Christabel laughed. "I've served my time. And I made chief investigator on merit alone. That's what I needed. For myself if not the Dynasty."

"You'll be a loss to the Directorate."

Christabel leaned in a fraction. "The Dynasty is going to need me. Our entire concept of security is going to have to be revised, thanks to our idiot founders giving in to Merioneth. I heard that everyone is now pouring funds into researching personal-sized force-field generators. And they're all beefing up the defenses on our private worlds."

"Typical. So am I allowed to ask what department you're joining?"

"Deputy manager EdenBurg protection."

"Wow. Big field."

"Yeah. Give me a couple of decades and I'll make it to chief of the division. After that . . ." She trailed off and drained her glass.

"You'll be locking horns with Nelson."

"Nhaaa. He's too smart. We'll get on, at that level you have to."

"Speaking of which—"

"Of course. We'll dataswap. Happy to. Unless dear old grandma Heather actually kills someone—then I'll be helping to cover her arse."

"It's not your Dynasty's founder I'm interested in."

"Oh?" Christabel plucked another glass from the bar.

Paula thought that she looked defensive. *How quickly alliances shift.* "If you get the chance to access your Dynasty's file on the Merioneth Isolation, I'd appreciate a summary."

"That kind of thing never gets put in a file, as you well know. What are you looking for? We got Fiech, for God's sake. Two and a half millennia in oblivion! It doesn't get better than that."

"Why did he do it?"

"What?"

"I don't understand his motivation."

"To liberate Merioneth from Dynasty oppression," Christabel recited viciously. "And the bastards won!"

"Yes, they did, but *Fiech* didn't. He was utterly committed to his cause, so much so that he perpetrates one of the worst atrocities in modern history. One that almost killed his precious movement stone dead. People were repelled by what he did. Even his old colleagues realized that was too much, which is why they quickly got professional. That's how they won. Continuing to wipe out the Dynasty kids and keep bystander body-loss to an absolute minimum was smart. It bought pressure to bear exactly where it was needed. Yet Fiech will never see the end result, he'll never live on his free, liberated Merioneth. Motivated people simply don't commit suicide, which is effectively what he's done. By the time he comes out of suspension, the Commonwealth won't be recognizable, even if it still exists. Damnit, we'll probably all be post-physical by then. He's sacrificed himself for something he'll never know. That doesn't make any sense."

"Fanatics never make any real sense to anyone except themselves. Don't look for logic here, you'll only be disappointed."

"There *was* logic behind this. I just don't understand it yet. And that bothers me. It means we've overlooked something. Whoever set this up expended a huge amount of effort. The Directorate ran checks on every planetary medical database in the Commonwealth. Nobody has any record of the doppelgänger's DNA, which is extremely unusual for this day and age. The nearest we can do is identify family traits; he has ancestry within a mix of Celtic, Northern Spanish, and Saudi ethnicities. We found what we believe is a possible cousin on Piura; it was certainly the closest genetic match. But the poor girl didn't recognize Dimitros. I ran her family tree as best I could, but if he's on it, I couldn't tell. We just don't know who he is. If we can't find out, then he's either the most important man in the Merioneth independence movement, or an absolute nobody. I don't believe either."

"Maybe you're right with the first one, and his pals in the Free Merioneth Forces are planning on springing him out of suspension just before CST shuts the wormhole."

"Not going to happen. Nothing and nobody can break into the Justice Directorate suspension facility."

"So what are you going to do?"

Paula saw a nervous-looking Aidan appear at the top of the stairs. She smiled. "What I always do; keep the file open, solve the case properly."

Christabel followed her gaze. "Of course, you always get your man."

"Yes. Always."

WHAT PAULA FOUND OUT

Nelson Sheldon was right about the timing. Twenty-one months after Fiech's court case, and three weeks after a planetary referendum officially denounced as a shambolic farce by Intersolar observers, the senator from Merioneth stood up in the Commonwealth Senate to declare that her planet was regretfully withdrawing from the Intersolar Commonwealth to "pursue our future independently." The Speaker wished her well, and there was a chilly silence as the Merioneth delegation dramatically walked out of the full chamber. CST immediately announced that the wormhole link to Merioneth would be withdrawn in three months, leaving enough time for anyone on the planet who didn't wish to be Isolated to return to the Commonwealth.

Out of a population of seventeen million, the number wanting to remain part of the Commonwealth was just over nine million. It took an awful lot of trains running round the clock to bring them out. Which made travel to Merioneth extremely easy, with an inbound train arriving every ten minutes. When Paula caught a train to Baransly, the capital, three weeks before the wormhole was due to be shut, she was the only passenger in first class. Most of the carriages were vehicle carriers. Émigrés favored big trucks crammed full with their possessions. Local shipping companies were charging a fortune to transport containers of larger items. And the emergent national government was getting difficult about letting industrial machinery leave. The latest batch of restrictions covered all types of agribots; a lot of farmers were heading back to the Commonwealth.

Paula stared out of the long window as they emerged through the wormhole's pressure curtain. It was winter outside, with flecks of snow drifting through an iron-gray sky. The landscape here outside the capital was arranged into neat fields given over entirely to row after row of some vine equivalent, with brown leafless stems stretched along wire frames. Hundreds of small agribots rolled slowly down the lines, their plyplastic tentacles pruning the vines back to their regulation two-meter length.

Baransly itself was a sprawl of housing estates and industrial zones clustered around a commercial center that had already started to put up skyscrapers. The architecture was a little bleak and functional perhaps, but the city's size was an excellent example of successful development for a world that had only been open to settlement for eighty years.

By the time the train reached the marshaling yard outside the station, there were signs of law and order beginning to break down. Streets were clogged with abandoned cars and vans. The crates and boxes that they'd carried were now strewn everywhere, broken open to spill their contents onto the icy enzyme-bonded concrete. It was as if the goods of a hundred department stores had been scattered across the district by a real live cargo cult god. Gangs of kids and some adults were foraging the bounty. Then the train drew into the marshaling yard itself, and Paula's view of the city vanished behind walls of metal containers stacked taller than the surrounding buildings, all waiting shipment out. Men in thick jackets with the Merioneth Nationalist Party logo on their sleeves patrolled the aisles.

The train drew in at one of the ten platforms under the cover of a sweeping green crystal canopy. Every square meter of the platforms and concourse was occupied by a bad-tempered crowd. Armor-clad CST security guards patrolled along narrow clearways, their jangler guns carried prominently.

Paula slipped off the carriage to be greeted by Byron Lacrosh, chief aide to the prime minister, Svein Moalem, who was also leader of the Merioneth Nationalist Party. Byron and an armed police escort guided her down one of the clearways. A large limousine took them from the CST station to the Parliament building along roads that were still being cleared of discarded vehicles. Every few minutes, they passed crews of men and bots lifting cars onto big tow trucks.

"You won't need to worry about mining any new metal for a few years," Paula observed.

"Material resources aren't our prime concern," Byron Lacrosh said. "We hope to establish a culture that isn't as technology-based as the Commonwealth."

"You're going to go the agrarian route?"

"We favor divorcing ourselves from the consumerist monoculture that dominates the Dynasty-ruled worlds, yes. We don't shun technology, we just don't see the necessity to incorporate it in every aspect of life."

"Appropriate sustainability, then?"

Byron gave her an interested look. "You understand the philosophy?"

"It's hardly new. My birthworld is based on it."

"Oh yes, of course. I'd forgotten where you came from, Investigator Myo."

The Parliament building was a concrete and glass monstrosity, intended as a vigorous statement of a new planet's identity and prosperity. The result was the kind of design-by-bureaucrat-committee that Paula always found depressing, representing the exact opposite of the ethos it had originally been commissioned to promote.

Svein Moalem's office was on the fifth floor, with a curving glass wall that opened onto the hanging rose garden—famous locally for its cost overruns and leaky troughs. He sat behind a dark desk made from native kajawood. A broad-shouldered man ten years out of rejuvenation, with a neatly trimmed beard—following current local tradition. His light blue eyes were strongly contrasted with dark skin and mousy hair. Paula saw tiny luminescent green lines flickering along his cheeks to curve around the back of his neck. More OCtattoos shone on his hands. When she ordered her inserts to scan the office, she found a considerable amount of encrypted electromagnetic traffic emanating from him, or, to be exact, from the necklace of flat opals he wore. It was the kind of emission level she usually associated with sensory drama actors, allowing the unisphere audience to experience their body's sensations. The two people, a man and a woman sitting in front of his desk, were also broadcasting an unusually large amount of data, from similar necklace arrays. Paula suspected that every aspect of her interview was to be recorded and analyzed. A high-capacity cybersphere node was discreetly incorporated into the floor-to-ceiling bookcase behind the desk, but apart from that and several security sensors, she couldn't detect any other active hardware. Not that she expected any weapons to be active.

"Thank you for agreeing to see me, Prime Minister," she said.

Svein Moalem nodded graciously but didn't get up. He gestured to an empty chair directly in front of his desk. "I asked for two representatives from the Attorney General's office to be present."

Paula glanced at the two lawyers flanking her as she sat down. "I'm not here to arrest you. In fact, nobody really knows if the Intersolar Commonwealth has jurisdiction here at the moment. You've declared independence, and we've agreed to recognize it in three weeks' time. Anything between those dates is a very gray legal area."

"Yes, but nonetheless, they will insure my reputation is protected from unfair allegations."

"Allegations are for tabloid shows. I'm only here to ask questions."

The green lines under Moalem's beard scintillated. "As a friend of the Commonwealth, I'm happy to oblige; we have nothing to hide from you. And of course, who can resist your personal notoriety? So let's get started, shall we? I can spare you thirty minutes."

"I am the appointed investigator for the Dimitros Fiech case. Did you know him, Prime Minister?"

"I know of him, sadly. His misguided organization was one of the main inspirations behind setting up our Nationalist Party. Of course, we completely repudiate the use of violence to achieve independence."

"So you didn't know him personally?"

"No. My party's goals were achieved by legitimate democratic ends."

"I accessed the report from the observer team on your referendum. They wouldn't agree."

"Biased vitriol from those who have a vested interest in our continuing dependence and integration with their monoculture."

"Whatever. Fiech and his colleagues proved exceptionally resourceful, and they certainly learned quickly from their mistakes. He is the only member of the Free Merioneth movement we have apprehended so far. What they did required a large amount of money, at the very least. Is your government aware of where that finance originated from?"

"Your pardon, Investigator, but right now the Treasury department has more pressing concerns than examining bank transactions from two years ago. Little matters like making sure we have a valid currency in place for the cutoff. You understand."

"Their money must have originated here."

"I'm sure you're right. If we find out in the next three weeks, we'll be sure to inform your Directorate."

"Could it have come from the same source as your Party's money?"

"We are not dignifying that with an answer," the female lawyer said sternly.

Svein Moalem gave Paula a small mocking shrug to say *Out of my hands.*

"You set up your party after Fiech's organization had already won Isolation from the Dynasties," Paula said.

"Interesting allegation, Investigator." Moalem glanced at the female lawyer. "Do you have proof of this?"

"At the moment, I'm purely interested in motives. As someone who embodies the Isolationist dream, can you tell me why Fiech sacrificed himself?"

"I'm sure old Earth history is full of martyrs, all neatly documented, if you are that interested. But I suspect he believed as I do. And those who truly believe in the cause of freedom will go to any lengths to see it become reality. I commend his bravery, though, of course, I cannot condone his method."

"Yet his methods secured your goals."

"They helped focus the imaginations and aspirations of everyone on this planet. He woke us up to the oppression we labored under."

"I don't believe the people of this planet are inspired by monstrous violence. Over a hundred and thirty people suffered severe bodyloss on the Nova Zealand plane alone. Your citizens would want justice for them and all the others whose blood was spilled."

"Justice, yes. But we equally disapprove of the vengeance we've seen your Directorate unleash."

"Excuse me?"

"Who did you find guilty of the Nova Zealand crime, Investigator? Not the person who pulled the trigger, at least not the whole person. The man you have in your suspension facility lived a different life on that day. Your prisoner is not guilty of bringing down that aircraft. You hold a prisoner of conscience.

A patsy whose sole purpose is to satisfy the masses to the benefit of your political masters."

"Dimitros Fiech committed that crime," Paula said, doing
her best to hold her temper in check. She knew that the prime
minister was provoking her, trying to throw her off track.
"There is no question of that."

"So already we see the difference between your culture's rigid
nature and our more liberal, progressive quality. Your laws cannot
adapt to new circumstances."

"Fiech's memories are an alibi, nothing more. It's no different from using cellular reprofiling to change your facial features."

"It is completely different; it is his mind. The mind of the
person you have suspended knows that he was on Ormal during the crime. You said it yourself in the deposition: He knows
his office screwed up sending him there, he knows he paid the
taxi fare in Harwood's Hill, he was the person who watched the
land roll past through the plane's window, he was angry and
frustrated when he arrived at the resort, he tasted the vodka
at the airport bar, he fancied the redheaded stewardess who
helped him on the plane, he had the hangover. That was Dimitros Fiech. Nobody else. *His* personality. Him! Your impru-
dent freedom fighter was someone else."

"Who was erased by his colleagues. And I will find them,"
Paula growled out. "In order to do that, I need to comprehend
the psychology behind all of this. So tell me, help mitigate
Dimitros Fiech's sentence: Why exactly do you want Isolation?
What can you possibly achieve here that requires this drastic
severance from the Commonwealth?"

"That's a very long list, Investigator. Starting with removing
the contamination of a morally bankrupt, decadent society."

"At the cost of medical benefits? Your industrial capability is
going to be reduced drastically."

"Not as much as your propaganda insists. We shall live here
peacefully and progress in our own way, a way not dictated by
the Dynasties or the Senate. Many people are attracted to such

a notion. Millions, actually. Do you really begrudge us such liberty?"

"No. I just don't see what ideology can't be pursued within the umbrella of the Commonwealth. It is not as oppressive as your party claims, as *you* are well aware. A great many reduced-technology communities flourish on Commonwealth worlds. What you have engineered here is radical. I'm trying to understand its rationale."

Svein Moalem sat back in his chair and gave Paula a thoughtful stare, very much the politician trying to convert another wavering voter. "You of all people struggle to understand? Forgive me, but that is hard to believe."

"Why?"

"You were created and birthed on Huxley's Haven, the most reviled planet in the Commonwealth. How the illiberal classes hated its founding. A world with everyone genetically predisposed to their job, a society in which everybody has a secure place. It is living proof that alternatives can work. Surely that's a concept to be welcomed and admired?"

"Its functionality is admirable. However, even I don't approve of its static nature. Those humans can no longer evolve."

"Yet they live perfectly happy lives."

"Yes," Paula said. "Within the parameters established by the Human Structure Foundation."

"You would want Huxley's Haven broken up and abandoned?" He sounded very surprised.

"Certainly not. Its citizens have a right to their existence. It is pure imperialist arrogance for outsiders to propose alteration."

"You see, Investigator, you make my argument for me! That is your answer. The right to self-determination is a human fundamental. Such a thing is not possible while under the financial hegemony of the Dynasties and Grand Families."

"Everything comes down to money in the end," Paula offered.

"Quite."

"I still can't believe some abstract ideology is enough for Fiech to sacrifice himself."

"Hardly abstract." Moalem waved at the city outside. "His wish has become our reality."

Paula pursed her lips, following his gesture. "I hope it's worth it."

"It is."

She stood and gave him a small bow. "Thank you for your time, Prime Minister."

"You're welcome, Investigator. In fact, I'd like to offer you a place here with us. Our police forces will need a substantial re-organization after the cutoff. Who better to manage that? You are celebrated and respected on every world in the Common-wealth. Your honesty and devotion to justice have broken the hatred and prejudice barrier. In a way, you are what we aspire to be."

"That's very flattering, but the answer is no."

"Why not? Indulge me, please. I am curious. You left Hux-ley's Haven, the only one of millions ever to do so. You found the Commonwealth more attractive. Why not us?"

"I didn't leave," Paula said, feeling her shoulder muscles tense up. "I was stolen from my birthing clinic. The political ac-tivists who took me wanted to make a point in their campaign to 'liberate' Huxley's Haven. Consequently, I was brought up in the Commonwealth. I chose to stay."

"You found it more desirable than the most secure civiliza-tion ever established?"

"I was created to be a police officer; it is what I am. There is more crime in the Commonwealth than on Huxley's Haven, and it is the culture I was brought up in. It was logical for me to stay. Here I would never lack for challenges."

"So the activists were right then? The manufactured people of Huxley's Haven would be able to settle in the Intersolar Commonwealth?"

"They could physically settle. Intellectually, I doubt they would be able to integrate. Myself and other police officers are a very small minority of the population. The exceptions. I understand that after my 'batch,' the Foundation changed the psychoneural profiling. Huxley's Haven police officers are no longer as liberal as me"—she licked her lips in amusement—"a notion that discomforts the Commonwealth even more. Can you imagine a less forgiving version of me, Prime Minister?"

"That's a tough one, I admit." Finally he stood, a faint smile on his lips. "Good day, Investigator."

Two days later, Paula woke up to a call request from Christabel flashing in her virtual vision. She yawned, stretched, and told her maidbot to bring some tea. Then her virtual finger touched Christabel's green icon.

"You made it back okay," Christabel said. "I heard it's getting tough in Baransly. CST asked for a week's extension before they switch off the wormhole; they're worried they won't be able to get everyone out before the cutoff."

"There's a lot of people there," Paula said, remembering the trip back to the CST station, the way her police escort had to force their way to a train for her. "What did the Merioneth government say?"

"No."

"Figures. Moalem has worked hard to reach this moment. He's not going to allow anything to stop it now. Especially now."

"Especially now? Did you get some useful information?"

"Very. He was the alibi memory. Svein Moalem went to Ormal and spent the day living Fiech's life."

"*What?* You've got to be fucking kidding me."

"No. I'm not."

"How do you know that?"

"He fancied a redhead."

"Come on, talk sense to me."

"Moalem told me the stewardess on the plane Fiech flew on from Essendyne back to Harwood's Hill was a redhead. He's right, too." Paula closed her eyes, recalling the memories that didn't belong to her, the ones she'd read from Fiech's brain. Seeing wavery images of the attractive woman in her neat blue and green uniform, Celtic-red hair all tied up with leather clips. Trying to smile as she supported his body up the stairs, and, amazingly, still calm when she deposited him in his seat and he made a crude drunken pass.

Paula had interviewed the woman a week later as she retraced the alibi, confirming the memory.

"So?" Christabel asked.

"That detail wasn't in the memory deposition filed with the court. I just said a stewardess."

"He could have found out."

Paula pulled the straps of her slip up properly on her shoulders as the maidbot came in with a large breakfast cup of green Assam tea. "Why would he?"

"Because they're obviously all part of the same group of Isolationists. He'd want to know everything connected with the case."

"No, this was a casual detail. I know it was. He was the one on Ormal."

"Oh bloody hell, so now what?"

"Obviously, he has to be arrested. He was a major part of the crime. If he was as deeply involved in the Free Merioneth Forces as I suspect, he could well expose the others with a memory read."

"Not going to happen. There's only two and a half weeks left to Isolation. You'll never get clearance for that. It would take a small army to go in there and arrest their new prime minister. Actually . . . how come you didn't try while you were there? I know you. You cannot stand back."

"I know. It's engineered into my nature. But the probability of a successful outcome if I'd tired to arrest him on the spot was zero. They would simply have eliminated me."

"So natural self-preservation is stronger than the rest of you after all. That's a relief to know."

"It was simply a decision based on common sense. I am going to arrange a meeting with Nelson. He may be able to secure me the return ability I need to complete the case."

"Damn, that's a long shot."

"Yes, but what else have I got? The Directorate won't be able to lift Moalem from Merioneth."

"I wouldn't count on the Sheldons doing it either. The political fallout would be too great: Lifting someone from an Isolated world and making them stand trial here all because they assassinated Dynasty members. That won't look good for the Dynasties, Paula, not politically. Isolation was the end of this, the deal."

"I know, but Nelson is the best option I've got." She sipped some of the tea. "What were you calling me about?"

"I've been digging around where I shouldn't have, as you asked. I'm not sure how relevant this is now, but the Dynasties know who's been backing the whole Merioneth independence movement."

"Who?"

"Now promise you won't shoot the messenger."

Paula grinned and took another sip. "I won't."

"The Human Structure Foundation."

The surprise made her start. "Damnit!" She struggled not to let the tea spill onto the bed.

"You okay?"

"Yes, yes." Beside her, Aidan stirred at the commotion.

"Look, I can maybe make some inquiries at this end, see if my Dynasty will go along with a covert extraction. The Free Merioneth Forces hurt a lot of Halgarths. Heather was not happy about giving them Isolation. We could put together an operation with the Sheldons."

"That's more like vengeance," Paula said quietly. "Not due process."

"You're running out of options."

"I know. I need to make a few more inquiries about this. I'll get back to you."

Aidan blinked round, lifting his head off the pillow. "Some-thing wrong?"

"No." She ran her hand through his disheveled hair. "Early start, that's all. Something unexpected came up. I've got to take a trip."

"Where to now? Other side of the Commonwealth again?"

"The Caribbean, actually."

The nearest city on the trans-Earth loop was New York. When she arrived at the Newark station, Paula took a cab over to JFK and flew a Directorate hypersonic parallel to the East Coast, then on south to Grenada. The Human Structure Foun-dation campus occupied a broad stretch of rugged land behind a series of curving beaches whose pale sand was just visible in the low moonlight. A circular white-glass tower formed the cen-ter, silhouetted by liquid bifluron tubes embedded in the struc-ture. The long sodium-orange web of streets radiating out from the base revealed the surrounding village of elaborate bunga-lows. Foundation members didn't reside in any of the island's ordinary towns; in the last century, few ventured out beyond the heavily guarded perimeter strip. It was a micronation of genetic ideologues, despised by just about everyone, yet contin-uing to operate under Senate-imposed research restrictions, re-strictions that had grown ever stronger since the establishment of Huxley's Haven.

Paula was familiar enough with the setup, though she'd never actually visited before. The notion of walking around the place that conceived her—intellectually and physically—was an experience she simply didn't want.

Her plane landed on a circular pad by the tower. Long ply-plastic petals unrolled from the edges to form a protective shell over her little craft. An astonishingly attractive woman named Ophelia escorted her up to Dr. Friland's office on the top floor of the tower. On the way through the atrium lobby, people stopped and stared at Paula. It was three o'clock in the morning local time; the tower should have been deserted. She was used to attention, but this was akin to religious respect. Some looked like they wanted to bow as she walked past. The effect was un-nerving—and she wasn't used to that feeling at all.

"You're the living proof that the concepts for which we stand have been successful," Ophelia murmured as they walked into the elevator. "There have been many sacrifices down the de-cades, so please excuse their wonder."

Paula sucked in her cheeks, unable to meet any of the ar-dent stares as the elevator doors slid shut.

According to his file, Justin Friland was born toward the end of the twentieth century. Meeting him in the flesh, Paula couldn't tell, and she normally prided herself in spotting the telltale mannerisms of the truly old. He didn't have any. His ef-fusive good nature matched his handsome adolescent appear-ance perfectly. Like the Foundation members down in the lobby, he gave Paula an incredulous smile as she came into his office.

"Director, I appreciate you seeing me," Paula said. "Espe-cially at this time of night."

"Not at all. This is an absolute honor," he said, shaking her hand too vigorously and beaming a wide smile.

"Thank you," Paula said gently, and removed her hand from his grip.

"I spent twenty-five years on Huxley's Haven, helping to establish the birthing centers," Justin Friland said. "And seeing you here is"—he spread his arms out—"astonishing. We never thought one of you could adapt to life offworld."

"One of *me*?" Paula arched an eyebrow.

"Sorry, sorry! It's just—we took so much shit over the Haven. Even fifty years ago, the perimeter here was sur-rounded by protestors. However, the days of the ten-thousand-strong mob have long gone. We still do have a hard core camped to the side of our main entrance. They're not . . . *pleas-ant* people. My thoughts are still in war mode. My fault."

"I see."

"Please, sit down." He hurried over to a wide couch. "What can I do for you?"

"I need information."

"Whatever I can provide." He was nodding enthusiastically as Paula sat beside him.

"There is a rumor that the Foundation financed Merioneth's Isolation."

"Not us," Friland said emphatically. He brushed some floppy chestnut hair from his forehead. "However, the Foundation has undergone considerable schism during the last quarter century. I now lead what you'd probably call a Conservative faction."

"What of the other factions?"

He sighed. "The person you want to talk to is Svein Moalem."

Paula gave Friland a surprised look. "He's a Foundation member?"

"An ex-colleague, yes. Now the leader of the New Immortals."

"We didn't know that. We don't have access to Merioneth files now."

"Wouldn't have done you any good. The New Immortals have coveted their own planet for some time. They did a lot more than simply finance the Isolation revolution on Merioneth. They infiltrated its civil service quite some time ago. Any records you did access through the unisphere merely say what they want them to say."

"And you didn't feel obliged to tell us this?"

"Us?" Justin Friland smiled faintly.

"The Intersolar Senate. The Serious Crimes Directorate."

"Ah. Your government? No. Pardon me, Paula. I wasn't about to come running to the organization that officially condemned my projects as the work of the devil. Besides, up until they started killing Dynasty members, our Immortal brethren didn't actually do anything illegal. Political shenanigans are perfectly permissible under our oh-so-liberal Intersolar constitution.

Manipulating public data for ideological ends is common practice. I assume you have better statistics than I do on the subject."

Paula thought about arguing but decided against it. The information might be useful later, if the Directorate decided to press complicity charges against Friland. "The New Immortals?" she asked. "I assume it's a relevant name. What method have they adopted? And why does it need an Isolated world?"

Julian Friland looked distinctly uncomfortable. "It's a modified version of today's re-life memory succession, which eliminates the requirement to rejuvenate a body."

"Thank you. You've just told me nothing."

"If you suffer bodyloss today, your insurance company grows a clone and downloads your secure memory store into it. Many people regard that as death. It's a question of continuity, you see. In rejuvenation, your body simply floats in a tank while its DNA is reset. The you that comes out is still the you that went in a year before, so there's no doubt about originality and identity. What Moalem and his group proposed was operating *continuous* bodies. A mental relay, if you like, with a personality twinned between an old and young version of the same person."

"So when the old physical body dies, the young one carries on."

"With continuity intact," Friland emphasized. "I acknowledge the concept is an elegant one."

"Not entirely original," Paula said, thinking about the emissions she'd detected coming from Moalem. She frowned, trying to follow the idea through to its conclusion. "Surely, the two bodies would have to be close together. If they started to diverge, see and react to different things, then the personality would also start to fraction."

"Good point. The New Immortals claimed that was actually a desirable outcome. Moalem decided that a singular personality input-point was a primitive notion. The human mind should be able to expand to encompass many bodyforms, all inputting their experiences to the unifying mind."

"That has to be unstable. Bipolar disorder and multiple personalities are notoriously erratic."

"I've been through these arguments so many times with Svein. He maintains that inherent mental illness is completely avoidable in these circumstances, that the human mind can evolve in conjunction with its physical environment. The host personality has to be willing and receptive to change, to want to learn how to be different. He's probably right."

"I'm sorry, I don't follow. You say the Foundation split because of this? I thought you were all about exploring new forms of human existence."

"We are. I set up the Foundation to advance humanity through genetic modification. But change in isolation is not a desirable thing. Hence Huxley's Haven. Not only are its citizens perfectly adjusted to their jobs, the entire society is designed to be stable, so that only the professions and abilities we have allowed for are needed. There are human clerks who make electronics, especially computers, redundant. Engineering is constitutionally fixed to equal early-twentieth-century development, so mechanics are capable of performing all repairs, rather than writing software for maintenance bots. It's a level that was specifically chosen to give everyone a decent quality of life without dependence on cybernetics. Which is what makes Huxley's Haven a perfectly integrated society. It doesn't change because there is no requirement for change. That is what Commonwealth citizens found so disturbing; it's also why it works. Within the Foundation, we had a very large debate as to whether we should Isolate it once it was established."

"Why didn't you? A society like that can only be challenged by an outside force, so why risk continued exposure? There are plenty of idealists even today who would like it stopped."

"I didn't believe we had the right. Maybe in a few hundred years' time, the Haven will choose to isolate itself from what the Intersolar Commonwealth will become. Who knows?"

"And if it starts to fail, you can fix it," Paula guessed. He had that kind of egotism.

"That's what the freethinkers are for," Friland said. "And to a lesser degree, the police such as yourself. All societies should include a mechanism for self-correction."

"You're distracting me," Paula said. "Why the split with the New Immortals?"

"Very well," Friland said. "I owe you of all people that explanation, if nothing else."

"How ironic for you, having to explain yourself to your creation!"

"I'm not a Frankenstein, Investigator."

"Of course not. The split?"

"First, the prospect of a hive mind is one I resist. Call me old-fashioned, but I don't regard it as a human goal. Yet there is that danger. Svein knows that you need more than two bodies to guarantee life-continuity. The more you have, the higher the personality's survival probability. There is no theoretical limit. He can possess hundreds, thousands, of bodies. More still. Exponential growth rates are a favorite politician's scare image, and I don't like to use it, but something close to exponential expansion is a very real threat in this case. What happens to individual, normal humans if a New Immortal expands its nest of selves? An Immortal by his or her nature becomes focused on survival. That will trigger competition for resources, possibly as bad as it was in the twenty-first century before Ozzie and Nigel developed wormhole technology. Would the singulars survive? Would they be *allowed* to survive? And what about other nest Immortals? One route is merger. The universal monomind. Again, something I instinctively shy away from. Svein was not complimentary about what he perceives as my outdated reactionary thinking."

"That must have been painful for you."

"Quite. The other problem I have is the method that the New Immortals have chosen. It is not pure genetic evolution, which is our creed."

"Now you've really lost me."

"If you have children, Investigator, they will remain true to your nature. They will inherit the genetic and psychoneural profiling that make you the perfect law enforcement officer. We set the traits that make you what you are; they are dominant. Even if all our fabulous society should fall, if the wormholes are closed, the factories break down, electricity cease to flow; if the human race enters into a new age of barbarism—what the Foundation created will remain. Our heritage is written in our genes. When we define an advancement, we incorporate it in our DNA. It can never be lost. An equal science can remove it, but our advances would endure a dark age. Svein's system will not. He shares his thoughts and memories with his other bodies via the unisphere. He needs OCtattoos and inserts to transmit and receive. He needs clone vats to grow new bodies. His is a cybernetic, technological future. It is a very short step from what he wishes to become to simply downloading your thoughts into a machine, like today's uniheads do with the SI. After all, a machine can be made far stronger than human flesh. This is not the route I wish the Foundation to go down. At the far end, it is not a human outcome that awaits."

"Surely, that's all contrary to the stasis of Huxley's Haven?"

"The Haven provides us with a proof of concept. We know we can match our genetic and societal requirements synergistically. That sets the stage for our next advances."

"Which are?" she asked sharply.

"Development along all fronts. Extreme longevity—ultimately, self-rejuvenation. Increased intelligence. Huge disease resistance."

"Bigger. Stronger. Better," she murmured.

"Yes. These advances are slowly seeping into the human genome. Parents have baseline procedures carried out on their embryos to give their offspring healthier physiques. Reprofiling is commonplace in rejuvenation tanks, at least for those who can afford it. We are a slow revolution, Paula. People find our long-term aims uncomfortable, but they continue to incorporate our immediate successes into their very selves. Given such development, society will inevitably adapt and evolve. Which is why I reject the obsessional goal of the New Immortals. I will happily continue my rejuvenation treatments every thirty years because they will ultimately be temporary. In four or five hundred years' time, I will be beginning my senior life span, which will be measured in millennia. Can you imagine what kind of culture that will play host to?"

"Even if I could, I obviously wouldn't have a place in it. I'm just a halfway stage experiment, remember."

"Oh no, Paula, you've become much more than that. You've humbled us by showing how adaptive humanity is. You are an inspiration that we can all exceed our perceived limits."

"How very lovely for you," she said acerbically, and stood up.

Justin Friland looked up at her. "What will you do to Svein Moalem now that you know what he is?"

"I'm not sure," she replied truthfully. "I'm sure I'll *adapt* my nature somehow, and bring him to justice."

He smiled sadly. "We're not adversaries, Paula, not you and me."

"Not yet. Not quite. But keep on going the way you are, and we'll wind up facing each other in court. The Senate has strict laws concerning genetic manipulation outside designated human parameters."

"I know. And I'm very tired of them, which is why we're finally leaving altogether."

She narrowed her eyes. "Are you going to Isolate another world?"

"No, we don't have to. The Commonwealth is desperate to make a success of Far Away; the Senate spent so much money getting there, they have to justify it to the taxpayer. It's a blank canvas of a world, thanks to the solar flare that eliminated its indigenous life. My remaining colleagues are moving there with me. The Senate's authority and its laws are confined to one city; out in the wild, we'll be free of the petty regulations that restrict us here, and we can design a new biosphere environment to complement whatever enhancements we build into our bodies. The ultimate synergy, eh?"

"That sounds like a project that will keep you occupied for a few decades."

"We would be honored if you'd join us. You would be an enormously valuable asset to any community, Paula."

"Thank you, but no. I have work to do in this society." She started toward the door.

"There could be tens of him by now," Friland called out after her. "Dozens. You'll never get them all."

"Nonetheless, he will face justice. You know that. That's how you made me."

WHAT HAPPENED NEXT

The countryside outside Baransly was certainly a lot more hospitable in summer. A warm G-class star shone in a deep ocean-blue sky. High wispy clouds laced the horizon ahead as Paula walked down the narrow farm track that cut through the big fields, pushing her lightweight p-bike over the scattered stone. The air was thick and warm, heavy with the sugary scent of the fireflower vine. She knew the name now. It was the district's main crop. In the summer's warmth and humidity, the rows of wire frames were transformed into long dunes of vivid crimson flowers with thick yellow stamen. Petals were already starting to crisp and brown at the edges as midsummer approached; in another month, the fruit would ripen to fist-sized globes a dull purple in color. The pulp was a local staple, equivalent to meat-potato, though the fruit could be crushed for oil as well.

She reached the concrete road at the end of the track and straddled the p-bike. There was no traffic. She twisted the throttle and set off toward Baransly's outskirts, five miles ahead.

The city's traffic management network was still functioning. It registered her p-bike as she crossed into the official city boundary. By now, she was on Route Two, one of the main highways into the city, with the midafternoon traffic starting to build up around her. She told the network that she wanted Lislie Road and received a route authorization. Her vehicle license had been accepted as current.

Lislie Road was in the middle of a pleasant residential suburb, with small dome-roofed houses grown out of air coral. Paula turned off the tree-shaded road itself onto the broad pavement and started peddling the p-bike. That way, she was no longer monitored by the traffic network. She stopped outside number 62 and wheeled the p-bike up to the front door. It accepted the code she put in and swung open for her.

Nelson Sheldon had paid Terrie Ority, the previous occupant, a handsome sum for his codes, just as he'd paid another Merioneth refugee for a bike license. The preparations had taken over a month. Paula and Nelson had put the operation together on Augusta, the Sheldon Dynasty's industrial world. It was the first time in nine decades that Paula had taken a holiday from the Directorate. She'd accrued eight years' leave. The personnel office was delighted—her director curious.

Inside number 62, the air was musty. Terrie Ority was a fussy man—he'd turned off all the power before he left. He had also left behind most of the furniture. Paula switched the air-conditioning back on and ran the taps to cycle the plumbing system. A couple of ancient maidbots were sitting in their alcoves, fully charged, so she ordered them to start cleaning.

She spent the rest of the day establishing her legend identity in the civil and commercial systems. Her bank account was opened and loaded from a card. She registered with several local stores and had food delivered. Then she sat back and accessed the planetary cybersphere, with her e-butler extracting news summaries to build a picture of Merioneth after the wormhole had closed five months earlier.

It was like losing a short, brutal war. With half the population gone, whole towns had been abandoned. New consumer items were hard to find. Not that it mattered, people simply reclaimed and recycled products from deserted homes. Food hadn't quite been rationed in the winter, but a lot of favorites were no longer commercially available. She was interested to see that medical services, including rejuvenation clinics, had been nationalized on a temporary basis, so that they could be reorganized for fair and equal distribution. Whole fleets of bots, especially civic ones, were breaking down; there were too few service and repair companies to keep them functional. Public transport was patchy, with priority given to maintain strategic links. Cars and trucks were also in need of maintenance, but again, there were a huge number of abandoned vehicles that could be utilized. But on the plus side, this summer's crops were going to produce big surpluses—nobody would go hungry. The tidal and hydropower stations were all functioning efficiently. Local currency was stabilizing after months of disastrous inflation. People were starting to adapt to their new life.

She started to research Svein Moalem. He was still prime minister, with his Nationalist Party holding two thirds of the remaining seats in Parliament. There were due to be elections in two years, when the new constituency boundaries had been established. The party had spent the months since Isolation revoking a whole host of "oppressive Commonwealth restrictions," the majority of which were regulations covering genetic modifications and cloning. Helpfully, Moalem's office provided a diary listing events he was due to attend.

The next day, Paula started observing his movements within the city. They were typical of any high-ranking politician. Speeches to civic and community leaders, meetings with party officials. Parliamentary debates. Voter-friendly visits to schools, hospitals, and selected business. Trips to provincial towns.

He had bodyguards, of course, good ones. When he was due at an event, crowds were scanned using feature recognition software to check for repeat observers. The traffic network was analyzed for any vehicle that kept cropping up in his vicinity. If he took a train or plane, passenger lists were reviewed. All well-established midlevel protocols.

As a consequence, she kept her distance, content to follow his routes via some very sophisticated software her e-butler manipulated in the planetary cybersphere.

After a week, she'd confirmed that he would often abandon his official residence next to the Parliament building in favor of a grand private house in Baransley's most exclusive LakeHill district, where the last remaining multimillionaires resided. It was a perfect place for his nest to operate from.

On the eighth night, with her monitor routines confirming his presence at a late-night Cabinet session, Paula broke in.

The perimeter alarm circuits and sensors were utterly ineffectual against her superior software and the active stealth covering of her light-armor suit. She started walking through the formal grounds, tracking the sentinel dogs prowling around. Thickets of local trees provided excellent cover. The house was squatting on the summit of a mound that had been sculpted with high terracing. To Paula's suspicious eye, the mound would be perfect cover for an underground complex.

She climbed the dry-stone wall of the last terrace. Ahead of her, the house was a three-story construction of dark gray stone, crowned with a lantern tower. The lawn between her and the wall was completely devoid of cover and dotted with sensors. She used her inserts to neutralize several in her path. Her e-butler told her that several motion trackers up on the eves were locking on as she jogged forward. Data traffic in and out of the house began to increase.

Paula scurried up to a large French door and used a compact power blade to cut a circle through the glass. She found herself in a big hall that followed the principals of High Renaissance architecture, with square columns and a vaulting ceiling of decorated panels.

The lights came on when she was halfway to the vast curving stairs at the far end. Five security staff with high-rated maser rifles were lined up behind the polished stone banister.

"Hold it right there."

More armed security staff scurried in from ground-floor rooms and surrounded her. Their armor suits were a lot heavier than hers. She raised her hands as eleven energy weapons lined up on her, any one of which could probably cut through her protection.

"Do not move. Deactivate all your systems."

Paula switched the shimmering stealth layer off, then slowly reached up and removed her helmet. One of the armored figures up on the stairs stood up, lowering his rifle. Paula's inserts detected a large emission of encrypted data emerging from him, and suppressed a smile.

"Investigator Myo," he said, taking off his own helmet. There was no resemblance to Svein Moalem in his features and his skin was the pale brown of a North African.

"Correct," she said. "And whom am I addressing?"

"Agent Volkep. I'm in charge of the prime minister's security." He walked down the stairs. Paula's e-butler told her the nodes in the house had closed their links to the cybersphere. More suppression shielding came on, sealing up the hall from any communication.

"That's convenient for you," Paula said archly as Volkep stood in front of her. His expression gave nothing away.

"Take her over to the holding center," he told the armed squad. "I want a full scan for weapon inserts, and be very thorough. Hell knows what her Directorate equipped her with. Then bring her down to secure facility three. I'll interrogate her there."

Two electromuscle-enhanced gauntlets gripped Paula's arms, almost lifting her off the ground. She turned her head to look at Volkep as she was hauled away across the hall's marble flooring. "Nice seeing you again, Svein," she called out loudly.

That brought a flicker of annoyance to his face.

The holding center was a simple concrete room with a cage door and a single medical-style chair in the middle. It was equipped with malmetal restraints.

Four of the armored bodyguards came in with her, powered up and shielded. They ordered her to strip. Paula obediently removed her own armor. "Keep going," they told her. She pulled off her sweatshirt and slipped her long shorts down her legs. The OCtattoo glowed sapphire and jade on her abdomen, a circle encasing a tight geometry of intersecting curves that undulated slowly. Four gun muzzles lined up on the gentle light.

"What's that?"

"Sensory booster," Paula said. "It's wetwired into my nerves so I can receive a bigger sensation when I'm accessing porn from the unisphere. Don't you have them here?"

"Just get the rest of your clothes off, lady."

She shrugged out of her bra and took her panties off. One of the suited bodyguards dropped all her garments into a big bag and carried it out. Paula was left standing in the cold concrete cell with the remaining three agents.

"Not bad," one remarked.

"You wouldn't need a booster for anything with me," his colleague said. The others laughed.

Paula gazed at his blank shiny helmet and gave a small snort of contempt. Perhaps she had given the secret service agents too much credit after all.

A female technician came in, followed by a trollybot loaded with sensor equipment. She frowned when she saw Paula's OC-tattoo. "Put her in the chair."

The malmetal manacles flowed over Paula's wrists and ankles. Sensor pads were applied to her skin over the twisting luminescence. More scans swept across her limbs and torso. Then her skull was given a thorough examination. The woman took samples of her blood and saliva. Nails were tested for toxins. Even the air she exhaled was sampled for any abnormality.

Finally, the technician nodded at the armored figures. "She's clean. Her inserts are sophisticated, but they're all sensors, memory chips, and processor systems; no weapons of any kind. You can take her down to Volkep."

"So what's that thing?" one of the agents asked, pointing at Paula's abdomen.

"Receiver circuitry wired into her spinal cord, just like she said."

Paula was marched back through the grandiose hall to a room at the back of the house. An elevator took her deep underground. She wasn't at all surprised when it opened on a junction of corridors. Volkep took over, dismissing the bodyguards. He took Paula by the arm and led her to a simply furnished office. Svein Moalem was waiting there, his opal necklace just visible inside the open collar of his shirt. Two other youths were with him, one obviously a full clone with identical features to Svein, just five years younger, the other having East Asian features; the one thing they had in common was a necklace. Volkep was still in his armor, so she couldn't tell if he was wearing any kind of array.

"I like the whole underground citadel thing," Paula said, looking around the office with its drab ceiling and dilapidated couch. "Quite the retro Criminal Mastermind secret headquarters." Her abdominal OCtattoo showed her that the four of them were exchanging data at a huge rate, all of which originated from the ornamental arrays around their necks. She opened the additional bioneural chips in her cortex and started recording their emissions.

"Why are you here?" Volkep asked.

"I talked to Dr. Friland."

"Ah," Svein said, an exclamation simultaneously uttered by his youthful clone.

"You fired the missile on Nova Zealand," Paula said.

"Well, that's open to debate."

"In fact, I suspect your nest *is* the Free Merioneth Forces in their entirety."

"Not completely. My Foundation colleagues are fully supportive in every respect."

"I see."

"Would you like to arrest them as well?"

"I might get around to it."

"I'm fascinated by how you got here. Did you come back before or after the wormhole closed?"

"After. You killed a lot of Sheldons."

"Old concept," the East Asian youth said dismissively. "They're all alive today."

"Interesting," Paula said. "Did you know your inflections are the same?"

Svein walked around in front of her. "Did you know I don't care? Why are you here? Even with Sheldon support, you can't possibly expect to snatch all of me back to the Commonwealth. After all, you don't even know how many of me there are."

"True. Did you get hot while you waited for the plane to take off? I did while I was out there. That desert has a terrible climate."

"You'd have to send a small army here for that, and even if Sheldon was determined enough, there's no guarantee he'd succeed. Were you sent to try to find out how much I've grown?"

"I don't care how many there are in your nest. Was the missile heavy when you lifted up and aimed it at the plane?"

"What do you mean, you don't care? Why are you here then? Why did you break into my home? Is it to snatch data on me?"

"I have all the data I need. It was the reason for the Isolation that puzzled me. Now that I know it wasn't a financial or political ethos, it makes perfect sense. Did you build the missile here? Did it kick when you launched it? Was the exhaust plume loud?"

"Not political?" Svein said it, but all four of the nest raised their eyebrows in unison, sharing the same slightly mocking expression. "What could be more political than developing a new kind of life–effectively, a new species?"

"Friland called you obsessional," Paula said. "I think he's right. Did you actually watch the plane falling out of the sky? I bet you did. Who could resist that? No matter what type of human you are."

"Paula"–all four of him assumed a mock-indignant expression–"are you trying to *provoke* me?"

"Did you feel satisfaction when it exploded?"

"Two can play this game. Did Friland tell you we're related, you and me?" The Svein body grinned.

The Volkep body stood beside Svein. "And he was the original," Volkep said, tapping Svein on the shoulder. "Our minds are rooted in the same ancestor, Paula."

"I didn't know that," she admitted. "Were you nervous when you ran back to the boat? That was a weak point. Someone might have seen you."

"Friland originally funded the Foundation from the clinic he used to run in Granada back in the twenty-first century," Svein said. "He sold baseline germ treatments to wealthy Westerners whose own countries banned such tinkering. That way, he amassed a massive germ bank. A good percentage of the wealthy and powerful people of the day came to visit at some time and have their children enhanced. Their money and DNA was a good foundation for his Foundation."

"Standing on Ridgeview station platform waiting for the train, you must have been buzzing on adrenaline," Paula persisted. "You'd know that I or someone like me would have the trains stopped. You might have been stranded there, with the police closing in. No way to get back to Sydney and establish your alibi."

"I looked up the records in Granada. Our ancestor is Jeff Baker; apparently, he invented crystal memories. A famous man in his time. A very smart man, too. Friland needed that level of intelligence in his research team, which is why I was created from Baker's old sperm samples. You, I imagine, require a similar analytical ability. A lot of other sequences were included, which is where we start to diverge, but genetically, he's equivalent to our grandfather. Which makes us cousins, Paula. We're family. And you always thought you were unique, isolated, and alone. You're not, Paula. We not only share flesh, we think the same way."

"Were you watching when my Directorate team arrested your Fiech body? Some clever little vantage point nearby, perhaps?"

Svein pressed his face up close to Paula, his mouth parting with an angry snarl. "That *obsession* you mock in me is exactly the same one that runs through you, Investigator Myo! Friland didn't have to sequence it into your genome quite as much as you were led to believe. It's not artificial, it's *you*. It's your heritage. It's my heritage. It's what we are. And this is our world. You're home, Paula. Welcome back."

She smiled lightly. "I know what I am, and I know where my home is. Good luck finding yours."

The Svein body took a half step back from her. All four of the nest were frowning in annoyance now. "Why are you here?" they demanded in unison.

"To ensure that the sentence passed on Fiech is carried out in full," Paula told them.

"I thought it had been," the Volkep body said coldly.

"It hasn't been yet, because you made sure that part of you didn't remember. But memory's a funny thing, it's triggered by association. And your mind is *shared*." Paula gestured around at the empty air. "It's all around us, if you know how to look." Her virtual hand touched Nelson's communication icon.

"I've got enough," she said out loud.

"What—" all four nestlings grunted.

The wormhole opened behind her, expanding out from a micron-wide point to a two-meter circle. Bright light shone through, silhouetting Paula's naked body. She stepped backward, crossing the threshold to be enveloped by the light. She lost her footing as Augusta's slightly heavier gravity claimed her, and fell on her arse in a completely undignified manner. Svein and his nestlings never saw that. The wormhole closed the instant she was through.

She was sitting in the middle of the alien environment confinement chamber of the CST Augusta Exploratory Division, a huge dome-shaped chamber with dark radiation-absorptive walls. In front of her was the five-meter-wide blank circle of the wormhole gateway, its gray pseudosubstance emitting strange violet sparkles. Halfway up the curving surface behind her was a broad band of reinforced windows with the big operations center behind it. Nelson Sheldon was pressed up against the superstrength glass, grinning down at her. Behind him, the hundred-strong staff controlling the wormhole were peering over the tops of their tiered rows of consoles, curious and eager to see the conclusion to their oddest operation ever. Tracking her movements on Merioneth and keeping the wormhole close by had stretched the machinery to its limit.

"You okay?" Nelson's amplified voice boomed down from the ceiling.

"Yeah," Paula said, climbing to her feet. "I'm okay."

WHAT I KNOW REALLY HAPPENED

The court guards were utter bastards to me. After that idiot judge passed sentence they dragged me down to the holding cell while I shouted that I was innocent. They just laughed as they slung me inside. I heard them later. Deliberately. They said that the Justice Directorate had developed a suspension system that allows a tiny part of your mind to stay awake during the sentence, so you're aware of each long year as it passes. It's part of the punishment, knowing all the opportunities you've lost, the life you've missed.

Not true. Just another unisphere myth.

After, they put me down on the bed in the preparation room. No. I'll be honest. After, they *held* me down. I fought them, *Damnit,* I'm innocent! I was a classic case of someone who went down screaming and kicking. They won't ever forget me. It took six Directorate orderlies to hold me in place while the malmetal restraints wrapped around my limbs. And after that, I still shouted. I cursed them and their families. I swore vengeance, that in two and a half thousand years I'd become the killer they wrongly thought I was, and I'd hunt down their descendants and torture them to death.

No use. They still infused the drugs. Consciousness faded away.

I woke up. The room that slowly came into focus around

me was very similar to the preparation room I'd gone to sleep in. Stupidly, I was bloody grateful that I hadn't known all that time flowing around me. The waste of my potential lives. But I was alive. Warm. And pleasantly drowsy.

There was something around my neck that seemed familiar somehow, something from the time in my life I'd lost. Icons in my virtual vision were blinking green, showing that the memorycell channels into my neural structure were wide open.

Then that queen bitch Paula Myo came in. I tried to get up to throttle her. That's when I found I was still restrained, with malmetal coiled around my arms and legs.

"What the fuck is this?" I shouted. My voice was weak.

"I had you woken," Myo told me. "I have something for you, something you've forgotten."

"What? What is this?"

"You," she said, and took off her suit jacket. Something was glowing underneath her white cotton blouse. I could see shapes moving.

"Help," I cried. "Someone. Help me." The colored shadows on her abdomen began to writhe faster and faster. My virtual icons changed from green to blue, showing incoming impulses.

"What is that?" I whispered in fright.

She glanced down, as if only becoming aware of the light. Her smile made her face ugly. "A kind of prison, I suppose. You know, in ancient times necromancers used to draw pentagrams to trap demons in. They thought that if they were imprisoned, they could use their powers. A very misplaced notion, I suspect. In this case, geometry isn't important. I simply had to have a large receiving element. Your thoughts are big, after all. But I managed to catch them. Not all of them, just the right ones. Those that were relevant to the crime."

"My thoughts?" The icons expanded abruptly, wiping out my sight. Then faces emerged through the blue mist. Four of them in some kind of dilapidated room. Faces I knew. Svein. I remembered him. I remembered . . . *being* him.

I was the one standing in the desert outside Ridgeview

while the rest of me lived our life. It was hot out there. Bloody unpleasant, actually. The sun burned my arms and face. I took a leak against some local plant. That way if the forensic team were any good, they'd find it and confirm the Fiech body's DNA.

Then the air traffic control data playing in my virtual vision showed me that the plane was taxiing to the runway. I took a breath and got the missile ready. A simple thing, really, three of me had built it in the engineering center under the Lake Hill house. Most of the components were off-the-shelf, and the custom ones were easy enough for the bots to manufacture. We built quite a few.

The finished product was a simple blue-gray launch tube over a meter long, with a shoulder saddle and a handle. It was heavy when I rested it on my shoulder; I squatted down on the stony sand to make the weight easier. I could see the big old Siddeley-Lockheed lift into the sky, with its engine rumble faint in the hot desert air. It took what seemed like an age to climb up to its cruise altitude, curving around the city in a wide arc. The passenger list said it was just about full, over a hundred and thirty people. It would be quick. Death in such a fashion always is. And the passenger list confirmed the Dynasty scum were on board. The missile's sensors locked on. There wasn't anything else in the sky to confuse them.

I fired the missile. The bloody launch tube slammed into my shoulder. If I hadn't been bracing myself, it would have knocked me down. The roar of the solid rocket booster was obscenely loud. For a couple of seconds, I was overwhelmed. It was like being hit on the side of the head. Smoke was seething all around me. I crouched, staggered about. Then I recovered enough to stand still and look up into the wide open sky. The hyperram had kicked in, which made the missile just about impossible to see.

I expected the explosion to be bigger. This was just a white pinpoint flash, no fireball. But behind the blaze, the plane started to disintegrate, tumbling out of the sky, dark fragments twirling away from the main body.

There was no way I could move. Actually, my whole nest of bodies froze up as I watched the spectacle. There was something obscenely beautiful about the sight, and better still was the knowledge that *I* had created it. If I could do this, I could do anything! I'd be able to force through Merioneth's Isolation now. I had the courage and determination.

The first fragments hadn't even reached the ground when I turned and hurried down to the shore where the boat was anchored. This point was critical. The whole area would be swarming with people. The unisphere was already flinging out alarms. Rescue crews and police would be dispatched within minutes. And any local citizens nearby would no doubt rush to help. My Volkep body released the warning message into the unisphere as I reached the shoreline.

After that, it was a quick trip across the sea to Ridgeview. I waited on the station platform for my train back to Earth. It was an eerie experience. Everyone around me was accessing the unisphere reports of the plane crash. Nobody said anything; they were all too shocked at the disaster just outside town.

When I got back to Sydney, I took a cab straight to the apartment. The rest of me were a pleasant sensation of reassurance as I took the memory wipe drugs. The Volkep body took the array necklace from my neck and smiled proudly. I could feel the connection with myself reducing, darkness replacing the joy and color of my true memories. One contact remained, a single thread of experience: the alibi trip to Ormal. Damn, that stewardess was great-looking. I wish I hadn't been so wrapped up on a mission.

Then I was alone. And the drugs kicked in, and I knew nothing more.

Then I was without one of me. Just for an instant, I felt regret. But I am many. The loss of a single body is irrelevant. That's what I am, a New Immortal. That's *why* I am. I continue even after the loss of one, or more. I *live*.

I was shivering when the glare of color and sensation subsided into simple knowledge. Paula Myo was looking down at me, pulling her suit jacket back on. The flare of activity within her OCtattoo was subsiding.

"Bitch!" I couldn't sense me. For the first time since I nested, I was devoid of myself. One body with a single mind, completely alone.

"Good-bye," said Paula Myo.

"No. No!" A Justice Directorate orderly had entered the room. He was carrying an infuser. Paula Myo nodded at him. "Carry on," she ordered.

"Why have you done this to me?" I cried. "This is inhuman!"

She turned in the door, her face blank as she stared at me. "You are the person who committed the crime. The *whole* person, now. This is your sentence. The sentence you tried to avoid. Justice has prevailed."

The orderly pressed the infuser against my neck. I screamed, my mind crying out to the rest of me, to help me, to comfort me. There was no answer.

WHAT HAPPENED AFTER

Nelson Sheldon was waiting in the entrance hall of the Justice Directorate as Paula came out of the elevator. "How did it go?" he asked.

"Successfully. The true Dimitros Fiech is now serving his sentence."

"Shame about the rest of him."

"Not really."

"Oh?"

"When suspension was first introduced, the Justice Directorate examined the idea of leaving convicts aware while their bodies slept. It was abandoned almost immediately. The experience was too much like sensory deprivation. The minds went insane very quickly under such circumstances."

"So how does that help us?" Nigel asked curiously.

"Dimitros Fiech is now unaware of his predicament. He'll sleep soundly for the next two and a half millennia, and he'll be offered extensive therapy when he gets out–assuming the Commonwealth is still around. Meanwhile, on Merioneth–"

"Ah. Svein Moalem's nest knows part of him is in suspension. And as an Immortal–"

"He'll endure those two and a half thousand years aware of the Fiech body's state. The punishment is shared. Or rather, it isn't, because it's all his. Just experienced in different ways."

Nelson smiled. "We can live with that."

"Good, because I have no intention of returning to Merioneth."

"Thank you for going in the first place," Nelson said. "The Dynasty is most grateful. We don't forget who our friends are."

Paula grinned back shrewdly. "I'll remember that."

OWNER SPACE

Neal Asher

Born and still living in Essex, England, Neal Asher started writing at the age of sixteen but didn't explode into public print until a few years ago; a quite prolific author, he now seems to be everywhere at once. His stories have appeared in Asimov's, Interzone, The Agony Column, Hadrosaur Tales, *and elsewhere, and have been collected in* Runcible Tales, The Engineer, *and* Mason's Rats. *His extremely popular novels include* Gridlinked, Cowl, The Skinner, The Line of Polity, Brass Man, The Voyage of the Sable Keech, The Engineer Reconditioned, *and* Prador Moon: A Novel of the Polity. *Coming up is a new novel,* Hilldiggers.

In the wild and pulse-poundingly-suspenseful adventure that follows, he vividly demonstrates that it might be a good idea for the citizens of opposing Galactic Empires to stay well away from each other—especially when there are deep, bitter, and long-lasting grudges between them.

K elly Haden worked herself into a sweat on the training machines positioned in the outer ring of the *Breznev*'s spin section, the scars on her arms and chest tightening. She would have preferred to use free weights, but such were not allowed aboard ships like this, since a malfunction of the spin section or, for that matter, of the ship entire, could result in heavy lumps of iron hurtling about like chaff. There was also the matter of the weight itself, when a lightly constructed training machine like the one she was using could stand in for a few hundreds pounds of iron.

Finishing her workout, she picked up her towel and headed for the ladder leading up to the inward hatch, but the exercise had not dispelled the taut feeling of frustrated anger in her stomach. She climbed up into the sleeping quarters.

"Feeling better now, Societal Asset Haden?" enquired Longshank from his bunk. He was reading his notescreen again–some esoteric biological text, no doubt. She glanced at him, took in his long gray hair tied back with some confection of colored beads, at his graywear deliberately altered for individuality: sleeves cut away above the elbow, red fabric from the three Collective flags they found aboard sewn around the collar and waistband. They all did this sort of thing. Kelly had been one of the lucky ones to have found an old Markovian uniform jacket, which she had altered to fit, and had cut off her graywear trousers at just below the knee. It was a form of escape–the only escape for them that seemed likely now.

"No, I don't feel much better, Societal Ass Longshank," she replied.

What had once been a humorous exchange now contained a hint of bitterness.

The inner ring of the spin section was the bridge. It was without a ceiling, and while working at any of the consoles it was possible to see one's fellows upside down overhead. Kelly, being a ship's engineer, had been quite accustomed to this sort of thing, but it had taken some getting used to for the other escapees, and the vomit vacuums had seen plenty of work.

"How are we doing?" she asked Traviss, who in the low grav sat strapped into his chair at the center of a horseshoe of navigation consoles before the projection cylinder.

Traviss was a young hyperactive man who had been in the Collective military until he showed a talent with computers and spatial calculus and was reclassified as a "societal asset." Like them all, he had resented the resultant scrutiny from the

Doctrinaires. He touched a control and the projection cylinder filled with stars.

"Our slingshot around Phaeton is taking us nicely out of the system's gravity sink and we'll be able to U-jump in sixteen hours." One of the stars flashed red, and, a little way out, flashed the blue spinning-top icon of the *Breznev*. Between the two lay three icons representing the Collective pursuit vessels from Handel. They weren't the problem. The problem was a green icon accelerating out from the nearest star to Phaeton. The *Lenin,* though not as close to them as the other ships, would now easily be able to intersect their course. It was also faster, so there would be no outrunning it.

Traviss continued, "I calculate that the *Lenin* will be able to knock us back into the real in three days if we continue along our present course."

The others were gathering around now: Slome Terl, astrophysicist and their paternal figurehead; Olsen Marcos, who was a geneticist and an amateur historian, though that was a pursuit now strictly controlled in the Collective; and Elizabeth Terl, Slome's daughter and plain physicist in her own right. Of the fifty people aboard, everyone was an expert of some kind, and everyone had been reclassified as a "societal asset" and come under doctrinal scrutiny and control. To say the Collective was ruled would be to deny what it claimed to be, but it *was* ruled, by those who did all they could to skew reality to fit doctrine. The Doctrinaires knew that anyone above a certain intelligence level was a danger, yet also essential for a space-faring civilization, so such people had to be *managed.*

"Space has, by definition, three dimensions," said Slome. He was old, bald, and running to fat, and possessed a mind that sliced through problems like a microtome.

"Somewhat more than that, I would suggest," said Elizabeth, young, arrogant, and, though intelligent, more intent on displaying that intelligence than using it.

"Shut the fuck up, Liz," said Kelly distractedly.

The girl gave Kelly a superior look, then reached up to flick a lock of her bright ginger hair aside. She was pretty, too, which Kelly also found annoying.

"Our options are limited," said Traviss. He touched another control and areas of the cylinder were shaded in different colors. Their ship was within a blue hemisphere that disappeared off-cylinder—the Collective. A red area impinged from above and other discrete red areas were scattered below, with one large red hemisphere filling the lower right of the cylinder.

"If you would run through those options," said Slome, and Kelly got the suspicion that Slome and Traviss had already done so, and that a decision had already been made.

Traviss touched controls and numbers appeared in each of the colored areas. "Red signifies danger," he said needlessly. "Area One is what's left of the Grazen Empire. If we head that way, we'll either run straight into their defenses or their wormships will catch up with us." He glanced around. "And if we're lucky, they'll blow us out of space rather than capture us." They all knew what happened to humans caught by the Grazen.

"Area Two?" Slome prompted.

"Areas Two, Three, and Five are asteroid fields," Traviss explained. "We would have to drop out of U-space to navigate them." He highlighted some stars in the Collective adjacent to Area Three. "Even if we tried to get through Three, which is the smallest, the Collective could send ships from the bases indicated and intercept us."

"Six?"

"Grazen outposts scattered in an asteroid field and extended dust cloud."

"You surprise me," said Slome.

Kelly interjected, "Collective problems at home ended that mission. In my opinion, the area wasn't worth taking—nothing there remotely human-habitable and it would have taken years at the cost of many ships. But the Doctrinaires don't let facts get in the way of ideology—there'll be another attack on it."

Slome nodded, then pointed a gnarled finger at the hemisphere of red. "And that?"

Traviss hesitated for a moment and Kelly knew precisely why. She also knew that Slome's prompting and Traviss's hesitation were just a performance. They both knew where this was leading. Kelly wondered what it was they were yet to reveal.

"That's been under Interdict since before the Markovians," Traviss replied. "I can't really find out much about it."

"But you've found something," said Slome.

"Yes," Traviss said. He appeared distinctly uncomfortable with the act. "That area is classified as Owner Space."

After a brief, almost embarrassed silence, Elizabeth laughed knowingly, then said, "The Markovians were not noted for their rationality."

Kelly felt the need to defend Traviss, despite the fact that he and Slome were playing some game. "Yes, which is why they were slaughtered by our oh-so-rational Collective."

Elizabeth shot back, "The Collective is a doomed ideology, but their rationality is superior to the myth-making and religions of the Markovians."

"Well, I can always drop you in one of the escape pods if you want to go back," said Kelly. "That's supposing the Doctrinaire aboard the *Lenin* thinks you a valuable enough asset to pick up."

Elizabeth began to bristle until Olsen interrupted heavily, "The Owner is no myth, though some people's conception of him may stray into the territory of religion."

Holding up a finger to silence his daughter, Slome turned to the geneticist and sometime historian. "I heard something about all this when I was a student under the Markovians. Perhaps you could elaborate?"

Olsen shrugged. "Highlight the Sabalist System, would you, Traviss?"

Traviss complied, picking out a star sitting just on the Grazen side of the border between the Grazen Empire and the Collective.

"Owner Space extended to here. The Owner apparently ceded the area to us in the pre-Markovian era. The Markovians lost it to the Grazen over a century ago, but we still have a lot of data and biological samples from Sabal itself. Those samples indicate a great deal of adaptation from ancient Terran forms."

"That was almost certainly our work," said Elizabeth.

"We aren't in that league," Olsen replied.

"But perhaps we were?"

Olsen shook his head.

"Though I know some of the details, this is the first I've heard about the Sabal connection," said Slome.

"It's in some very old data files—I did some research," Olsen replied. "Those same files were secured by the Collective, and I came under the scrutiny of Doctrinaires long before they invented the concept of 'societal assets.' Some of my fellows weren't so lucky."

"So we are now to believe in immortal superbeings?" enquired Elizabeth.

"We don't have to," said Kelly.

They all turned to look at her.

She continued. "The Grazen avoid that place. When I was engineer aboard the *Mao,* a Grazen scoutship faced us down rather than enter there. We tore it apart. Grazen ships get destroyed if they try to enter that area, and Collective ships get flung out—their drive systems wrecked."

"This was when you were fighting for the Collective," said Elizabeth.

"This was when I was an engineer groveling in radioactive sludge below the *Mao*'s engines."

Elizabeth did not have much more to say about that—they could all see the shiny scar tissue down the side of Kelly's face, her neck, and disappearing under her jacket.

After an embarrassed silence, Slome said, "Well, as you say, Traviss, 'limited options.' But we must make a decision." He turned to Kelly. "I defer to you on this, since without you we would never have escaped the Commutank, and since you have greater experience in these matters"—Kelly knew that a "however" was due—"however, the Grazen would peel off our skins over a slow fire, while the Collective would peel our minds and we'd soon all become obedient little citizens after they fitted us with strouds." He gestured toward the viewing cylinder. "As I see it, when we drop into U-space, we should run for the edge of the Grazen outpost, where we will be in their territory only briefly before reaching the . . . Interdict Area."

Hints, rumors, stories–nothing clear and nothing proven–that's all Kelly had ever heard while in the Collective fleet. The whole, however, had left an impression on her, an idea that the Owner was something to be feared, something that even the *Grazen* feared. Perhaps that was just the fear of the unknown.

"We won't be able to enter there," she said–not entirely sure of her facts. "We'll get crippled and flung out, and those aboard the *Lenin* will capture us, if the Grazen don't get to us first."

Slome gave a weak smile. "Yes, that would have been true."

"*Would have* been true?"

Slome gestured to the cylinder. "Show them the message, Traviss."

Traviss cleared the cylinder. Then, after a moment, he brought up a brief text message: "Escapees from the Collective, Owner Space is open to you. Welcome."

Traviss said, "Its source was deep inside Owner Space."

"Very well," said Kelly, her spine crawling. "Owner Space it is."

Clinging to the handholds, Doctrinaire Shrad gazed at flecked void through the thick portholes of the *Lenin* and ground his teeth. A stupid waste of resources, he felt, specifically himself. He should have been back with the Central Committee, planning the coming attack on the Grazen Empire, not out here chasing after a few assets gone bad. It was the other Doctrinaires in the Committee who had driven him out–fools whose ideology was unsound, who did not understand precisely how things should run in the Collective. They called his leadership of the previous campaign "disastrous" and did not understand how working with the old Markovian command structures in the fleet had hindered him. Well, he would bring these assets back, strouded and subservient, then return to his place in the Committee and bring to fruition his vision of the New Deal. Meanwhile—he turned from the viewing window—he would have to see about correcting the ideological aberrations he had found aboard this vessel.

The engineer, his hands bound behind his back, was being held between two of the Guard. Shrad pushed himself over and caught hold of some of the masses of pipe work running from the reactor cylinder. Then, with an exclamation, he snatched his hand away and had to stop himself by grabbing the shoulder of one of the Guard, who, as ever, just silently maintained his position.

"Those pipes are hot, Doctrinaire Shrad," observed the engineer. "If you must grab pipes, I suggest you grab the ones painted white."

"Thank you, Citizen Rand." Shrad took hold of a white pipe and hauled himself back. "Now, Citizen, I expect you are wondering why the Guard have detained you."

"I am overcome with curiosity, Doctrinaire Shrad."

Shrad could feel his rage growing but, as usual, kept it locked inside. "I am presuming you understand the ideological concept behind graywear?"

"I do: it being doctrine that all people are equal, all people must also appear so."

"Yet here you are wearing Markovian overalls!"

It was an unusual contrast: a citizen of the Collective dressed in Markovian overalls, held between two of Shrad's own unit of graywear-clad Guard—men who had once been Markovians.

"I don graywear when I go off-shift. Unfortunately, it is not practical in the engineering environment."

"Are you saying that Committee instructions are wrong?"

"No, Doctrinaire Shrad, I am saying that in the engineering environment, I would soil and destroy my graywear, which perhaps the Committee would consider an insult, though, of course, I don't presume to know what the Committee would think. I just try to do my best for the good of the Collective."

The words were as correct as they could be under the circumstances, but Shrad could detect a note of forbidden Irony and perhaps Sarcasm. He knew that it would be necessary to modify the behavior of this man.

"Doctrinaire Shrad."

Shrad turned. "Citizen Astanger," he said, feeling an immediate increase in his annoyance. Astanger was a societal asset—a synthesist who, under the Markovians, would have been called captain of the *Lenin.*

"Is there a problem?" asked Astanger.

Shrad gazed at the man. He was gray-haired, tall and thin, possessed piercing blue eyes, and what, in another time, would have been called a noble face. Shrad had his suspicions that Astanger's ancestry was, in fact, Markovian—he possessed a similarity of facial structure to those in Shrad's Guard unit—and that his outer appearance stemmed from the genetic tweaks those rulers had made to their line. It further annoyed Shrad that though Astanger's hair and graywear were utterly correct, he always looked sartorially impeccable.

"This engineer is incorrectly dressed," said Shrad.

Astanger turned his cold gaze on the man. "Rand, why are you wearing those overalls?"

"Graywear doesn't give enough freedom of movement, Ca . . . Citizen."

Ah, thought Shrad, smirking. As he had supposed, this ship being without doctrinal supervision throughout the last five years of the conflict with the Grazen, archaic and politically incorrect behavior had flourished. Rand had nearly called Citizen Astanger *Captain.*

"Be that as it may," continued Astanger, "you knew that wearing anything other than graywear is . . . ideologically incorrect." Astanger turned to Shrad. "As synthesist, I suggest, Doctrinaire Shrad, that for the good of this mission, Citizen

Rand be made to work 120 percent shifts on 75 percent rations."

"That will not be necessary," said Shrad. He turned to the two onetime Markovians, the two of the Guard—the only ones who wore a slightly different style of graywear in that theirs was armored. The two men were as stony-faced as ever, each of them bearing a stroud spread like a two-fingered steel hand up the side of one cheek and dividing at the temple to spread two fingers halfway along their foreheads. "Stroud him."

Citizen Rand bellowed and began to struggle but, being experienced at this sort of thing, in fact having experienced it themselves, the Guard held him, and one of them quickly slapped the stroud he had been holding into place. Rand shrieked, and now the Guard released him. For a moment, Shrad thought he saw something in the expression of the particular guard who had used the stroud—was he Evan Markovian, or one of the others? Shrad tended to get them confused now. After a moment, he dismissed the suspicion—there was hardly anything left inside their skulls of the people they had been.

Writhing like a maggot, Rand tumbled through the air, his face clenched in a rictus of agony and blood running from underneath the stroud. Then, abruptly, his face went slack, moronic. The probes, about two thousand of them in all, had found their required locations in his brain, in some of those locations killing brain matter and in others injecting certain combinations of neurochemicals. Now the recordings would be playing. The indoctrination process would take about three hours and Rand would be a good citizen afterward, if he survived—only one in three did. Satisfied, Shrad turned to gaze at Astanger.

"It was foolish of him to flout the law," said Astanger, still watching Rand and seemingly unaffected by what had happened. He now turned to Shard. "As synthesist, I will now have to factor in that though we may have gained one good citizen, we have certainly lost one good engineer."

"Be careful what you say, Citizen Astanger."

"I am always careful, Citizen Shrad . . . now, perhaps you would like to come to the bridge. It would seem that the *Breznev* has now dropped into U-space and is taking a most unexpected route."

"Unexpected?"

"Well, let me say 'disconcerting'—their choices were limited."

The ovoid, eight miles long, looked like a furry egg from a distance, but closer it revealed itself to be a loose tangle of yard-wide pipes of a white coralline substance. Yig worms dwelt in the pipes and were currently extending the perimeter of the nest since it had encompassed another asteroid for them to grind up and digest after the nest's departure from the rookery. The Mother crouched in the center of the tangle, with sensory tendrils spread half a mile all around her and engaged into yig channels, which in turn led to exterior long-range sensors. Like a giant metallized crayfish with an extended body, she crouched, protected from hard vacuum by yig-worm opalized shields, tending her domain, cataloging her additions to the yig work, and raging.

Five million of her children were dead, and the Mother's rage was a terrible thing that she knew might last her for the rest of her millennia. After the Misunderstanding, this slaughter had been the worst thing that had ever happened to her. No other Grazen had lost so much, and she felt justified in breaking away from the rest of her kind and fleeing to this outpost. But she knew, deep in her fifth heart, that in Grazen terms she was not entirely sane.

When she saw the distortion of the undersphere that signified the presence of humans, she lashed out, the yig weaving a ripple into the undersphere and directing it along the course she set, and she relished the coming opportunity for vengeance. Human neurology was a simplistic and easily manipulated thing, and it was possible to exact punishment lasting even beyond the death of the neural network that formed the being. She still had some of the murderers with her now–forever shrieking in yig channels. Only when the ripple was away did she experience a sudden dread. The distortion was so close to *his* realm that this might lead to another Misunderstanding. She waited, observed the human vessel slam up into the oversphere, then observed it continuing on under conventional drive. She felt a moment of chagrin at her impulsive reaction. The ship would be crippled and flung back out, so there was no rush–it would soon be hers.

Then the other human vessel rose into the oversphere.

The Mother observed it for a little while. She surmised that once it saw what was about to happen to the one ahead of it, it might flee into the undersphere, so she sent another ripple to render its undersphere engines inert. Then she began to consolidate a kernel nest for travel. She withdrew her tendrils to the kernel, shifted supplies and the required devices inside, selected specific yig worms, and opalized the kernel. The nest yig opened a path through the outer opalized shields to the oversphere, and, clawing space, she shot out, wrapped in her kernel. The second human vessel, now limited to oversphere drive, was heading directly *there* too. She traveled slowly, waiting for both vessels to be expelled, and relished the prospect of revenge. Then, in horrified disbelief, she observed the two human ships enter *his* realm, unharmed!

———

Wearing a spacesuit, which gave her a lot more shielding than she had ever been allowed aboard the *Mao,* Kelly clung to a handhold in the drive penny and gazed at one drive unit–a teardrop of polished alloy ten feet long. There were three of them evenly spaced around the circumference of the penny, where they had been braced on bubblemetal beams at a distance apart precise to one ten-thousandth of an inch. The penny was temperature-controlled simply to maintain this accuracy, since variation in temperature would have resulted in disastrous metal expansion. It was all irrelevant now. The drive unit she was studying obviously lay out of true with the rest, and if that wasn't enough, the smoke coiling from a blown-away inspection hatch certainly was.

"What's the problem, Kelly?" asked Slome over the suit radio.

Kelly pushed herself away from her handhold over to the central cleanlock and went through; once out the other side, she began undogging her helmet. There were three of them awaiting her in the drive annex—no room for any more: Slome, his daughter, and Olsen.

"The problem is," she replied at length, "no more U-space drive."

"What?" said Elizabeth. "You're saying you can't repair it?"

The girl was really starting to irritate Kelly now. "A U-space drive is fitted and tuned in the Gavarn station complex. It takes about eight months just to balance it, and all the processing power of the complex itself. If I took back what we've got in there"—Kelly stabbed a thumb over her shoulder—"they'd likely scrap it and start again."

"Well," said Slome, listening to his headset, "it may all be irrelevant now." He gestured to the ports over to one side, and Kelly pushed herself over, dreading that she was about to see one of those shimmering tangles of pipes that the Collective called a Grazen dreadnought, although probably that wasn't an apt description at all. The things had only appeared occasionally during the war, and not one had ever been destroyed. If the Grazen had used them properly, she reckoned, there would be no Collective by now, but that was something you weren't ever allowed to say out loud aboard the *Mao*. But the Grazen had *not* used them, just their wormships, which, though dangerous, the human ships were able to destroy. However, the sight that greeted her eyes wasn't a Grazen dreadnought, but something she had only ever seen in very hazy high-magnification pictures.

"Border post," said Olsen.

"A what?" asked Elizabeth.

Why was she here? Someone more senior should have been here.

"Something I read about. They were also called death posts, though since we're sailing on past it without getting killed, I suppose the description is inapt."

"Or they have been deactivated by whoever sent us that invitation," said Slome.

It certainly looked a bit like a post, though one with streamlined ovoids attached at each end. It was huge—as Kelly recollected, the high magnification scan readout put these objects at two miles high, and there were thousands of them. The Doctrinaires aboard *Mao* told everyone they were the product of the ancient Collective from Earth that had been betrayed by the humans who took control before the Markovians. No one believed that; too many of the crew had heard the rumors about the entity called the Owner, though, of course, no one said so.

"That could have been what hit us," said Elizabeth.

Kelly shook her head. "I don't think so—that felt like something the Grazen did. Usually, after a strike like that, the wormships would be all over us. Maybe they're not attacking because of our location." She didn't feel as sure as she sounded, but felt the need not to let any of Elizabeth's statements go unchallenged.

Slome was listening to his headset again, nodding to himself. After a moment, he said, "Seems the same thing just happened to the *Lenin,* and now it's heading directly toward us."

Kelly rested her head against the port. It was quite simple—they'd gambled and lost.

Slome continued. "We're on the edge of a solar system here—one with a habitable world. Under conventional drive, we could be there in eight months."

"Do we have the supplies for that?" asked Kelly.

"Water and air recyling will last that long; the food will just have to."

"Then what?"

"We land."

"I don't see what good that will do us."

"Would you rather the *Lenin* caught up with us out here? At least down on a planet there's some chance of evading the Guard."

"Yeah, right."

The Grazen U-space weapon had knocked out the U-space drives of both the *Breznev* and the *Lenin,* and Astanger had thought they were all about to die. Owner Space would fling them out if they headed that way, and, anyway, they would never be able to flee the aliens using conventional drive through realspace. Whether they continued on their course after the *Breznev* had seemed irrelevant, but, in the end, that was what saved them from the Grazen. Owner Space flung out human ships, yet it destroyed the Grazen ones. This time it did not do the first, and fear of the second was, Astanger suspected, what was keeping the Grazen away.

However, their situation was now dire, and Shrad's insistence on pursuing those assets and punishing them seemed quite insane. With a Grazen dreadnought sitting in vacuum behind them, reversing their course would have been stupid. Taking some other course out of Owner Space would have taken years under conventional drive, and they just did not have the supplies for that. Heading straight for the same planet to which the other ship was heading seemed the best course available, but still, Shrad was as mad as a box of frogs.

Citizen Shrad—the one everyone knew was responsible for the war against the Grazen, even if Collective society doctrine had it that individual responsibility was an outmoded concept, and that there were no such things as leaders.

Shrad had ordered all of the strouded, except for the Guard, to stop eating, and, good little robots that they were, that is precisely what they had done. Now, a month into their slog insystem, some of those people were dying. Astanger felt much regret for their straits, since though the strouding process made good little robots of them, it did not relieve them of suffering—that would have been too much to ask of the Collective. However, all those who were dying were not crew but nonessential personnel, because those who were strouded did not have sufficient independence of thought to be essential. They were also, in Astanger's opinion, better off dead. At least Engineer Rand had not suffered death by slow starvation—his stroud had not taken, and he had died before they could get him to the medbay.

Everyone else was on half rations, except of course for Shrad himself, he being the most *essential* person aboard. Astanger could think of numerous people aboard who were more essential . . . the entire crew, for example. And as it was now seeming likely that there might be no return to the Collective—it struck him as improbable that a rescue ship would be sent, what with Shrad having been blackballed from the Committee—Astanger was attracted to the idea of depriving Shrad of his ability to eat. This was a position he'd never imagined himself to be in when he'd received his military call-up. As a misty-eyed youth, he had known himself to be a member of an advanced and rational political system.

The Collective had taken power before he was born, and he'd grown up in a still relatively free society, for it took quite some time for the dictates applied to actually take effect. That effect was first felt on the Capital World and took some years to reach his borderland homeworld. He grew up with the changes, the indoctrination and propaganda, and the kowtowing to the Doctrinaires. He crewed on Fleet ships that were still run the old Markovian way and because of his indoctrination thought the system bankrupt. As a ship's security officer, he applied the dictats of the new Doctrinaires to each ship now acquired. This was probably what accelerated his ascent up the promotion ladder to the position of captain. Then came the war with the Grazen.

As captain, he then had a greater overview of everything that was happening, and though Shrad's propaganda talked of Grazen assaults on Collective worlds, Astanger knew otherwise. It started to nag him, the way a straightforward assault on the

Grazen was by Shrad and his lackies called a "defensive maneuver." Plain aggression was couched in terms of Collective-
speak, thus the bombardment of a Grazen nest was a "tactical
clearance" and the incineration of a planet-based alien nursery—one of Shrad's "special projects"—was "groundwork procedure." This elicited his dislike of Shrad, the Committee, the
Collective, and himself. Being older, and wiser, he began to re-
assess his life. But what could he do? He was but a small cog
in the Collective machine. The introduction of graywear and
the gradual dismantling of the Markovian command structure
elicited his disgust and contempt, and the use of the strouds
finally aroused in him a cold hatred. But, again, what could
he do?

Five years before the end of the war, a wormship attack de-
prived *Lenin* of its Doctrinaire. He'd spent the rest of the war
ensuring that the ship didn't get another one. The Grazen withdrew from numerous worlds, then consolidated their nests
around the core of their empire—if "empire" was the correct description of their system of governance, which he frankly
doubted. Supplies to fleet ships were low, resources scant. The
Committee called it a "victory of political rationality over ani-
malistic imperialism" and recalled the fleet. Seeing through to
the reality, Astanger counted the cost: on the Grazen side,
twenty out of tens of thousands of their nests destroyed and a
nursery world burned; on the Collective side, fifteen hundred
and six capital ships destroyed, numerous support vessels gone,
ground assault troops exterminated in great numbers (some of
them burned on the nursery world in the common kind of
screwup occurring when military tactics became subject to political control). The total human cost was somewhere in the
hundreds of thousands, though it was impossible to get an accu-
rate count.

Victory indeed.

But now, here aboard the *Lenin*, he wanted to *do* something.
Many of the crew agreed with him—the exceptions being new
personnel who had not been aboard during those five years—

but there simply weren't enough of them. The crew complement consisted of fifty-eight people, all, by Committee ruling,
unarmed. Shrad had one hundred of the utterly loyal Guard
with him, all of them armed with handguns and carbines, and
with access to even more powerful weapons than those. It
seemed hopeless, and would become more so in the months to
come as his crew steadily starved.

———

The Mother retreated to the nest, but could not bring herself to
finally return her vessel to its structure. Only partially reconnecting her tendrils into the yig channels and thus to the nest's
long-range sensors, she gazed at the two human ships as they
moved beyond the barrier. No reaction, nothing. She could not
believe this: every wormship sent through there had been destroyed, the posts had fried *all* the drive systems of every human ship that strayed that way and then flung them back out.
Why not now?

She seethed as the two human ships made for the nearest
world within *his* domain. She gazed at them throughout the
months of their journey, her frustration growing at letting two
such easy targets—now they had lost the ability to travel in
U-space—escape. But she was also frightened: there was the
Misunderstanding to consider.

Then it started again.

Through long-unused yig channels, she received the news
that the humans were preparing for another attack on the Grazen.
Watch stations peppered throughout the Collective reported un-
controlled industrialization and the effective rapine of worlds.
They reported massive movements of supplies, ships, and human
warriors. Apparently, these last were different somehow, and this,
too, was a worrying development. Such an effort had been predicted as a remote possibility when the Grazen, taking a long view
of things, had withdrawn to wait for the inevitable collapse of a societal experiment that seemed doomed to failure. Analysis of this
new effort showed that it would bankrupt the Collective and bring

about its predicted collapse early, but that would be no consolation if another nursery world was burned.

Though she had physically separated her nest from the rest of the Grazen, she could not separate herself from her kind's racial will, the purpose, the gestalt that was the Grazen. While others of her kind prepared with cold efficiency to hold the Collective at bay until it collapsed, the Mother raged. She wanted to strike out, to damage, to hurt, and the nearest humans to her were but a few weeks away through the undersphere, then the oversphere.

The posts had not touched them, so perhaps they would not touch her? Maybe *he* was looking away, maybe *he* was gone? It was said by some that he took the form of a human, so maybe he was as short-lived as that kind and had died? While one part of her mind was so foolishly wishful, another part reasoned that something like *him* would not die and would not be caught with his guard down.

Then came the communication.

Though couched perfectly in the language of the yig channels, the Mother knew its source to be alien. Tracing back through the undersphere to its source, she felt a moment of pure dread. *Him?*

But the Misunderstanding? was the essence of her reply.

He explained, and she felt a sudden overwhelming joy.

She once again detached her consolidated kernel for oversphere travel and fell away from her main nest. Clawing through vacuum between asteroidal debris until she found clear space, she dropped into the undersphere. Yes, she had always felt that humans must pay for the deaths of her children and the other deaths sure to come, and pay, and pay. However, this was different, this was *personal.*

———

Kelly gazed at the images displayed in the viewing cylinder. The two probes showed the world ahead to be beautiful, warm and burgeoning with life. Bands of forest rimmed the continents, enclosing prairies and mountain ranges. Vast herds of grazing beasts, sometimes tens of miles across, were visible in flowing patterns across the prairies, cutting swathes of brown through the green. One close view showed a predator–some kind of massive reptile standing up on its hind legs–bringing down one of these grazing beasts. It was just a microcosm of the huge ebb and flow of life spread across the landmasses.

The oceans seemed equally as bountiful. Shoals of fish spumed the sea across areas as large as those landward herds. Giant cetaceans hunted and played, enormous sharks the color of polished copper cruised shorelines swamped by either basking amphibians or swimming mammals come ashore to mate and lay eggs.

Birds and flying reptiles swirled across the sky. Tropical seas gleamed sapphire. Snowcapped peaks glistened pure white. Salmon leaped in a million miles of clean rivers. It all looked so wonderfully natural, an untouched paradise.

"Do you even begin to comprehend the kind of engineering involved in creating something like that?" enquired Olsen.

"If it *is* engineered," said Elizabeth dismissively.

"Tell me about the engineering," said Slome.

"Think of the migratory patterns–it all has to be programmed in. Not only has life been created down there from base genetic imprints, it's been programmed to integrate into the entire artificial environment. And you know, there's things down there that went extinct back on Terra and others that simply never existed."

"Then perhaps they were here before any engineering commenced," suggested Elizabeth, playing her preferred devil's advocate role.

"No, you see, they're suited to their environment."

"Precisely." Elizabeth was triumphant.

Olsen shook his head at her and turned to Slome. "Everything down there is suited to that environment. Yet, unless a lot of Markovian records are wrong, that environment was a lot colder about three hundred years ago."

"Go on," said Slome, his eyes narrowing.

"This world is not where it's supposed to be—it's much closer to the sun."

Elizabeth barked a laugh. "So, this immortal superbeing is also capable of moving worlds? I think it more likely that initial Markovian studies were inaccurate and that inaccuracy was simply copied."

Olsen shrugged. "That's always possible."

Kelly continued gazing at the images and compared what she was seeing to the incompleteness of many Collective worlds, where near-Terran environments were maintained by gas extraction and fixing plants, the importation of essential minerals from elsewhere, the resowing of certain biologicals, the endless war against alien biologicals—whole industries working to prevent, in human terms, planetary ecological collapse. This world, though, seemed to function perfectly. There was no sign of atmosphere plants or any other support technology—no sign, in fact, of any technology at all . . . until Traviss spoke.

"I've found something," he said.

The images in the cylinder blurred for a moment, then settled on a high view of a coastline. Traviss focused in by stages, each time allowing the ship's computers to clean up the image presented. The final image was of an estuary where a river cut down into a wide blue bay. On one side of the estuary, on a blunt peninsula, it seemed evident that there was a large building of some kind. Squinting, Kelly was also sure she could make out a jetty with what appeared to be a large twin-hulled boat moored beside it, projecting from a rocky shore just beside a white sand beach.

"Someone living down there?" wondered Slome.

Kelly shivered. The *Owner*?

"I'm getting stuff in infrared and some other EMR," said Traviss. "Nothing substantial, but it does seem likely there's someone down there."

"Can you give us a closer view?" Slome asked.

"If I do, we'll lose this probe—it won't have enough fuel to pull up again."

"Do so."

They all stood watching as the probe obviously headed in a course out to sea and down, the view flicking back to the building and clarifying intermittently. The image shuddered for a little while as the probe's stabilizers failed to compensate for its declerating burn as it curved around and headed back in. Kelly felt both a growing excitement and trepidation, but really did not know what she expected to see. The final views in the probe's life were clear, and puzzling; something so prosaic in so unusual a location. Nestled in rocky slopes scattered with gnarled trees was a large building, a house, something like the kind of place the Markovians might have used as a country retreat. It was sprawling, fashioned of the surrounding stone, with turrets and towers rising here and there, red tiles on the roofs and many baroquely shaped windows. Tracks led down from it to the shore, to some wooden buildings from which a jetty projected out into the sea. Moored next to the jetty was a large catamaran. As the probe sank down toward the sea, she was sure she could discern a figure sitting on the jetty.

"That last image," said Slome. "Can you repeat it and clean it up?"

Traviss complied, and they all gazed at a human figure—difficult to tell if it was male or female—sitting on the jetty, fishing—and waving, too. No one seemed able to say anything about that—it all just seemed too incongruous. They had arrived at a world that had been under interdict for longer than any of them had been alive because it was owned by some dangerous being . . . then this.

"Give us that first orbital view again," said Slome.

Once again they gazed down from upon high.

Slome pointed. "On the other side of the estuary, the forest comes nearly down to the shore. On the side where the house lies, it's hilly for a few miles back before leveling into prairie—

that's one of the few areas where forest doesn't cover the land to the rear of the shore."

"No coincidence, I would suggest," said Elizabeth, now somehow subdued.

"No," said Slome. He turned and checked each face in turn. "I suggest we land on that prairie—as close to the house as we can get. Then I suggest we go and see who is living there."

"Is that a good idea?" wondered Kelly.

"I don't know. However, what I *do* know is that once this ship is down, we'll not be able to take it back up again, and I do know that the *Lenin* is not far behind us and will almost certainly land near to us. A Doctrinaire and the Guard will come looking for us. If we were to land anywhere else, our only choice would be to run, and keep on running. There"—he stabbed a finger at the projection—"some alternative might lie open to us."

"The Owner might save us," said Elizabeth flatly.

"Or we might be bringing the Guard down on an innocent lone settler," said Kelly.

Slome shook his head. "No one is innocent. Haven't you been reading your Committee dictats?"

The *Breznev* headed toward the world tail first, poised on the bright flare of its main drive. Behind the half hemisphere of the thrust plate and the conglomeration of fuel tanks, reactor, lithium pellet injectors, and ignition lasers lay the drive penny for the U-space engines. Beyond this stretched a long reinforced framework holding an access tunnel from the now stationary spin section—a cylinder eighty feet wide and a hundred feet long—inside which the escapees were being crushed into acceleration chairs. Next along from the spin section was the giant brick of the storage section and holds, capped off by the heavy reentry shield and underslung reentry plate. The ship left an ionized trail past the world's single cratered moon, the four big reaction thrusters positioned at the four corners of the frame holding the spin section belching chemical flame to force the ship into an inward curve.

Further brighter ionization in the world's disperse exosphere sketched the vessel's course around the world and deeper toward the thermosphere. When its speed reached a predetermined level, the main drive cut out and the thrusters flared again, turning the ship nose to tail to present its reentry shield to the steadily thickening air. The flip-over had its usual effect internally, and clamping down on her churning guts, Kelly knew the vomit vacuums would again be required. Explosive bolts blew, clamps detached, especially weakened structural members broke where they were supposed to, and the entire drive section detached, small steering thrusters slightly altering its course to throw it into orbit around the world. Landing with a U-space engine and fusion reactor had never been an option.

The reentry shield smoked as its layer of soft ceramic began baking hard. It soon began to emit a dull red glow. Then fire flared out and back from it, enclosing the ship, podlike. It hurtled down, planing on fire. Then the thrusters adjusted its course to bring it down on the underslung reentry plate and steadily began firing to slow the ship even further. As the ship penetrated cloud, sealed containers positioned all around the spin section opened like buds to spew parachutes. Using a combination of these and the big thrusters, the ship descended on prairie, scattering herds of buffalo, and one herd of unicorns. Grass fires ignited underneath as it finally began to settle, but they were short-lived, for this vegetation was spring green. With a final whump and a settling of parachutes all around, the *Breznev* was down.

Her fingers digging into the arms of her acceleration chair, Kelly thought about the logistics of relaunch and knew that the *Breznev* would never be leaving this world. And she vowed to become part of the earth here rather than be subject to strouding by those who would soon be coming here after them.

The gas content of the air was breathable, but it might be packed with lethal microbes and biotoxins. They had no way of analyzing the air and there weren't enough spacesuits to go around, and no one wanted to walk out there in the cumbersome things anyway. No one wanted to stay in the ship—not when seeming freedom awaited outside. Kelly was damned if she was going to wait until Slome and the others came to a decision about what to do next. While they squabbled, she collected all her stuff in a shoulder bag, including her Sancha carbine and her father's antique sidearm, and headed for the airlock leading into the storage and cargo section.

"Not inclined to debate, SA Haden?"

Standing below the ladder leading up to the airlock, Kelly turned to gaze at Longshank. He was carrying a large backpack, wore some large walking boots in addition to his usual attire, and carried his notescreen clipped to his belt.

"Staying inside this ship is not an option—if something out there kills me, I would rather have that happen than wait here for one of the Guard to fit me with a stroud."

"My thoughts precisely. Anyway, this Owner-constructed world seems eminently human-habitable. Maybe we'll pick up a few bugs along the way, but I doubt there's anything out there we can't handle in usual immune-response way."

"You seem very confident."

"No—resigned."

Kelly mounted the ladder and climbed, stepped up onto the platform, and hit the door control as Longshank stepped up behind her. They crammed into the airlock together, and after Longshank closed the first door, Kelly opened the second door leading into the forward cargo section of the ship. It opened with a slight hiss of pressure differential. Kelly clamped her nose and blew until her ears popped.

"There's an ATV packed away in here," she said while stepping out onto the next platform. She breathed carefully, wondering if anything would affect her right away, since they were now breathing the air of this world, the cargo section being vented to the outside.

"Let's walk," suggested Longshank.

"Where?"

"Where else?"

Many of the pressure-sealed crates in the section were open, their food contents all used up during the trip here. Other crates, once containing a cargo of freeze-dried ration packs destined for a Collective space station, were also empty. Kelly felt a pang of hunger, but it quickly passed—it had been some days since she felt really hungry. They moved past other sealed crates and Kelly hit the control to lower the loading ramp. Its locks clumped open and slowly it began to descend, exposing painfully bright blue sky. It finally hit down on vivid green dotted with blue and pink flowers. The intensity of light and color hurt her eyes, but seemed to balm something behind them.

"Come on." Longshank led the way out.

To their right, the silvery material of a parachute rippled in a soft caressing breeze. Longshank pointed to where trees dotted a distant slope. "Just beyond there—a few hills, a bit of a trudge."

As they walked through the thigh-high grass, birds racketed into the sky to scold them and, on one occasion, a large flightless bird leapt up from a nest full of brown-speckled eggs and charged away hooting in indignation. On the slope, the vegetation was shorter—the grass cropped down by some animal and large areas covered by mosses or mats of low-growing vines. Kelly stared at the first squat tree they came to and recognized the green orbs it bore as walnuts. Higher on the slope, there were almond and olive trees and others she did not recognize.

Weariness soon set in, and Longshank's "bit of a trudge" became a growing struggle until the splashing of a stream attracted them to a hollow.

"Shall we?" Longshank enquired.

The water tasted delicious and afterward they ate some of the walnuts, even though they were unripe. An eagle soared above, and short-eared rabbits scattered and observed them from ridges. Eventually they hit a track, and, in dry mud, Kelly observed the impressions of the soles of boots little different from the kind she was wearing. The track wound down through a sparse scattering of trees, beyond which she could see the multiple roofs of the house they had observed from orbit, and terminated against an ironwork gate set into a hedge of copper birch. Something like a chrome spider was working along the hedge far to their right, pruning it back with multiple gleaming pincers. A simple latch admitted them to perfect lawns and rose gardens.

"Well, hello," said a man, standing up from inspecting a large red rose. "Goodness me, I haven't had any visitors here in what"—he turned to gaze at a huge gnarled oak standing within its own circular border in the middle of one of the lawns—"well, since I planted that."

"Are you the Owner," said Longshank.

The man, a stocky gray-haired individual with a deep tan and eyes like green chips of glass, gazed about himself for a moment. "I guess so . . . sort of."

———

Slome gazed about himself, the tightness in his guts increasing, then peered back at the loading ramp as he heard the sound of an electric motor. The ATV—basically an aluminium box able to hold six people and some cargo, suspended on four independent rubber wheels—rolled down onto the grass. Now that it was down, the fifty escapees began unloading supplies and placing them in makeshift packs. Slome turned from the scene and peered down at the notescreen Traviss was holding, which was displaying a map of the area. He tapped a finger against forest just back from the peninsula on this side of the estuary.

"There, I think," he said. "If they head toward the estuary they could end up trapped against it by the Guard."

"Peerkin said the same," Traviss replied, adding, "They've voted him temporary leader, what with his experience of wild environments."

"Good. They need to go deep and keep under cover—we'll

update them on whatever happens at the house and warn them if they need to run."

"They'll probably run when the *Lenin* comes down anyway."

Slome nodded.

"So it'll be me, you, Elizabeth, and Olsen in the ATV. Anyone else?"

"No, we'll need the space for Haden and Longshank if we have to run."

Slome was all too aware that that might be the case. Why would this "Owner," supposing him able, want to help them anyway? He had deliberately remained out of contact with the human race for longer than living memory, and, though initially human himself, was supposedly no longer of that kind. Why had the Owner allowed them, and the *Lenin,* through? Maybe the Owner no longer existed, maybe the individual they had seen from the probe was someone who had come here in the intervening time?

"We're ready," Elizabeth called.

He glanced over and saw that the steps were now folded down from the ATV and the others were climbing aboard. Snatching up his pack, he ambled over and boarded, too, taking the seat saved for him by Elizabeth behind the driver, Traviss. They headed away, leaving the other escapees to grab up what they could and head for the hideaway in the forest. Traviss accelerated the vehicle through the tall grass and soon hit the slope, navigating fast amid the trees and obviously enjoying himself. It took them very little time to come upon a track and within sight of the house.

"Take us around to the front," said Slome upon seeing the hedge.

Traviss took them around, then down beside a stream, up through an orchard, then onto another track. Visible through the apricot trees to their left was an arch, to which they headed. This led into a stone courtyard. Traviss parked the ATV before steps leading up to a heavy wooden door. Even as they climbed out of the vehicle, the door began opening and a man stepped out.

"Hello and welcome," he said.

Slome studied the man and thought he looked just too damned ordinary to be this "Owner."

"I have some of your fellows here already," the man said. "Come in. Are you hungry?"

The others looked to Slome for guidance and, after a moment, he led the way up the steps and held out his hand. "Slome Terl. My companions"—he gestured at each in turn—"are my daughter, Elizabeth, Olsen Marcos, and Traviss Painter. Who might you be?" A rough calloused hand and a strong grip—the hand of a laborer. The Owner? It seemed unlikely.

The question seemed to puzzle the man for a moment, then he said, "Call me Mark—that would be best, I think."

"Are you the Owner?" asked Elizabeth, somewhat querulously, Slome thought.

Mark grinned. "You could say that, and you would be both right and wrong." Now he looked up. "Are these with you, too?"

Slome abruptly gazed up into cerulean sky, but for a moment he could see nothing. Then, the flare of steering thrusters.

"No," said Slome. "That is the *Lenin*—a Collective ship containing those who intend to either kill or enslave us. Can you help? Because if you cannot, we had best start running now."

"Oh, I can help," said Mark. He looked up again. "Seems they have a shuttle."

Again, Slome could see nothing for a moment or two. Then he was able to discern a brief glint departing the position of the steering flame and the vague darkness of the *Lenin*. His eyes weren't bad—he'd recently had an optic nerve cellular stimulation and corneal cleaning—he should in fact be able to see better than anyone else here.

"You have good vision," he commented.

"Positively omniscient," Mark replied. "Do come in."

He led the way into a well-lit entry hall, floored in polished wood and surrounded by statues carved from the native stone. Slome recognized only one of them: the legendary beauty Alison Markovian. From the hall, he took them through double doors into a plushly furnished living area.

"Ancient Earth," said Olsen. "I think."

Slome's gaze fell on Haden and Longshank, who were standing by an oval table before the window, steadily working their way through bowls piled with food. On the table there were platters heaped with comestibles. As the smell reached his nostrils, his stomach immediately rumbled and his mouth started watering.

"Help yourself," said Mark.

"Thank you." Slome led the way over to the table. He wanted to say something to Haden and Longshank, but that want was secondary to his hunger. They all quickly tucked in, and when a small amount of food in Slome's shrunken stomach satisfied his hunger, he finally turned to them.

"You didn't wait for a decision," he said.

"Decision about what?" Kelly asked. "About whether or not to stay at the ship and wait for a Doctrinaire to come along and scrub our brains?"

Slome nodded, turning to glance over his shoulder and note that the man, Mark, had left the room. "What have you learned about him?"

"Very little. He's been here a long time, or so he claims, but he's equivocating about whether or not he's the Owner."

"With us, too, but he says he can help us."

"Do you think him capable of helping us?" Elizabeth interjected. "I've seen no evidence here that he can do anything about the Guard, and that shuttle will be here soon."

Slome shook his head. He didn't know what to think.

Kelly shrugged. "Despite his equivocation, I trust him. I don't know why."

"And on that basis we should risk ending up under the stroud?"

Olsen now said, "I've told you all what would be involved

in creating something like this world. The Guard should be no threat to someone that capable."

In the viewing cylinder, Astanger watched the shuttle descending toward the incongruous house on the planet below. Shrad had taken fifteen of the Guard with him, and, perhaps sensing Astanger's intentions, had set the rest patrolling or guarding the most critical areas of the ship—twenty of them were here on the bridge, ever watchful, their damaged minds rendered incapable of suffering boredom. Two of them stood behind each of the crew and four of them were standing watch about the weapons system controls—those consoles now abandoned by Chadrick, the weapons officer.

Now, having flown into low orbit to drop the shuttle, it was time to move the *Lenin* back out. Astanger turned to his bridge crew.

"Okay, bring us out," he instructed.

"Where to?" enquired Citizen Grade, the helmsman.

"Precisely to where Doctrinaire Shrad instructed us to wait: the Lagrange point between this world and its moon." He shot a glance at the two of the Guard standing behind him, then at the two standing behind Grade, and observed them studying the course alterations the man made. Were they even capable of knowing what he was doing? Of course they were. On many occasions, he had taken the opportunity to speak to some of them. Though devoid of any social ability or any understanding of plain conversation, they were intelligent and focused in other almost-enviable ways. They were good little robots.

And they were an atrocity.

Since Astanger had started questioning *everything,* he'd also started questioning his inculcated hatred and contempt of the Markovians. Shrad's Guard had all once been Markovians, and since Shrad had boastfully mentioned this only a little while ago, Astanger had begun to recognize the bone structure and features of those he had been taught to hate. Now he didn't hate them, just felt a huge sadness and pity, but he *did* hate Shrad. What the man had done, what the Committee had done, had nothing to do with social engineering, nothing to do with making a better world, nothing to do with *doctrine*. Shrad and his kind were rulers who were substantially less restrained about how they used their power than the Markovians had been. Astanger's disgust for Shrad and his kind was only exceeded by his self-disgust.

As his men bent to their task, Astanger, with a bitterness in his mouth, returned his attention to his controls and tried to concentrate on what he had been doing before. In the cylinder, he pulled up a view of the moon. It was a cratered monster over two thousand miles in diameter, and only after scanning the planet below had Astanger now turned his attention to it. As yet no evidence of technology had been picked up, but there was something odd about the astrogation data that just kept on niggling at him, so, barring some opportunity to disarm the Guard aboard his ship and then incinerate Shrad's shuttle on its return journey, he focused on that sphere.

Now under drive again, the *Lenin* headed for the Lagrange still point. The Guard, Astanger noted, seemed rooted to the deck despite the sideways drag of acceleration. On his screens, he decided to call up Markovian data on this sector of space, despite the watchful eyes behind him. Very quickly, he found the first discrepancy: the world wasn't in the right place. He felt a surge of awe, then immediately told himself not to be stupid– the data were obviously wrong. Then another glaring error became evident. According to the Markovians, this world should not even have a moon. He speculated about the possibility of it being recently captured in orbit and thus also repositioning the world, but that didn't gel. If such a thing had happened between the time these data were recorded and now, there would be huge volcanic activity below and other massive damage. Nothing like that was evident. But he realized that all this had nothing to do with what was niggling him.

Astanger called up the astrogation data again and kept on

going through it. He gazed at the position of the Lagrange point, and suddenly realized what was bothering him: it was too close to the moon. Now calling up data on a similar orbital setup within the Collective, he confirmed this, then began to make his own calculations. The moon, he soon realized, must mass considerably less than a sphere of rock over two thousand miles across should mass, and yet, the data they had gathered on it showed it to be precisely that.

Abruptly, he canceled out the data on his screens, then just called up prosaic stuff about their current trajectory. He leaned back and considered some possibilities. Either the scanners were malfunctioning—a not unusual occurrence under Collective rule— or that moon was definitely not what it appeared to be.

He reckoned that it was hollow. He also reckoned that Doctrinaire Shrad might be heading for a rude awakening. He smiled to himself at the prospect, which seemed the best he could hope for. Then the U-signature detection alarm wiped the smile from his face, and horror bloomed in his chest as the ship's scanners automatically redirected, and displayed the source of that signal in the viewing cylinder.

A Grazen dreadnought had just arrived.

Doctrinaire Shrad crouched behind the perfectly manicured rose bed and watched his men close in on either side of the window, then, raising his thumb telescope to his eye, he observed those inside—clicking up the light amplification since the greenish yellow sun was now setting and stars were beginning to blink into view on the far horizon.

What were they doing in there, having a party? He had already seen Slome Terl standing near the window picking at a plate of food while talking to the traitor Kelly Haden. It had to be some kind of trap. They must have seen his shuttle coming in to land and known that justice was snapping at their heels. He lowered his telescope. And what about this place?

Shrad could not quite equate the massive technology of

those constructs they had passed while heading into "Owner Space" with this house. He'd thought long and hard about what he had read in secret Collective records and come to some conclusions. Though it was doctrine that those structures were the product of a previous collective from ancient Earth, he was of a sufficiently high rank to know the truth. There had been an Owner who once had contact with the Markovians—though details were sketchy since many records had been destroyed during the "transition of power"—and during the recent "victorious conflict" with Grazen, those "posts" had damaged and repelled human vessels and destroyed Grazen wormships. However, nothing had been heard about the Owner for longer than living memory. It struck him as likely that though the being had once existed, he or it did not exist now. The action of the posts? Automated systems that were obviously breaking down. He surmised that during the "transition of power," some high-ranking Markovians had fled out this way and managed to get to this world during some periodic malfunction of the posts. This residence looked distinctly Markovian—like one of those country retreats where Shrad had obtained the base material of his Guard.

Shrad smiled to himself. If he could capture some high-ranking Markovians that could be put on trial, the Committee would be much more inclined to send a rescue ship and their "resources are presently unavailable" and their "tactical requirements do not permit" would probably change. Also, his discovery about the malfunctioning of the posts opened up massive new territories to the Collective.

"We are in position," Citizen One of the Guard informed him through his earpiece.

"Commence action—I repeat: subdue and restrain them. Do not, I repeat, do not kill any of them, even in the likelihood of losing Guard strength."

Raising his thumb telescope again, he now observed one of the Guard beside the window slap something against the glass, then lower his breather mask over his face. The blast disintegrated the window, and the men to either side now tossed in flash and gas grenades. After the subsequent detonations, and while numb-smoke belched from the house, the fifteen Guard piled inside. Shrad waited for a moment, but though he heard shouting from inside, there was no shooting. He stood, and, pulling his own breather mask up into place, drew his sidearm and headed over.

Broken glass crunched underfoot. The table had been tipped to one side and food and dishes spilled across a carpet patterned with geometric shapes. Kelly Haden was still fighting, but three of the Guard had her pinned and were cuffing her hands behind her back. Slome Terl just lay there, fighting for breath. All six of the figures on the floor wore disheveled gray-wear modified in ways that would be a stroudable political offense in themselves. All six, then, were escapees—there had to be others here.

Abruptly, Shrad realized that the smoke was clearing. He glanced up to see it being drawn away into holes in the ceiling—interspersed between the inset lights that were now slowly growing brighter as it grew darker outside—then returned his attention to the captives as the Guard hauled them up onto their knees. He holstered his sidearm.

"Seven of you, search the rest of this place and bring here anyone you find—stay in contact," he instructed.

Seven departed, but the eight remaining were certainly enough to keep under control the patently subdued captives. The smoke had now all but cleared—it had a short active life anyway—so Shrad removed his mask. He sniffed at the burnt hair smell, realizing it came from where the flash grenades had seared the carpet. Then he strode forward to stand before the six kneeling figures.

"Did you think the Collective would allow its Societal Assets to escape?" he enquired.

None said anything.

"You, Kelly Haden, you betrayed the Collective, stole its property, and, as I understand it, you killed two of the Guard."

Haden shrugged and looked away. Shrad gave a muted nod to the guard standing beside her, who stooped and drove the butt of his carbine into her stomach. She groaned and went down with her forehead on the carpet.

"It strikes me as evident that your obvious external ugliness reflects the ugliness inside you," said Shrad.

"Fuck . . . you . . . and your little robots," she managed.

Shrad nodded to himself. "Under Collective authority, I have a choice about what I should do with you. For the murder you committed, the sentence should be death, but I have the leeway to make my own decisions in this matter." He nodded to the Guard. "Stroud her."

One of the Guard hauled her up by the hair while another righted the table and placed a case on the surface, which he opened to reveal twenty strouds lying in the foam packing like a collection of steel prosthetic feet for birds. He took out one of these and placed it in a programming slate—these strouds needing to be prepared as had been the one Shrad had instructed to be placed on the *Lenin*'s engineer.

"Going to help us!" spat Elizabeth Terl somewhat hysterically, gazing beyond Shrad.

Slome Terl bowed his head, a look of pain on his face. Shrad turned and saw four of his Guard returning, leading a man into the room—his hands cuffed behind his back.

"Put him with the rest," he instructed. "Is there anyone else?"

"We have found no one else yet, but there is still much to search," replied Citizen Five of the Guard.

"Very well. You four remain here." Shrad now watched as the man was brought over and forced to his knees beside Haden. "Who are you?" he finally asked.

"My name is Mark," the man replied calmly.

Shrad felt a sense of victory upon hearing the name. In the back of his mind, he had held the suspicion that his reasoning about this house might have been at fault. Now he felt sure he was right.

"Mark as in Markovian, I've no doubt," he said. "How did you come to be here?"

"Well, my mother met my father–"

Shrad gave that muted nod and a carbine butt smacked across the man's mouth. He went over, spitting blood, and remained there until hauled back up onto his knees again.

"Was there any need for that?"

"There was." Shrad turned to the guard who had now prepared the first stroud. "Go ahead."

The guard walked over as two others restrained Haden. Abruptly the man, Mark, burst out laughing.

"I fail to see the reason for your amusement," said Shrad.

"Oh, I'm just amused at the rather crude technology. Do you honestly think your Collective will survive after lobotomizing most of it citizens? Do you honestly think its economy and whole social structure could survive your coming attack on the Grazen? Though of course, that's not something you'll find out about, since the Grazen will stop playing their waiting game . . . just like the one that's coming here."

"Explain yourself."

"Gladly. Your social system is bankrupt and bound to fail. The Grazen withdrew to their heartlands to await that failure, since it would have been less costly to them than continuing to fight you. Now that they have seen that the Collective is about to attack again, they'll come out fighting, and this time they won't be sending those insentient and easily mass-manufactured wormships."

"How do you know all this?"

"I'm the Owner–haven't you figured that out."

The others were now looking at the man with something approaching hope. Shrad felt another sudden doubt of his earlier reasoning. Maybe this man did have some power and, if so, Shrad must clamp down on it fast. The man looked human enough, so a bullet in the brain would soon solve any problem he might cause. And there was also that "crude technology." Perhaps that was the better option–even strouded, the man could still stand trial for his crimes against the collective will. The Committee much preferred to put those before the cameras who said what they were told to say.

"You are Markovian scum and a liar. Now tell me about the Grazen coming here."

The man shrugged. "They normally keep away. We had a bit of a misunderstanding about a thousand years ago . . . or rather they misunderstood what I meant when I said no, keep out, these star systems are mine. I thought I put it to them quite clearly, but apparently not."

"It's a good act, Markovian, but you're on your knees with broken teeth."

"Yeah, bastard that."

"You were saying?"

"Oh yeah . . . well, they normally keep out, but the one whose nest you passed on the way in here lost all her children on the nursery world in the bombardment you instigated. She's not happy—especially now that the Collective is preparing to attack again. I rather think she would like to have you all screaming in her shig-ware."

"You babble."

Even so, Shrad removed his communicator from his belt and opened a channel to the shuttle uplink. "Citizen Astanger—report."

After a short delay: "Tell your fucking Guard to let us get out of here! And tell them to let Citizen Chadrick back to his weapons console!"

"Give me your situation."

"Sitting here with our thumbs up our arses watching a Grazen dreadnought approach. It's already fired a ranging shot."

"Where would you go, given the opportunity to run?"

"Down to where you are. If we stay out here, we're dead!"

The communicator was slippery in his palm and he felt someone trying to wind his insides around a stick. This should not, could not, be happening.

"Put me on . . . general address," he managed.

"You're on."

"Guard–" Could this be some sort of ploy by Astanger? No, Astanger would have called him first. "Guard, allow Citizen Chadrick back to the weapons console and allow Citizen Astanger to move the *Lenin* out of danger. Astanger, I will keep this channel open–keep me informed of events."

"Oh yes, like I'm going to have time for that!"

Shrad lowered the communicator and clipped it back on his belt. This Mark had *known,* and the Markovians had never been above using additional cerebral wiring–it was from the remaining files on that technology that Collective Social Assets had managed to work out how to make strouds. What else could the man control, influence? He turned and pointed.

"Use the stroud on him! Now!"

From his knees, Mark launched himself to his feet, but the Guard brought him down.

"Keep that fucking thing away from me!" he bellowed.

Shrad smiled. He had correctly understood what was happening here; this man was not the Owner, but just some Markovian refugee. He fought, but soon the stroud was in place and he was kicking on the floor, his face clenched up in agony as blood ran from underneath the device. Shrad stepped past him.

"So, you see your all-powerful Owner." He gestured dismissively to the prostrate form. "Now, I can find them of course, but I want you to tell me where the rest of the escapees are. Obviously I don't want to waste societal assets, but I will have each of you strouded in turn if you do not tell me."

"Did your father fuck your mother up the arse to produce you?" asked Haden.

Shrad sighed, then gave the nod to the guard beside her.

Nothing happened.

He gave the nod again, but the guard seemed to not be paying attention.

"Strike her," he instructed.

The guard lifted his carbine and gazed down at it, then looked up at Shrad. Tears were pouring from the man's eyes.

Abruptly he went down on his knees and slowly bowed his head.

What?

A clattering, then the sound of bodies hitting the floor. Two of the Guard had collapsed. Another two went over even as he watched. Others were sinking to their knees like the first, or just suddenly finding somewhere to sit down. Some were crying, others grinning idiotically.

"It is, actually, not a crude technology at all. The Markovians obtained it from the Grazen, who, though they would not admit to it, obtained it from an excavation of some ruins left by those I called the jelly people—they were okay, but tended to be a bit impetuous. Anyway, I needed to see one of your strouds from the inside to be sure of the structure. I've U-transmitted the signal now, so that every single strouded human being in the Collective just woke up to what has been done to them or, if the damage is too severe, died."

It felt to Shrad as if ice was forming down his spine. He reached down, drew his sidearm, turned. The man, Mark, was on his feet facing him. Shrad fired once, the bullet snapping the man's skull back and blowing its contents out behind him. The head slowly swung forward again. One eye was missing.

"And that completes the deal," said Mark.

Shrad shot him four more times, the shots smashing into the man's chest and knocking him staggering back. Mark grinned. Then his legs gave way and he slumped to the floor.

Astanger secured his strap as the *Lenin* turned hard. The sound of the ship's guns impinged—an accelerating drone—and the power drain momentarily dimmed the lighting.

What happened to the Guard?

Some of them had just collapsed where they stood. One of those nearest him, a woman, was crouching beside a console, clinging with both hands, her weapon abandoned on the floor and sliding away from her. Her expression was one of horrified amazement, yet someone strouded usually didn't show emotion. Another, over near where Chadrick had taken position at the weapons console, was kneeling, his carbine propped upright before him. He seemed to be crying.

No matter. It might be that the *Lenin* would not even survive the next few minutes, so the condition of those aboard would cease to be of relevance. Again came the detonation of something that got too close before the guns took it out. The ship shuddered and smoke began crawling through the air from the bridge exit.

"It's going to be a hard reentry!" shouted Grade over the racket.

"Go to earpieces and mikes," said Astanger.

"Okay—I'm on," replied Grade.

"We've still got to drop velocity."

"Yup."

As they slowed into atmosphere, they would become a much easier target for the pursuing alien vessel, but Astanger knew that out in space the *Lenin* would end up smeared across the vacuum. Collective ships had encountered these dreadnoughts on a few occasions and been destroyed almost out of hand.

The *Lenin* began shaking, and Astanger recognized the muted but growing roar of atmosphere. Inertial forces tried to drag him out of his chair as the ship flipped nose-to-tail. He saw a member of the Guard slam into the ceiling above, then lost sight of him in smoke. Someone was shrieking, short jerky shrieks like those you might hear in an asylum, not from anyone in pain. A body slammed down with a wet crunch nearby, then smeared blood across the floor as deceleration dragged it away. Grade had gone for a full emergency landing: not dumping the drive section, but decelerating down toward the planet on the drive flame.

"Will you bring us down close to the *Breznev*?" Astanger inquired.

"Within a few miles of it—if we don't get hit on the way down," Grade replied.

"Chadrick—status?"

"It seems to be holding off, I don't know why."

I do, thought Astanger. *If it destroys the* Lenin, *then we all die. The Grazen wants us alive to play with. I wonder how long—*

"Captain!" Chadrick shouted.

What now, some weapon he can't stop? Astanger knew that Chadrick must be in considerable emotional distress to use the old politically incorrect title, even if the Guard were down.

"What is it, Chadrick," he said calmly.

"The moon . . . look at the moon."

What?

Astanger cleared the pursuing alien vessel from the viewing cylinder and trained the ship's scanners on the moon, and then just stared in shock, even though he had known there was something odd about that satellite. There was a line drawing across the surface, longitudinally. It flickered—an arrow-straight firestorm. On one side of the line was the surface he had earlier viewed, on the other side . . . on the other side was something else. He saw massive pylons, steel plains, and valleys cutting through either buildings or clustered monolithic machines, transmission or reception dishes the size of calderas, giant throats glimmering with lights and webworks of scaffold, ships bigger than anything he had ever seen gathered in frameworks like bullets in an ammunition clip. It was impossible to take in the vast complexity of it all. The moon was obviously some vast vessel or station.

Owner space?

Yeah, now he knew for certain why it remained so. Whoever had constructed this thing possessed more resources, more plain unadulterated power, than entire galactic civilizations.

But how did it affect them, right now, aboard the *Lenin*? It didn't. If they didn't get down to the surface of that planet soon, they would be dead. Moon or otherwise.

"Keep your scanners focused on the Grazen, Chadrick," said Astanger. Then switching to general address, he said, "When we're down, I want someone to break open the weapons locker. We grab what we can and we get out–that ship will be on us in minutes."

"What about . . . the Guard?" inquired Chadrick.

"What about them?"

"I . . . I don't know."

"We ignore them." Astanger took a steady breath. The G-forces were high now and it was becoming difficult to talk. "Something's got to them . . . through their strouds . . . maybe some Grazen . . . viral weapon."

The muted roar had now become a full-throated one. And the ship was shuddering around them. The Guard were probably irrelevant, since anyone not strapped in an acceleration chair when they began their descent was probably either dead now or suffering from multiple fractures. Maybe he and his crew should be merciful and kill them on the way out. No, they wouldn't have the time.

Blackout.

When consciousness began to fade back in, Astanger realized that the roaring he could hear now was only from the engines. He felt the pressure rapidly dropping away from him. Judging by the pull of gravity, the ship was coming down at a steep angle. This was going to be bad. The *Lenin* settled with an almighty crash and the drive cut out. Then, with an awful creaking and groaning, the ship toppled and slammed down flat on whatever it had landed on. The impact flung Astanger sideways in his chair, but the side padding absorbed most of the shock. He was now sideways to the pull of gravity. Peering down to the bottom of the spin section, he saw a tangle of bodies, blood, and some exposed broken bone where the Guard had ended up. Some of them had landed on Citizen Breen–Astrogation–but she seemed okay because she was pushing them away and unstrapping herself. She climbed through the tangled mass over to the spin-section controls and hit the step-motor button. The section shuddered and began to turn, and she walked around with it. Step by step it brought sets of acceleration chairs down to ground level, and the crew unstrapped. Astanger released himself from his chair last and eyed the bodies that had tumbled around like stones in a polisher. A few of them were still breathing. One was bubbling blood from her mouth and muttering.

"Okay, let's get out of here."

Those from Engineering had broken open the weapons locker and, when Astanger arrived, were passing out carbines, sidearms, and loading up two shoulder-held missile launchers.

"Should we get food?" enquired someone.

"No time," Astanger replied.

The loading ramp was nearly underneath the ship, but its hydraulics managed to lift the cargo section enough for them to crawl out. Outside, a pall of smoke obscured much, and the ground was blackened and in places still burning. Checking a notescreen map and positional indicator, Astanger led the way toward where the *Breznev* was down, and toward where that house lay. After a few hundred yards, light penetrated–reflected from that awesome terrible moon as it breached the horizon–then a breeze began sweeping the pall aside to reveal a nightmare perhaps a mile to their left.

The Grazen ship.

The thing possessed no aerodynamics, no recognizable engine or drive section, nothing remotely equateable with human technology. It was a loose tangle of meter-wide pipes, the color of charred bone, nearly half a mile across. Within this tangle was a nacreous and vaguely spherical core. Some of the pipes, their mouths open to the air, were moving as if questing for the scent of something. Astanger had a fair idea what they were searching for.

"No–keep moving." He slapped an engineering assistant on the back as the man raised and aimed the missile launcher at the ship. "You'll only attract its attention."

But what was "it"? Was he talking about the ship itself or what it contained? He'd seen pictures of organic fragments from destroyed nests, but there were so many different kinds of those that no Collective Societal Asset had managed to put together an entire Grazen. He had little idea of what they actually looked like, how big they were—anything, really. The Collective described them as alien maggots—but that description was politically motivated and predicated on charred evidence gathered from the bombed nursery world.

"Keep moving."

Surely their luck could not hold for much longer.

It didn't.

A sound issued from the ship—the sighing groan of caves. Astanger glanced back at it and saw some of those pipes inclining toward the ground, coming together, then leveling so that he could see straight down their throats.

"You two! Hit that!" he shouted at the two carrying the missile launchers.

Both of them turned and went down on one knee, their shoulder launchers bucking. There was something coming down the pipes as the four missiles struck. Red fire bloomed, spraying bony fragments everywhere, but out of that flame a twiggy wheel two meters across rolled at speed toward them.

"Run!"

The thing seemed to hesitate for a moment, then it made its choice. It accelerated up behind one of those with a launcher and slammed down on the man. Astanger skidded to a halt, then ran back to look down into a terrified face. Encaged in the gnarled jointed mass the man struggled. Astanger had heard about this; the man would begin to scream in a moment, for spikes would soon begin easing into his flesh. He drew his sidearm and shot the man twice through the forehead—the only mercy possible. Then, looking back toward the ship, he saw its core open and its pipe components snake across the ground toward them—the whole mass disassembling and turning into a rolling avalanche of alien technology. And within that mass, commanding it, swept along with it, controlling it, came the

Grazen itself. Obeying his own command, he turned and ran just as hard as he could.

Kelly guessed it didn't really matter what had happened. Though the Guard were completely out of it, the Doctrinaire still held a gun and she and her companions were still bound.

"Astanger! Report!" Shrad kept screaming into his communicator.

Any minute now, that would change. Either this Astanger would report or he wouldn't. Afterward, Doctrinaire Shrad would return his attention to his prisoners and, strouds no longer being an option, he would probably settle the matter with his gun. Kelly knew him. He represented everything she hated about the system she had tried to escape. He was also the one who had led them into the fight against the Grazen in which many of her friends had died, quite often as a result of his incompetence. She strained at her cuffs, but they were still hardened steel and unbreakable. Maybe if she could get to her feet, she could kick the weapon out of his hand. Maybe the others . . .

She turned and looked at the other five. Elizabeth was down on her side, her head in her father's lap. Slome looked ill, and anyway, he was old and fat and would probably be no help. That left Traviss and Longshank. Both of them were focused on the Doctrinaire. Kelly caught their attention and nodded her head toward Shrad. Longshank, who was closest, began to ease a leg forward, ready to hurl himself at the man. The sidearm abruptly whipped around, the barrel aimed straight at Longshank's forehead.

"I don't think so," said Shrad. He lowered his communicator and clipped it back on his belt. Kelly felt herself deflate.

Shrad continued. "Obviously the *Lenin* has encountered some difficulties."

The man looks crazy, thought Kelly. *No telling what he might do now.*

"But difficulties aside, you are all still criminals and betrayers of the Collective. Unfortunately, it seems that the strouds no longer function correctly." Shrad gazed around at the Guard. Not one of them remained standing. Some were sitting, some sprawled and unmoving, some kneeling with their foreheads against the carpet. "No matter–this is easily settled." He focused his attention back on Longshank. "For your crimes against the collective will, Daniel Longshank, I now execute sentence on you."

Shrad pulled the trigger. There came a hollow thunk, and the Doctrinaire looked with puzzlement at his weapon. After a moment, puzzlement turned to shock. He yelled and flung the weapon away. Tracking its course, Kelly saw it bounce on the carpet and begin smoking, then, with a multiple crack, it exploded, flinging fragments in every direction.

Kelly began trying to get to her feet. Then she noticed something: the Guard, those of them that were not obviously dead, were all now standing. She hadn't even seen them move.

"Citizen Guard One!" said Shrad with relief.

The one he addressed shook his head. "No . . . I think . . . I was . . ." He gave a puzzled frown, looked to his fellows for a moment, then slowly returned his attention to Shrad. "There's holes, but he tells me I can fill them. I remember now: my name is Evan . . . Evan Markovian."

Markovian.

"Citizen Guard One!" said Shrad, backing up. "Kill the prisoners! At once!"

Kelly settled back down, the certain knowledge of what would soon ensue igniting a warm glow in her chest.

"Why should I do that?" enquired Evan–formerly Citizen Guard One.

"I order you to kill the prisoners!"

"No," said Evan. He glanced to his fellows and from them received nods of approval. After a moment, he reached up and pushed at one finger of his stroud with his thumb. The device lifted and, as if removing an irritating scab, he peeled it from his head.

"Do you know what's happening now?" Evan asked. Shrad could only shake his head mutely. Evan continued. "Tens of thousands of the Guard, all armed and ready for the new assault on the Grazen, have suddenly found themselves without strouds." He smiled. "I can see the images in my head, and they are beautiful. I see Doctrinaires being marched to the airlocks of ships and expelled into vacuum. I see them, on Capital World, being lined up and shot. Elsewhere, some have had the idea that sterilization is a better option, and flamethrowers are being used. And everywhere more personal, more painful, and more long drawn-out vengeances are being enacted." He paused contemplatively, gazing down at the stroud he held, then discarded it. "I think that last option is the one I want, Shrad." He looked up. "It's going to take you a long time to die."

Shrad turned and ran.

Get him, get him now, thought Kelly, but the newly awakened Evan Markovian just watched Shrad's departure with amused contempt. Almost without thinking, she brought her hands forward to push herself upright, then stopped and stared in confusion at her wrists. Where were the cuffs? Glancing back, she saw them lying in pieces on the carpet. No matter. She pushed herself to her feet, just as Longshank and Traviss were doing.

"Are you going to let him go?" she asked Evan. "Because I'm not."

The man still had that look on his face, but he was utterly motionless. Kelly walked over to him. She prodded his chest. He swayed but showed no other reaction. The other Guards were motionless, too. What was going on here? Fuckit. She could not work this out right now. But whatever was happening, she was not going to let that fucking Doctrinaire escape. She turned, scanning about her feet, then squatted down to pick up a carbine. She checked it over—just to be sure it was in working order.

"This cannot be happening," said Longshank.

What was the man on about?

A hand squeezed her shoulder. In annoyance, she turned, and then shock took over and she found herself dragging herself backward.

"It's all right," said the man who had named himself Mark, the man whose brains were all over the carpet nearby and whom she'd subsequently seen shot four times in the chest. He turned to glance over at the others and she could see that the occiput of his head was missing, exposing a gory hole the size of her fist.

"Conflicts outside my territory are usually of no interest to me, though I keep watch on them, just to be sure they don't come to represent a danger."

Kelly stared at the back of his head, watching as the hole just filled up and closed. He turned back toward her, and she saw bright pinpricks of light flickering around him. Both his eyes were in place, and red points advanced from deep inside to fill them out, turning them into something demonic. The man Mark seemed to be fading into the background, blurring, or perhaps another background was reaching out from somewhere to grab him back. Abruptly, the figure before her came back into focus and was no longer Mark. This individual's hair was bone white over a thin face. His simple attire transformed into something more like the inside of a machine than clothing for a human being. Trying to focus on him, Kelly realized she was looking into something . . . else.

Around him, indefinable engines lurked at the limit of perception, gathered and poised like a planetoid moments before impact. Vast energies seemed to be focused upon this one man, like a mountain turned onto its tip.

The Owner–Kelly had not the slightest doubt now.

"But I don't like conflicts upon my border. I find them . . . disturbing." He nailed her with viper eyes. "This Collective you fled is one of the most unsavory regimes I've seen in some time. It would have died eventually, but meanwhile it was stirring up the Grazen, who represent an altogether different danger."

There was a coldness here—an indifference to human suffering. Yet, he had saved them. Why did he do that? Kelly suspected that he had done so simply because the difference between saving them and not saving them was minuscule to him. She also felt he could annihilate them in a moment, at a whim.

"How can they be a danger to you?"

He paused contemplatively, then said, "Human speech—I have to slow myself down so much for it, have to hone down a fragment of myself for its purpose. The word should not have been danger but inconvenience. They inconvenienced me once before. They call it 'the Misunderstanding.' It resulted in me losing the biosphere of one of my worlds."

"What did *they* lose?"

"Half of their race . . . but that was long ago, when I was more impulsive."

Had he used the right words then?

"What about them?" Kelly pointed at the Guard.

"They are healing slowly—it's better to take them offline during the process. I used them to set Shrad running, just as I am using the rest of their kind to bring down the Collective."

He talked about human beings as if they were components in a machine.

"Yes, Shrad," said Kelly pointedly, gripping her weapon with more determination, but not yet ready to turn away from this being.

He looked at her as if he did not understand; then it seemed that the penny dropped. "I see, Shrad. You want to kill him." He turned toward the shattered window. "Walk with me." Glancing at the others, he instructed, "All of you."

They stepped out of his house and began crossing the rose garden. His walking, she saw, seemed okay at a brief glance, but closer inspection revealed that his feet weren't touching the ground. Kelly strode at his side; the others attentive all around.

"My god!" Olsen suddenly exclaimed.

Kelly glanced at him and saw that he was gazing up and to

her left. She glanced there, taking in the starlit darkness and the rising moon. It took a moment for what she had just seen to register, and then she looked back. That was no moon.

"My ship," stated the Owner.

His ship. Fucking hell.

"I don't like problems close to home," he went on. He glanced at Kelly and she thought, *He's more human now.* Perhaps he had refined that *fragment* he was using for communication.

"The Grazen are an inconvenience. A Grazen Mother who is grieving and half mad could become something more than that, especially when she positions herself right on my border."

"The one that's coming?" Kelly guessed.

"The one that is already here."

Kelly's sudden fear was muted by his presence. "Here?"

"Yes, here to find a cure for her ill, and a kind of justice."

Abruptly, Slome interjected, "Is vengeance a cure?"

The Owner gazed at him and Slome turned pale at what he saw, but the Owner nodded. "Yes, for that mind-set, and for the human mind, too, though humans would like to deny their own nature."

Vengeance?

Then Kelly understood.

———

Leaning against the trunk of a gnarled olive tree, Astanger caught his breath and gazed in horror at the thing poised on the slope below them. So this was a Grazen! He saw a giant crayfish head from which extended many wiry tendrils, many of them spearing away to connect into the writhing tangle of pipe-things, whose black-etched moon shadows now surrounded him and his crew. Unlike a crayfish, it did not seem to possess a jointed exoskeleton, but a slick and tough-looking red and brown skin. At the extremities of the multiple limbs arrayed down its long body, it possessed things like hands, or feet, with digits arrayed in rows under flat pads. Its tail was not a flat fish tail, but a long rattish thing coiled around its already coiled body. And the Grazen was the size of a space shuttle.

It had stopped, why had it stopped? Was it toying with them now?

"What do we do now?" asked one of the crew.

Astanger wanted to reply, *We die, probably very slowly,* but didn't think that would help much. He gazed down at the sidearm he clutched and wondered if it would be best to use it on himself now, or to wait until the monster sent one of those twiggy things for him.

Movement behind.

He looked upslope and saw the pipe-things withdrawing into the surrounding trees. Did it want them to run again? Had the chase thus far not been satisfying enough for it? Then he saw the figure hurtling toward them down the moon-silvered grass, and, after a moment, recognized the Doctrinaire. Obviously things had gone badly at the house—perhaps the Guard with Shrad had collapsed like those aboard the *Lenin.* Shrad must have used the tracer on Astanger's communicator and had come here because he thought he would be safe. Astanger felt like laughing, but knew it would come out hysterical.

When he saw what was awaiting beyond Astanger and the crew, Shrad came to an abrupt halt.

"Astanger! This way!" Shrad gestured imperiously.

Astanger just rested against his tree, watching the pipes moving in quietly behind the Doctrinaire. It was a small satisfaction to know that the man would be suffering a similar fate to them all.

"Come on!"

He started to gesture again, but then must have heard something. Turning, he saw one of the pipes rising up behind him, throated darkness bearing down on him. He fell back to the ground and scrambled downslope. He managed to gain his feet and break into a run. The pipe, like a confident python, came down and slowly writhed after him, then halted ten yards out from the first of the crewmen. Shrad kept running until he was up beside Astanger. Horrified, he stared downslope at the Grazen, then turned on Astanger.

"What the hell do you think you are doing, Citizen Astanger! You should've warned me! You should've run!"

Shrad's holster was empty. Astanger gazed at crewmen Breen, Chadrick, Grade, and the others who now gathered around. He read in them the contempt and hatred they felt for the Doctrinaire. Transferring his gaze to his own weapon, he swung it to one side in a leisurely motion, then brought it back hard across Shrad's face. The man went down and lay moaning, clutching at his cheek.

"He's unarmed," said Astanger to the others. "Instruct the others not to give him a weapon and not to give him a bullet when the time comes."

"Astanger!" Shrad was glaring at him from the ground.

In measured tones, Astanger said, "If you speak to me again I will shoot you in the kneecap." He returned his attention to the alien.

The Grazen seemed to be agitated—if he was interpreting correctly its jerky movements and the way it was reaching out with its insectile hands to touch the surrounding tangle. It had deliberately made a gap to let Shrad through, to get them all together in one place, so why was it not now attacking? Was it waiting for others to come this way? How likely was that? The Guard were screwed so it seemed unlikely to him that they would be coming after Shrad. Maybe the escapees, since their ship lay beyond the Grazen?

The ground shuddered and someone swore. What now? Astanger looked to where many of the crew were now gazing, as the shuddering of the ground increased. The moon was on the move, the glare of some titanic drive behind it. Slowly it shifted from its location above the horizon and grew visibly brighter. Astanger had no doubt it was moving into a position overhead.

"Please, you must listen to me, Astanger," said Shrad.

The man was crouching, desperate-looking. He hadn't even

noticed what was happening in the sky—it probably didn't fit his ideology.

"Do go on," said Astanger, almost too stunned to care anymore.

"If we make a concerted attack on the creature itself, it'll lose control of . . . those . . . things. We should be able to fight our way through—get to the ship."

Astanger considered that. They'd fired eight missiles at the creature and every one of those eight missiles had impacted on opalescent shields that abruptly sprang into being. Bullets just bounced off of the thing. Missiles into the tangle of pipework had shattered it, but the pipes just discarded the shattered sections, melded back together, and carried on. Now they were all out of missiles and the rest of their ammunition was depleted. He'd seen the others passing bullets to those who had run out. The bullets weren't for the Grazen. Astanger had four bullets left in his sidearm. He could spare one. He raised his weapon and fired once. Shrad went down yelling, clutching the mess of bone and blood that had been his kneecap. Astanger returned his attention to the alien.

Why was it holding back? Did it understand that its prey would kill themselves when it made its final assault? Was it trying to figure out a way of capturing them alive?

"Captain Astanger," said Grade, no longer worried about using a politically incorrect form of address.

Astanger turned to see the man pointing upslope. Looking there he saw a group of people approaching. He recognized graywear, then, after a moment, recognized some of the escapees. There was one other with them—something odd about him. Two of the pipe things reared back and the group passed between. Now Astanger could see the other individual more clearly. He seemed to be walking in a kind of hollow in the air and around him metallic things seemed to hover on the edge of visibility. Pale, white hair, eyes that seemed to open into the Pit. Astanger knew at once who this person must be.

The group approached, the escapees glancing warily at the

crewmen as they moved aside. Finally, they reached Astanger. The Owner glanced down at Shrad, then raised his gaze to Astanger.

"*Captain* Astanger," he said, then his mouth twisted in a cruel smile.

The moon now glared overhead, and the shuddering of the ground became a muted vibration, like the running of some vast engine, and one Astanger knew was shaking this whole world. That inconceivably gigantic vessel up there was *his.* Astanger was glad when the . . . man turned his attention toward the Grazen.

"The Mother," the Owner intoned.

Astanger looked in that direction, too, and to his horror saw that the Grazen was lining up some of those tube mouths, and that in them could be glimpsed twiggy insectile movement. He stepped back, brought his sidearm up to his head.

"That won't be necessary, *Captain.*"

Yeah, right.

One of the things spat out, rolled along the ground toward them, its pace leisurely. Astanger stepped back again, heard the sounds of weapons being cocked. The twiggy wheel slowed to a halt over Shrad, folded down into a kind of leggy cone.

"Astanger!" Shrad screamed.

It hesitated, wavering back and forth. The Owner gestured, and then the thing fell on the Doctrinaire. Shrad began yelling incoherently. Astanger gazed down at him without sympathy, then abruptly jerked his head up as the pipe that had fired the thing began to snake across the ground toward them. Now Shrad began screaming. The twigwork was extruding spikes like clawed fingers and they were slowly easing into the man's flesh. He was struggling but, thus encaged, there was nowhere for him to go. Astanger noted that the wounds did not bleed. He guessed that would be too easy.

The pipe reached Shrad and fibers speared out, glimmering like spider silk in the moonlight, from the seething multijawed face of something inside. The fibers attached all around the cage, dragged Shrad in. His screams disappeared up inside the pipe, becoming hollow and echoey.

"He ordered the bombing of the nursery world," one of the escapees said.

Astanger glanced at her, recognized Kelly Haden. Then he understood the implication of what she was saying. *The Mother*, he realized.

But it wasn't over. The other pipe-mouths were still there, those things still inside and ready to roll. Astanger was all too aware that though he personally did not take part in the bombing of the nursery world, he was part of the fleet that did, and that if he had been ordered to take part, he would have. The things began to ease out.

"It's been the best it could be," said Grade. The man brought his carbine up underneath his chin and pulled the trigger. Nothing happened.

The Owner glanced at him. "Hasty," he said, then returned his attention to the Grazen Mother. "Must I destroy you?"

Around him the metallic objects seemed to gain a greater solidity. He held out a hand to one side almost in sad entreaty. Astanger winced. It felt almost as if he was standing too close to a fire, yet what he was feeling was not exactly heat.

"Withdraw, now," said the Owner.

Like the heads of tubeworms, the twiggy wheels abruptly retracted out of sight. Movement all around. The pipes were all pulling back toward the Grazen and she began retreating downslope. She, and all her weird technology, gathered into a rolling wave falling away from them, then it all began to clump around her, opalescent shields flicking on in intervening spaces, gradually blotting her from sight. With a thrum that transmitted through the ground, the whole mass began to rise. Then, with a sighing groan, it shot up into the sky.

"Thank you," said Astanger.

The Owner held out a hand for silence, stillness, as he still gazed up into the sky. After about a minute, he returned his attention to them all.

"These," he gestured to the escapees, "you will not harm. Their ship is now fully functional and you will all return on it." He paused for a contemplative moment. "Your Collective is collapsing. At my request, the Grazen will not attack what remains."

"I have no love of the Collective," said Astanger.

The Owner nodded, and Astanger reckoned that he'd had no need to say that, for it was probably why he was still alive. He noted that though the . . . machines around the Owner were now plainly visible, he and they seemed to occupy some encystment in reality, something somehow excised.

The Owner said, "Leave now. You have one day to get beyond my border."

A star of darkness flickered within that encystment, and all it contained seemed to be stretching away. Somehow Astanger knew that it was connected to that vessel hovering above them like the steel eye of some vast god.

"Build something better this time—you have been warned," the Owner told them.

The encystment retracted into the star, disappeared.

Astanger guessed it was the best they could hope for.

"Well, Societal Assets," said Astanger to the escapees, "we'd best find the rest of your people and get out of here."

"Fuck you," said Kelly Haden. "I'm not a 'Societal Asset' and I don't take orders from you!"

Astanger held up his sidearm, reversed it, and held the butt out to her. "Then you must choose who you do take orders from, or choose to give them yourself."

Really, it was the best they could hope for.

THE MAN WITH THE GOLDEN BALLOON

Robert Reed

Robert Reed sold his first story in 1986, and quickly established himself as a frequent contributor to The Magazine of Fantasy and Science Fiction *and* Asimov's Science Fiction, *as well as selling many stories to* Science Fiction Age, *Universe,* New Destinies, Tomorrow, Synergy, Starlight, *and elsewhere. Reed may be one of the most prolific of today's young writers, particularly at short fiction lengths, seriously rivaled for that position only by authors such as Stephen Baxter and Brian Stableford. And—also like Baxter and Stableford— he manages to keep up a very high standard of quality while being prolific, something that is not at all easy to do. Reed stories such as "Sister Alice," "Brother Perfect," "Decency," "Savior," "The Remoras," "Chrysalis," "Whiptail," "The Utility Man," "Marrow," "Birth Day," "Blind," "The Toad of Heaven," "Stride," "The Shape of Everything," "Guest of Honor," "Waging Good," and "Killing the Morrow," among at least a half dozen others equally as strong, count as among some of the best short work produced by anyone in the '80s and '90s; many of his best stories were assembled in his first collection,* The Dragons of Springplace. *Nor is he nonprolific as a novelist, having turned out eight novels since the end of the '80s, including* The Lee Shore, The Hormone Jungle, Black Milk, The Remarkables, Down the Bright Way, Beyond the Veil of Stars, An Exaltation of Larks, Beneath the Gated Sky, Marrow, *and* Sister Alice. *His most recent books include two chapbook novellas,* Mere *and* Flavors of My Genius; *a collection,* The Cuckoo's Boys; *and a novel,* The Well of Stars. *Reed lives with his family in Lincoln, Nebraska.*

In 1994, Reed launched a long series of stories (including novels such as Marrow*) about the Great Ship: a Jupiter-sized starship found abandoned in deep space by exploring humans and retrofitted into a kind of immense interstellar cruise ship, off on a grand tour of the galaxy (circumnavigating it, in fact), with millions of human and alien customers of many different races aboard. In the intricate story that follows, he points out that even on a starship the size of a gas giant inhabited by millions of passengers, there will be hidden corners where nobody has ever gone before, and enigmatic surprises to be found there— including a lesson in just how far the arm of the Empire can stretch, and how subtle and profound its touch can be.*

I

Q uee Lee learned about the Vermiculate from an unlikely source—a painfully respectable gentleman who had never taken pleasure from adventuring or the unexpected. But their paths happened to cross during a feast given by mutual friends, and after the customary pleasantries, he pulled the ancient woman aside, remarking, "I have some news that might be of interest to you." Then, with a precise, mildly perturbed voice, he explained how one tiny portion of the Great Ship had never been mapped.

"How can that be?" Quee Lee asked skeptically. After all, the captains had made it a priority to investigate every shipboard cavern and tunnel, and today even the tiniest crevice wore its own intricate name.

"The captains were quite thorough," he admitted. "But the Ship is so very enormous."

That it was. With the mass and volume of Uranus, no machine was the Great Ship's equal. Its engines were as big as moons, its fuel tanks could drink oceans, and the variety and volume of its onboard habitats was nothing less than spectacular. Mapping such an enormous body proved a daunting challenge. Yet the early captains were clever and very stubborn souls. Their survey began with a few million robots–small, elegantly designed machines bristling with sensors and curious limbs. Scrambling through the Ship's interior, the robots memorized every empty volume, and whenever a passageway split in two, the robots would pause, feasting on the local rock and metal and then building copies of their obsessive selves. As prolific as carpenter ants or harum-scarum fleas, those early scouts soon numbered in the trillions, and, ruled by a set of simple unyielding instructions, they moved ever deeper inside the Ship, eventually scurrying down every hole and recording each turn and dead end, working with relentless unison to create a precise three-dimensional model of the Ship's vacant interior.

But the method had its limitations. Doorless bubbles and pockets and finger-wide seams lay out of reach; a few long caverns were sealed beneath kilometers of iron and hyperfiber. But with sonic probes and neutrino knives, the Ship's engineers eventually made even those buried places visible. The only major failure was hiding today in the Ship's distant core. But the peculiar world that would be known as Marrow lay in the remote future. The Master Captain was being honest when she stood on the bridge, proclaiming that her fabulous machine had been mapped in full, and its crew and countless passengers had little reason not to believe every promise that this voyage would remain routine–a blissful journey that would eventually circumnavigate the bright heart of the Milky Way.

"I understand how the Ship was mapped," remarked Quee Lee's companion. "What I am telling you is that despite everyone's best efforts, a few empty spaces are lurking out there."

"And how do we know this?" she asked, her tone politely curious.

"The Master Captain owns a team of AI savants," the gentleman replied. "They are brilliant machines designed to do nothing but ponder the Ship and its mysteries. One of those AIs recently made a thorough analysis of old data, and it discovered one glaring gap, one blank spot on the captains' map, and nobody seems to understand how this could have happened."

"And when did we learn this?"

"But we haven't learned anything," he countered, his calm voice breaking at the edges. "This is a very grave, very important business. Only the highest-ranking captains know about the flaw."

"And you," she pointed out.

"Yes, I know portions of the story. I can't tell how or why, however, and please don't ask me. But it occurred to me that you of all people would appreciate hearing this news."

Give a rich secret to the blandest soul, and he will dream of telling what he knows. And Quee Lee was a charming presence as well as a very desirable audience: a wealthy woman from Old Earth and one of a handful of humans on board the Ship who could remember that precious moment when their species turned a sensitive ear to the sky and heard intelligent sounds raining down from the stars. In that sense, she was a remarkable, and very rare, creature—a lady of genuine fame inside the human community. She was also beautiful and poised, socially gifted and universally liked. Given the chance, any healthy, mildly insecure heterosexual male would work hard to impress Quee Lee.

"Our captains are worried," her confidant mentioned. "The Master Captain even took the trouble of waking one of the old surveying robots and putting it down a promising hole. And do you know what happened?"

"You're going to tell me, I hope."

"The robot lost its way." The man sighed, rather bothered by this turn of events. "The machine fumbled around in the darkness, and then, with nothing to say for itself, it climbed back out of the hole again."

"Fascinating," she exclaimed.

"I knew you would enjoy this," he whispered, offering a smile and quick wink. After millennia of traveling together, he had finally managed to engage this beautiful creature.

"Perri will want to hear this story," she mentioned.

"But I wish you wouldn't mention it," the man sputtered. Then a worse possibility occurred to him. "I understood that your husband is traveling just now. He isn't here with us, is he?"

"Oh, but he is," she exclaimed. By chance, Perri had just entered the festival room. For the last several weeks, he had been riding a saddle strapped to the back of a porpoiselike alien called the Gi-Gee, enjoying wild swims in a frigid river of water and ammonia. Of course, Perri would want to learn of this man's news. A thousand souls were scattered across the room, human and otherwise. Most of the partiers were dressed in gaudy, look-at-me costumes—which was only proper, since these were among the wealthiest, most powerful individuals to be found in the galaxy. But Quee Lee looked past the towering egos, waving at the only human male dressed in plain, practical clothes.

Instantly, her companion warned, "I don't want this to be known. Not outside our circle, please."

The tone said it all: Perri was neither wealthy nor important, which made him unacceptable.

But Quee Lee laughed off the insult as well as the earnest pleas for silence. "Oh, I'm sure my husband's already heard about the Vermiculate," she remarked. "Believe me, Perri knows the Ship as well as any captain does, and he knows everyone on board who matters, too." She winked, adding sweetly, "He knows you, of course."

"Of course."

"This won't be news to him," she promised.

Yet, for some reason, Perri wasn't familiar with this particular rumor. He listened intently as Quee Lee related the mystery, and yes, he was very familiar with that region called the Vermiculate. It was an intricate nest of dry caves, very few entrances leading to a million dead ends. But he had never heard evidence that some portion of those caverns had escaped mapping.

"Tell it again," he demanded, tugging at the fellow's elbow. "From the beginning, everything you know."

But there weren't many new details to share.

"I think I see what's happening," Perri mentioned. "This is probably just an old rumor reborn. The first two passengers to come on board the Great Ship started this story. Over drinks or in somebody's bed, they convinced themselves there had to be secret places and unmapped corners lurking somewhere. It helped heighten the sense of adventure, don't you see? And that's why every century or two, that same old legend puts on a new costume and takes its walk in public."

"But this is no rumor," the man proclaimed. "And I don't approve of legends. What I told you is the truth, I swear it."

"Yet you won't name your source," Perri pointed out.

"I cannot," the man repeated. "Frankly, I wish I hadn't said this much."

Perri was a modern human, durable and functionally immortal. But unlike all of the well-moneyed souls in the room, he wore a boyish face and a pretty, almost juvenile smile. When it served his needs, he played the role of a smart child surrounded by very foolish adults. "It scares the hell out of you, doesn't it? You hear about this puzzle, and you're the kind of creature who won't fall asleep unless every puzzle is solved, every question mark erased."

"And what is wrong with that?" asked the rumor's source.

"What's right about it?" Perri countered.

Quee Lee had expected precisely that response, and when it came, she laughed softly.

The gentleman bristled. "My dear, I thought you would be interested in this matter. But if you're going to tease me—"

"I didn't mean that," she began.

But the man had his excuse to turn and march away. No doubt he would avoid Quee Lee for the rest of the day and, if genuinely angry, she wouldn't see him for the next fifty years.

"I shouldn't have laughed," Quee Lee admitted.

"He will forgive you."

True enough. Fifty years of chilled silence was nothing among immortals. All but the most malicious slights were eventually pardoned, or at least discarded as memories not worth carrying any farther. "It's too bad that the story isn't true," she said. "I wish there was some unmapped cave hiding out there."

"Oh, but there is," Perri replied.

Quee Lee worked through the possibilities. "You lied to me," she complained. "You'd already heard about the Vermiculate."

"I didn't, and I haven't."

"Then how can you say—?"

"Easily," he interrupted. "Your friend might be a wonderful soul. He might be charitable and sweet—"

"Hardly."

"But he has never once shown me the barest trace of imagination. I seriously doubt that he could dream up such a tale, and I know he wouldn't repeat any wild fable, unless it came from a reasonable, responsible source."

"Such as?"

"One of the captains," Perri allowed.

"But why would any rational officer take any passenger into his or her confidence?" She hesitated, and laughed. "I suppose my old friend is rather wealthy."

"Wealthier even than you," Perri agreed.

"And if he happened to be sleeping with a captain . . ."

"That's my cynical guess."

Quee Lee knew her husband's mind. "You already know which captain it is, don't you?"

"I have a robust notion," he allowed.

"Who?"

"Not here," he warned, stroking her arm with a fond hand. "But my candidate has rank and connections, and she's desperately fond of money. And if you mix those qualifications with the fact that she, like that prickly man sulking over there, doesn't appreciate mysteries . . ."

"Is the Vermiculate unmapped?" she asked.

"If any place is," Perri allowed. Then, with long fingers, he drew elaborate shapes in the air between them. "If you wove all of those empty caves together and straightened them out, you'd have a single tunnel long enough to reach from your Earth to Neptune and partway home again. So yes, it's easy to imagine that some AI expert could massage the old data, and guess that one corner here and one little room there might have escaped notice and naming. And maybe after fifty thousand years of sleep, one of the original survey robots was awakened and shoved down a hole, and, because of its age, it malfunctioned, making everything seem far more mysterious than it actually was."

On her own, Quee Lee had narrowed the list of suspect captains to three, perhaps four. With a quiet, conspiratorial voice, she asked, "Who's going to make our discreet inquiries, you or me?"

"Neither of us," Perri said.

"Then you're not my husband," she teased. "The man I married would want to finish the mapping himself."

Perri shrugged and grinned. "We can make our own good guesses where to look." Then with a fond whisper, he added, "Besides, if we get ourselves noticed, what began as a tiny data anomaly mentioned to a lover will become much more: an area of potential embarrassment to the godly rulers of the Great Ship. Then our nameless captain will personally march into that empty corner . . . and keep me from having my little bit of fun . . ."

"And me, too," said Quee Lee.

"Or quite a lot of fun," Perri added, wrapping an arm around his wife's waist. "If you're in the mood for a little darkness, that is."

II

Yet nothing was simple about this simple-sounding quest. Finding holes inside the existing maps proved difficult, requiring months of detailed analysis by several experts paid well for

their secrecy as well as their rare skills. Meanwhile, half a dozen
of Perri's best friends heard about his newest interest, and, by
turning in past favors, they earned slots on the expedition ros-
ter. Then Quee Lee decided to invite two lady friends who had
been pressing for centuries to join her on a "safe adventure,"
which was what this would be. The Vermiculate might be imperfectly known, but there was no reason to expect danger. The
dry caves were filled with the standard minimal atmosphere–
nitrogen and oxygen and nothing else. There were no artificial
suns or lights, and the only heat was thermal leakage from the
nearby habitats and reactors. But even if the worst happened–if
everyone lost their way and their supplies were exhausted–the
end result would be a bothersome thirst and gradual starvation.
Eventually, their tough bioceramic minds would sever all connections with their failing bodies, and, when no choice was left,
ten humans would sit down in the darkness and quietly turn
into mummies, waiting for their absence to be noted and a rescue mission to track them down.

But Perri didn't approve of losing his way. Meticulous in
recording their position on the new, modestly improved map,
he earned gentle and then not-so-gentle ribbing from the others. The Vermiculate was far too enormous to explore, even a
thousand years. But their flex-skin car took them to areas of interest, and before they stepped away from each base camp, he
made his team memorize the local layout of tunnels and chambers. He insisted that everyone stay with at least one companion. He begged for the others to carry several kinds of torches
as well as locator tools, noisemakers, and laser flares. But eighteen days of that kind of mothering caused one of Quee Lee's
friends to break every rule. She picked a random passageway
and ran for parts unknown, at least to her. She was carrying
nothing but one small torch and a half-filled water bottle, and
after ten hours of solitary adventuring, she discovered that she
had no good idea where she was in the universe.

One night alone was enough of a lesson. Perri and Quee
Lee found the explorer sitting in a dead-end chamber, shivering

inside her heated clothes—shivering out of hunger and anxiety. And from that moment on, everyone's wandering was done with at least the minimal precautions.

It was the boredom that began to defeat the explorers.

The Vermiculate's walls were stone buttressed with low-grade hyperfiber. No human eye had ever seen these tunnels, but the novelty was minimal. Some places were beautiful in their shape and proportions, but it was an accidental beauty. The Ship's builders might have had a purpose for each twist and turn, every sudden room, and for the little tubes that gave access to the next portion of the maze. But to most eyes, nothing here was strange or particularly interesting, and, after two months of wandering, the novice adventurers were losing interest.

One by one, the expedition shrank.

First to leave was the woman who hadn't gotten lost. Then Perri's friends complained about these dreary circumstances, each demanding a ride to the nearest exit point. The only ones left were identical twin brothers and that dear old friend of Quee Lee who had gotten lost and scared, and then discovered a genuine fondness for spelunking.

Or maybe it was the brothers who held her interest. One night, when the camp lights were dropping down to a nightly glow, Quee Lee spotted the twins slipping into her friend's little shelter—entering her home from opposite ends, and neither appearing again until morning.

Another month of wandering brought few highlights. Half a dozen tunnels showed evidence of foot traffic over the last few thousand years. The desiccated slime trail of a Snail-As-God was a modest surprise. Inside one cave, they discovered the broken scale from a harum-scarum shin, and a few meters farther along, a liter of petrified blood left behind by a human male. And then came that momentous afternoon when they discovered a graveyard of surveying robots—ten thousand machines that had pulled themselves into neat, officious piles before dropping into what had become an eternal sleep.

Two days later, Perri brought his team to the bottom of a deep, deep chimney. Mathematical wizards had labeled that location as "mildly interesting." The Vermiculate had patterns, predictable and occasionally repeatable, and, according to sophisticated calculations, that narrow hole should lead to a large "somewhere else." But the unknown refused to expose itself with a glance. Two little tunnels waited at the bottom of the chimney, but every sonic pulse and cursory examination showed that they were merely long and exceptionally ordinary.

The five humans broke into two groups.

Perri and Quee Lee slipped into the shorter tunnel. As always, they brought tracking equipment as well as the sniffers that constantly searched for organic traces left by past visitors, and along with heated clothes and survival rations, they carried a variety of lights to offer feeble glows or sun-blazing fires. But the most effective sensor came in pairs, and it was the bluish-yellow eyes that noticed the sudden hole in the floor.

"Stop," said Perri.

Quee Lee paused, one gloved hand dropping, fingertips reaching to within a hairsbreadth of the emptiness.

"Look," he advised.

"I see it," she said. But she didn't know what she saw. After days and weeks of staring at structural hyperfiber, she recognized that something here was different. It was the area surrounding the hole that was peculiar. Holding a variable beam to the floor, she slipped through a series of settings. Hyperfiber was the strongest baryonic substance known—the bones of the Ship and the basis of every star-faring civilization—yet she had never seen light flickering against hyperfiber quite like it did just then. It was as if the floor was feeling their weight, and the photons were betraying the vibrations.

"Do you know what this is?" Perri asked.

"Do you?"

"The source," he announced. "The source of our rumor."

She shone a second light up and down the tunnel. There was no sign of disabled robots or the detritus left by mapping crews. But the captains could have cleaned up their trash, since captains liked to keep their secrets secret, particularly when it came to curious passengers.

"This hole is fresh," Perri decided. And when Quee Lee reached toward the edge, he said, "Don't. Unless you want to cut off a finger or two."

The floor was pure hyperfiber—a skin only a few atoms thick at its thickest. Because the stuff was so very thin, the light flickered. What they were trusting with their weight was close to nothing, like worn paint stretched across empty air, and the edge of the revealed hole was keener than the most deadly sword.

"But a robot should have noticed," she guessed. "If we can see that the floor here is different . . ."

"I've given that some thought," Perri offered. "We're about as deep into the Vermiculate as you can go, or so we thought. A few surveyors probably started working above us, and when they were overwhelmed, they stopped and ate the rock and replicated themselves."

"Imperfect copies?" she guessed.

"Maybe." He shrugged, enjoying the game but taking nothing too seriously. "Whatever the reason, the machine that first crawled into this tunnel wasn't paying close attention. It didn't notice what should have been obvious, and that's why the Ship's map was incomplete."

"Just like the rumor says," Quee Lee agreed. "Except there isn't much mystery, is there? Because if the captains had found something remarkable down here—"

"We wouldn't get within ten kilometers," Perri agreed.

With every tool, including her warm brown eyes, Quee Lee examined the floor and the hole and the blackness below.

Perri did the same.

And then, for the first time in perhaps a thousand years, one of them managed to surprise the other.

It wasn't the adventurous spouse who spoke first.

Pointing down, Quee Lee said, "That hole's just wide enough for me."

"If we string tethers to the ceiling," Perri mentioned, "and if there's another floor worth standing on below us."

"What about our friends?" she asked.

"I'll go gather them up," he began.

"No." Then, for the second time, she surprised her husband. "We'll leave a note behind. We can tell them to follow, if they want."

Perri smiled at the ancient creature.

"This is *our* adventure," she concluded. "Yours, and mine."

III

What lay below was very much the same as everything above. Which was what they had expected. The only difference was that no public map showed these particular cavities and chimneys, and the long tunnels and little side vents always led to a wealth of new places devoid of names. According to Perri's navigational equipment, they had wandered nearly twelve kilometers before beginning their hunt for a campsite. A series of electronic breadcrumbs led back to the original hole and their left-behind note, and, speaking through the crumbs, Quee Lee discovered that her lady friend and the twins hadn't bothered to come looking for them. She speculated as to why that might be, and they enjoyed a lewd laugh. Then, following one promising passageway around its final bend, they entered what seemed to be the largest room they had seen for weeks.

The floor of the room was an undulating surface, like water stirred by deep currents. They selected a spacious bowl of cool gray hyperfiber, and, with the camp light blazing beside them, they made love. Then they ate and drank their fill, and at a point with no obvious significance, Perri strolled over to his pack and bent down, intending to snatch some tiny item out of one of the countless pockets.

That was the moment when every light went out.

Quee Lee was sitting on her memory chair, immersed in sudden darkness. Her first instinct was to believe that she was to blame. Their camp light was in front of her. Had she given it some misleading command? But then she thought about their other torches and, realizing that the night was total, she naturally wondered if for some peculiar reason she had gone completely blind.

Then from a distance, with a moderately concerned voice, her husband asked, "Darling? Are you there?"

"I am," she remarked. Perri was blind too, or every one of their lights had failed. Either way, something unlikely had just occurred. "What do you think?" she asked.

"That it's ridiculously dark in here," Perri allowed.

Perfectly, relentlessly black.

"Do you feel all right?" he inquired.

"I feel fine," she said.

"I do, too." He was disappointed, as if some little ache might help answer their questions. "Except for being worried, I suppose."

One of Perri's feet kicked the pack.

"Darling?" she asked.

He said, "Sing to me. I'll follow your voice."

Softly, Quee Lee sang one of the first tunes that she had ever learned—a nursery rhyme too old to have an author, its beguiling lyrics about rowing and time wrapped around a language long considered dead.

Moments later, she heard Perri settle on the ground directly to her right.

She stopped singing.

Then Perri called from somewhere off to her left, from a distance, telling her, "Don't quit singing now. I'm still trying to find you, darling."

For a long moment, nothing happened. The darkness remained silent and unknowable. And then from her right, from a place quite close, a voice that she did not recognize softly insisted, "Yes, please. Sing, please. I rather enjoy that wonderful little tune of yours."

IV

Quee Lee began to jump up.

"No, no," the voice implored. "Remain seated, my dear. There is absolutely no reason to surrender your comfort."

She settled slowly, warily.

Perri said her name.

Clearing her throat, Quee Lee managed to say, "I'm here. Here."

"Are you all right?"

"Yes."

"But I thought I heard–"

"Yes."

"Is somebody with you?"

In the same moment, two voices said, "Yes."

Then the new voice continued. "I was hoping that your wife would sing a little more," it remarked. "But I suppose I have spoiled the mood, which is my fault. But please, Perri, will you join us? Sit beside Quee Lee, and I promise: Neither of you will come to any harm. A little conversation, a little taste of companionship . . . that's all I wish for now."

Again, with urgency, Perri asked, "Are you all right?"

How could she answer that question? "I'm fine, yes." Except that she was startled, and for many rational reasons, she was scared, and with the darkness pressing down, she was feeling a thrilling lack of control.

Her husband's footsteps seemed louder than before. In the perfect blackness, he stepped by memory, and then, perhaps sensing her presence, he stopped beside her and reached out with one hand, dry warm fingertips knowing just where her face would be waiting.

She clung to his hand with both of hers.

"Sit, please," the stranger insisted. "Unless you absolutely must stand."

Perri settled on one edge of her soft chair. His hand didn't leave her grip, and he patted that knot of fingers with his free hand. As well as she knew her own bones, Quee Lee knew his. And she leaned into that strong body, glad for his presence and confident that he was glad for hers.

"Who are you?" Perri asked.

Silence answered him.

"Did you disable our lights?" he asked.

Nothing.

"You must have," Perri decided. "And my infrared corneas and nexus-links, too, I noticed."

"All temporary measures," the stranger replied.

"Why?"

Silence.

"Who are you?" Quee Lee asked. And in the same breath, she added, "What is your name?"

Something about that innocuous question was humorous. The laughter sounded genuine, weightless, and smooth, gradually falling away into an amused silence. Then what might or might not have been a deep breath preceded the odd statement, "As a rule, I don't believe in names."

"No?" Quee asked.

"As a rule," the voice repeated.

Perri asked, "What species are you?"

"And I will warn you," the voice added. "I don't gladly embrace the concept of species either."

The lovers sat as close as possible, speaking to each other with the pressure of their hands.

Finally, Quee Lee took it upon herself to say, "We're human. If that matters to you, one way or another."

Silence.

"Do you know our species?" she asked.

And then Perri guessed, "You're a Vapor-track. Nocturnal to the point where they can't endure even the weakest light—"

"Yes, I know humans," the stranger responded. "And I know Vapor-tracks, too. But I am neither. And believe me, I am neither nocturnal nor diurnal. The time of day and the strength of the ambient light are of absolutely no concern to me."

"But why are you down here?" Quee Lee asked.

Their companion gave no response.

"This is a very remote corner of the Ship," Perri said. "Why would any sentient organism seek out this place?"

"Why do you?" was the response.

"Curiosity," Perri confessed. "Is that your motivation?"

"Not in the least." The voice was more male than female, and it sounded nearly as human as they did. But those qualities could be artifacts of any good translator. It occurred to Quee Lee that some kind of deception was at work here, and that what they heard had no bearing at all on what was beside them. "I could imagine that I am a substantial puzzle for the two of you," the voice allowed.

The humans responded with their own silence.

"Fair enough," their companion said. "Tell me: Where were each of you born?"

"On the Great Ship," Perri volunteered.

"I come from Earth," Quee Lee offered.

"Names," the stranger responded. "I ask, and you instantly offer me names."

"What else could we say?" asked Quee Lee.

"Nothing. For you, there are no other polite options. But as a rule, I prefer places that don't wear names. Cubbyholes and solar systems that have remained uncataloged, indifferent to whichever label that a passerby might try to hang on its slick invisible flesh."

Quee Lee listened to her husband's quick, interested breathing.

After reflection, Perri guessed, "And that's why you're here, isn't it? This is one place inside the Great Ship that has gone un-noticed. Until now."

"Perhaps that is my reason," the voice allowed.

"Is there a better answer?" Perri asked.

Silence.

"You have no name?" Quee Lee pressed.

The silence continued, and then, suddenly, an explanation was offered. "I don't wear any name worth repeating. But I do have an identity. A self. With my own history and limitations as well as a wealth of possibilities, most of which will never come to pass."

They waited.

The voice continued. "What I happen to be is a government official. A harmless and noble follower of rules. But when neces-sary, I can become a brazen, fearless warrior. Except when my best choice is to be a determined coward, in which case I can flee any threat with remarkable skill. Yet, in most circumstances, I am just an official: the loyal servant to a exceptionally fine cause."

"Which cause?" both humans asked.

"In service to the galactic union," the entity replied. "That is my defining role . . . a role that I have played successfully for the last three hundred and seven million years, by your arbi-trary and self-centered count."

Surprise and doubt ran through their bodies.

Quee Lee took it upon herself to confess, "I'm sorry. But we don't entirely believe you."

"You claim you were born on Earth. Is that true, my dear?"

She hesitated.

" 'Earth.' Your home planet carries a simple utterance. Am I right?"

She said, "Yes."

"I do happen to know your small world. But when I made my visit, the stars were completely unaware of that self-given name."

"And what do you know about Earth?" Perri asked.

"Actually, I know quite a lot," their companion promised. Then once again, it fell into a long, long silence.

V

Separately, Quee Lee and Perri had come to identical conclusions: The voice was rhythmic and deep, not just easy to listen to but impossible to ignore. Every word was delivered with clarity, like the voice of a highly trained actor. But woven through that perfection were hints of breathing and little clicks of tongues or lips, and, once in a great while, a nebulous sound that would leak from the mouth or nostrils . . . or some other orifice hiding in the darkness. Whatever was speaking to them was slightly taller than their ears, and their best guess was that the creature was sitting on a lump of hyperfiber less than three meters from them. There was mass behind the voice. Sometimes a limb would move, or maybe the body itself. Perhaps they heard the creak of its carapace or the complaining of stiff leathery clothes, or maybe a tendril was twisting back against itself–unless there was no sound, except what the two humans imagined they could hear out in the unfathomable blackness.

As far as they could determine, their nameless companion was alone. There wasn't any second presence or a whisper of another voice. And it somehow had slipped into their camp, perhaps even before the lights died, and neither one of them had perceived anything out of the ordinary.

Maybe the voice was just that.

Sound. Or a set of elaborate sounds, contrived for effect and existing only as so much noise, produced by nothing but the unlit air or the fierce motions of individual atoms.

Perhaps somebody was playing an elaborate joke on the two of them. Perri had many clever friends. A few of them might have worked together, going to the trouble necessary to bring him and Quee Lee into this empty hole, snatching them up in some game that would continue until the fun was ex-

hausted and the lights returned. Quee Lee could envision just
that kind of trick: One moment, a mysterious voice. And then,
just as suddenly, a thousand good friends would be standing
around them, congratulating the married pair on one or another minor anniversary.

"Is this a special occasion?" Quee Lee asked herself.

That route seemed lucrative. She smiled, and the nervousness in her body began to drain away. How many months and
years of work had gone into this silly joke? But she had seen
through all of the cleverness, and, for an instant, she considered
a preemptive shout and laugh, perhaps even throwing out the
names of the likely conspirators.

The creature continued explaining what might or might not
be real. "My preferred method of travel," it proclaimed, "is to
move alone, and always by the most invisible means. This is
standard behavior for officials like myself. We will finish one
task in some portion of the Union, and, with that success, another task is supplied. Since news travels slowly across the
galaxy, an entity like myself is granted considerable freedom of
action. Few organizations are confident enough to tolerate such
power in their agents."

"What kind of tasks?" Perri asked.

"Would you like an example?"

"Please."

"I am thinking now of a warehouse that I had built and
stocked. A hidden warehouse in an undisclosed location. And
in the very next moment, I was suddenly dispatched into my
next critical mission."

"A warehouse?" Perri asked.

"A vast, invisible facility full of rare and valuable items.
I haven't returned to that particular location since, but it most
likely remains locked and unseen today. Unused, but always at
the ready. Waiting for that critical, well-imagined age when its
contents help with some great effort. But that is the Union's
way: We have an elaborate structure, robust and overlapping.
Enduring and invincibly patient. Which is only natural, since

we happen to be the oldest, most powerful political entity within this galaxy."

"The Union?" Perri said dubiously.

"Yes."

"That's a name," he pointed out. "I thought you didn't approve of such things."

"I offer it because you expect some kind of label. But like all names, 'the Union' doesn't truly fit what is real." A smug, superior tone had taken hold, but it was difficult for the audience to take offense. After all, this was just a voice in the night, and who could say what was true and what was sane?

"Simply stated," their companion continued, "my Union is a collection of entities and beliefs, memes and advanced tools, that have been joined together in a common cause. And what you call the Milky Way happens to be our most important possession. The central state inside a vast and ancient empire."

"No," Perri said. "No."

Silence.

Quee Lee felt her husband's tension. Leaning forward, she told their companion, "There are no empires."

A long black silence held sway, and then came a sound not unlike the creak of a joint needing oil.

"Many, many species have tried to build empires," she continued, naming a few candidates to prove her knowledge of the subject. "The galaxy's first sentient races accomplished the most, but they didn't do much. The galaxy is enormous. Its planets are too diverse and far too numerous to be ruled by any one government. And starflight has always been a slow, dangerous business. When a species rises, it can gain control of only a very limited region. When you measure the history of empires against the life stories of suns and worlds, even the most enduring rule is a temporary, very tiny business."

Quee Lee concluded by saying, "No single authority has ever controlled any significant portion of the galaxy."

"I applaud your generous sense of doubt," the stranger replied. "May I ask, my dear? What are you?"

"What do you mean?"

"By blood, I think you must be Chinese. Am I right?"

"Mostly, yes," she admitted.

"And the city of your birth?"

"Hong Kong," she whispered.

"Hong Kong, yes. A place I know of, yes. Of course you understand that your China was a great empire, and more than once. And as I recall from my long-ago studies of Earth, there was a period–a brief but not unimportant time–when the port of Hong Kong belonged to the greatest empire ever to exist on your little world. There was a minor green island sitting in a cold distant sea. It called itself Great Britain, and, with its steam-driven fleets, it somehow managed to hang its flag above a fat fraction of the world's population."

"I know about Britain," she replied.

"Now tell me this," their companion continued. "There lives an old rickshaw driver who plies his trade on the narrow Hong Kong streets. Does that lowly man care who happens to serve as governor of his home city? Does it matter to him if the fellow on top happens to have yellow hair, or is a Mongol born on the plains of Asia, or even a Han Chinese who is a third cousin to him?"

"No," she admitted. "He probably didn't think much about those matters."

"And what about the peasant farmer struggling to feed himself and his family from a patch of land downstream from Everest . . . the ruler of a farm that has never even once fallen under the indifferent gaze of the pale northern man who works inside a distant government building? Does that farmer concern himself with the man who signs a long list of decrees and then dies quietly of malaria? And does he care at all about the gentleman who comes to replace that dead civil servant . . . another northern man who bravely signs more unread decrees before he dies of cholera?"

Quee Lee said nothing.

"Consider the Mayan woman nursing her daughter in Belize, or the Maasai cattle herder in Kenya who happens to be the tall strong lord to his herd. Do they learn the English language? Can they even recognize their rulers' alphabet? And then there is the Aboriginal hunter sucking the precious juice out of an emu egg. Is he even aware that fleets of enormous coal-fired ships are landing and then leaving from his coast each and every day?

"These souls are busy, embroiled in their rich and complex, if painfully brief, lives. Within the British Empire, hundreds of millions of citizens go about their daily adventures. The flavor of each existence is nearly changeless. Taxes and small blessings come from on high, but these trappings accomplish little, regardless of which power happens to be flying the flags. A peasant's story is usually the same as his forefathers' stories. And if the peasant's children survive, they will inherit that same stubborn, almost ageless narrative."

Neither human spoke.

"Do these little people ever think of that distant green island?"

"I wouldn't be surprised if they didn't," Quee Lee allowed.

"But if they did think of Britain," the stranger began.

"What?" Perri prompted.

"Would they love the Empire for its justice, order, and the rare peace that it brings to the human world?"

Neither responded.

"Of course, they do not. What you do not know, you cannot love. This is true of emperors as well as mates. So long as the peasants' lives remain small and steady, they won't be capable of hating the British.

"Which is not to say they are unsophisticated souls. They are far from simple, in fact. But their lives are *confined.* By necessity, the obvious and immediate are what matter to them. And the colors and shape of today's flag could not have less meaning."

"Suppose we agree," said Perri. "We accept your premise: For humans, empires tended to be big, distant machines."

"As they are for most other species," was the reply.

In the dark, Quee Lee and her husband nodded.

"But I don't agree with that word 'big,' " the stranger continued. "I believe that even the greatest empire, at the height of its powers, remains vanishingly small. Nearly invisible, even."

"I don't understand," confessed Quee Lee.

"Let me remind you of this: Several million whales swam in your world's little ocean. They were great beasts possessing language and old cultures. But did even one species of cetaceans bow to the British flag? And what about the tiger eating venison on the Punjab? Did he dream of the homely human queen? And what role did the ants and beetles, termites and butterflies, play in the world? They did nothing for Britannia, I would argue . . . except for what they would have done anyway if left to their own marvelous devices."

Perri tried to laugh.

Quee Lee could think of nothing useful to say.

"The trouble," the voice began. Then it paused, perhaps reconsidering its choice of words. "Your mistake," it continued, "is both inevitable and comforting, and it is very difficult to escape. What you assume is that the *names* in history are important. Because you have smart, educated minds, you have taught yourselves much about your own past. But even the most famous name is lost among the trillions of nameless souls. And every empire that you think of when the subject arises . . . well, that political entity, no matter how impermanent and trivial, was visible only because it wasted its limited energies making certain that its name would outlive both its accomplishments and its crimes."

"Maybe so," Quee Lee allowed.

"Names," the voice repeated. "The worlds you know share that unifying trait. A name brings with it a sense of purpose and a handle for its recorded history. Attached to one or a thousand words waits some center of trade, a nucleus of science, and you mistakenly believe that the most famous names mark the hubs of your great cosmopolitan galaxy."

Perri squeezed his wife's hand, fighting the temptation to speak.

"But the bulk of the galaxy . . . its asteroids and dust motes, sunless bodies and dark corners without number . . . those are the features that truly matter."

"To whom?" Quee Lee asked.

"To the ants, of course. And the lowly fish. The beetles and singing whales, and our rickshaw driver who knows the twisting streets of Hong Kong better than any Chinese emperor or British civil servant. The nameless citizens are those who matter, my dear." Their companion shifted its weight. Perhaps. Something creaked, and the voice drifted slightly to one side. "And I will confess that my empire is like all those others, if not more so. The Union that I love . . . that I have served selflessly for eons . . . is vast and ancient. But where England made maps and gave every corner its own label, my Union has wisely built itself upon places unknown."

Husband and wife contemplated that peculiar boast.

Then Quee Lee remembered an earlier thread. "You have visited Earth, you claimed."

"I did once, yes."

"Before or after your invisible warehouse?"

"After, as it happens. Soon after."

"You mentioned receiving a new mission then," Perri coaxed.

"Which leads directly to an interesting story, I believe." The next sound was soft, contented. "My new orders came by a most usual route. Whispered and deeply coded. Instructions from my superiors that were designed to resemble nothing but a smeared flicker of light thrown out from a distant laser array." The words were strung together with what felt like a grin. "Alone, I left my previous post. Alone, I rode inside a tiny vehicle meant to resemble a shard of old comet, using a simple ion motor to boost my velocity to where my voyage took slightly less than forty centuries–"

"By our arbitrary and self-centered count," Perri interjected.

"Which is not a very long time." Those words were ordinary and matter-of-fact, yet somehow with the sound of them—in their clarity and decidedly slow pace—the voice conveyed long reaches of time and unbounded patience. "I traveled until I came to a nameless world. There was one ocean and several continents. The forests were green, the skies blue with white watery clouds. To fulfill the demands of my new mission, I selected an island not far from the world's main continent: a young volcanic island where the local inhabitants built boats driven by oars and square sails, and they put up houses of wood and stone, and they planted half-wild crops in the fertile black soil. And their moments of free time were filled with the heartfelt worship of their moon and sun—the two bodies that ruled a sky that they would never truly understand."

"Was this Earth?" Quee Lee asked.

There was a pause.

In the darkness, motion.

And then the voice told them, "When these particular events occurred, my dear, there was no world called 'Earth.' "

Quee Lee wrapped both hands around her husband's arm.

"Remember this," the voice continued. "The Union is the only power that truly matters. And the Union is interested only in those dark realms that appear on no worthwhile map."

VI

"A king happened to rule that warm, sun-washed island. He was simple and rather old, and I was tempted to kill him in some grand public fashion before taking his throne for myself. Yet my study of his species and its superstitions showed me a less bloody avenue. The king's youngest wife was pregnant, but the child would be stillborn. It was a simple matter to replace that failed infant and then bury what was Me inside its healthy native flesh. Once born, I proved to the kingdom that their new prince was special. I was a lanky boy, physically beautiful, endowed with an unnatural strength and the gentle grace of wild birds. I didn't merely walk at an early age, I danced. And with a bold musical voice, I spoke endlessly on every possible subject, people fighting to kneel close to me, desperate to hear whatever marvel I offered next.

"The wise old women of my kingdom decided that I must be a god's child as much as a man's.

"On a daily basis, I predicted the weather and the little quakes that often rattled the island. I boasted that I could see far into the skies and over the horizon, and to prove my brave words, I promised that a boat full of strangers would soon drift past our island.

"I made my prediction in the morning, and by evening I was proved right. The lost trireme was filled with traders or pirates. On a world such as that, what is the difference between those two professions? Whatever their intentions, my people were waiting for them, and after suitable introductions, I ordered the strangers murdered and their possessions divided equally among the general populace."

The voice paused.

In the darkness, Quee Lee leaned hard against her husband.

Then, without comment, the story continued. "I was almost grown when that little old king stood before his people and named his heir. Two of my brothers were insulted, but I had anticipated their clumsy attempts at revenge. In a duel with bronze swords, I removed the head of the more popular son. Then I turned my back, allowing my second brother to run his spear through my chest—a moment used to prove that I was, as my people had always suspected, immortal.

"With my own hands, I yanked the spear from my heart.

"In anguish, my foe flung himself off one of our island's high cliffs.

" 'Someday I will follow my brothers into the Afterlife,' I promised the citizens. 'But for the rest of your days, I will remain with you, and together we shall do the work of the gods.'

"And that was the moment, at long last, when the heart of my mission finally began."

Their companion paused.

Finally Perri asked, "Are you going to explain your mission?"

"Hints and teases. I will share exactly what is necessary to explain myself, or at least I will give you the illusion of insights, placing you where your imaginations can fill in the unnamed reaches."

"About these natives," Quee Lee began. "Your people . . . what did they look like?"

Quietly and perhaps with a touch of affection, the voice explained, "They were bipedal, as you are. And they had your general height and mass, hands and glands. Like you, they presented hairless flesh to the world, except upon their faces and scalps and in their private corners. As a rule, most were dirty and drab, and on that particular island, their narrow culture reached back only a few generations. But their species had potential. Following ordinary pathways, natural selection had given them graceful fingers and an evolving language, busy minds and a compelling sense of tribe. In those following years, I showed my people how to increase the yields and quality of their crops. I taught them how to purify their water, how to carve and lift gigantic stones, and I helped them build superior ships that could chase the fat fish and slow leviathans that could never hide from my godly eyes. Then, in the shadow of their smoldering volcano, I laid out a spacious palace surrounded by a solid home and wide avenues, and for three generations, my devoted followers built the finest city that their species had ever known."

Once again, the voice ceased. But the silence was neither empty nor unimportant, accenting a sense of time crossed with clear purpose. Then came a smooth laugh, and their companion remarked, "If the two of you were dropped into similar circumstances, you would accomplish most if not all of my tricks. You are borderline immortals. Spears through your hearts would be nuisances at day's end. Armed with the knowledge common to your happy lives, you could visit some nameless world and convince its residents that you were divine, and in the next breath you could call for whatever riches and little pleasures that your worshippers might scratch together for you.

"What pleasures *me* is serving the Union.

"What I wanted . . . what my orders demanded from this one place, inside this single moment . . . was the construction of a significant machine, a device that would demand the full focus of a half-born civilization."

"What kind of machine?" asked Perri.

"If it proves important to know that, then I will tell you."

Except Perri couldn't accept that evasive answer. "How many people lived in your city? Five thousand? Fifty thousand? I don't know what you were building. Granted. But you're implying advanced technologies, and I'd have to guess that you'd need a lot more hands and minds than you would ever find on a tiny island in the middle of the sea."

The first answer was prolonged silence.

Then came the sharp creak of a limb or cold leather, and with quiet fury the entity replied, "You have not been listening carefully enough, sir. Pay strict attention to everything that I tell you."

"Remind me what you said," Perri snapped.

Another pause.

Then the voice continued, explaining, "I sat on my throne for seventy summers and several months. Then one day I abruptly announced that my city was failing me. With a wave of my fist, I told my followers that they were not truly devoted, that they were not sufficiently thankful for my wise counsel, and I was contemplating the complete obliteration of their island-nation.

"With the next sunrise, the great volcano erupted. The rich rocky earth split wide. Ash was coughed into the sky, lava flowed into the boiling sea, and boulders as big as houses dropped onto the cowering, inadequate heads around me. But then I pretended a sudden change of mind. I showed pity, even empathy. On the following day, after the dead were buried and the damage assessed, I dressed in a feathered robe and walked to the summit, where I told the mountain to sleep again. Which it would have done on its own, since the eruption had run its course. But a single moment of theater erased the last shreds of doubt. Again, I had convinced my followers that I was supreme. You could not hear one muttered complaint about me, or doubts about my powers, or the slightest question concerning each of my past decisions.

"That seamless devotion was necessary.

"You see, the eruption was not a random event. And I didn't make the mountain tremble and belch just to scare the local souls.

"Even as I sat on my throne, I had been working. My assignment demanded the kinds of energy generated by top-grade fusion reactors. But reactors produce signatures visible at a great distance. Neutrinos are difficult to shield, and I didn't want prying eyes to notice my industrial plant. So instead of a reactor, I employed the lake of magma directly beneath our feet, creating an inefficient but enormous geothermal plant. When that plant awoke—when the first seawater poured down the pipes and into the reaction vessels—my island was shoved upward like a balloon inflating. Watchful eyes noticed that every tide pool was suddenly baking in the sun. Our island was significantly taller, a thousand hot springs flowed out of the high crevices, and the black ground was itself warm to the touch.

"On that good day, I ordered every woman of breeding age to come to the palace, to arrive with the evening bell, and I welcomed each of them individually, giving them a feast and plenty to drink, as well as jewelry and robes finer than anything they had known. Then to this nervous, worshipful gathering, I announced that each of them was carrying a child now. My offspring were riding contentedly inside them.

"I promised my wives untroubled pregnancies and healthy, superior babies.

"Both promises came true.

"And you are correct, Perri. Sir. Fifty thousand followers would never have been enough. No natural species can bring the mental capacity demanded by this kind of delicate, highly technical work. So I enlarged the natives' craniums and restructured their neural networks, flinging them across fifty thousand generations of natural selection. Then I served as the children's only teacher. I taught them what they needed to know about the high sciences, and I made them experts in engineering, all while carefully preparing my kingdom for the next change."

Perri said, "Wait."

In the dark, Quee Lee felt her husband's body shifting. She recognized his excitement and interest, his emotions mirroring her own.

Again, he said, "Wait."

"Yes?"

"I've been thinking about what you've told us."

"Good."

"Where your logic leads . . ."

Silence.

"If you were willing to rewrite the biology of one species," Perri began, "you could just as well reshape others, too."

"Ants?" Quee Lee blurted. "Were you a god to the island's ants?"

"Ants have no need for gods," the voice corrected. "They demand nothing but a queen blessed with spectacular fertility. But you've seen my logic, yes. You are paying attention. But then again, I sensed that the two of you would prove to be a worthy audience."

Some small object clattered against hyperfiber—a clear, almost bell-like sound expanding and diminishing inside the gigantic room.

Then the voice returned, explaining, "By the time my first grandchildren were born, the ocean around my island was lit from below. Which was only reasonable, since the city above was just one portion of a much greater community—a nation numbering in the billions. My people supplied the genius, but to serve them, I had built a multitude of obedient minds trained for narrow, exceptionally difficult tasks. A full century of careful preparation had made me ready to begin the construction of a single mechanical wonder.

"Which was the moment, I should add, when my troubles began."

VII

In the smothering blackness, Quee Lee held her husband by an arm, by his waist. And then she twisted her body in a particular way, inviting a groping hand, not caring in the least that the nameless entity might be able to make out their timeless, much-cherished intimacies.

Perri started to offer a new question.

"What troubles—?" he began.

But the voice interrupted him, claiming, "Human beings are an extraordinarily fortunate species. Wouldn't you agree?"

"I feel lucky," Quee Lee said.

"Lucky because of the Great Ship?" Perri asked.

"Tell me your opinion: Is this vessel a blessing for you?"

Perri laughed. "I know at least a thousand other species that could have found it first. That should have found it before us. They were more powerful than we, and far more numerous. One of them should have grabbed it up before we ever knew it existed."

"It's a magical machine," Quee Lee offered.

The entity made a few soft, agreeable noises. Then it continued, saying again, "Our galaxy has stubbornly refused to be dominated by any single species. But your kind stumbled across the Ship while it was still drifting on the outskirts of the galaxy. You claimed the prize first, and you have held on to it since. A single possession has lifted the human animal into an exceptionally rare position. Your best captains have no choice but to thank the stars and Providence for this glorious honor. Today, your artisans and scientists are free to drink in the wisdom of the galaxy. Your wealthiest citizens can make this journey in safety, sharing their air with the royalty of a hundred thousand worlds. But I think your greatest success rises from the hungriest, bravest souls among you.

"Each year, on average, seventeen and a third colonial vessels push away from the Ship's ports. How many of your willing cousins are dropped to the surface of wild worlds and lucrative asteroids? How many homes and shopes are being erected, entirely new societies sprouting up in your wake? Now multiply those impressive numbers by the hundreds of thousands of years that you plan to invest in this circumnavigation of the galaxy. The totals are staggering. No society or species or even any compilation of cooperative souls has enjoyed this human advantage.

"And now consider this: How many aliens buy berths on board the Ship? Thousands arrive each year, and, in trade for a safe journey, they surrender every local map, plus cultural experiences and open-ended promises of help. That's why each of your new colonies has a respectable, even enviable, chance of survival. And that's why your species is hugging a small but respectable probability of dominating the richest portions of the galaxy.

"So now I ask you: When will this wilderness of ours, from its dwarf satellites to its black core, be known everywhere and to every species as 'the Milky Way'?

"In other words, when will the galaxy be your possession?"

Considering that possibility, the humans couldn't help but smile.

But then Quee Lee sighed, shaking her head as she said, "Never? Is that the answer you want?"

Quietly, the voice explained, "That kind of success shall never happen. Never, no. Even in your blessed circumstances, this little whirlpool of creation remains too vast and far too complex for any single species to dominate. And your makeshift empire is doomed at its birth. The best result that you might achieve—and even this is an unlikely future—is for the Great Ship to complete its full circuit of the galaxy without being stolen from you, and for you to leave behind twenty million human worlds. But what are twenty million worlds against those trillions of rocks big enough to be called planets? And I can promise that no matter the blessings it starts with, each one of your colonies will struggle to survive. It is inevitable. Your species is relatively late on the scene; easy rich worlds are scarce and typically belong to someone else. By the minute, our galaxy grows older. And with every breath, the sky grows slightly more crowded. New species are constantly evolving, thinking machines are being born every moment, and almost everything that lives strives hard to live forever, or nearly so."

The smiles had vanished.

For a long moment, neither human spoke.

Then Quee Lee suggested, "Maybe our empire should stop naming our worlds. If we emulated your Union . . . if human beings decided to rule the dark and empty and the unmapped–"

"No," the voice interrupted.

Then, with a palpable scorn, it added, "I will share with you one common principle known by every true empire. Whether you are British or Mongolian, Roman or American: You may never, ever allow any competing empire to sprout within your sacred borders.

"My Union stands alone.

"Never forget that.

"And when the inevitable future arrives . . . when the final star burns out and the universe pulls itself into a great empty cold . . . my Union will persist, and it will thrive, living happily on this galaxy's black bones: a force as near to Always as that word might ever allow."

VIII

The humans felt chastened and a little angry, powerless to respond but nonetheless intrigued by the stark implications. They held each other in ways that spoke—the touch of fingers, the pressure of a plump knee, and the shared tastes of expelled air carrying odors that could only come from Perri, and only come from Quee Lee.

The voice returned, quietly mentioning, "My mission had begun so easily, with much promise. Yet now its nature changed. In relatively quick succession, three problems emerged, each one capable of threatening the project and my sterling reputation."

A thoughtful pause ended with a brief, disgusted sound.

"Remember the pirates mentioned before? The seafarers whom I let my people kill? They had floated out from the main continent, and with another hundred years of experience, their descendants were eager to return. That rocky green wilderness still lay over the horizon, but now it was speckled with dirty cities and fledging nations. Unlike my little island, those far places had always enjoyed culture and a deep history, every corner of their rich landscape adorned with some important little name.

"Bronze-and-brick technology was at work. Kings and educated minds were beginning to piece together the first, most obvious meaning of the universe. Their largest triremes could wander far from land, and their captains knew how to navigate by the stars and moon. That those captains would try to visit my island was inevitable, which is why I took precautions. The leviathans patrolling my bright waters were instructed to scare off every explorer, and, should fear not work, they were entitled to crush the wooden hulls and drown those stubborn crews.

"A few ships were sunk off our coast.

"The occasional corpse washed up on shore, swollen by rot and chewed upon by curious or vengeful mouths.

"One of the dead had been a scientist and scholar, and, while he drowned, he managed to grab hold of his life's work—a long roll of skin covered with dense writing and delicate sketches.

"The body was looted, and the book eventually found its way into the appreciative hands of one of my grandchildren.

"The island's original natives could never have understood the intense black scribblings. But my grandchild wasn't merely intelligent and highly creative, he was also curious and unabashedly loyal to me. Using code-breaking algorithms, he taught himself the dead man's language. In his spare moments, he managed to translate the text in full. His purpose, it seems, was to make me proud of his genius. He was certainly thrilled of his own accomplishment, which was why he shared what he had learned with close friends and lovers. Then he walked to the palace and kneeled before my throne, presenting both the artifact and his translation for my honest appraisal.

" 'They speak of us,' the young man reported. 'The rest of our world believes that we are gods or the angels of gods, or that we have descended from the stars. They have convinced themselves that if they defeat the sea monsters and outsmart the currents, they can row into our harbor and stand among us, and they will be heroes in the gods' eyes. And for their extraordinary bravery, we will award them with the secrets of All.' "

A brief pause.

"I'll ask this question again," said Perri. "This species you're telling us about . . . were they human?"

There was a sound, soft but disgusted.

"Atlantis?" Quee Lee whispered. "Is that what this story is?"

"My thought exactly," Perri confessed, hugging her until her ribs ached. Then he said the ancient word for himself, pronouncing, "Atlantis," in the appropriate dead language.

"Once again," the voice replied, "you have forgotten: The galaxy had no name for that world, much less for that long-ago island. But I cannot stop you from imagining your Earth and its legendary lands. And I won't fight the labels that help you follow what I happen to say."

In the darkness, Perri squeezed his wife again, and she pushed her mouth into his ear, saying, "It must be," with relish.

They had decided, together.

Atlantis, yes.

"My grandchildren," the voice continued. "Several generations had passed since the first of them were born, and I should confess to one inevitable event. I have always taken lovers from the locals. A lover serves as a source of information, and oftentimes a tool for good methodical management. Bedding those who are most beautiful and intriguing is just a natural consequence of my station. But one of those grandchildren proved more irresistible than usual. She was a young woman, as it happened. Though it's just as likely that she could have been a man.

"By the standards of her species, she was small and exceptionally lovely.

"Among her gifted peers, she was considered brilliant and singularly blessed. The finest of the fine.

"That I took her into my bed was perfectly natural. That she retained her virginity until that night only enhanced her reputation with her own people and, to a degree, with me. The bloodied sheet was hung from the palace wall for a full day, and when she appeared again in public, cheers made her stand tall as a queen–the center of attention smiling at her appreciative world.

"I was very fond of that little creature.

"As a lover, she was fearless and caring, bold and yet compliant, too. And when we were not making love, she would ask me smart little questions about all matters of science and engineering. Her particular expertise involved the heart of the device that we were building together. There were puzzles to work through, matters that I didn't understand fully myself. I had never built such an object, you see. That's why the brilliant grandchildren were critical to me. But even though she understood many of the ideas behind our work, she always wanted to know more and, if possible, hold what she knew more deeply.

"Charming and crafty, she was, and I let myself be fooled. I confessed that there were subjects that could never, ever be discussed with her people. 'You will not repeat any of this again,' I warned. 'Not even to the wind.'

"She promised to remain mute.

"Then I explained to her the true shape of the galaxy, and its great age, and I told the violent history of our glorious universe.

"And yes, there were occasions when I mentioned the Union and my small, critical role within it.

"Then, because she seemed so very interested in the subject of Me, I confessed my true age and delivered a brief but thorough accounting of past missions as well as some of the tricks that I was capable of."

The voice fell away.

In the blackness, a body stretched until the bones or carapace creaked and gave a sharp dry crack.

"That lover was my second challenge," said the voice. "Although at that particular moment, I didn't appreciate the danger."

Quee Lee leaned away from Perri, begging her dark-adapted eyes to find any trace of wayward light. If she could just make out the creature that was sitting so close to them—

No. Nothing.

"One of our shared nights never seemed to end," the voice offered. "Normal fatigues don't trouble me, but my lover, no matter how much improved genetically, needed sleep. She lived for dreams. Yet the girl somehow resisted every urge to close her lovely dark eyes. Twice in the dark, she managed to surprise me with tricks she had never shown before. I was appreciative. How could I not be? But then as the full moon set and the bright summer sun began to rise, she whispered, 'I was wondering my lord . . . about something else.'

" 'What?' I asked.

" 'But maybe I shouldn't,' she conceded.

" 'Ask me anything,' I said, never voicing the obvious possibility that I wouldn't reply, or that I might simply lie.

" 'I am curious,' my lover confessed, her voice sleepy and

slow. 'When you speak of old missions, you usually seem to be out between the stars, or huddled beside some dying star, or cloaked inside a storm cloud of interstellar dust.'

"For a moment, she seemed to drop into sleep.

"But then she roused herself with a gasp, straightening her little body and asking, 'Why come here? Why visit our little world, my lord?'

" 'It suits my present mission,' I conceded. 'Your volcano and the seawater are rich with rare elements and useful minerals–'

" 'But you have told me before this . . . on other nights, you explained that in the baby days of any solar system, some, if not most, of the new worlds are flung out into the night. Their oceans freeze. Their atmospheres fall as snow. But radiation keeps their iron cores molten, and volcanoes still bubble up beneath the bitter ice, and a god like you could surely bring a temporary life to those unnamed realms.'

"I listened, perhaps not quite believing just how bright she was.

"Then, very quietly, I reminded her, 'Like those cold places, this world possesses no name. As far as the universe is concerned, your home is a random lump of dust and still-simple life-forms.'

"For a long while, she stared at me.

"Those beautiful dark eyes . . . I cannot mention those eyes and not feel shame . . . a burning shame that keeps me from describing to you just how deep their hold was on me . . .

"But then the eyes closed, and my lover drifted into a rich, much deserved sleep. I thought the matter was finished. I didn't want to entertain any other possibility. And really, what reason did I have to believe that this worshipful little creature was a threat, or, even if she was, that she could be ever be a genuine danger to the likes of me?

"I covered her with a fine linen sheet.

"Then, for the following days and months, and years, nothing changed. No word or incident raised even the tiniest suspicion on my part. My lover was the same to me as she had always been, and I was as pleasant and giving to her and to all of my people.

"And then my third challenge arrived. This danger came from the sky and, even at a great distance, it brought the worst possible trouble. Out on the edge of the solar system was an automated probe. A harum-scarum probe, as it happened, moving at a small fraction of lightspeed. The harum-scarums have always been aggressive in their explorations and colonizations, and now one of their sharp-eyed robots was plunging out of the darkness, threatening to fly past my world while taking note of everything that might bear interest.

"I couldn't allow myself or my good work to be seen.

"And sadly, the machines that I had left in orbit couldn't protect me. I needed to leave the island. Wisely, I didn't offer reasons or predict when I would return. As far as my people knew, I would be back among them with the next sunset or the coming full moon. But I begged them to continue our work—the delicate fabrication of a single machine that meant everything to me and to them."

In the dark, the voice seemed to sigh.

Then quietly, but with an unhealed pain, their companion said, "This was the moment when the rebellion began. And I think you can guess who stood on the silk cushions of my empty throne, whirling a titanium hammer above her head, shouting to the throng, 'It is time to save our world, my friends! To rescue our futures and gain control over our souls!' "

IX

Within the silence lay emotions rich and fresh, born out of a sadness that could not be forgotten. Or maybe there was only silence, black and seamless, and the misery and burning sense of loss were supplied entirely by the human audience. It was impossible to tell which answer was correct, or if both were a little true. But then the humans heard a limb flex, the invisible body creaking as it shifted, not once but three times in quick succession. When the voice returned, it seemed slower. Each word was delivered alone, and between one word and the next lay a tiny silence, like a cold black mortar pushed between warm red bricks.

"I could have destroyed the automated probe at a distance. I could have used methods that would have made harum-scarum scientists believe that bad luck was responsible. Just some random rock, a cosmic hazard that slipped past the machine's various armors. Nothing would seem too unusual about that. But erasing the danger was not the only problem. Harum-scarum probes are relatively common in our galaxy, and if I blithely obliterated them whenever our paths crossed, somebody would eventually see the pattern in my clumsiness.

"No, what I did was rise up into the sky to meet the danger directly.

"Like you, I am the loyal subject to a variety of laws concerning motion and energy. I had to race out into the solar system for a considerable distance, and then, with methods that I cannot share, I invisibly changed my trajectory, racing back again, making certain that my momentum carried me close to the probe's vector.

"Together, that machine and I dove into the hot glare of the sun. I studied my opponent while it absorbed images of the two inner worlds. Then we climbed away from the sun and, at a moment when I would escape notice, I drifted close and touched the machine with a thousand fingers, allowing its giant eyes to do their work even as I changed a small portion of what it could see.

"Together, we passed between the gray moon and my blue-green world.

"Soon the danger was finished. The probe turned its attentions to the little red world coming up next, and, with my chore accomplished, I happened to glance backward, examining my home with my own considerable eyes.

"The rebellion was well under way.

"Twenty different security systems had been fooled or, by various means, disabled. And now my clever little grandchildren had full control over their land and the ocean around them.

"Feigning loyalty, they had continued to build the machine.

"Pretending subservience, most of them moved through their lives in the expected ways. But others openly prayed that I was dead, even while they planned my murder should I return. And still others pretended to die, their names removed from the city's rosters, freeing them to journey over to the mainland, taking with them tools and skills as well as a story that would inspire the primitive souls they would find waiting there.

"I was furious.

"In ways quite rare to me, I felt a powerful, consuming need for revenge.

"But motion and energy still held sway. I could not roar home in the next instant, and if I didn't wish to be noticed by the probe beside me, I would have to be patient enough to obey my original plan.

"Easing out the probe's view consumed many days.

"I spent another month pushing against the universe, slowing myself to a near halt before turning and plunging back into the brilliant sunshine.

"By then, the harum-scarum eyes were distant. If the probe happened to glance back at my world, it could have noticed an island exploding, a dark cloud spreading, and a deep bubbling caldera left in the island's place. But I resisted that instinctive violence. Destroying my own work would have been an unacceptable cost, and worse, it would have been graceless.

"And I could have remotely shut down the entire operation, protecting my investment from malicious hands. But that meant new risks as well as long delays.

"Instead, I decided to dance with complete disaster, but aiming for total success."

After those words, a long pause seemed necessary.

Finally Perri said, "You won't tell us. I know. But we would appreciate knowing what the stakes were."

"I'd like to know," Quee Lee voted.

"What exactly you were building?" her husband pressed.

"Britannia," the voice replied. "Like any empire worth its salt." A weak laugh washed over them. "How can you separate a true empire from all of the little pretenders? What did the British possess that their vanquished opponents lacked? Why were those northern men superior to the peasants in the field and the dogs in the street?

"Any good empire holds at least one skill that is its own.

"The Greeks had their highly trained hoplites and several unique if competing forms of government. The Chinese had the most enduring civil services ever seen on your world. Romans were possessed of their engineering and their brutal legions. And so long as British boats owned the seas, their power was accepted by a world that saw no option but bow in their mighty presence.

"An empire is always smarter than its competition.

"And my Union is far, far smarter than the human species. Or any other species you can name, for that matter.

"The device I was building? Well, I will tell you that it was just a single component meant to be set inside a much larger machine. And that it was extremely rare and very valuable, embodying sciences that you have never mastered. Once assembled, the full apparatus can wield principles that your most brilliant minds might recognize as possible, but only that. The apparatus is magic. It is gorgeous. It was, and is, worth every cost."

A brief pause ended with Quee Lee's voice.

"So you returned to Earth," she said. "To Thera, or Atlantis. Although it wore different names then, I suppose."

"Whatever the world, whatever the island," said the voice. "Yes, I returned, yes. To find my grandchildren engaged in an artful rebellion."

There was a long, contemplative pause.

Finally Perri asked, "And what happened?"

"Worth every cost," the entity said once again. "I speak without doubts, telling you what I did that day. And for that matter, what I would do on this day, in an instant, if I saw that there was any threat to my enduring Union."

X

Until that moment, the voice had been just so much noise. It was interesting and entertaining noise, the words intriguing if not completely believable. The narrative was compelling enough, the humans feeling empathy and hope for the creatures that could well have been their own ancestors. They listened carefully to every portion of the disjointed tale, trying to guess what would happen next and then next after that; but there was no moment when they stopped wondering what kind of body was connected to the voice. Until then, that was the central question that kept begging to be answered.

Then they heard the words "To protect the Union," and that simple utterance changed everything.

Wrapped around a bald statement was stiff, unyielding emotion. Quee Lee and Perri heard the threat, the promise, the conviction and purpose—and they instantly believed what they heard. Now both of them were considering what it would mean if this story, as unlikely as it seemed, was in some fashion or another true. And that was when the formless entity beside them—mysterious and unknowable, bristly and proud—became markedly less interesting than the grim bit of history it was sharing with them now.

Human hands grabbed one another.

Each lover felt the other's body bracing for whatever came next.

Another silence was what the voice decided to offer. And then, from the perfect darkness, came a sound not unlike a tongue or two licking against lips threatening to grow dry.

Quee Lee and Perri had been married for tens of thousands

of years. But as long as that might seem to be, marriage was infinitely older than their single relationship. And there were species that took intimacy to higher levels than humans could manage. The Janusians, for instance: Their little husbands rooted into the body of female hosts, literally joining into One. But among human animals, Quee Lee and Perri were famous. Their relationsihp had evolved gradually, becoming something complex and robust, enduring and very nearly impossible to define. There were a few humans who spent more time together than the two of them. Unlikely as it seemed, some married souls enjoyed their physical lives even more than these two managed to. But no one could believe that any other human pair, on the Ship and perhaps anywhere else in the universe, was emotionally closer than that ancient Earth-born lady and her boyish life-mate.

At some point, everybody tried to tease them.

The happy couple generally welcomed good-natured barbs and admiring glances. But when asked to explain their success—when some friend of a friend insisted on advice for less perfect relationships—they grew testy and impatient, and even a little defensive. The truth was that they were helpless to define their relationship. A marriage was always larger than its participants, and what they possessed here was as mysterious and unlikely to them as it seemed to distant eyes. They couldn't understand why they had drawn so closely together. They didn't see why life had not yet found the means to yank them apart. But they were undeniably intimate and deeply dependent, up to the point where Quee Lee and Perri could never imagine being separated from each other in any lasting, meaningful way.

"Can you read each other's thoughts?" people wanted to know.

Not at all, no.

"But it seems like you can," some maintained. "The way you each know what the other wants, what they're about to say and do."

Did they do that?

"There's a trick at work," a few declared. "Dedicated nexuses that do nothing but let your minds share thoughts and feelings. Is that what you're doing right now?"

Not at all, no. In fact, they made a point of avoiding mechanical shortcuts to real conversation.

Eventually, somebody would ask, "When did you feel closest?"

What did that mean? Close how?

"When was the day—the incident—when you felt as if you were a single brain shared by two independent bodies?"

There were thousands of stories worth repeating, each able to satisfy their audience. They had a few dozen favorites that had become minor legends among the passengers. But the best answer was never offered, not even to the closest, dearest friends. It happened on that particular evening as they sat in that perfect darkness, deep inside the unmapped Vermiculate, immersed in the most isolated corner yet discovered within the Great Ship. That proud and stern and eternal voice told them that it would do anything to protect the Union, and for that singular moment, Quee Lee and Perri were one irreducible soul.

That was when they finally believed the unlikely story.

Then they heard the unseen tongues licking at dry lips, and the two lovers held each other with strong arms, sharing a flurry of thoughts, speaking with nothing but the touch of fingers, the sound of breathing.

"There *is* a Union," they decided voicelessly together. "It is real."

And, in the next moment, it occurred to them that the Union's loyal servant did nothing that did not, in small ways or great, help its ageless cause.

Quee Lee pressed hard against her husband, and she shivered, and just before the voice spoke again, she pushed an obvious thought into her husband's skull:

"Our new friend is on a mission! Now!"

And, in the next instant, with thrilled horror, Perri replied, "It's telling us the story for a reason . . . we *are* the mission!"

XI

With a sense of deeply buried pain, or at least an old, much practiced anger, the voice continued once again.

"At last, I returned to the island. At last, I touched down in the Sunset Plaza, on an ellipse of crimson glass brick reserved for my shuttle and my immortal body. The plaza was flanked by tall apartment buildings buried beneath masses of vines—engineered greenery that thrived in the volcanic warmth, producing enough fruit and sweet nuts to feed the residents within. A thousand of my grandchildren quickly gathered around me, while thousands more sneaked looks from behind the curtains of their comfortable little homes. Every face made an effort to smile. Every head dipped in a show of respect—gestures that I had never demanded from my subjects, that arose naturally long ago on their own. Only one important face was missing. But the brave traitors anticipated my first question. Several knelt before me, palms to the sky, and they explained that I had been gone longer than anticipated, and my arrival had proved quite sudden, but yes, my mistress was as happy as anyone could be. In fact, she was waiting for me at the palace, rapidly making herself ready for my pleasures.

"The avenue was lined with pruned trees thriving inside big copper pots and rows of intricate geometric sculptures cut from the black native stone. The smallest citizens barely noticed my passing. They were the ants and fat beetles that I had reinvented for the purpose of little jobs, and, unburdened by the demands of awe, they continued cutting down the weeds and disposing of trash. But a crew of enhanced crabs was pulling superconductive cables under the pavement, and when I passed nearby, they paused long enough to salute me with their elegant pincers.

"The grandchildren continued to stare, all working to appear nothing but worshipful, to shine with joy, and a few of them even managing to convince themselves that they were being honest.

" 'You were gone too long,' several complained, at different moments, but always with the same worried, slightly put-upon tone. And then one or two remarked, 'We feared you were lost, that some horrid disaster had claimed you.'

"If hope lay inside those voices, it was kept hidden.

"Then, at the mouth of an alleyway, I noticed a very young grandchild standing in the shadows, waiting for something. Not for me, it seemed . . . but in his stance and attitude, I could see anticipation.

"I paused and asked his name, even though I had already found his face in the public files. He introduced himself, and, with a charming little smile, mentioned that he had no memory of me. I had left for my errand among the stars while he was still just a toddler.

"He was barely more than that now. I smiled, telling him that it was my pleasure to meet him.

"He mentioned that I looked exactly as he expected me to look, except that I wasn't tall enough, and then his gaze drifted off toward the island's slumbering volcano.

" 'What are you waiting for?' I inquired.

" 'For you,' he replied. But before there was any misunderstanding, he added, 'I'm waiting for you to pass, and then I can go about my business.'

" 'Which is?'

" 'To walk down to the Sunset Plaza and watch the night come,' he explained.

" 'You like the setting sun, do you?'

"The young eyes smiled, and the mouth, too. Then a smart little voice said, 'Yes,' and nothing else.

"The bodies surrounding us began to relax.

"With a fond hand, I stroked the boy's thick black hair and

kissed him on the nose, and then continued with my triumphant stroll to the palace.

"No one was invited to follow me inside, and no one asked to join me. My shadow passed first through the iron gates and beneath the brass arches and into the grand hall. The air was scented with spice and smoke. The floor and walls and high ceiling were tiled in a fractal pattern, cultured sapphires and diamonds lending accents to an example of mathematical beauty that I have always appreciated. My throne stood at the end of the hall–the oldest object in the palace, gold flourishes and silk laid over my adoptive father's original chair.

"My shadow hesitated, and so did I.

"My grandchildren stood in a crowd outside, waiting for me to vanish.

"Suddenly a great damp shape emerged from a back door, walking on long mechanical legs. The creature was a leviathan whose ancestors had swum in the local sea. I had made him small while changing his lungs and flesh to where he could thrive indoors, adeptly serving me with whatever little duty that I might require.

"With a high-pitched warble, he welcomed me home.

"Whatever plots were lurking about, I sensed that he was not involved and almost certainly unaware of them.

"I asked if I had been missed.

" 'Always,' he replied with a quick series of clicks.

" 'Where is she now?' I inquired.

" 'In your quarters, lord.'

" 'And has she been faithful to me?'

" 'No,' the creature replied, without hesitation. 'I have seen her use her hands and several plastic devices. And once, the edge of a large pillow.'

" 'Thank you for your honesty,' I said. 'And good evening to you.'

"No shadow led the way now. Alone, I climbed a long flight of dimly lit steps and entered a narrow hallway that only seemed endless . . . an illusion lined with tall doors meant to impress and confuse the rare visitor. I walked a short distance and opened what seemed to be a random door. There was only one bedroom inside the palace, and it never occupied the same position twice. I entered through a random wall, and my lover flinched in surprise, starting to pull the sheets over her naked body before realizing that it was me, only me.

"Together, we celebrated my return.

"I had been absent even longer than I had anticipated. The young creature that I had left in this bed was noticeably older. A few white hairs and a hundred little erosions marked the natural decline of a creature not born immortal and never told to expect such blessings. But she was just as fierce a lover as always, and maybe more so. She insisted on satisfying herself by various means, and whenever my attentions seemed to waver, she would offer encouragements or measured complaints.

" 'What kind of god are you?' she teased me once, in the dark. 'Are you going to let this old lady beat you at your game?'

" 'I am tempted to lose, yes,' I confessed.

"Perhaps she heard more than one message in those words, because she paused and pulled away from me. Then, like a hundred times before, she settled on my chest, legs spread, the smell of her thick and close.

"In a whisper, she mentioned, 'Your journey must have been considerable.'

" 'My task was difficult,' I replied.

" 'We have continued with our work.' She said, 'Our work,' to make certain that I would hear the loyalty in those words. Then, after a pause, she added, 'But of course you kept track of our progress.' "

" 'Always,' I said.

" 'Have we missed any goals?'

" 'Never.'

" 'Are you proud of us?'

" 'Along the narrowest tangents, yes. Yes, I am very proud.'

"She refused to be surprised by my measured answer. And what worry she let show was small and easily controlled. The creature was exceptionally bright, after all. And she was wise in rare, precious ways. Extraordinary dangers were lurking about, and she realized that there was no way to keep me from seeing pieces of her scheme.

"Silently, she dropped her face to my face and kissed me.

"Then I placed my hand against her little throat, feeling her breath and the flinching of soft muscles, and I eased her back up into a sitting position. Then with a flat, cool tone, I said, 'It was sensible, holding to the work schedule. And I was most impressed with the methods you used, how you managed to fool my security systems.'

"Perhaps her plan was to claim innocence. 'I didn't try to fool anything,' she might have said. 'I don't know what you're accusing me of.' Denial might have given the plotters precious time. But it might have angered me, which would have brought my wrath down on them even sooner than they had planned.

"So instead of lying, my lover decided on poise. She shrugged her shoulders, asking, 'What do you know?'

" 'That the good machine being built inside our mountain is almost finished. But your lieutenants have surreptitiously slipped other devices into its workings. You devised some very clever, extremely powerful bombs that you hope will obliterate the purpose of my coming to this world.'

"Most souls would have tensed, hearing those words. Many would have panicked. But for my lover, that moment brought relief. Her duplicity was laid bare, and the simple fact that she was alive meant that perhaps she still retained some little chance of success here.

"I felt her throat relax against my hand.

"Then with great seriousness, I added, 'I also know you hope to murder me. Tonight, if possible. You have an array of weapons hiding here, and you have modified any piece of machinery that might injure me. I can even see dangers inside *you*, darling. Your body fat has been laced with acids that can be set free with a thought . . . turning you into a burning puddle that falls over my writhing, helpless body.'

"She stared down at me.

"In her gaze, I could see her asking herself if this was the moment for suicide. But why would I lie beneath her if I felt at all at risk?

"With a reasonable tone, she asked, 'Can we kill you?'

" 'If I was foolish and a little blind, perhaps. But I am not, and I am not.'

"She nodded, accepting that verdict.

"And then she tensed through the shoulders and along her back, and with a voice that was small and furious, she asked, 'But why shouldn't we try to kill you? When your work is finished, you intend to murder all of us. Isn't that so?'

"I didn't respond immediately.

" 'You told me as much,' she claimed. 'When you sang about your secret Union and your need for nameless places . . . you practically confessed that when you were finished with this place, you wouldn't leave any witnesses behind.'

" 'You don't understand,' I warned her.

"Then I dropped my hand, the fingers and broad palm stroking her body down to the point where her legs joined together. 'You are a special, special soul,' I told her. 'My work would have been finished in another few years, and my plan was to take you with me. Out to the stars, out into the rich cold darkness.'

"The shock rolled across her features.

"Quietly, almost angrily, she said, 'No, you're lying.'

"But I was speaking the truth.

"With a fond, slightly paternal voice, I asked, 'How do you think I was brought into the Union? No one is born into this noble service. The rank and responsibilities are earned only on exceptionally rare occasions. In my case, another servant visited my home world and built several marvels before retreating back into the darkness with his treasures, including the man lying beneath you now.'

" 'No,' she whispered.

"And then, in pain, she said, 'Maybe. But this changes nothing. I wouldn't abandon my world, and I certainly won't let you to blow up this volcano and make it as though this place never was.'

" 'Is that what you think will happen?' I asked. 'That I would slaughter you and yours for no reason but my convenience?'

"She hesitated. Then with a figurative acid on her tongue, she asked, 'What do you mean?'

" 'Unless provoked, I will not murder.'

"By the light of the moon, my lover looked into my face. And then the beginnings of an explanation occurred to her. 'You won't murder, but you might take back all of your gifts. Our minds. The genetic manipulations. Wipe clean the ideas and concepts you brought down here to serve your damned Union.'

"I interrupted her by throwing my palm across her mouth.

"Then I yanked her close, and said, 'Yes. That was my kind, responsible plan. You would come with me, and my magical device would come with us, and the other grandchildren would wake that following morning to discover . . . nothing. Nothing but a shared dream of a magical civilization . . . a public memory that would turn to legend in another day, and, in another ten generations, vanish into a muddled, impossible story.'

"She lay against me, her heart beating against what passed for my ribs.

" 'I am sorry,' she told me.

"Into my ear, she said, 'Really, we haven't done anything wrong. Not yet. I can give commands, and every weapon will be put away, and you won't have to worry about any of us lifting so much as a lard knife against you.'

" 'That is not enough,' I replied.

" 'And you can kill me,' she promised. Then she repeated her offer, sounding as if she was begging. 'Kill me, and maybe the other adults. But leave our children. They don't know anything.'

" 'Like the boy I spoke to? The child waiting between the plaza and the palace?'

"She hesitated.

" 'At this moment,' I said, 'that tiny fellow is sitting beside the water, bare toes in the surf. And do you know what he is watching with all of his interest, every shred of passion? He watches the sky.'

"She did not move.

" 'The sky,' I repeated. 'And in particular, this night's very bright stars.'

"The woman could not breathe.

" 'You are a crafty soul, my dear. My darling.' I told her, 'I am extremely impressed by the thoroughness and audacity of your plan. Threatening the machine as well as my own immortal self . . . well, those are the tactics that anyone would expect. But you also dispatched a team of technicians to the mainland. You convinced the worshipful souls living there that they should help you. Since then, our people and theirs have been living in a distant valley, secretly fabricating an amazing machine of their own.

" 'A radio beacon, as it happens.

" 'To the best of your ability, you have been marking my passage across the heavens. You guessed that I was subverting a set of prying eyes, and you were correct. Your hope was to broadcast a huge, important signal. You wanted to be noticed. By the probe, perhaps. Or if you missed that mark, then at least there would exist a loud intelligent scream that would race its way through the heart of our galaxy.

" 'Your secret hope was to accomplish what I would never allow.

" 'You wanted to name your world, and to name it in exactly the way that would make the universe take note of your presence.

" 'You were right, my sweet darling. That would have been your only genuine hope of salvation.

" 'But just this morning, I visited that far valley and your secret beacon, and I destroyed the dishes and power plant, and I have slaughtered everyone in my reach, but left the local communication system intact. During these last hours, every time you spoke to your fellow rebels, you were actually speaking to me.' "

Finally, the voice paused.

In the perfect darkness, a deep useless breath was taken.

Then the entity was speaking again, quietly admitting, "I gave my lover one last freedom. She could be the last to die, or first. She chose to be first, and she did that herself, releasing the acids inside her body. But I was already standing at a safe distance from our bed, my back to the carnage. Hearing the screams and smelling the blistered flesh, I kept my eyes averted, reminding myself that the worst of this awful night was finally finished."

XII

The two humans clung to each other.

In the same moment, in a rough chorus, they asked, "What happened? What did you do? What about the other people? What?"

A tight slow creak was audible, old leather or old bones moving.

From a point markedly closer than before, a mouth opened and breathed and then breathed again.

"I did exactly what I promised." The voice seemed to be within arm's reach. "However imperfectly, I have always strived to serve my cause, and that includes punishing those who dare rise up against me. I had no choice but to gather the worst of the offenders on the Sunset Plaza, and, with the rest of the grandchildren watching, I removed them from the living world. Then I ordered the low animals to clean the bricks of blood and pink tissues, and the dead bones were ground up and piled high on the nearest beach. And within five years, those who had survived my justice had managed to make up for lost time. Within ten years, my work was finished, and I carved away the gray summit of the volcano and pulled from the hot workroom a single machine encased in the finest hyper-fiber—a wonder of genius and competence that made my stay on that world worth any cost."

The voice drifted even closer and, feeling the intrusion, Quee Lee instinctively leaned away.

Perri held her and spoke past her, asking, "When did the mountain erupt?"

Nothing.

"After you abandoned the world, did the island explode?"

A sound of amusement, weary and cool, ended with the simple pronouncement, "Never, no."

They waited.

"Your assumption has been that this was Earth. And that is a reasonable, wrong assumption. But I let you believe what you wanted. As a rule, every species, no matter how open to odd notions and alien fancies, will find its own stories to be the most compelling.

"No, this wasn't your cradle world. And its people were perhaps not quite as human as I might have let on."

"What happened to them?" Quee Lee pressed.

"As I promised my lover, I undid my fancy tinkering. I made her citizens simple again, just as I pulled back the engineering of the other species. The population scattered. The palace was abandoned. Without trained hands to make repairs, the city fell into ruins. Within a few years of my departure, the island was a mystery already famous across half of that world. But its mountain would never erupt. My work had stolen away too much heat, and the magma lake below had cooled and turned to stone."

The voice paused.

Then, with a matter-of-fact tone, it explained, "Earth is blessed in many ways. It has a mature, very stable sun. Comets are rare beauties in the sky, not constant hazards. And it possesses a relatively thin crust, easily pierced and quick to bleed. But this world that I speak of was notably different. Its skin is much thicker than Earth's, and much more resilient. As its core generates heat, oceans of magma build up slowly, millions of years required to reach that critical point when a thousand eruptions come at once.

"That harum-scarum probe surely recognized the inevitable— a world perched on the margins of a grand, yet thoroughly natural, disaster.

"I left that world and placed my magical machine in a secret place. A new mission called to me from the sky, and I was en route when that nameless world suddenly and violently attacked itself.

"The sulfurous gases and blistering lava flows achieved everything that I had counted upon. Every convincing trace of my visit was erased. The continents were wracked by quakes. Ten thousand volcanoes spat ash and fire, and then they exploded, flinging their poisons into the stratosphere. Every forest burned. Every breath brought blisters and misery. The ocean floors were wrenched upward, forcing salt water over the coastlands. My little island was washed clean beneath a quick succession of tsunamis, erasing even the palace. The humanlike creatures were reduced to a few scattered populations, ignorant and desperate. And after another thousand years of geologic horror—when the skies finally cleared and the lava cooled to glass—not a single example of that very promising species could be found in Creation."

Those deadly words were absorbed in silence.

Then Quee Lee said, "How awful."

Softly, the voice asked, "In what way is this awful?"

"You allowed that to happen," she began.

"But the people were doomed long before I knew of their existence. And despite my considerable powers, there was little I could have done, except delaying the story's end by one day, or maybe two."

The humans said nothing.

"If you need righteous anger," it continued, "direct your emotions toward the harum-scarums. Their probe saw the same future that I saw. Three of their colonies were near enough and powerful enough to launch rescue missions. Better than I, they could have saved a worthy sampling of those people before they passed out of existence. But no missions were launched. The costs and the benefits were too much and too little, respectively. The battered world remained nameless until a starship eased its way into orbit. That particular ship was bringing colonists, I should mention—people who didn't care about the bones under their feet, people who wanted nothing but to start new lives on this rich empty place."

Quietly, Perri asked, "Is it another harum-scarum world?"

"No," the voice replied, "it is not."

"Then who?"

"Who else would be a likely suspect, my friend? Remembering all that we have discussed by now . . ."

Humans had claimed the empty world. The colonists might even be humans that had come from the Great Ship . . . people whom Quee Lee and Perri had met and even known well at one time or another.

Quee Lee was desperate to talk about anything else.

And Perri was, too. With a scornful, demanding tone, he said, "I still don't believe in your Union."

"No? In what ways do you doubt it?"

"When you describe this organization, it sounds like an exclusive club or somebody's secret society. Not the imperial underpinnings of a powerful political machine."

There was a long pause, and then the voice said, "Power," four times, each utterance employing a different emotion. Amusement was followed by disgust, and then came contempt, and finally, a different species of amusement. A joyful, almost giddy rendering of the word "Power." After that, there was a laugh that lingered until the voice decided to speak again.

"As you must have guessed by now," it told them, "I am

embroiled in a new task in the service of my Union. A mission full of facets and difficult challenges, yes."

The humans held their breath.

And now the voice pushed even closer, less than an arm's length away, and from a mouth that they could only imagine came the reminder, "I did once visit your cradle world. Your Earth. Yes, I did."

Quee Lee nodded.

"Before it was named," Perri recalled.

"Moments before," the voice added. And then the bulk of an invisible body drifted even closer, hovering within a tongue's length of Quee Lee's ear, and an intimate whisper offered her a single date. A specific time. Then a place inside a city that she would never see again.

Quee Lee shivered.

Perri reached out with one arm, aiming for the face that had to be lurking in the blackness . . . but his hand closed on nothing, and nothing else came from the voice, and, after a few moments more of clinging comfort, their camp lights returned— a scorching white glare of photons that left them blinking, blinded in a new way altogether.

XIII

They didn't sleep that night, and they didn't start missing sleep until the middle of the following morning. By then, Perri and Quee Lee had thoroughly explored the enormous room and most of the little tunnels leading out from it. But they didn't find any traces of visitors other than themselves. Their sniffers tasted surgically clean surfaces and cold air uncluttered by even a single flake of lost skin, and, just as puzzling, none of their machines could explain why they had failed last night. Whatever the voice was, it had been careful. With its absence, it proved its great powers . . . at least when it came to fooling a couple of peasants who were ignorant of the real powers of a galaxy that they had barely begun to know.

There was talk about returning to the flex-car, or at least contacting their missing friends.

But one last tunnel needed a quick examination. And with Perri at the lead, they marched up into an increasingly narrow space that turned sharply, revealing a pair of security robots waiting for anyone who might wander where they didn't belong.

The robots were in slumber mode, facing in the opposite direction.

Perri retreated, pulling his wife along behind him. "They're the last in a string of sentries," he decided. "I bet if we could find our way to the other side, we'd come across barricades and official warnings from the captains not to take one step farther."

"The captains don't know about our route?"

"Not yet," he allowed. Then, with a soft conspiring voice, he added, "Maybe we should hurry home. Now. Before we get noticed."

They discovered their friends waiting at the flex-car. An argument had just ended, and one of the twin brothers refused to say anything to anyone. Apparently he had lost out on the competition for the rich woman's affections, and his anger helped avoid any of the usual questions.

The tiny expedition abandoned the Vermiculate before evening.

Home again, the old married couple made love and ate enough for ten hungry people, and throughout the sex and the dinner, they constantly discussed what they should do next, if anything. And then Quee Lee slept hard for three dream-laced hours. When she woke up, Perri was standing over her. He was smiling. But it was a grim, concentrated smile—the look of a man who knew something enormous but unsatisfying.

"Want to hear a rumor?" he asked.

She sat up in bed, answering him with a look.

"Like we heard before, the captains did discover the hole in their maps, and they sent an old robot down into the hole. But it got lost and climbed out again, and it couldn't explain where it had gone wrong."

"That's the story I remember," she allowed.

"Engineers tore open the robot. Just to identify the malfunction. And that's when they found a message."

Quee Lee blinked, and waited.

"Addressed to the Master Captain," he continued, his smile growing warmer by the moment. "After a thousand security checks, the invitation was delivered. Except for the Master Captain, and maybe a few Submasters, nobody knows what the message said. But a few days later, alone, the Master Captain walked down that tunnel and vanished for nearly five hours. And when she emerged again, she looked sick. Shaken sick. The rumor claims that she actually cried in the presence of her security troops, which is why the whole story refuses to get wings and soar. It doesn't sound at all like the benign despot we know so well."

His wife agreed with a nod. Then she asked, "When did this happen?"

"Ten years ago, nearly."

"And since then?"

"Well," Perri allowed, "the Master Captain has quit weeping. If that's what you're curious about."

She lay back on her pillows.

"No," her husband said.

"Why not?"

"I didn't wake you just to tell you something that might have happened. Or even to give you another mystery to chew on."

"Then why am I awake?"

"I know a man," Perri said. "And he's very good at pulling old memories out of very old skulls."

———

The magician was named Ash.

He was human, but he lived inside an alien habitat where

the false sun never set. Sitting in a room full of elaborate machinery, Ash told his newest clients, "I can make promises, but they don't mean much. This date is a very big problem, madam. You were alive then, yes. But barely. This is a few years before bioceramic brains came into existence. You could have been the brightest young thing, but my tricks work best with the galactic-standard minds . . . brains that employ quantum many-world models to interface with a trillion sister minds."

Perri asked, "Can you do anything?"

"I can take your money," Ash replied. "And I can also dig into the old data archives. You claim you have a place in mind?"

"Yes," Quee Lee said. Then she repeated the location exactly as the voice had given it to her.

"I assume you think you were there then," Ash said.

"I don't know if I was."

"And this is important?"

"We'll see," she remarked.

Ash began to work. He explained that on Earth, for this very brief period of history, security systems as well as ordinary individuals tried to keep thorough digital records of everything that happened and everything that didn't happen. The trouble was that the machinery was very simple and unreliable, and the frequent upgrades as well as a few nasty electromagnetic pulses had wiped clean a lot of records. Not to mention the malicious effects of the early AIs—entities who took great delight in creating fictions that they would bury inside whatever data banks would accept their artistic works.

"The chances of success," Ash began to say.

Then he saw something entirely unexpected and, lifting his gaze, he mentioned to Quee Lee, "You were a pretty young lady."

"Did you find me?" she asked expectantly.

"Too easily," he allowed. Then he showed her a portion

of the image—a girl who was nine or maybe eight years old, dressed in the uniform mandated by a good private school.

With a shrug, Ash allowed, "No need for paranoia. This does happen. On occasion." He gave commands to a brigade of invisible assistants and then said, "If I can dig up a few more records, I think I can piece together what you and the man talked about."

"What man?" she asked.

Perri asked.

"The man standing beside you," Ash remarked. "The man with the golden balloon." Then he showed them an image captured by a nearby security camera, adding, "I'm assuming he's your father, judging by his looks."

"He's not," she whispered.

"And now we have a second digital record," Ash said happily. "Hey, and now a third record. See the adolescent boy down the path from you? Wearing the medallion on his chest? Well, that was a camera and a very good microphone. His video has been lost, but not the audio. I can't tell you how unlikely it is to have this kind of recording survive long enough, in any usable form."

"What is the man saying to me?" Quee Lee asked nervously.

"Let me see if I can pull it up."

And suddenly, a voice that she hadn't thought about for several seconds returned. The young girl and the stranger were standing in Hong Kong Park, on the cobblestone path beside the lotus pond. A short white picket fence separated them from the water. In the background stood towers and a bright blue sky. With the noise of the city and other passersby erased, the voice began by saying, "Hello, Quee Lee."

"Hello?" the young girl replied, nervous in very much the same fashion that the old woman was now. "Do I know you?"

"Hardly at all," the man replied.

The girl looked about, as if expecting somebody to come save her now. Which there ought to have been: Quee Lee was the only child of a very wealthy couple who didn't let her travel anywhere without bodyguards and a personal servant. "Where are my people now?" she seemed to ask herself.

The voice said, "I will not hurt you, my dear."

Hearing that promise didn't help the girl relax.

"Ask me where I came from. Will you please?"

The youngster decided on silence.

But the strange man laughed and, pretending that the question had been asked, he remarked, "I came from the stars. I am here on a great, important mission, and it involves your particular species."

The girl looked up at a face that possessed a distinct resemblance to her face. Then she looked back down the path, hoping for rescue.

"In a little while," said the stranger, "my work here will be complete."

"Why?" the girl muttered.

"Because that is when one of your mechanical eyes will look at the most lucrative portion of the sky, at the perfect moment, and almost everything that you will need to know about the universe will be delivered to your doorstep."

The pretty black-haired girl hugged her laptop bag, saying nothing.

"When that day comes," said the man, "you must try to remember everything. Do you understand me, Quee Lee? This will be the most important moment in your species' history."

"How do you know my name?" she asked again.

"And that is not all I am doing on your world." The man was quite handsome but ordinary, nothing about him hinting at anything that wasn't human. He was wearing a simple suit, rumpled at the edges. His right hand held the string that led up to a small balloon made from helium and gold Mylar. He smiled with fierce joy, telling her, "It has been decided. Your species has a great destiny in service of the Union."

In the present, two people gasped quietly.

"What's the Union?" the girl asked.

"Everything," was the reply. "And it is nothing."

The girl was prettiest when she was puzzled, like now.

"You won't remember any portion of this conversation," the man promised. "Ten minutes from now, you won't remember me or my words."

One hand smoothed her skirt, and she anxiously stared at her neat black shoes.

"But before I leave you, I wanted to tell you something. Are you listening, Quee Lee?"

"No," she claimed.

The man laughed heartily. Then he bent down, placing their faces on the same level, and when he had her gaze, he said, "You were adopted, only your parents don't know that. The baby inside your mother had died, and I devised you out of things that are human, but also elements that were inspired by an old friend of mine."

The girl tried to step back but couldn't. Discovering that her feet were fixed to the pavement, she looked down and then up at the other adults walking past the long brown pond. When she tried to scream, no sound came from her open mouth.

"I am not gracelessly cruel," the stranger told her. "You may think that of me one day. But even though I live to aid the workings of an enormous power, I make certain that I find routes to kindness and, when it offers itself, to love."

The little girl couldn't even make herself cry.

"Part of you," he said. Then he paused, and from two different perspectives, the audience watched as his free hand touched the girl's bright black hair. "The shape of your mind was born on another world, a world too distant to be seen today. And I once lied to that mind, Quee Lee. I told it that I could stand aside and watch it die forever."

But the man was crying, his face wet and sorry.

"I wish I could offer more of an apology," he said. And then he rose up again, pulling the balloon's string close to his chest while wiping at his wet face with a wrinkled sleeve. "But much is at stake . . . more than you might ever understand,

Quee Lee . . . and this is as close to insubordination as this good servant can manage."

Then he glanced at the security camera hidden in the trees and handed the string and balloon to the girl beside him. "Would you like this, Quee Lee? As a little gift from your grandfather?"

The girl discovered that she could move again.

"Take it," he advised.

She accepted the string with one little hand.

For a brief instant, they were posing, staring across the millennia in a stance that was strained but sweet nonetheless—the image of a little girl enjoying the park with some undefined adult relative.

"I will see you later," he mentioned.

Quee Lee released the string, watching the gold ball rise faster than she would have expected—shooting into the sky as if it weighed nothing at all.

When her eyes dropped, the stranger had stepped out of view.

A few moments later, her father ran up the path to join her, asking, "Where did you go? I couldn't find you anywhere."

"I didn't go anywhere," the girl replied.

"Tell me the truth," the scared little man demanded. "Did you talk to somebody you shouldn't have talked to?"

She said, "No."

"Why are you lying?" he asked.

"But I'm not lying," she protested. Then with a wide, smart grin, the young Quee Lee added, "The sky is going to talk, Father. Did you know that? And he promised me that I am going to see him again later!"

THE SIX DIRECTIONS OF SPACE

Alastair Reynolds

Alastair Reynolds is a frequent contributor to Interzone *and has also sold to* Asimov's Science Fiction, Spectrum SF, *and elsewhere. His first novel,* Revelation Space, *was widely hailed as one of the major SF books of the year; it was quickly followed by* Chasm City, Redemption Ark, Absolution Gap, *and* Century Rain, *all big sprawling Space Operas that were big sellers as well, establishing Reynolds as one of the best and most popular new SF writers to enter the field in many years. His other books include a novella collection,* Diamond Dogs, Turquoise Days. *His most recent books are a novel,* Pushing Ice, *and two new collections,* Galactic North *and* Zima Blue and Other Stories. *Coming up is a new novel,* The Prefect. *A professional scientist with a Ph.D. in astronomy, he comes from Wales, but lives in the Netherlands, where he works for the European Space Agency.*

Reynolds's work is known for its grand scope, sweep, and scale (in one story, "Galactic North," a spaceship sets out in pursuit of another in a stern chase that takes thousands of years of time and hundreds of thousands of light-years to complete; in another, "Thousandth Night," ultrarich immortals embark on a plan that will call for the physical rearrangement of all the stars in the Galaxy. In the hard-hitting and disquieting story that follows, Reynolds shows us a brutal Galactic Empire embattling itself to defend against attacks by other Empires that come not just from elsewhere in the Galaxy, but from other universes altogether!

We had been riding for two hours when I tugged sharply on the reins to bring my pony to a halt. Tenger, my escort, rode on for a few paces before glancing back irritatedly. He muttered something in annoyance–a phrase that contained the words "stupid" and "dyke"–before steering his horse back alongside mine.

"Another sightseeing stop?" he asked, as the two mismatched animals chewed their bits, flared their nostrils, and flicked their heads up in mutual impatience.

I said nothing, damned if I was going to give him the pleasure of an excuse. I only wanted to take in the view: the deeply shadowed valley below, the rising hills beyond (curving ever upward, like a tidal wave formed from rock and soil and grass), and the little patch of light down in the darkness, the square formation of the still-moving caravan.

"If you really want to make that appointment–" Tenger continued.

"Shut up."

Tenger sniffed, dug into a leather flap on his belt, and popped something into his mouth.

"On your own head be it, Yellow Dog. It certainly won't be my neck on the line, keeping the old man waiting."

I held both reins in one hand so that I could cup the other against my ear. I turned the side of my head in the direction of the caravan and closed my eyes. After a few moments, I convinced myself that I could hear it. It was a sound almost on the edge of audibility, but which would become thunderous, calamitous, world-destroying, as they drew nearer. The sound of thousands of riders, hundreds of wheeled tents, dozens of monstrous siege engines. A sound very much like the end of the world itself, it must have seemed, when the caravan approached.

"We can go now," I told Tenger.

He dug his spurs in, almost drawing blood, his horse pounding away so quickly that it kicked dirt into my eyes.

Goyo snorted and gave chase. We raced down into the valley, sending skylarks and snipe barreling into the air.

———

"Just going by the rules, Yellow Dog," the guard said, apologizing for making me show him my passport. We were standing on the wheeled platform of the imperial *ger*. The guard wore a knee-length blue sash-tied coat, long black hair cascading from the dome of his helmet. "We're on high alert as it is. Three plausible threats in the last week."

"Usual nut jobs?" I said, casting a wary glance at Tenger, who was attending to Goyo with a bad-tempered expression. I had beaten him to the caravan and he did not like that.

"Two Islamist sects, one bunch of Nestorians," the guard answered. "Not that I'm saying that the old man has anything to fear from you, of course, but we have to follow protocol."

"I understand fully."

"Frankly, we were beginning to wonder if you were ever coming back." He looked at me solicitously. "Some of us were beginning to wonder if you'd been disavowed."

I smiled. "Disavowed? I don't think so."

"Just saying, we're all assuming you've got something suitably juicy, after all this time."

I reached up to tie back my hair. "Juicy's not exactly the word I'd use. But it's definitely something *he* has to hear about."

The guard touched a finger to the pearl on his collar.

"Better go inside, in that case."

I did as I was invited.

My audience with the khan was neither as private nor as lengthy as I might have wished, but, in all other respects, it was a success. One of his wives was there, as well as Minister Chiledu, the national security adviser, and the khan was notoriously busy during this ceremonial restaging of the war caravan. I thought, not for the first time, of how old he looked: much older than the young man who had been elected to this office seven years earlier, brimming with plans and promises. Now he was graying and tired, worn down by disappointing polls and the pressures of managing an empire that was beginning to fray at the edges. The caravan was supposed to be an antidote to all that. In this, the nine hundred and ninety-ninth year since the death of the Founder (we would celebrate this birthday, but no one knows when it happened), a special effort had been made to create the largest caravan in decades, with almost every local system commander in attendance.

As I stepped off the *ger* to collect Goyo and begin my mission, I felt something perilously close to elation. The data I had presented to the khan—the troubling signs I had detected concerning the functioning and security of the Infrastructure—had been taken seriously. The khan could have waved aside my concerns as an issue for his successor, but—to his credit, I think—he had not. I had been given license and funds to gather more information, even if that meant voyaging to the Kuchlug Special Administrative Volume and operating under the nose of Qilian, one of the men who had been making life difficult for the khan these last few years.

And yet my mood of elation was short-lived.

I had no sooner set my feet on the ground than I spied Tenger. He was bullying Goyo, jerking hard on his bridle, kicking a boot against his hocks. He was so preoccupied with his business that he did not see me approaching from behind his back. I took hold of a good, thick clump of his hair and snapped his head back as far it would go. He released the bridle, staggering back under the pressure I was applying.

I whispered in his ear. "No one hurts my horse, you ignorant piece of shit." Then I spun him around, the hair tearing out in my fist, and kneed him hard in the groin, so that he coughed out a groan of pain and nausea and bent double, like a man about to vomit.

———

Some say that it is Heaven's Mandate that we should have the stars, just as it was the will of Heaven that our armies should bring the squabbling lands of Greater Mongolia under one system of governance, a polity so civilized that a woman could ride naked from the western shores of Europe to the eastern edge of China without once being molested. I say that it is simply the case that we—call us Mongols, call us humans, it scarcely matters now—have always made the best of what we are given.

Take the nexus in Gansu system, for instance. It was a medium-sized moon that had been hollowed out nearly all the way to its middle, leaving a shell barely a hundred *li* thick, with a small round kernel buttressed to the shell by ninety-nine golden spokes. Local traffic entered and departed the nexus via apertures at the northern and southern poles. Not that there was much local traffic to speak of: Gansu, with its miserly red sun—only just large enough to sustain fusion—and handful of desolate, volatile-poor, and radiation-lashed rocky worlds, was neither a financial nor military hub, nor a place that figured prominently in tourist itineraries. As was often the case, it was something of a puzzle why the wormlike *khorkoi* had built the nexus in such a miserable location to begin with.

Unpromising material, but in the five hundred years since we first reopened a portal into the Infrastructure, we had made a glittering bauble out of it. Five major trunk routes converged on Gansu, including a high-capacity branch of the Kherlen Corridor, the busiest path in the entire network. In addition, the moon offered portals to a dozen secondary routes, four of which had been rated stable enough to allow passage by juggernaut-class ships. Most of those secondary routes led to stellar population centers of some economic importance, including the Kiriltuk, Tatatunga, and Chilagun administrative volumes, each of which encompased more than fifty settled systems and around a thousand habitable worlds. Even the routes that led to nowhere of particular importance were well traveled by prospectors and adventurers, hoping to find *khorkoi* relics or, that fever dream of all chancers, an unmapped nexus.

We did not know the function of the ninety-nine spokes, or of the core they buttressed. No matter; the core made a useful foundation, a place upon which to build. From the vantage point of the rising shuttle, it was a scribble of luminous neon, packed tight as a migraine. I could not distinguish the lights of individual buildings, only the larger glowing demarcations of the precincts between city-sized districts. Pressurized horseways a whole *li* wide were thin, snaking scratches. The human presence had even begun to climb up the golden spokes, pushing tendrils of light out to the moon's inner surface. Commercial slogans spelled themselves out in letters ten *li* high. *On Founder's Day, drink only Temujin Brand Airag. Sorkan-Shira rental ponies have low mileage, excellent stamina, and good temperament. Treat your favorite wife: buy her only Zarnuk Silks. During hunting season, safeguard your assets with New Far Samarkand Mutual Insurance. Think you're a real man? Then you should be drinking Death Worm Airag: the one with a sting at both ends!*

I had spent only one night in Gansu, arranging a eunuch and waiting for the smaller ship that would carry us the rest of the way to Kuchlug. Now Goyo, the eunuch, and I were being conveyed to the *Burkhan Khaldun,* a vessel that was even smaller than the *Black Heart Mountain* that had brought me to Gansu. The *BK* was only one *li* from end to end, less than a quarter of that across the bow. The hull was a multicolored quilt of patch repairs, with many scratches, craters, and scorches yet to be attended to. The lateral stabilization vanes had the slightly buckled look of something that had been badly bent and then hammered back into shape, while the yaw dampeners appeared to have originated from a completely different ship, fixed on with silvery fillets of recent welding work. A whole line of windows had been plated over.

As old as the *BK* might have been, it had taken more than just age and neglect to bring her to that state. The Parvan Tract was a notoriously rough passage, quickly taking its toll on even a new ship. If the Kherlen Corridor was a wide, stately river that could almost be navigated blindfold, then the Tract was a series of narrow rapids whose treacherous properties varied from trip to trip, requiring not just expert input from the crew, but passengers with the constitution to tolerate a heavy crossing.

Once I had checked into my rooms and satisfied myself that Goyo was being taken care of, I made my way back to the passenger area. I bought a glass of Temujin *airag* and made my way to the forward viewing platform, with its wide sweep of curved window–scratched and scuffed in places, worryingly starred in others–and leaned hard against the protective railing. The last shuttle had already detached, and the *BK* was accelerating toward the portal, its great human-made doors irising open at the last possible moment, so that the interior of Gansu was protected from the Parvan Tract's unpredictable energy surges. Even though the Infrastructure shaft stretched impossibly far into the distance, my mind kept insisting that we were about to punch through the thin skin of the moon.

The ship surged forward, the sluggish artificial gravity generators struggling to maintain the local vertical. We passed through the door, into the superluminal machinery of the Infrastructure. The tunnel walls were many *li* away, but they felt closer–as they raced by at increasing speed, velocity traced by the luminous squiggly patterns that had been inscribed on the wall for inscrutable reasons by the *khorkoi* builders, I had the impression that the shaft was constricting, tightening down on our fragile little ship. Yet nothing seemed to disconcert or even arouse the interest of my fellow passengers. In ones and twos, they drifted away from the gallery, leaving me alone with my eunuch, observing from a discrete distance. I drank the *airag* very slowly, looking down the racing shaft, wondering if it would be my fortune to see a phantom with my own eyes. Phantoms, after all, were what had brought me here.

Now all I had to do was poison the eunuch.

The eunuch answered to "eunuch," but his real name (I learned after a certain amount of probing) was Tisza. He had not been surgically castrated; there was an implant somewhere in his forearm dispensing the necessary cocktail of androgen-blockers, suppressing his libido and lending him a mildly androgynous appearance. Other implants, similar to those employed by government operatives, had given him heightened reflexes, spatial coordination, and enhanced night vision. He was adept with weapons and unarmed combat, as (I had no cause to doubt) were all Batu eunuchs. I had no need of his protection, of course, but appearances were paramount. I was posing as a woman of means, a well-healed tourist. No women in my circumstances would ever have traveled without the accompaniment of a man such as Tisza.

He served my purpose in another way. We shared the same rooms, with the eunuch sleeping in a small, doorless annex connected to mine. Because I might (conceivably) be drugged or poisoned, Tisza always ate the same meals as me, served at the same time and brought to my cabin by one of the *BK*'s white uniformed stewards.

"What if you get poisoned and die on me?" I asked, innocently, when we were sitting across from each other at my table.

He tapped a pudgy finger against his belly. "It would take a lot to kill me, Miss Bocheng. My constitution has been tailored to process many toxins in common circulation among would-be assassins and miscreants. I will become ill much sooner than you would, but what would kill you would merely make me unwell, and not so unwell that I could not discharge my duties."

"I hope you're right about that."

He patted his chin with napkin. "It is no occasion for pride. I am what I am because of the chemical intervention and surgery of the Batu Escort Agency. It would be equally pointless to understate my abilities."

Later, feigning nervousness, I told him that I had heard a noise from his annex.

"It is nothing, I assure you. No one could have entered these rooms without our knowing it."

"It sounded like someone breathing."

He smiled tolerantly. "There are many foreign sounds on a

ship like this. Noises carry a great distance through the ducts and conduits of the air-circulation system."

"Couldn't someone have crawled through those same conduits?"

He rose from the table without a note of complaint. "It is unlikely, but I shall investigate."

As soon as he had vanished through the door into his annex, I produced a vial from my pocket and tipped its sugary contents onto the remains of his meal. I heard him examining things, pulling open cupboard doors and sliding drawers. By the time he returned, with a reassuring expression on his face, the toxin crystals had melted invisibly into his food and the vial was snug in my pocket.

"Whatever you heard, there's no one in there."

"Are you sure?"

"Completely. But I'm willing to look again, if it would put your mind at ease."

I looked abashed. "I'm just being silly."

"Not at all. You must not be afraid to bring things to my attention. It is what you have hired me for."

"Tuck in," I said, nodding at his meal, "before it gets cold."

———

Tisza was moaning and sweating on the bed, deep in fever, as Mr. Tayang appraised him warily. "Did he tell you he could detect poisons? They don't all come with that option."

"He can. Isn't that the point?"

"It could just be a bug he's picked up. On the other hand, he may have been hit by something intended for you that his system wasn't designed to filter out."

"A poison?"

"It's a possibility, Miss Bocheng."

Tayang was a steward, a young man with a pleasant face and a highly professional manner. I had seen him around earlier, but—as was the case with all the crew—he had steadfastly refused to engage in any conversation not related to my imme-

diate needs. I had counted on this, and contrived the poisoning
of the eunuch to give me heightened access to one or more of
the crew. It need not have been Tayang, but my instincts told
me that he would serve excellently.

"Then why isn't it affecting me?" I asked.

"I don't wish to alarm you, but it could be that it's going to
in a very short while. We need to get both of you into the sick
bay. Under observation, we should be able to stabilize the eunuch and ensure you come to no harm."

This was the outcome I had been hoping for, but some indignation was called for. "If you think I'm going to spend the
rest of this trip in some stinking sick bay, after I've paid for this
cabin . . ."

Tayang raised a calming hand. "It won't be for long. A day
or two, just to be on the safe side. Then you can enjoy the rest
of the trip in comfort."

Another pair of stewards was summoned to help shift the
hapless Tisza, while I made my way to the sick bay on foot.
"Actually," I said, "now that you mention it . . . I do feel a little
peculiar."

Tayang looked at me sympathetically. "Don't worry, Miss
Bocheng. We'll have you right as rain in no time."

The sick bay was larger and better equipped than I had
been expecting, almost as if it belonged in a different ship entirely. I was relieved to see that no one else was using it. Tayang
helped me onto a reclined couch while the other stewards
pulled a screen around the stricken eunuch.

"How do you feel now?" Tayang asked, fastening a black
cuff around my forearm.

"Still a bit funny."

For the next few minutes, Tayang—who had clearly been
given basic medical training—studied the readouts on a hand-
held display he had pulled from a recess in the wall.

"Well, it doesn't *look*—" he began.

"I should have listened to my friends," I said, shaking my
head. "They told me not to come here."

He tapped buttons set into the side of the display. "Your friends warned you that you might end up getting poisoned?"

"Not exactly, no. But they said it wasn't a good idea traveling on the *Burkhan Khaldun,* down the Parvan Tract. They were right, weren't they?"

"That would depend. So far, I can't see any sign that you've ingested anything poisonous. Of course, it could be something that the analyzer isn't equipped to detect–"

"And the eunuch?"

"Just a moment," Tayang said, leaving the display suspended in the air. He walked over to the other bed and pulled aside the curtain. I heard a murmured exchange before he returned, with a bit less of a spring in his step. "Well, there's no doubt that something pretty heavy's hit *his* system. Could be a deliberate toxin, could be something nasty that just happened to get into him. We're not far out of Gansu; he could have contracted something there that's only just showing up."

"He's been poisoned, Mr. Tayang. My bodyguard. Doesn't that strike you as a slightly ominous development?"

"I still say it could be something natural. We'll know soon enough. In the meantime, I wouldn't necessarily jump to the conclusion that you're in immediate peril."

"I'm concerned, Mr. Tayang."

"Well, don't be. You're in excellent hands." He leaned over to plump my pillow. "Get under the blanket if you feel shivery. Is there anything you'd like me to fetch from your room?"

"No, thank you."

"In which case, I'll leave you be. I'll keep the analyzer attached just in case it flags anything. The other stewards are still here. If you need anything, just call."

"I will."

He was on the verge of leaving–I had no doubt that he was a busy man–when something caused him to narrow his eyes. "So if it wasn't about being poisoned, Miss Bocheng, why exactly was it that your friends didn't want you taking this ship?"

"Oh, that." I shook my head. "It's silly. I don't know why I mentioned it at all. It's not as if I believe any of that nonsense."

"Any of *what* nonsense, exactly?"

"You know, about the phantoms. About how the Parvan Tract is haunted. I told them I was above all that, but they still kept going on about it. They said that if I took this ship, I might never come back. Of course, that only made me even more determined."

"Good for you."

"I told them I was a rationalist, not someone who believes in ghosts and goblins." I shifted on the couch, giving him a sympathetic look. "I expect that you're fed up with hearing about all that, especially as you actually work here. I mean, if anyone would have been likely to see something, it would be *you,* wouldn't it, or one of the other crew?"

"That would make sense," he said.

"Well, the fact that you obviously *haven't* . . . there can't be anything to it, can there?" I crossed my arms and smiled triumphantly. "Wait until I tell my friends how silly they've been."

"Perhaps," he began, and then fell silent.

I knew that I had him then; that it would be only a matter of time before Tayang felt compelled to show me evidence. My instincts proved correct, for within a day of my discharge from the sick bay (the eunuch was still under obervation, but making satisfactory progress), the steward contrived an excuse to visit my quarters. He had a clean towel draped over his arm, as if he had come to replace the one in my bathroom.

"I brought you a fresh one. I think the cleaning section missed this corridor this morning."

"They didn't, but I appreciate the gesture all the same."

He lingered, as if he had something to get off his chest but was struggling to find the right words.

"Mr. Tayang?" I pressed.

"What we were talking about before."

"Yes?" I inquired mildly.

"Well, you're wrong." He said it nicely enough, but the defiance in his words was clear. "The phantoms exist. I may not have seen anything with my own eyes, but I've seen data that's just as convincing."

"I doubt it."

"I can show you easily enough." He must have been intending to say those words from the moment he had decided to come to my cabin, yet now that he had spoken them, his regret was immediate.

"Really?"

"I shouldn't have."

"Tell me," I said forcefully. "Whatever this is, I want to see it."

"It means your friends were right; and you were wrong."

"Then I need to know that."

Tayang gave me a warning look. "It'll change the way you think. At the moment, you have the luxury of not believing in the phantoms. I know that there's something out there that we don't understand, something that doesn't belong. Are you sure you want that burden?"

"If you can handle it, I think I can. What do I have to do?"

"I need to show you something. But I can't do it now. Later, during the night shift, it'll be quieter."

"I'll be ready," I said, nodding eagerly.

Close to midnight, Tayang came for me. Remembering to keep in character for someone half convinced she was the target of an assassin, I did not open up immediately.

"Yes?"

"It's me, Tayang."

I cracked open the door. "I'm ready."

He looked me up and down. "Take off those clothes, please."

"I'm sorry?"

He glanced away, blushing. "What I mean is, wear as much or as little as you would wear for bed." I noticed that he had a jacket draped over his arm, as if he was ready to put it around my shoulders. "Should we meet someone, and should questions be asked, you will explain that I found you sleepwalking, and that I'm taking you back to your cabin via the most discrete route I can think of, so you don't embarrass yourself in front of any other passengers."

"I see. You've given this some thought, haven't you?"

"You aren't the first skeptical passenger, Miss Bocheng."

I closed the door and disrobed, then put on thin silk trousers and an equally thin silk blouse, the one scarlet and the other electric yellow, with a design of small blue wolves. I untied my hair and messed it to suggest someone only recently roused from the bed.

Outside, as was customary during the night shift of the *BK*'s operations, the corridor lights were dimmed to a sleepy amber. The bars, restaurants, and gaming rooms were closed. The public lounges were deserted and silent, save for the scurrying mouselike cleaning robots that always emerged after the people had gone away. Tayang chose his route well, for we did not bump into any other passengers or crew.

"This is the library," he said, when we had arrived in a small, red-lit room, set with shelves, screens, and movable chairs. "No one uses it much—it's not exactly a high priority for most of our passengers. They'd rather drink away the voyage with Temujin *airag.*"

"Are we allowed here?"

"Well, technically there'd be nothing to stop you visiting this room during normal ship hours. But during normal ship hours, I wouldn't be able to show you what I'm about to." He was trying to be nonchalant about the whole adventure, but his nervousnous was like a boy on a dare. "But don't worry, we won't get into trouble."

"How is a library going to change my mind about the phantoms?"

"Let me show you." He ushered me to one of the terminals, swinging out a pair of hinged stools for us to sit on. I sat to the left of him, while Tayang flipped open a dust cover to expose a keyboard. He began to tap at the keys, causing changes to the hooded data display situated at eye level. "As it happens, these consoles are connected to the *Burkhan Khaldun*'s own computers. You just have to know the right commands."

"Won't this show up?"

He shook his head. "I'm not doing anything that will come to anyone's attention. Besides, I'm perfectly entitled to access this data. The only thing wrong is you being with me, and if anyone comes down here, we'll have time to prepare for them, to make it look as if I caught you sleepwalking." He fell silent for a minute or so, tapping through options, obviously navigating his way through to the information stored in the computer's memory bank. "I just hope the company spooks haven't got to it already," he murmured. "Every now and then, someone from Blue Heaven comes aboard and wipes large chunks of the *BK*'s memory. They say they're just doing routine archiving, clearing space for more data, but no one believes that. Looks like we're in time, though. I didn't see any spooks nosing around when we were in Gansu: they'll probably come aboard next time we're back." He glanced over his shoulder. "I'll show it to you once. Then we go. All right?"

"Whatever you say, Mr. Tayang."

"The *BK* has cameras, pointed into the direction of flight. They detect changes in the tunnel geometry and feed that data to the servomotors driving the stabilizing vanes and yaw dampers, so that they can make adjustments to smooth out the turbulence. They're also there as an emergency measure in case we encounter another ship coming the other way, one that isn't on schedule or hasn't got an active transponder. The cameras give us just enough warning to swerve the *BK* to one side, to give passing clearance. It's bumpy for the passengers when that happens, but a lot better than a head-on collision at tunnel speeds."

"I take it the cameras saw something," I said.

Tayang nodded. "This was a couple of trips ago, about halfway between Gansu and Kuchlug. They only got eight clear frames. Whatever it was was moving fast, much quicker than one of our ships. The fourth, fifth, and sixth frames are the sharpest."

"Show me."

He tapped keys. A picture sprang onto the display, all fuzzy green hues, overlaid with date stamps and other information. It took a moment before I was sure what I was looking at. There was some kind of pale green smudge filling half the frame, a random-looking shape like the blind spot one sees after looking at the sun for too long, and beyond that, a suggestion of the curving squiggles of the tunnel's *khorkoi* patterning, reaching away to infinity.

I pressed a finger against the smudge. "That's the phantom?"

"This is frame three. It becomes clearer on the next one." He advanced to the next image and I saw what he meant. The smudge had enlarged, but also become sharper, with details beginning to emerge. Edges and surfaces, a hint of organized structure, even if the overall shape was still elusive.

"Next frame," Tayang mouthed.

Now there could be no doubt that the phantom was some kind of ship, even if it conformed to the pattern of no vessel I had ever seen. It was sleek and organic-looking, more like a darting squid than the clunky lines of the *BK*.

He advanced to the next frame, but—while the image did not become substantially clearer—the angle changed, so that the three-dimensional structure of the phantom became more apparent. At the same time, hints of patterning had begun to emerge: darker green symbols on the side of the hull, or fuselage, or body, of whatever the thing was.

"That's about as good as it gets," Tayang said.

"I'm impressed."

"You see these armlike appendages?" he asked, pointing to part of the image. "I'm guessing, of course, but I can't help wondering if they don't serve the same function as our stabilization vanes, only in a more elegant fashion."

"I think you could be right."

"One thing I'm sure of, though. *We* didn't build that ship. I'm no expert, Miss Bocheng, but I know what counts as cutting-edge ship design, and that thing is way beyond it."

"I don't think anyone would argue with that."

"It wasn't built by the government, or some mysterious splinter group of Islamist separatists. In fact, I don't think it was built by humans at all. We're looking at alien technology, and they're using our Infrastructure system as if they own it. More than that: every now and then you hear about entire ships and message packets going missing. They're not just trespassing in our network, they're stealing from it as well."

"I can see Blue Heaven would rather this didn't get out."

Tayang closed the display. "I'm sorry, but that's all I can show you. It's enough, though, isn't it?"

"More than enough," I said.

Of course, I had my doubts. Tayang could have easily faked those images, or been the unwitting victim of someone else's fakery. But I did not think that was the case. I had been looking at genuine data, not something cooked up to scare the tourists.

I was just beginning to plot my next move—how I would get a copy of the data, and smuggle it back to NHK while I continued with my investigations in Kuchlug space—when I became aware of a presence behind me. Tayang must have sensed it, too, for he turned around as I did. Standing in the doorway to the library was one of the other stewards, an older man whose name I had yet to learn. I noticed that the sleeves of his uniform were too short for him.

Wordlessly, he raised a hand. In it glinted the smooth alloy form of a small, precise weapon: the kind often carried by government spies such as myself. He shot me; I had a moment to stare at the barb embedded in my thigh, and then I passed out.

———

I came around in my cabin, gripped by a vile nausea, a headache like a slowly closing iron vice, and no conception of how much time had passed since Tayang and I had been disturbed in the library. Getting out of bed–I had been placed on top of the sheets–I searched the adjoining annex for the eunuch, before I remembered that he was still in the sick bay. I tried my door and found that it had been locked from the outside; there was no way for me to leave my room.

Understand, I did not accept my imprisonment lightly, but understand also that all my attempts at escape proved futile. I could not even squeeze through the conduit I had mentioned to the eunuch: such methods succeed in adventure stories, but not in real life.

Of course, it was desired that I be kept alive. The man who had shot me could have administered a fatal dose simply by twisting a dial in the grip of his weapon. He had chosen not to, and it was no accident that food and water appeared in the room's serving hatch at regular intervals. But as to who had chosen to detain me, I was uninformed.

I could guess, though.

He was the first to see me when the ship docked in Kuchlug space. He came to my room, accompanied by guards. He was as squat and muscled as a wrestler, his bare arms fully as thick as my thighs. He wore a leather jerkin, crisscrossed by thick black belts to which were fastened various ceremonial weapons and symbols of martial authority. A carefully tended mustache curled down on either side of his mouth, with a tiny but deliberate tuft of hair preserved under his lower lip. A stiff leather helmet, long at the sides and back, covered the rest of his head. The only visible part of his hair was a blunt, wedge-shaped fringe terminating just above his eyebrows, which were at once finely drawn, expressive, and deeply quizzical.

Of course, I knew the face.

"Commander Qilian," I said.

"Yes, I get about." His hands were impressively hairy, scarred and knotted like the roots of a very old tree. He snapped his fingers at the guards. "Have her brought to the debriefing facility on the Qing Shui moon. Bring the pony as well." Then he poked one of those fingers under my chin, lifting it up so that our eyes met. "Give some thought to the particulars of your story, Miss Bocheng. It may make all the difference."

They took me down to the moon. We landed somewhere and I was carried through dark, rusting corridors to a windowless holding cell. The floor rocked with a slow, sickening motion, as if I was on a ship at sea in a high swell—even though there were no oceans on the Qing Shui moon. They stripped me, took away my belongings, and gave me prison clothing to wear: a simple one-piece affair in orange silk. I pretended to be shocked and disoriented, but I was already summoning my training, recollecting those stratagems I had been taught to withstand prolonged detention and interrogation. As the guards were shutting the door on me, I contrived to slip a finger into the crack between the door and its frame. When the door closed, I yelped in pain and withdrew my hand with the fingertip squashed and red from the pressure.

I sucked it in my mouth until the pain abated.

"Stupid bitch," someone said.

There was a bunk, a spigot in the wall that dribbled tepid, piss-colored water, and a hole in the floor, with chipped ceramic sides stained an unspeakable brown. Light seeped in through a grille in the door. Neither willing nor able to sleep, I lay on the bunk and shivered. Presently—no more than two or three hours after my arrival—men came to take me down the corridor, to an interrogation room.

It is not necessary to document all that happened—the many weeks that it took for me to permit them to peel back the layers of identity I had wrapped around myself, each time thinking that the victory was theirs.

Suffice it to say that most of what they did to me involved electricity and chemicals in varying combinations. They did break two fingers on my left hand, including the one I had trapped in the door, but when they pulled out one of my finger-nails, it was from the other hand, not the one I had hurt. They beat me around, broke my teeth, extinguished Yesugei brand cigarettes on my skin, but only cut me superficially, to demon-strate that they could and would. Then they had other men come in to sterilize and dress the wounds. Once in a while, a gowned doctor with a Slavic face came to the cell and gave me a thorough, probing medical examination.

It was during one of the doctor's examinations that I elected to reveal myself as a government spy. As the doctor was examining me, I allowed my hair—stiff and greasy with dirt—to fall away from the nape of my neck. I knew instantly that he had taken the bait. I felt his fingers press into the area around the subcutaneous device, feeling for the hard-edged component lodged under the skin.

"What is this?"

"What is what?" I asked, all innocence.

"There's something under your skin."

They took me back to the interrogation room. My hair was shaved and my neck swabbed. The Slavic doctor dithered over the medical tools on the shelves until he found the bundle he wanted. He brought the instruments onto the table, unrolling the towel so that I could see what lay in store for me. When he was done, the implant was placed on a piece of clean towel in front of me. It was bloodied, with bits of whitish flesh still at-tached to its feelerlike input probes.

"Looks like government," someone said.

I did not admit to it immediately; that would have made them rightfully suspicious. It was a matter of judging the mo-ment, making my confession appear natural, rather than a scripted event.

In hindsight, I wish that I had arranged my confession sooner.

I was brought to a different room. There was a window in the wall, before which I was encouraged to sit. A clamp was fitted around my eyes so that I could not look away. The doctor dripped some agent into my eyes that had the effect of paralyzing the lids, preventing me from blinking. When the lights came on in the room on the other side of the window, I found myself looking at Goyo.

He was upside down, suspended in a sling, rotated on his back in the manner that horses are prepared for veterinary work. The sling was supported from a heavy white framework mounted on trolley wheels. Goyo's legs had been bound together in pairs using thick adhesive material. Even his head and neck had been braced into position using cushioned supports and clamps. A leathery girth strap enclosed his waist, preventing him from thrashing around. His abdominal region, between fore and hind limbs, had been shaved to the skin. A white sheet, not much larger than a towel, had been draped over part of that shaven area. There was a red stain in the middle of the sheet, where it formed a depression.

Goyo's eye, the one that I could see, was white and wild and brimming with fear.

Qilian walked into the room. He was dressed as I remembered him from our encounter on the *BK,* except that his hands and forearms were now gloved. The gloves had a heavy, martial look to them, with curved steel talons on the ends of the fingers. He stopped next to Goyo, one hand resting on the frame, the other stroking my pony's neck, as if he sought to placate him. When he spoke, his voice came through a microphone.

"We think we know who you are, but some corroboration would be welcome. What is your operational code name? To which section are you assigned? Are you one of the Thirteen?"

My mouth had turned dry. I said nothing.

"Very well," Qilian continued, as if he had expected as much. He reached over and whisked the white sheet away from

Goyo's abdomen. There was a wound there, a red sucking hole wide enough to plunge a fist through.

"No," I said, trying to break free of the straps that bound me to the chair.

"Before you arrived," Qilian said, "certain surgical preparations were made. A number of ribs have already been removed. They can be put back, of course, but their absence now means that there is an unobstructed path through to your pony's heart."

With his right hand, he reached into the wound. He frowned, concentrating on the task. He delved in slowly, cautiously. Goyo responded by thrashing against his restraints, but it was to no more avail than my own efforts. In a short while, Qilian's entire fist was hidden. He pushed deeper, encountering resistance. Now the fist and fully half of his forearm were gone. He adjusted his posture, leaning in so that his chest was braced against Goyo's shoulder. He pushed deeper, until only the top extremity of the glove remained visible.

"I am touching his beating heart now," Qilian said, looking directly at me. "He's a strong one, no doubt about that. A fine pony, from good Mongol stock. But I am stronger, at least when I have my hand on his heart. You don't think I can stop it beating? I assure you I can. Would you like to see?" The expression on his face altered to one of concentrated effort, little veins bulging at the side of his temple. Goyo thrashed with renewed energy. "Yes, he feels it now. He doesn't know what's happening, but a billion years of dumb evolution tells him something's not right. I don't doubt that the pain is excruciating, at least in animal terms. Would you like me to stop?"

The words spilled out, feeling like a genuine confession. "I am Yellow Dog. I am a government operative, one of the Thirteen."

"Yes, we thought you were Yellow Dog. We have the nonofficial cover list for all of the Thirteen, and we know that Ariunaa Bocheng is a name you've used before, when posing as a journalist." He broke off, took a deep breath, and seemed to redouble his efforts. "But it's good to get it from the horse's mouth, so to speak."

"Stop now."

"Too late. I've already started."

"You said you'd stop," I replied, screaming out the words. "You promised you'd stop!"

"I said nothing of the sort. I said the ribs could be put back. That remains the case."

In an instant, Goyo stopped thrashing. His eye was still open, but all of a sudden there was nothing behind it.

———

Several weeks later—I could not say precisely how many—Qilian sat opposite me with his big hairy hands clasped in silent contemplation. The documents on his desk were kept in place by grisly paperweights: little plinth-mounted bones and bottled, shrunken things in vinegary solution. There were swords and ceremonial knives on the wall, framing a familiar reproduction watercolor showing the landing of the invasion fleet on Japanese soil.

"You were good," he said eventually. "I'll give you that. My men genuinely thought they'd hit bottom when they got you to confess to being the journalist. It was a surprise to all concerned when that identity turned out to be a cover."

"I'm glad I provided you with some amusement," I said.

"If it hadn't been for that implant, we might never have known. Your people really should give some thought into making those things less detectable."

"My people?" I asked. "The last time I checked, we were all working for the same government."

"I don't doubt that's how it feels in New High Karakorum. Out here, it's a different story. In case you hadn't realized, this is a special administrative volume. It's part of the empire, but only in a very tenuous, politically ambiguous sense. They want what we can give them—raw materials, cheaply synthesized chemicals, mass-produced low-bulk consumer goods—but they don't want to think too hard about what we have to do to keep that river of commerce flowing. Laws have to be bent here, because otherwise there'd *be* no here. Look out the window, Yellow Dog."

Visible through the partially shuttered window of his office, a good four or five *li* below, was a brutal, wintery landscape of stained ice, reaching all the way to the horizon. The sky was a rose pink, shading to midnight blue at the top of the window. Cutting through it along a diagonal was the twinkling, sicklelike curve of a planetary ring system. Canyon-deep fissures cracked the surface, leaking feathery quills of yellow-white steam into the thin, poisonous atmosphere of that windswept sky. Here and there, an elbow of splintered rock broke the surface. There were no fixed communities on the moon. Instead, immense spiderlike platforms, mounted on six or eight intricate jointed legs, picked their way across the ever-shifting terrain in awesome slow motion. The platforms varied in size, but at the very least each supported a cluster of squat civic buildings, factories, refineries, and spacecraft handling facilities. Some of the platforms had deployed drilling rigs or cables into the fissures, sucking chemical nourishment from under the icy crust. A number were connected together by long, dangling wires, along which I made out the tiny, suspended forms of cable cars, moving from platform to platform.

"It's very pretty," I said.

"It's a hellhole, frankly. Only three planets in the entire volume are even remotely amenable to terraforming, and not one of those three is on track for completion inside five hundred years. We'll be lucky if any of them are done before the Founder's two thousandth anniversary, let alone the thousandth. Most of the eighty million people under my stewardship live in domes and tunnels, with only a few *alds* of soil or glass between them and a horrible, choking death." He unclasped his hands in order to run a finger across one of his desktop knickknacks. "It's not much of an existence, truth be told. But that doesn't mean we don't have an economy that needs fueling. We have jobs. We have vacancies for skilled labor. Ma-chines do our drilling, but the machines need to be fixed and programmed by *people,* down at the cutting face. We pay well, for those prepared to work for us."

"And you come down hard on those who displease you."

"Local solutions to local problems, that's our mantra. You wouldn't understand, cozied up in the middle of the empire. You pushed the dissidents and troublemakers out to the edge and left us to worry about them." He tapped a finger against his desk. "Nestorian Christians, Buddhists, Islamists. It's a thou-sand years since we crushed them, and they *still* haven't got over it. Barely a week goes by without some regressive, funda-mentalist element stirring up trouble, whether it's sabotage of one of our industrial facilities or a terrorist attack against the cit-izenship. And yet you sit there in New High Karakorum and shake your heads in disgust when we have the temerity to im-plement even the mildest security measures."

"I wouldn't call mass arrests, show trials, and public execu-tions 'mild,' " I said tartly.

"Then try living here."

"I get the impression that's not really an option. Unless you mean living in prison, for the rest of my life, or until NHK sends an extraction team."

Qilian made a pained expression. "Let's be clear. You aren't my enemy. Quite the contrary. You are now an honored guest of the Kuchlug special administrative volume. I regret what happened earlier, but if you'd admitted your true identity, none of that would have been necessary." He folded his arms behind his neck and leaned back in his chair with a creak of leather. "We've got off on the wrong footing here, you and I. But how are we supposed to feel when the empire sends undercover agents snooping into our territory? And not only that, but agents who persist in asking such puzzling questions?" He looked at me with sudden, sharp intensity, as if my entire future hung on my response to what he was about to say. "Just what *is* it about the phantoms that interests you so much, Yellow Dog?"

"Why should you worry about my interest in a phenomenon that doesn't exist?" I countered.

"Do you believe that, after what you saw on the *Burkhan Khaldun*?"

"I can only report what I saw. It would not be for me to make inferences."

"But still."

"Why are we discussing this, Commander Qilian?"

"Because I'm intrigued. Our perception was that NHK probably knew a lot more about the phenomenon than we did. Your arrival suggests otherwise. They sent you on an intelligence-gathering mission, and the thrust of your inquiry indicates that you are at least as much in the dark as we are, if not more so."

"I can't speak for my superiors."

"No, you can't. But it seems unlikely that they'd have risked sending a valued asset into a trouble spot like Kuchlug without very good reason. Which, needless to say, is deeply alarming. We thought the core had the matter under control. Clearly, they don't. Which only makes the whole issue of the phantoms even more vexed and troubling."

"What do you know?"

He laughed. "You think I'm going to tell you, just like that?"

"You've as much as admitted that this goes beyond any petty political differences that might exist between NHK and Kuchlug. Let me report back to my superiors. I'll obtain their guarantee that there'll be a two-way traffic in intelligence." I nodded firmly. "Yes, we misjudged this one. I should never have come under deep cover. But we were anxious not to undermine your confidence in us by revealing the depth of our ignorance on the phenomenon. I assure you that in the future everything will be aboveboard and transparent. We can set up a bilateral investigative team, pooling the best experts from here and back home."

"That easy, eh? We just shake hands and put it all behind us? The deception on your part, the torture on ours?"

I shrugged. "You had your methods. I had mine."

Qilian smiled slightly. "There's something you need to know. Two days ago—not long after we dug that thing out of you—we did in fact send a communiqué to NHK. We informed them that one of their agents was now in our safekeeping, that she was being more than helpful in answering our questions, and that we would be happy to return her at the earliest opportunity."

"Go on."

"They told us that there was no such agent. They denied knowledge of either Ariunaa Bocheng or an operative named Yellow Dog. They made no demands for you to be returned, although they did say that if you were handed over, you'd be of 'interest' to them. Do you know what this means?" When I refrained from answering—though I knew precisely what it meant—Qilian continued. "You've been disavowed, Yellow Dog. Left out in he cold, like a starving mongrel."

His men came for me again, several days later. I was taken to a pressurized boarding platform, a spindly structure cantilevered out from the side of the government building. A cable car was waiting, a dull gray, bulbous-ended cylinder swaying gently against its restraints. The guards pushed me aboard, then slammed the airtight door, before turning a massive wheel to lock it shut. Qilian was already aboard the car, sitting in a dimpled leather chair with one leg crossed over the other. He wore huge fur-lined boots equipped with vicious spurs.

"A little trip, I thought," he said, by way of welcome, indicating the vacant seat opposite his.

The cable car lurched into motion. After reaching the limit of the boarding area, it passed through a long glass airlock and then dropped sickeningly, plunging down so far that it descended under the lowest level of buildings and factory structures perched on the platform. One of the huge, skeletal legs was rising toward us, the foot raised as if it intended to stomp

down on the fragile little cable car. Yet just when it seemed we
were doomed, the car began to climb again, creaking and swaying. Qilian was looking at something through a pair of tiny
binoculars, some piece of equipment—a probe or drill head, I
presumed—being winched up from the surface into the underside of the platform.

"Is there a point to this journey?" I asked.

He lowered the binoculars and returned them to a leather
case on his belt. "Very much so. What I will show you constitutes a kind of test. I would advise you to be on your guard
against the obvious."

The cable car slid across the fractured landscape of the
moon, traversing dizzyingly wide crevasses, dodging geysers,
skimming past tilted rockfaces that seemed on the verge of
toppling over at any moment. We rose and descended several
times, on each occasion passing over one of the walking platforms. Now and then, there was an interruption while we were
switched to a different line, before once more plunging down
toward the surface. After more than half an hour of this—just
when my stomach was beginning to settle into the rhythm—we
came to a definite halt on what was in all respects just another
boarding platform, attended by a familiar retinue of guards and
technical functionaries. Qilian and I disembarked, with his spurs
clicking against the cleated metal flooring. With a company of
guards for escort, we walked into the interior of the platform's
largest building. The entire place had an oily ambience, rum-
bling with the vibration of distant drilling processes.

"It's a cover," Qilian said, as if he had read my thoughts.
"We keep the machines turning, but this is the one platform that
doesn't have a useful production yield. It's a study facility instead."

"For studying what?"

"Whatever we manage to recover, basically."

Deep in the bowels of the platform, at a level that must
have meant they were only just above the underside, was a
huge holding tank that—so Qilian informed me—was designed

to contain the unrefined liquid slurry that would ordinarily have been pumped up from under the ice. In this platform, the tank had been drained and equipped with power and lighting. The entire space had been partitioned into about a dozen ceilingless rooms, each of which appeared to contain a collection of garbage, arranged within the cells of a printed grid laid out on the floor. Some of the cells held sizable clusters of junk; others were empty. Benches arranged around the edges of the cells were piled with bits of twinkly rubbish, along with an impressive array of analysis tools and recording devices.

It looked as if it should have been a literal hive of activity, but the entire place was deserted.

"You want to tell me what I'm looking at here?"

Qilian indicated a ladder. "Go down and take a look for yourself. Examine anything that takes your fancy. Use any tools you feel like. Look in the notebooks and data files. Rummage. Break stuff. You won't be punished if you do."

"This is phantom technology, isn't it? You've recovered pieces of alien ships." I said this in a kind of awed whisper, as if I hardly dared believe it myelf.

"Draw whatever conclusion you see fit. I shall be intensely interested in what you have to say."

I started down the ladder. I had known from the moment I saw the relics that I would be unable to resist. "How long have I got? Before I'm judged to have failed this test, or whatever it is."

"Take your time," he said, smiling. "But don't take *too* much."

There seemed little point agonizing over which room to start with, assuming I had the time to examine more than one. The one I chose had the usual arrangement of grid, junk, and equipment benches. Lights burned from a rack suspended overhead. I stepped into the grid, striding over blank squares until she arrived at a promising little clump of mangled parts, some of them glittery, some of them charred to near blackness. Gingerly, I picked up one of the bits. It was a curving section of metallic foil, ragged along one edge, much lighter and stiffer than I felt it had any right to be. I tested the edge against a finger and drew a bead of blood. No markings or detail of any kind. I placed it back down on the grid and examined another item. Heavier this time, solid in my hands, like a piece of good carved wood. Flowing, scroll-like green patterning on one convex surface: a suggestion of script, or a fragmented part of some script, in a language I did not recognize. I returned it to the grid and picked up a jagged, bifurcated thing like a very unwieldy sword or spearhead, formed in some metallic red material that appeared mirror-smooth and untarnished. In my hands, the thing had an unsettling buzzing quality, as if there was still something going on inside it. I picked up another object: a dented blue-green box, embossed with dense geometric patterns, cross-woven into one another in a manner that made my head hurt. The lid of the box opened to reveal six egglike white ovals, packed into spongy black material. There were six distinct spiral symbols painted onto the ovals, in another language that I did not recognize.

I perused more objects in the grid, then moved to the benches, where more items were laid out for inspection.

I moved into one of the adjoining rooms. There was something different about the degree of organization this time. The grid was the same, but the objects in it had been sorted into rough groupings. In one corner cell was a pile of spiky, metallic red pieces that obviously had something in common with the swordlike object I had examined in the other room. In another lay a cluster of dense, curved pieces with fragmented green patterning on each. Each occupied cell held a similar collection of vaguely related objects.

I examined another room, but soon felt that I had seen enough to form a ready opinion. The various categories of relic clearly had little in common. If they had all originated from the phantoms—either wrecked or damaged or attacked as they passed through the Infrastructure—then there was only one conclusion to be drawn. There was more than one type of phantom, which, in turn, meant there was more than one kind of alien.

We were not just dealing with one form of intruder. Judging by the number of filled cells, there were dozens—many dozens—of different alien technologies at play.

I felt the hairs on the back of my neck bristle. Our probes and instruments had swept the galaxy clean and still we had found no hint of anyone else out there. But these rooms said otherwise. Somehow or other, we had managed to miss the evidence of numerous other galaxy-faring civilizations, all of which were at least as technologically advanced as the Mongol Expansion.

Other empires, somehow coexisting with ours!

I was ready to return to Qilian, but, at the last moment, as I prepared to ascend the ladder, something held me back. It had all been too simple. Anyone with a pair of eyes in their head would have arrived at the same conclusion as I had. Qilian had said it would be a test, and that I must pass it.

It had been too easy so far.

Therefore, I must have missed something.

When we were back on the cable car, nosing down to the geysering surface, Qilian stroked a finger against his chin and watched me with an intense, snakelike fascination.

"You returned to the rooms."

"Yes."

"Something made you go back, when it looked as if you'd already finished."

"It wouldn't have been in my interests to fail you."

There was a gleam in his eye. "So what was it, Yellow Dog, that made you hesitate?"

"A feeling that I'd missed something. The obvious inference was that the collection implied the presence of more than one intruding culture, but you didn't need me to tell you that."

"No," he acknowledged.

"So there had to be something else. I didn't know what. But when I went back into the second room, something flashed through my mind. I knew I had seen something in there before, even if it had been in a completely different context."

I could not tell if he was pleased or disappointed. "Continue."

"The green markings on some of the relics. They meant nothing to me at first, but I suppose my subconscious must have picked up on something even then. They were fragments of something larger, which I'd seen before."

"Which was?"

"Arabic writing," I told him.

"Many people would be surprised to hear there was such a thing."

"If they knew their history, they'd know that the Arabs had a written language. An elegant one, too. It's just that most people outside of academic departments won't have ever seen it, any more than they know what Japanese or the Roman alphabet looks like."

"But you, on the other hand—"

"In my work for the khanate, I was obliged to compile dossiers on dissident elements within the empire. Some of the Islamist factions still use a form of Arabic for internal communications."

He sniffed through his nostrils, looking at me with his penetrating blue eyes. The cable car creaked and swayed. "It took my analysis experts eight months to recognize that that lettering had a human origin. The test is over; you have passed. But would you care to speculate on the meaning of your observation? Why are we finding Arabic on phantom relics?"

"I don't know."

"But indulge me."

"It can only mean that there's an Islamist faction out there that we don't know about. A group with independent spacefaring capability, the means to use the Infrastructure despite all the access restrictions already in place."

"And the other relics? Where do they fit in?"

"I don't know."

"If I told you that, in addition to items we consider to be of unambiguously alien origin, we'd also found scraps of other vanished or obscure languages—or at least, scripts and symbols connected to them—what would you say?"

I admitted that I had no explanation for how such a thing might be possible. It was one thing to allow the existence of a secret enclave of technologically advanced Islamists, however improbable that might have been. It was quite another to posit the existence of *many* such enclaves, each preserving some vanished or atrophied branch of human culture.

"Here is what's going to happen." He spoke the words as if there could be no possibility of dissent on my behalf. "As has already been made clear, your old life is over, utterly and finally. But there is still much that you can do to serve the will of Heaven. The khanate has only now taken a real interest in the phantoms, whereas we have been alert to the phenomenon for many years. If you care about the security of the empire, you will see the sense in working with Kuchlug."

"You mean, join the team analyzing those relics?"

"As a matter of fact, I want you to lead it." He smiled; I could not tell if the idea had just occurred to him, or whether it had always been at the back of his mind. "You've already demonstrated the acuteness of your observations. I have no doubt that you will continue to uncover truths that the existing team has overlooked."

"I can't just . . . take over, like that."

He looked taken aback. "Why ever not?"

"A few days ago, I was your prisoner," I said. "Not long before that, you were torturing me. They've no reason to suddenly start trusting me, just on your say-so."

"You're wrong about that," he said, fingering one of the knives strapped across his chest. "They'll trust who I tell them to trust, absolutely and unquestioningly."

"Why?" I asked.

"Because that's how we do things around here."

So it was. I joined Qilian's investigative team, immersing my-self in the treasure trove of data and relics his people had pieced together in my absence. There was, understandably, a degree of reluctance to accept my authority. But Qilian dealt with that in the expected manner, and slowly, those around me came to a pragmatic understanding that it was either work with me or suffer the consequences.

Relics and fragments continued to fall into our hands. Sometimes the ships that intruded into the Infrastructure were damaged, as if the passage into our territory had been a violent one. Often, the subsequent encounter with one of our ships was enough to shake them to pieces, or at the very least dislodge major components. The majority of these shards vanished with-out a trace into the implacable machinery of the Infrastructure. Even if the *khorkoi* apparatus was beginning to fail, it was still more than capable of attending to the garbage left behind by its users. But occasionally, pieces lingered in the system (as if the walls had indigestion?), waiting to be swept up by Qilian's ships, and eventually brought home to this moon.

As often as not, though, it was a trivial matter to classify the consignments, requiring only a glance at their contents. The work became so routine, in fact—and the quantity of consign-ments so high—that eventually I had no choice but to take a step back from hands-on analysis. I assembled six teams and let them get on with it, requiring that they report back to me only when they had something of note: a new empire, or something odd from one of those we already knew about.

That was when the golden egg fell into our hands. It was in the seventh month of my service under Qilian, and I immedi-ately knew that it originated from a culture not yet known to us. Perhaps it was a ship, or part of one. The outer hull was almost entirely covered in a quilt of golden platelets, overlapping in the manner of fish scales. The only parts not covered by the platelets were the dark apertures of sensors and thruster ports, and a small, eye-shaped area on one side of the teardrop that we quickly identified as a door.

Fearing that it might damage the other relics if it exploded under our examinations, I ordered that the analysis of the egg take place in a different part of the mining structure. Soon, though, my concern shifted to the welfare of the egg's occupants. We knew that there were beings inside it, even if we could not be sure if they were human. Scans had illuminated ghostly structures inside the hull: the intestinal complexity of propulsion subsystems, fuel lines, and tanks packed ingeniously tight, the fatty tissue of insulating layers, the bony divisions of armored partitions, the cartilaginous detailing of furniture and life-support equipment. There were even ranks of couches, with eight crew still reclining in them. Dead or in suspended animation, it was impossible to tell. All we could see was their bones, a suggestion of humanoid skeletons, and there was no movement of those bones to suggest respiration.

We got the door open easily enough. It was somewhat like breaking into a safe, but once we had worked out the underlying mechanism—and the curiously alien logic that underpinned its design—it presented no insurmountable difficulties. Gratifyingly, there was only a mild gust of equalizing pressure when the door hinged wide, and none of the sensors arrayed around the egg detected any harmful gases. As far as we could tell, it was filled with an oxygen-nitrogen mix only slightly different from that aboard our own ships.

"What now?" Qilian asked, fingering the patch of hair beneath his lip.

"We'll send machines aboard now," I replied. "Just to be safe, in case there are any booby traps inside."

He placed a heavy, thick-fingered hand on my shoulder. "What say we skip the machines and just take a look inside ourselves?" His tone was playful. "Not afraid, are we, Yellow Dog?"

"Of course not," I answered.

"There's no need to be. I'll go in first, just in case there *are* surprises."

We walked across the floor, through the cordon of sensors, to the base of the attenuated metal staircase that led to the open door. The robots scuttled out of the way. My staff exchanged concerned glances, aware that we were deviating from a protocol we had spent weeks thrashing out to the last detail. I waved down their qualms.

Inside, as we already knew from the scans, the egg was compartmented into several small chambers, with the crew in the middle section. The rear part contained most of the propulsion and life-support equipment. Up front, in the sharp end, was what appeared to be a kind of pressurized cargo space. The egg still had power, judging by the presence of interior lighting, although the air aboard it was very cold and still. It was exceedingly cramped, requiring me to duck and Qilian to stoop almost double. To pass from one compartment to the next, we had to crawl on our hands and knees through doors that were barely large enough for children. The external door was larger than the others, presumably because it had to admit a crew member wearing a spacesuit or some other encumbrance.

Qilian was the first to see the occupants. I was only a few seconds behind him, but those seconds stretched to years as I heard his words.

"They are aliens after all, Yellow Dog. Strapped in their seats like little pale monkeys. I can see why we thought they might be human . . . but they're not, not at all. So much for the theory that every empire must represent a human enclave, no matter how incomprehensible the artifacts or script."

"That was never my theory, sir. But it's good to have it dismissed."

"They have masks on. I can see their faces, but I'd like a better look."

Still on my knees, I said, "Be careful, sir."

"They're dead, Yellow Dog. Stiff and cold as mummies."

By the time I reached Qilian, he had removed one of the intricate masks from the face of his chosen alien. In his hands, it was tiny, like a delicate accessory belonging to a doll. He put it down carefully, placing it on the creature's lap. The alien was dressed in a quilted gold uniform, cross-buckled into the couch. It was the size of an eight-year-old child, but greatly skinnier in build, its torso and limbs elongated to the point where it resembled a smaller creature that had been stretched. Though its hands were gloved, the layout of the long, dainty-looking digits corresponded exactly to my own: four fingers and an opposed thumb, though each of the digits was uncommonly slender, such that I feared they might snap if we attempted to remove the gloves. Its head—the only part of it not covered by the suit—was delicate and rather beautiful, with huge, dark eyes set in patches of black fur. Its nose and mouth formed one snoutlike feature, suggestive of a dog or cat. It had sleek, intricate ears, running back along the sides of its head. Save for the eye patches, and a black nose at the tip of the snout, its skin varied between a pale buff or off-white.

The alien's hands rested on a pair of small control consoles hinged to the sides of the couch; the consoles were flat surfaces embossed with golden ridges and studs, devoid of markings. A second console angled down from the ceiling to form a blank screen at the creature's eye level. The other seven occupants all had similar amenities. There were no windows, and no controls or readouts in the orthodox sense. The aliens were all alike, with nothing on their uniforms to indicate rank or function. From what little I could see of their faces, the other seven were identical to the one we had unmasked.

I suppose I should have felt awed: here I was, privileged to be one of the first two people in history to set eyes on true aliens. Instead, all I felt was a kind of creeping sadness, and a tawdry, unsettling feeling that I had no business in this place of death.

"I've seen these things before," Qilian said, a note of disbelief in his words.

"These aliens, sir? But this is the first time we've seen them."

"I don't mean that. I mean, isn't there something about them that reminds you of something?"

"Something of what, sir?"

He ignored my question. "I also want this vehicle stripped down to the last bolt, or whatever it is that holds it together. If we can hack into its navigation system, find an Infrastructure map, we may be able to work out where they came from, and how the hell we've missed them until now."

I looked at the embossed gold console and wondered what our chances were of hacking into anything, let alone the navigation system.

"And the aliens, sir? What should we do with them?"

"Cut them up. Find out what makes them tick." Almost as an afterthought, he added, "Of course, make sure they're dead first."

The aliens were not the greatest surprise contained in the egg, but we did not realize that until the autopsy was under way. Qilian and I observed the procedure from a viewing gallery, looking down on the splayed and dissected creature. With great care, bits of it were being removed and placed on sterile metal trays. The interior organs were dry and husklike, reinforcing the view that the aliens were in a state of mummification: perhaps (we speculated) some kind of suspended animation to be used in emergency situations. But the function and placement of the organs were all too familiar; we could have been watching the autopsy of a monkey and not known the difference. The alien even had a tail, lightly striped in black and white; it had been contained within an extension of the clothing, tucked back into a cavity within the seat.

That the creatures must have been intelligent was not open to dispute, but it was still dismaying, when they were cut up, to learn how human their brains looked. Small, certainly, yet with clear division of brain hemispheres, frontal and temporal lobes, and so on. Yet the real shock lay in the blood. It was not neces-

sarily a surprise to find that it had DNA, or even that its DNA
appeared to share the same protein coding alphabet as ours.
There were (I was led to believe) sound arguments for how that
state of affairs might have arisen independently, due to it being
the most efficient possible replicating/coding system, given the
thermodynamic and combinative rules of carbon-based bio-
chemistry. That was all well and good. But it entirely failed to
explain what they found when they compared the alien's chromosomes to ours. More on a whim than anything else, they had
tested the alien blood with human-specific probes and found
that chromosomes 1 and 3 of the alien were homeologous to
human chromosomes 3, 9, 14, and 21. There were also unex-
pectedly strong signals in the centromeric regions of the alien
chromosomes when probed for human chromosomes 7 and 19.
In other words, the alien DNA was not merely similar to ours;
it was shockingly, confoundingly, alike.

The only possible explanation was that we were related.

Qilian and I were trying to work out the ramifications of
this when news came in from the team examining the pod. Uugan—my deputy—came scuttling into the autopsy viewing room,
rubbing sweaty hands together. "We've found something," he
said, almost tongue-tied with excitement.

Qilian showed him the hot-off-the-press summary from the
genetics analysis. "So have we. Those aliens aren't alien. They
came from the same planet we did. I *thought* they looked like
lemurs. That's because they *are.*"

Uugan had as much trouble dealing with that as we did.
I could almost hear the gears meshing in his brain, working
through the possibilities. "Aliens must have uplifted lemur stock
in the deep past, using genetic engineering to turn them into intelligent, tool-using beings." He raised a finger. "Or, other aliens
spread the same genetic material on more than one world. If that
were the case, these lemurs need not be from Greater Mongolia
after all."

"What news do you have for us?" Qilian asked, smiling
slightly at Uugan's wild theorizing.

"Come to the egg, please. It will be easier if I show you."

We hastened after Uugan, both of us refraining from any speculation as to what he might have found. As it happened, I do not think either of us would have guessed correctly.

In the sharp end of the egg, the investigators had uncovered a haul of cargo, much of which had now been removed and laid out on the floor for inspection. I glanced at some of the items as we completed the walk to the pod, recognizing bits and pieces from some of the other cultures we already knew about. Here was a branching, sharp-tipped metallic red thing, like an instrument for impaling. Here was a complexly manufactured casket that opened to reveal ranks of nested white eggs, hard as porcelain. Here was a curving section of razor-sharp foil, polished to an impossible luster. Dozens more relics from dozens of other known empires, and still dozens more that represented empires of which we knew nothing.

"They've been collecting things, just like us," I said.

"Including this," Uugan said, drawing my attention to the object that now stood at the base of the egg.

It was the size and shape of a large urn, golden in construction, surfaced with bas-relief detailing, with eight curved green windows set into its upper surface. I peered closer and rested a hand against the urn's throbbing skin. Through the windows burbled a dark liquid. In the dark liquid, something pale floated. I made out the knobbed ridge of a spine, a backbone pressing through flawless skin. It was a person, a human, a man judging by his musculature, curled into fetal position. I could only see the back of his head: bald and waxy, scribed with fine white scars. Ridged cables dangled in the fluid, running toward what I presumed was a breathing apparatus, now hidden.

Qilian looked through one of the other windows. After a lengthy silence, he straightened himself and nodded. "Do you think he was their prisoner?"

"No way to tell, short of thawing him and out and seeing what he has to say on the matter," Uugan said.

"Do what you can," Qilian told Uugan. "I would very, very much like to speak to this gentleman." Then he leaned in closer, as if what he was about to say was meant only for Uugan's ears. "This would be an excellent time not to make a mistake, if you understand my meaning."

I do not believe that Qilian's words had any effect on Uugan; he was either going to succeed or not, and the difference between the two outcomes depended solely on the nature of the problem, not his degree of application to the task. As it happened, the man was neither dead nor brain dead, and his revival proved childishly simple. Many weeks were spent in preparation before the decisive moment, evaluating all known variables. When the day came, Uugan's intervention was kept to a minimum: he merely opened the preservation vat, extracted the man from his fluid cocoon, and (it must be said, with fastidious care) removed the breathing apparatus. Uugan was standing by with all the tools of emergency medical intervention at his disposal, but no such assistance was required. The man simply convulsed, drew in several gulping breaths, and then settled into a normal respiratory pattern. But he had yet to open his eyes, or signal any awareness in the change of his surroundings. Scans measured brain activity, but at a level indicative of coma rather than consciousness. The same scans also detected a network of microscopic machines in the man's brain and much of his wider nervous system. Though we could not see these implants as clearly as those we had harvested from the lemur, they were clearly derived from a different technology.

Where had he come from? What did he know of the phantoms?

For weeks, it appeared that we would have no direct answer to these questions. There was one thing, one clue, but we almost missed it. Many days after the man's removal from the vat, one of Uugan's technicians was working alone in the laboratory where we kept our new guest. The lights were dimmed and the technician was using an ultraviolet device to sterilize some culture dishes. By chance, the technician noticed something glowing on the side of the man's neck. It turned out to be a kind of tattoo, a sequence of horizontal symbols that was invisible except under ultraviolet stimulation.

I was summoned to examine the discovery. What I found was a word in Arabic, *Altair,* meaning eagle, and a string of digits, twenty in all, composed of nine numerical symbols, and the tenth, what the pre-Mongol scholars called in their dead language *theca* or *circulus* or *figura nihili,* the round symbol that means, literally, nothing. Our mathematics incorporates no such entity. I have heard it said that there is something in the Mongol psyche that abhors the very concept of absence. Our mathematics cannot have served us badly, for upon its back we have built a five-hundred-year-old galactic empire—even if the *khorkoi* gave us the true keys to that kingdom. But I have also heard it said that our system would have been much less cumbersome had we adopted that Arabic symbol for nothing.

No matter; it was what the symbols told me that was important, not what they said about our choice of number system. In optimistic anticipation that he would eventually learn to speak, and that his tongue would turn out to be Arabic, I busied myself with preparations. For a provincial thug, Qilian had a library as comprehensive as anything accessible from NHK. I retrieved primers on Arabic, most of which were tailored for use by security operatives hoping to crack Islamist terror cells, and set about trying to become an interpreter.

But when the man awoke—which was weeks later, by which time it felt as if I had been studying those primers for half my life—all my preparations might as well have been for nothing. He was sitting up in bed, monitored by machines and watched by hidden guards, when I came into the room. Aside from the technician who had first noticed his return to consciousness, the man had seen no other human being since his arrival.

I closed the door and walked to his bedside. I sat down next to him, adjusting the blue silk folds of my skirt decorously.

"I am Yellow Dog," I told him in Arabic, speaking the words slowly and carefully. "You are among friends. We want to help you, but we do not know much about you."

He looked at me blankly. After a few seconds I added: "Can you understand me?"

His expression and response told me everything I needed to know. He spoke softly, emitting a string of words that sounded superficially Arabic without making any sense to me at all. By then I had listened to enough recordings to know the difference between Arabic and baby talk, and all I was hearing was gibberish.

"I'm sorry," I said. "I do not understand you. Perhaps if we started again, slower this time." I touched a hand to my breast. "I am Yellow Dog. Who are you?"

He answered me then, and maybe it was his name, but it could just as easily have been a curt refusal to answer my question. He started looking agitated, glancing around the room as if it was only now that he was paying due regard to his surroundings. He fingered the thin cloth of his blanket and rubbed at the bandage on his arm where a catheter had been inserted. Once more I told him my name and urged him to respond in kind, but whatever he said this time was not the same as his first answer.

"Wait," I said, remembering something, a contingency I had hoped not to have to use. I reached into my satchel and retrieved a printout. I held the filmy paper before me and read slowly from the adhan, the Muslim call to prayer.

My pronunciation must still not have been perfect, because I had to repeat the words three or four times before some flicker of recognition appeared behind his eyes and he began to echo what I was saying. Yet even as he spoke the incantation, there was a puzzlement in his voice, as if he could not quite work out why we should be engaged in this odd parlor game.

"So I was half right," I said, when he had fallen silent again, waiting for me to say something. "You know something of Islamic culture. But you do not understand anything I say, except when I speak words that have not been permitted to change in fifteen centuries, and even then you only just grasp what I mean to say." I smiled, not in despair, but in rueful acknowledgment that the journey we had to make would be much longer and more arduous than I had imagined. Continuing in Mongol, so that he could hear my tongue, I said: "But at least we have something, my friend, a stone to build on. That's better than nothing, isn't it?"

"Do you understand me now?" he asked, in flawless Mongol.

I was astonished, quite unable to speak. Now that I had grown accustomed to his baldness and pallor, I could better appreciate those aspects of his face that I had been inclined to overlook before. He had delicate features, kind and scholarly. I had never been attracted to men in a sexual sense, and I could not say that I felt any such longing for this man. But I saw the sadness in his eyes, the homesick flicker that told me he was a long way from family and friends (such as I have never known, but can easily imagine), and I knew that I wished to help him.

"You speak our language," I said eventually, as if the fact of it needed stating.

"It is not a difficult one. What is your name? I caught something that sounded like 'filthy hound,' but that cannot have been correct."

"I was trying to speak Arabic. And failing, obviously. My name is Yellow Dog. It's a code, an operational identifier."

"Therefore not your real name."

"Ariunaa," I said softly. "I use it sometimes. But around here they call me Yellow Dog."

"Muhunnad," he said, touching his sternum.

"Muhunnad," I repeated. Then: "If you understood my name—or thought you understood it—why didn't you answer me until I spoke Mongolian? My Arabic can't be that bad, surely."

"You speak Arabic like someone who has only heard a whisper of a whisper of a whisper. Some of the words are almost recognizable, but they are like glints of gold in a stream." He offered me a smile, as if it hurt him to have to criticize. "You were doing your best. But the version of Arabic I speak is not the one you think you know."

"How many versions are there?"

"More than you realize, evidently." He paused. "I think I know where I am. We are inside the Mongol Expansion. We were on the same track until 659, by my calendar."

"What other calendar is there?"

"You count from the death of a warrior-deity; we count from the flight of the Prophet from Mecca. The year now is 1604 by the Caliphate's reckoning; 999 by your own, 2226 by the calendar of the United Nations. Really, we are quibbling over mere centuries. The Smiling Ones use a much older dating system, as they must. The—"

I interrupted him. "What are you talking about? You are an emissary from a previously hidden Islamic state, that is all. At some point in the five hundred years of the Mongol Expansion, your people must have escaped central control to establish a secret colony, or network of colonies, on the very edge of the Infrastructure."

"It is not like that, Ariunaa. Not like that at all." Then he leaned higher on the bed, like a man who had just remembered an urgent errand. "How exactly did I get here? I had not been tasked to gather intelligence on the Mongols, not this time around."

"The lemurs," I answered. "We found you with them."

I watched him shudder, as if the memory of something awful had only just returned. "You mean I was their prisoner, I think." Then he looked at me curiously. "Your questions puzzle me, Ariunaa. Our data on the Mongols was never of the highest quality, but we had always taken it for granted that you understood."

"Understood *what?*"

"The troubling nature of things," he said.

The cable car pitched down from the boarding platform, ducking beneath the base of the immense walking platform. After a short while, it came to an abrupt halt, swaying slightly. Qilian pulled out his binoculars and focused on a detail under the platform, between the huge, slowly moving machinery of the skeletal support legs.

"There," he said, passing me the binoculars.

I took them with trembling hands. I had been on my way to Muhunnad for one of our fruitless but not unpleasant conversational sessions, when Qilian's men had diverted me to the cable car platform.

"What am I supposed to be looking at?"

"Press the stud on the side."

I did so. Powerful gyroscopes made the binoculars twist in my hands, tracking and zooming in on a specific object, a thing hanging down from the underside like the weight on the end of a plumb line. I recalled now the thing I had seen the first time Qilian had accompanied me in the cable car, the thing that he had been examining with the binoculars. I had thought it was some kind of test probe or drilling gear being winched back into the platform. I saw now that I had been wrong.

I did need to see his face to know that I was looking at Muhunnad. He had been stuffed into a primitive spacesuit, blackened by multiple exposures to scorching heat and corrosive elements. They had him suspended from his feet, with his head nearest the ground. He was being lowered down toward one of those outgassing rifts in the surface of the Qing Shui moon.

"You can't be doing this," I said.

"If there was any other way," Qilian said, in a tone of utter reasonableness. "But clearly there isn't. He's been dragging his heels, giving us nothing. Spoke too soon early on, confided too much in you, and chose to clam up. Obviously, we can't have that." Qilian opened a walnut-veneered cabinet and took out a microphone. He clicked it on and tapped it against his knee before speaking. "Can you hear me, Muhunnad? I hope your view is as spectacular as ours. I am speaking from the cable car that you may be able to see to your right. We are about level with your present position, although you will soon be considerably lower than us."

"No," I said.

Qilian raised a calming hand. He hadn't even bothered to have me tied into the seat. "Do you hear that, Muhunnad? You still have an admirer." Then he said: "Lower the line, please. Take him to half his present elevation."

"Can you see that he's told you everything he knows?" I asked, tossing the binoculars against the floor.

"He's told us as little as he could get away with," Qilian replied, placing a hand over the end of the microphone to muffle his words. "We could go through the usual rigmarole of conventional interrogation, but I think this will prove much more effective."

"We'll learn far more from him alive than dead."

He looked at me pityingly. "You think I don't know that? Of course I'm not going to kill him. But very soon—unless he chooses to talk—he'll be wishing I did."

The winch dropped Muhunnad to within fifteen or twenty *alds* of the surface, just above the point where the outgassing material became opaque.

"I can hear you," a voice said over the cable car's speaker system. "But I have told you everything I intend to. Nothing you can do now will make any difference."

"We'll see, won't we," Qilian said. To me, confidingly, he said: "By now, he will be in extreme discomfort. You and I are fine, but we have the benefit of a functioning life-support system. His suit is damaged. At the moment, his primary concern is extreme cold, but that will not remain the case for very much longer. As he nears the fissure, it is heat that will begin to trouble him."

"You can tell the woman–Ariunaa–that I am sorry it was necessary to withold information from her," Muhunnad said. "Her kindness was appreciated. I think she is the only one of you with a heart."

"There's no need for me to tell her anything," Qilian replied. "She's listening in. Aren't you, Yellow Dog?" Somewhat to my surprise, he passed me the microphone. "Talk to him. Reason with your favorite prisoner, if you imagine it will help."

"Muhunnad," I said. "Listen to me now. I have no reason to lie to you. Qilian means what he says. He's going to put you through hell until he finds out what you know. I've seen him murder people already, just to get at the truth."

"I appreciate the concern for my welfare," he said, with a sincerity that cut me to the bone.

"Lower him to five *alds*," Qilian said.

———

Is it necessary to document all that happened to Muhunnad? I suppose not; the essential thing is that the pain eventually became intolerable and he began to tell Qilian some of the things my master was desirous of knowing.

What we learned was: Muhunnad was a pilot, a man surgically adapted for optimum control of a ship with extreme Infrastructure agility. His implants were part of the interface system by which he flew his vehicle. It turned out that Muhunnad's people had become aware of the breakdown of Infrastructure integrity many decades ago, long before it had come to our attention. The difference was, rather than pretending that the problem did not exist, or entrusting it to a single agent like myself, they had dedicated almost their entire state apparatus to finding a solution. Think of Qilian's research, multiplied by a thousand. There were countless men and women like Muhunnad, brave angels tasked with mapping the weak spots in the

Infrastructure, the points of leakage, and learning something of the other empires beginning to spill into their own. They knew enough about the properties of those weak points; enough to slip through them, gather intelligence, and still return home. The rate of attrition was still high. Muhunnad was a criminal, convicted of a crime that would have been considered petty in our own society, but normally merited the death penalty in his. In his case, he had been offered the chance to redeem himself, by becoming a pilot.

They knew about us. They had been intercepting our lost message packets for years, and had even found a couple of our ships with living crew. That was how they had learned Mongolian. They also knew about dozens of other empires, including the lemurs.

"They caught me," Muhunnad said, "as they catch any unwary traveler. They are to be feared."

"They look so harmless," Qilian answered.

"They are vicious beyond words. They are a hive society, with little sense of self. The beings you found, the dead ones, would have sacrificed themselves to ensure their cargo returned home intact. It did not mean that they did so out of any consideration for my well-being. But there are worse things than the lemurs out there. There are the beings we call the Smiling Ones. You will meet them sooner or later. They have been in space for millions of years, and their technology is only matched by their loathing for the likes of you and me."

"Tell us about your state," Qilian probed.

"We call it the Shining Caliphate. It is an empire encompassing seven thousand star systems, comprising twenty thousand settled worlds, half of which are of planet class or at least the size of major moons. A third of those worlds are terraformed or on the way to completion."

"You are lying. If an empire of that size already existed, we would have seen signs of it."

"That is because you are not looking in the right place. The Shining Caliphate is *here,* now, all around you. It occupied much the same volume as your own empire. It even has the same home world. You call it Greater Mongolia. We call it Earth."

"Lies!"

But I knew Muhunnad was not lying to us. I think it likely that even Qilian knew it, too. He was a brutal man, but not a stupid or unimaginative one. But I do not think he could bare to contemplate his place in a universe in which Muhunnad spoke the truth. Qilian was a powerful man, with an empire of his own on the very edge of the one he was meant to serve. If our empire was a map spread across a table, then he controlled more than could be covered by the palm of a hand. Yet if what Muhunnad said was correct, then that map was but one unexceptional page in a vast atlas, each page a dominion in its own right, of which our own was neither the most powerful nor the most ancient. Set against such immensity, Qilian controlled almost nothing. For a man like him, that realization would have been intolerable.

But perhaps I am crediting him with too much intelligence, too much imagination, and he was simply unable to grasp what Muhunnad was telling us.

What he *could* grasp, however, was an opportunity.

I was with them when we brought Muhunnad to the room where the couch had been prepared. I had heard of the existence of the couch, but this was my first sight of it. Even knowing its function, I could not help but see it as an instrument of torture. Muhunnad's reaction, to begin struggling against the guards who held him, showed that he saw the couch in similar terms. Behind the guards loomed white-coated doctors and technicians, including the Slav who had torn out my implant.

"This isn't to hurt you," Qilian said magnanimously. "It's to help you."

The couch was a skeletal white contraption, encumbered with pads and restraints and delicate hinged accessories that would fold over the occupant once they had been secured in place.

"I do not understand," Muhunnad said, although I think he did.

"We have studied your implants and deduced something of their function," Qilian said. "Not enough to learn everything about them, but enough to let you control one of our ships, instead of the one you were meant to fly."

"It will not work."

"No one is pretending it will be easy. But it is in your interests to do what you can to make it succeed. Help us navigate the Infrastructure—the way you do, finding the weak points and slipping through them—and we will let you return home."

"I do not believe you."

"You have no option but to believe me. If you cannot assist me in this matter, you will have concluded your usefulness to me. Given the trouble I would get into if New High Karakorum learned of your existence, I would have no option but to dispose of you."

"He means it," I said forcefully. "Help us fly the ships, Muhunnad. Whatever happens, it's better than staying here."

He looked at me as if I was the one thing in the universe he was willing to trust. Given all that had happened to him since leaving his people, it did not surprise me in the slightest.

"Plug him in," Qilian told the technicians. "And don't be too tender about it."

The name of the ship was the *River Volga*. She was half a *li* in length, her frontal stabilization spines suggesting the curving whiskers of a catfish. She had been a merchant vehicle once; later, she had been equipped for scouring the Parvan Tract for phantom relics, and, most recently, she had been hardened and weaponed for an exploratory role. She would carry six of us: Muhunnad, Qilian, Uugan, and two more members of the technical staff—their names were Jura and Batbayar—and myself. Next to her, identical in almost all respects, was the *Mandate of Heaven*. The only significant distinction between the two craft was that Muhunnad would be piloting the *River Volga,* while the *Mandate of Heaven* followed close behind, slaved to follow the same trajectory to within a fraction of an *ald.* The navigation and steering mechanisms of both ships had been upgraded to permit high-agility maneuvers, including reversals, close-proximity wall skimming, and suboptimal portal transits. It did not bear thinking about the cost of equipping those two ships, or where the funds had been siphoned from, but I supposed the citizens of the Kuchlug special administrative volume would be putting up with hardships for a little while longer.

We spent five days in shakedown tests before entering the Tract, scooting around the system, dodging planets and moons in high-gee swerves. During that time, Muhunnad's integration into the harness was slowly improved, more and more ship systems brought under his direct control, until he reported the utmost confidence in being able to handle the *River Volga* during Infrastructure flight.

"Are you sure?" I asked.

"Truly, Ariunaa. This ship feels as much a part of me as anything I ever flew in the Shining Caliphate."

"But indescribably less sophisticated."

"I would not wish to hurt your feelings. Given your resources, you have not done too badly."

The transit, when it came, was utterly uneventful. The *Mandate of Heaven* reported some minor buffeting, but this was soon negated following a refinement of the control linkage between the two ships. Then we had nothing to do but wait until Muhunnad detected one of the points of weakening where, with a judicious alteration in our trajectory, we might slip from one version of the Infrastructure to another.

Did I seriously think that Qilian would keep his promise of returning Muhunnad to his own people? Not really, unless my master had hopes of forging some kind of alliance with the Shining Caliphate, to use as leverage against the central authority of New High Karakorum. If that was his intention, I did not think he had much hope of succeeding. The Caliphate would have every reason to despise us, and yet—given the demonstrably higher level of both their technology and their intelligence—there was nothing they could possibly want from us except craven submission and cowering remorse for the holocaust we had visited upon their culture nearly a thousand years earlier.

No; I did not think Muhunnad stood much chance of returning home. Perhaps he knew that as well. But it was better to pretend to believe in Qilian's promises than incur his bored wrath back on the Qing Shui moon. At least this way, Muhunnad could continue to be materially useful to Qilian and, therefore, too valuable to hurt.

The detection of a weakening in the tunnel geometry, Muhunnad explained, was only just possible given the blunt sensibilities of our instruments. The Caliphate kept detailed maps of such things, but no record had survived his capture by the lemurs, and the information was too voluminous to be committed to memory. He recalled that there were four weak points in the section of Infrastructure we called the Parvan Tract, but not their precise locations or detailed properties.

No matter; he had every incentive to succeed. We overshot the first weakening, but the incident gave Muhunnad a chance to refine the manner in which he sifted the sensor data, and he was confident that he would not make the same error twice. Rather than attempt a reversal, it was agreed to push forward until we encountered the next weakening. It happened two days later, halfway to the Gansu nexus. This time, Muhunnad started to detect the subtle changes in the properties of the tunnel in time to initiate a hard slow-down, echoed by the *Mandate of Heaven* immediately to our stern.

We had been warned that the passage would be rough; this was an understatement. Fortunately, we were all braced and ready when it came; we had had two minutes' warning before the moment arrived. Even then, the ship gave every indication of coming close to breakup; she whinnied like a horse, her structural members singing as if they had been plucked. Several steering vanes broke loose during the swerve, but the *River*

Volga had been equipped to withstand losses that would have crippled a normal ship; all that happened was that hull plates swung open and new vanes pushed out to replace the missing ones. Behind us, the *Mandate of Heaven* suffered slightly less damage; Muhunnad had been able to send correctional steering signals to her guidance system, allowing her to follow a less treacherous path.

And then we were back in the tunnel, traveling normally. To all intents and purposes, it was as if nothing had happened. We appeared to be still inside the Parvan Tract.

"We have become phantoms now," Muhunnad informed us. "This is someone else's Infrastructure."

Qilian leaned over the control couch, where our pilot lay in a state of partial paralysis, wired so deeply into the *River Volga*'s nervous system that his own body was but an incidental detail. Around us, the bridge instruments recorded normal conditions of Infrastructure transit.

"Where are we?"

"There's no way of telling, not with these sensors. Not until we emerge."

"In the Gansu nexus?"

"Yes," he replied. "Or whatever *they* call it. There will be risks; you will not have seen many phantoms emerge into your version of the nexus because most such ships will make every effort to slip through another weakening."

"Why?"

He spoke as if the answer should have been obvious. "Because unless they are pilots like me, on specific intelligence-gathering missions, they would rather keep transitioning between versions of the Infrastructure, than emerge into what is likely to be a densely populated interchange. Eventually, they hope to detect the microsignatures in the tunnel physics that indicate that they have returned home."

"Signatures that we can't read," I said.

"I will attempt to refine my interpretation of the sensor

data. Given time, I may be able to improve matters. But that is some way off."

"We'll take our chances with Gansu," Qilian said.

There was, as I understood it, a small but nonnegligible possibility that the weakening had shunted us back into our own version of the Tract—we would know if we emerged into the nexus and I saw advertisements for *Sorkan-Shira* rental ponies. Muhunnad assured us, however, that such an outcome was very unlikely. Once we were elsewhere, we would only get home again by throwing the dice repeatedly, until our own special number came up.

For all that, when we did emerge into the Gansu nexus, my first thought was that Muhunnad had been wrong about those odds. Somehow or other, we had beaten them and dropped back into our own space. As the door opened to admit us back into the spherical volume of the hollowed-out moon, I had the same impression of teeming wealth; of a city packed tight around the central core, of luminous messages rising up the ninety-nine golden spokes, of the airspace thick with jewel-bright ships and gaudily patterned, mothlike shuttles, the glittering commerce of ten thousand worlds.

And yet, it only took a second glimpse to see that I was wrong.

This was no part of the Mongol Expansion. The ships were wrong; the shuttles were wrong: cruder and clumsier even than our most antiquated ships. The city down below had a haphazard, ramshackle look to it, its structures ugly and square-faced. The message on the spokes were spelled out in the angular letters of that pre-Mongol language, Latin. I could not tell if they were advertisements, news reports, or political slogans.

We slowed down, coming to a hovering standstill relative to the golden spokes and the building-choked core. The *Mandate of Heaven* had only just cleared the portal entrance, with the door still open behind it. I presumed that some automatic system would not permit it to close with a ship still so close.

Qilian was a model of patience, by his standards. He gave

Muhunnad several minutes to digest the information arriving from the *River Volga*'s many sensors.

"Well, pilot?" he asked, when that interval had elapsed. "Do you recognize this place?"

"Yes," Muhunnad said. "I do. And we must leave, now."

"Why so nervous? I've seen those ships. They look even more pathetic and fragile than ours must have seemed to you."

"They are. But there is no such thing as a harmless interstellar culture. These people have only been in space for a couple of hundred years, barely a hundred and fifty since they stumbled on the Infrastructure, but they still have weapons that could hurt us. Worse, they are aggressors."

"Who are they?" I whispered.

"The culture I mentioned to you back on the Qing Shui moon: the ones who are now in their twenty-third century. You would call them Christians, I suppose."

"Nestorians?" Qilian asked, narrowing his eyes.

"Another offshoot of the same cult, if one wishes to split hairs. Not that many of them are believers now. There are even some Islamists among them, although there is little about the Shining Caliphate that they would find familiar."

"Perhaps we can do business with them," Qilian mused.

"I doubt it. They would find you repulsive, and they would loathe you for what you did to them in your history."

It was as if Muhunnad had not spoken at all. When he alluded to such matters, Qilian paid no heed to his words. "Take us closer to the core," he said. "We didn't weld all this armor onto the *Volga* for nothing."

When Muhunnad did not show readiness to comply with Qilian's order, a disciplinary measure was administered through the input sockets of the harness. Muhunnad stiffened against his restraints, then—evidently deciding that death at the hands of the Christians was no worse than torture by Mongols—he began to move us away from the portal.

"I am sorry," I whispered. "I know you only want to do what's best for us."

"I am sorry as well," he said, when Qilian was out of earshot. "Sorry for being so weak, that I do what he asks of me, even when I know it is wrong."

"No one blames you," I replied.

We had crossed five hundred *li* without drawing any visible attention from the other vessels, which continued to move through the sphere as if going about their normal business. We even observed several ships emerge and depart through portals. But then, quite suddenly, it was as if a great shoal of fish had become aware of the presence of two sleek, hungry predators nosing through their midst. All around us, from one minute to the next, the various craft began to dart away, abandoning whatever course or errand they had been on before. Some of them ducked into portals or lost themselves in the thicket of spokes, while others fled for the cover of the core.

I tensed. Whatever response we were due was surely on its way by now.

As it happened, we did not have long to wait. In contrast to the civilian vessels attempting to get as far away from us as possible, three ships were converging on us. We studied them on high magnification, on one of the display screens in the *River Volga*'s bridge. They were shaped like arrowheads, painted with black and white stripes and the odd markings of the Christians. Their blade-sharp leading edges bristled with what could have been sensors, refueling probes, or weapons.

From his couch, Muhunnad said: "We are being signaled. I believe I can interpret the transmission. Would you like to see it?"

"Put it on," Qilian said.

We were looking at a woman who was wearing a heavy black uniform, shiny like waxed leather. She was pinned back into a heavily padded seat: I did not doubt that I was looking at the pilot of one of the ships racing to intercept us. Much of her face was hidden under a globular black helmet, with a red-tinted visor lowered down over her eyes. On the crown of the helmet was a curious symbol: a little drawing of Earth, overlaid with lines of latitude and longitude, and flanked by what I took to be a pair of laurel leaves. She was speaking into a microphone, her words coming over the bridge speaker. I wished I had studied more dead languages at the academy. Then again, given my lack of success with Arabic, perhaps I would still not have understood her Latin either.

What was clear was that the woman was not happy; that her tone was becoming ever more strident. At last, she muttered something that, had she been speaking Mongol, might have been some dismissive invitation to go to hell.

"Perhaps we should turn after all," Qilian said, or started to say. But by then, the three ships had loosed their missiles: four apiece, grouping into two packs of six, one for the *Mandate of Heaven* and one for us.

Muhunnad needed no further encouragement. He whipped us around with all haste, pushing the *River Volga*'s thrust to its maximum. Again, the stress of it was enough to set the ship protesting. At the same time, Muhunnad brought our own weapons into use, running those guns out on their magnetic cradles and firing at the missiles as they closed distance between us and the Christians. Given the range and efficacy of our beam weapons, it would not have troubled him to eliminate the three ships. In concentrating on the missiles, not the pursuers, he was doing all that he could not to inflame matters further. As an envoy of Greater Mongolia, I suppose I should have been grateful. But I was already beginning to doubt that the fate of my empire was going to be of much concern for me.

Because we had turned around, the *Mandate of Heaven* was the first to reach the portal. By then, the door had begun to close, but it only took a brief assault from the *Mandate*'s chaser guns to snip a hole in it. Muhunnad had destroyed nine of the twelve missiles by this point, but the remaining three were proving more elusive; in witnessing the deaths of their brethren, they appeared to have grown more cunning. By the time the *Mandate* cleared the portal, the three had arrived within fifteen *li* of the *River Volga*. By switching to a different fire pattern, Muhunnad succeeded in destroying two of them, but the last one managed to evade him until it had come within five *li*. At that point, bound by the outcome of some ruthless logical decision-making algorithm, the missile opted to detonate rather than risk coming any closer. It must have hoped to inflict fatal damage on us, even at five *li*.

It very nearly did. I recalled what our pilot had said about there being no such thing as a harmless interstellar culture. The blast inflicted severe damage to our rear shielding and drive assembly, knocking off another two stabilization vanes.

And then we were through, back into the Infrastructure. We had survived our first encounter with another galactic empire.

More were to follow.

In my mind's eye, I have an image of a solitary tree, bare of leaves, so that its branching structure is laid open for inspection. The point where each branch diverges from a larger limb is a moment of historical crisis, where the course of world events is poised to swerve onto one of two tracks.

Before his death, our founder spoke of having brought a single law to the six directions of space, words that have a deep resonance for all Mongols, as if it was our birthright to command the fundamental fabric of reality itself. They were prescient words, too, for the bringing of unity to Greater Mongolia, let alone the first faltering steps toward the Expansion, had barely begun. Fifty-four years after his burial, our fleet conquered the islands of Japan, extending the empire as far east as it was possible to go. But the day after our fleet landed, a terrible storm battered the harbors of those islands, one that would surely have repelled or destroyed our invasion fleet had it still been at sea. At the time, it was considered a great good fortune; a sure sign that Heaven had ordained this invasion by delaying that storm. Yet who is to say what would have become of Japan, had it not fallen under Mongol authority? By the same token, who is to say what would have become of our empire if its con-

fident expansion had been checked by the loss of that fleet? We
might not have taken Vienna and the cities of western Europe,
and then the great continents on the other side of the ocean.

I thought of Muhunnad's Shining Caliphate. The common
view is that the Islamists were monotheistic savages until swept
under the tide of the Mongol enlightenment. But I am mindful
that history is always written by the victors. We regard our
founder as a man of wisdom and learning first and a warrior
second, a man who was respectful of literacy, was curious about
the sciences, and possessed a keen thirst for philosophical inquiry. Might the conquered have viewed him differently, I
wonder? Especially if our empire fell, and we were not there to
gilden his name?

No matter; all that need concern us is that solitary tree, that
multiplicity of branches, reaching ever upward. After the moment of crisis, the point of bifurcation, there should be no further contact between one branch and the next. In one branch,
the Mongols take the world. In another, the Islamists. In another, some obscure sect of Christians. In another, much older
branch, none of these empires ever become a gleam in history's
eye. In an even older one, the lemurs are masters of Creation,
not some hairless monkey.

But what matters is that all these empires eventually find
the Infrastructure. In some way that I cannot quite grasp, and
perhaps will never truly understand, the *khorkoi* machinery exists across all those branches. Not simply as multiple copies of
the same Infrastructure, but as a single entity that in some way
permits the reunification of those branches: as if, having grown
apart, they begin to knot back together again.

I do not think this is intentional. If it were, the leaky nature of
the Infrastructure would have been apparent to us five hundred
years ago. It seems more likely to me that it is growing leaky;
that some kind of insulation is beginning to wear away, an insulation that prevents history short-circuiting itself, as it were.

But perhaps I am wrong to second-guess the motives of
aliens whose minds we will never know. Perhaps all of this is

unfolding according to some inscrutable and deliriously protracted scheme of our unwitting wormlike benefactors.

I do not think we will ever know.

I shall spare you the details of all the encounters that followed, as we slipped from one point of weakness to another, always hoping that the next transition would be the one that brought us back to Mongol space, or at least into an empire we could do business with. By the time of our eighth or ninth transition, I think, Qilian would have been quite overjoyed to find himself a guest of the Shining Caliphate. I think he would have even settled for a humbling return to the Christians: by the time we had scuttled away from empires as strange, or as brazenly hostile, as those of the Fish People or the Thin Men, the Christians had come to seem like very approachable fellows indeed.

But it was not to be. And when we dared to imagine that we had seen the worst that the branching tree of historical possibilities could offer, that we had done well not to stray into the dominion of the lemurs, that Heaven must yet be ordaining our adventure, we had the glorious misfortune to fall into the realm of the Smiling Ones.

They came hard and fast, and did not trifle with negotiation. Their clawlike green ships moved without thrust, cutting through space as if space itself was a kind of fluid they could swim against. Their beam weapons etched glimmering lines of violet across the void, despite the fact that they were being deployed in hard vacuum. They cut into us like scythes. I knew then that they could have killed us in a flash, but that they preferred to wound, to maim, to toy.

The *River Volga* twisted like an animal in agony, and then there was a gap in my thoughts wide enough for a lifetime.

The first thing that flashed through my mind after I returned to consciousness was frank amazement that we were still alive;

that the ship had not burst open like a ripe fruit and spilled us all into vacuum. The second thing was that, given the proximity of the attacking vehicles, our stay of execution was unlikely to be long. I did not need the evidence of readouts to tell me that the *River Volga* had been mortally wounded. The lights were out, artificial gravity had failed, and in place of the normal hiss and chug of her air recirculators, there was an ominous silence, broken only by the occasional creak of some stressed structural member, cooling down after being heated close to boiling point.

"Commander Qilian?" I called, into the echoing darkness.

No immediate answer was forthcoming. But no sooner had I spoken than an emergency system kicked in and supplied dim illumination to the cabin, traced in the wavery lines of fluorescent strips stapled to walls and bulkheads. I could still not hear generators or the other sounds of routine shipboard operation, so I presumed the lights were drawing on stored battery power. Cautiously, I released my restraints and floated free of my chair. I felt vulnerable, but if we were attacked again, it would make no difference whether I was secured or not.

"Yellow Dog," a voice called, from further up the cabin. It was Qilian, sounding groggy but otherwise sound. "I blacked out. How long was I under?"

"Not long, sir. It can't have been more than a minute since they hit us." I started pulling myself toward him, propelling myself with a combination of vigorous air-swimming and the use of the straps and handholds attached to the walls for emergency use. "Are you all right, sir?"

"I think–" Then he grunted, not loudly, but enough to let me know that he was in considerable pain. "Arm's broken. Wasn't quite secure when it happened."

He was floating with his knees tucked high, inspecting the damage to his right arm. In the scarlet backup lighting, little droplets of blood, pulled spherical by surface tension, were pale, colorless marbles. He had made light of the injury but it was worse than I had been expecting, a compound fracture of the radius bone, with a sharp white piece glaring out from his skin. The bleeding was abating, but the pain must have been excruciating. And yet Qilian caressed the skin around the wound as if it was no more irritating than a mild rash.

I paddled around until I found the medical kit. I offered to help Qilian apply the splint and dressing, but he waved aside my assistance save for when it came time to cut the bandage. The *River Volga* continued to creak and groan around us, like some awesome monster in the throes of a nightmare.

"Have you see the others?"

"Uugan, Jura, and Batbayar must still be at their stations in the midship section."

"And the pilot?"

I had only glanced at Muhunnad while I searched for the medical kit, but what I had seen had not encouraged me. He had suffered no visible injuries, but it was clear from his extreme immobility, and lack of response as I drifted by him, that all was not well. His eyes were open but apparently unseeing, fixated on a blank piece of wall above the couch.

"I don't know, sir. It may not be good."

"If he's dead, we're not going to be able to cut back into the Infrastructure."

I saw no point in reminding Qilian that, with the ship in its present state, Muhunnad's condition would make no difference. "It could be that he's just knocked out, or that there's a fault with his interface harness," I said, not really believing it myself.

"I don't know what happened to us just before I blacked out. Did you feel the ship twist around the way I did?"

I nodded. "Muhunnad must have lost attitude control."

Qilian finished with his dressing, inspecting the arm with a look of quiet satisfaction. "I am going to check on the others. See what you can do with the pilot, Yellow Dog."

"I'll do my best, sir."

He pushed off with his good arm, steering an expert course through the narrow throat of the bridge connecting door. I wondered what he hoped to do if the technical staff were dead, or injured, or otherwise incapable of assisting the damaged ship. I sensed that Qilian preferred not to look death in the eye until it was almost upon him.

Forcing my mind to the matter at hand, I moved to the reclined couch that held Muhunnad. I positioned myself next to him, anchoring in place with a foothold.

I examined the harness, checking the various connectors and status readouts, and could find no obvious break or weakness in the system. That did not mean that there was not an invisible fault, of course. Equally, if a power surge had happened, it might well have fried his nervous system from the inside out with little sign of external injury. We had built safeguards into the design to prevent that kind of thing, but I had never deceived myself that they were foolproof.

"I'm sorry, Muhunnad," I said quietly. "You did well to bring us this far. No matter what you might think of me, I wanted you to make it back to your own people."

Miraculously, his lips moved. He shaped a word with a mere ghost of breath. "Ariunaa?"

I took hold of his gloved hand, squeezing it as much as the harness allowed. "I'm here. Right by you."

"I cannot see anything," he answered, speaking very slowly. "Before, I could see everything around me, as well as the sensory information reaching me from the ship's cameras. Now I only have the cameras, and I am not certain that I am seeing anything meaningful through them. Sometimes I get flashes, as if *something* is working . . . but most of the time, it is like looking through fog."

"Are you sure you can't make some sense of the camera data?" I asked. "We only have to pass through the Infrastructure portal."

"That would be like threading the eye of a needle from halfway around the world, Ariunaa. Besides, I think we are paralyzed. I have tried firing the steering motors, but I have received no confirmation that anything has actually happened. Have you felt the ship move?"

I thought back to all that had happened since the attack. "In the last few minutes? Nothing at all."

"Then it must be presumed that we are truly adrift and that the control linkages have been severed." He paused. "I am sorry; I wish the news was better."

"Then we need help," I said. "Are you sure there's nothing else out there? The last time we saw it, the *Mandate of Heaven* was still in one piece. If she could rendezvous with us, she might be able to carry us all to the portal."

After a moment, he said: "There is something, an object in my vicinity, about one hundred and twenty *li* out, but I only sense it intermittently. I would have mentioned it sooner, but I did not wish to raise your hopes."

Whatever he intended, my hopes were rising now. "Could it be the *Mandate?*"

"It is something like the right size, and in something like the right position."

"We need to find a way to signal it, to get it to come in closer. At the moment, they have no reason to assume that any of us are alive."

"If I signal it, then the enemy will also know that some of us are still alive," Muhunnad answered. "I am afraid I do not have enough directional control to establish a tight-beam lock. I am not even certain I can broadcast an omnidirectional transmission."

"Broadcast what?" Qilian asked, drifting into the bridge.

I wheeled around to face him; I had not been expecting him to return so quickly. "Muhunnad says there's a good chance the *Mandate of Heaven* is nearby. Since we don't seem to able to move, she's our only chance of getting out of here."

"Is she intact?"

"No way to tell. There's definitely something out there that matches her signature. Problem is, Muhannad isn't confident that we can signal her without letting the enemy know we're still around."

"It won't make any difference to the enemy. They'll be coming in to finish us off no matter what we do. Send the signal."

After a moment, Muhunnad said: "It's done. But I do not know if any actual transmission has taken place. The only thing I can do is monitor the *Mandate* and see if she responds. If she has picked up our signal, then we should not have long to wait. A minute, maybe two. If we have seen nothing after that time, I believe we may safely assume the worst."

We waited a minute, easily the longest in my life, then another. After a third, there was still no change in the faint presence Muhunnad was seeing. "I am more certain than ever that it is the *Mandate*," he informed us. "The signature has improved; it matches very well, with no sign of damage. She is holding at one hundred and twenty *li*. But she is not hearing us."

"Then we need another way of signaling her," I said. "Maybe if we ejected some air into space . . ."

"Too ambiguous," Qilian countered. "Air might vent simply because the ship was breaking up, long after we were all dead. It could easily encourage them to abandon us completely. What do we need this ship for in any case? We may as well eject the lifeboats. The *Mandate of Heaven* can collect them individually."

After a instant of reflection, Muhunnad said: "I think the commander is correct. There is nothing to be gained by staying aboard now. At the very least, the lifeboats will require the enemy to pursue multiple targets."

There were six lifeboats, one for each of us.

"Let's go," Qilian replied.

"I'll see you at the lifeboats," I said. "I have to help Muhunnad out of the harness first."

Qilian looked at me for a moment, some dark calculation working itself out behind his eyes. He nodded once. "Be quick about it, Yellow Dog. But we don't want to lose him. He's still a valued asset."

With renewed strength, I hauled the both of us through the echoing labyrinth of the ship, to the section that contained the lifeboats. It was clear that the attack had wrought considerable damage on this part of the ship, buckling wall and floor plates, constricting passageways, and jamming bulkhead doors tight into their frames. We had to detour halfway to the rear before we found a clear route back to the boats. Yet although we were ready to don suits if necessary, we never encountered any loss of pressure. Sandwiched between layers of the *River Volga*'s outer hull was a kind of foam that was designed to expand and harden upon exposure to vacuum, quickly sealing any leaks before they presented a threat to the crew. From the outside, that bulging and hardening foam would have resembled a mass of swollen dough erupting through cracks in the hull.

There were six lifeboats, accessed through six armored doorways, each of which was surmounted with a panel engraved with both operating instructions and stern warnings concerning the penalities for improper use. Qilian was floating at the far end, next to the open doorway of the sixth boat. I had to look at him for a long, bewildered moment before I quite realized what I was seeing. I wondered if it was a trick of my eyes, occasioned by the gloomy lighting. But I had made no mistake. Next to Qilian, floating in states of deceptive repose, were the bodies of Jura and Batbayar. A little further away, as if he had been surprised and killed on his own, was Uugan. They had all been stabbed and gashed: knife wounds to the chest and throat, in all three instances. Blood was still oozing out of them.

In his good hand, Qilian held a bloody knife, wet and slick to the hilt.

"I am sorry," he said, as if all that situation needed was a reasonable explanation. "But only one of these six boats is functional."

I stared in numb disbelief. "How can only one be working?"

"The other five are obstructed; they can't leave because there is damage to their launch hatches. This is the only one with a clear shaft all the way to space." Qilian wiped the flat of the blade against his forearm. "Of course, I wish you the best of luck in proving me wrong. But I am afraid I will not be around to witness your efforts."

"You fucking–" I began, before trailing off. I knew if I called him a coward he would simply laugh at me, and I had no intention of giving him even the tiniest of moral victories. "Just go," I said.

He drew himself into the lifeboat. I expected some last word from him, some mocking reproach or grandiloquent burst of self-justifying rhetoric. But there was nothing. The door clunked shut with a gasp of compressed air. There was a moment of silence and stillness and then the boat launched itself away from the ship on a rapid stutter of electromagnetic pulses.

I felt the entire hull budge sideways in recoil. He was gone. For several seconds, all I could do was breathe; I could think of nothing useful or constructive to say to Muhunnad, nothing beyond stating the obvious hopelessness of our predicament.

But instead, Muhunnad said quietly: "We are not going to die."

At first, I did not quite understand his words. "I'm sorry?"

He spoke with greater emphasis this time. "We are going to live, but only if you listen to me very, very carefully. You must return me to the couch with all haste."

I shook my head. "It's no good, Muhunnad. It's all over."

"No, it is not. The *River Volga* is not dead. I only made it seem this way."

I frowned. "I don't understand."

"There isn't time to explain here. Get me back to the bridge, get me connected back to the harness, then I will tell you. But make haste! We really do not have very much time. The enemy are much nearer than you think."

"The enemy?"

"There is no *Mandate of Heaven*. Either she scuttled back to the portal, or she was destroyed during the same attack that damaged us."

"But you said . . ."

"I lied. Now help me move!"

Not for the first time that day, I did precisely as I was told.

Having already plotted a route around the obstructions, it did not take anywhere near as long to return to the bridge as it had taken to reach the lifeboats. Once there, I buckled him into the couch—he was beginning to retain some limb control, but not enough to help me with the task—and set about reconnecting the harness systems, trusting myself not to make a mistake. My fingers fumbled on the ends of my hands, as if they were a thousand *li* away.

"Start talking to me, Muhunnad," I said. "Tell me what's going on. Why did you lie about the *Mandate*?"

"Because I knew the effect that lie would have on Qilian. I wished to give him a reason to leave the ship. I had seen the kind of man he was. I knew that he would save himself, even if it meant the rest of us dying."

"I still don't understand. What good has it done us? The damage to the ship . . ." I completed the final connection. Muhunnad stiffened as the harness took hold of his nervous system, but did not appear to be in any obvious discomfort. "Are you all right?" I asked warily.

"This will take a moment. I had to put the ship into a deep shutdown, to convince Qilian. I must bring her back system by system, so as not to risk an overload."

The evidence of his work was already apparent. The bridge lights returned to normal illumination, while those readouts and displays that had remained active were joined by others that had fallen into darkness. I held my breath, expecting the whole ensemble to shut back down again at any moment. But I should have known better than to doubt Muhunnad's ability. The systems remained stable, even as they cycled through start-up and crash recovery routines. The air circulators resumed their dull but reassuring chug.

"I shall dispense with artificial gravity until we are safely under way, if that is satisfactory with you."

"Whatever it takes," I said.

His eyes, still wide open, quivered in their sockets. "I am sweeping local space," he reported. "There was some real damage to the sensors, but nowhere as bad as I made out. I can see Qilian's lifeboat. He made an excellent departure." Then he swallowed. "I can also see the enemy. Three of their ships will shortly be within attack range. I must risk restarting the engines without a proper initialization test."

"Again, whatever it takes."

"Perhaps you would like to brace yourself. There may be a degree of undamped acceleration."

Muhunnad had been right to warn me, and even then it came harder and sooner than I had been expecting. Although I had managed to secure myself to a handhold, I was nearly wrenched away with the abruptness of our departure. I felt acceleration rising smoothly, until it was suppressed by the dampeners. My arm was sore from the jolt, as if it had been almost pulled from its socket.

"That is all I can do for us now," Muhunnad said. "Running is our only effective strategy, unfortunately. Our weapons would prove totally ineffective against the enemy, even if we could get close enough to fire before they turned their own guns on us. But running will suffice. At least we have the mass of one less lifeboat to consider."

"I still don't quite get what happened. How did you know there'd still be one lifeboat that was still working? From what I saw, we came very close to losing all of them."

"We did," he said, with something like pride in his voice. "But not quite, you see. That was my doing, Ariunaa. Before the instant of the attack, I adjusted the angle of orientation of our hull. I made sure that the energy beam took out five of the six lifeboat launch hatches, and no more. Think of a knife fighter, twisting to allow part of his body to be cut rather than another."

I stared at him in amazement, forgetting the pain in my arm from the sudden onset of acceleration. I recalled what Qilian had said, his puzzlement about the ship twisting at the onset of the attack. "You mean you had all this planned, before they even attacked us?"

"I evaluated strategies for disposing of our mutual friend, while retaining the ship. This seemed the one most likely to succeed."

"I am . . . impressed."

"Thank you," he said. "Of course, it would have been easier if I had remained in the harness, so that we could move immediately once the pod had departed. But I think Qilian would have grown suspicious if I had not shown every intention of wanting to escape with him."

"You're right. It was the only way to convince him."

"And now there is only one more matter that needs to be brought to your attention. It is still possible to speak to him. It can be arranged with trivial ease: despite what I said earlier, I am perfectly capable of locking on a tight beam."

"He'll have no idea what's happened, will he? He'll still think he's got away with it. He's expecting to be rescued by the *Mandate of Heaven* at any moment."

"Eventually, the nature of his predicament will become apparent. But by then, he is likely to have come to the attention of the Smiling Ones."

I thought of the few things Muhunnad had told us about our adversaries. "What will they do to him? Shoot him out of the sky?"

"Not if they sense a chance to take him captive with minimal losses on their own side. I would suggest that an unpowered lifeboat would present exactly such an opportunity."

"And then?"

"He will die. But not immediately. Like the Shining Caliphate and the Mongol Expansion, the Smiling Ones have an insatiable appetite for information. They will have found others of his kind before, just as they have found others of mine. But I am sure Qilian will still provide them with much amusement."

"And then?" I repeated.

"An appetite of another kind will come into play. The Smiling Ones are cold-blooded creatures. Reptiles. They consider the likes of us—the warm, the mammalian—to be a kind of affront. As well they might, I suppose. All those millions of years ago, we ate their eggs."

I absorbed what he said, thinking of Qilian falling to his destiny, unaware for now of the grave mistake he had made. Part of me was inclined to show clemency: not by rescuing him, which would place *us* dangerously close to the enemy, but by firing on him, so that he might be spared an encounter with the Smiling Ones.

But it was not a large part.

"Time to portal, Muhunnad?"

"Six minutes, on our present heading. Do you wish to review my intentions?"

"No," I said, after a moment. "I trust you to do the best possible job. You think we'll make it into the Infrastructure without falling to pieces?"

"If Allah is willing. But you understand that our chances of returning to home are now very slim, Yellow Dog? Despite my subterfuge, this ship *is* damaged. It will not survive many more transitions."

"Then we'll just have to make the best of wherever we end up," I said.

"It will not feel like home to either of us," he replied, his tone gently warning, as if I needed reminding of that.

"But if there are people out there . . . I mean, instead of egg-laying monsters, or sweet-looking devils with tails, then it'll be better than nothing, won't it? People are people. If the Infrastructure is truly breaking down, allowing all these timelines to bleed into one another, than we are all going to have get along with each other sooner or later, no matter what we all did to each other in our various histories. We're all going to have to put the past behind us."

"It will not be easy," he acknowledged. "But if two people as unalike as you and I can become friends, then perhaps there is hope. Perhaps we could even become an example to others. We shall have to see, shan't we?"

"We shall have to see," I echoed.

I held Muhunnad's hand as we raced toward the portal, and whatever Heaven had in store for us on the other side.

THE SEER AND THE SILVERMAN

Stephen Baxter

Like many of his colleagues here at the beginning of a new century, British writer Stephen Baxter has been engaged for more than a decade now with the task of revitalizing and reinventing the "hard-science" story for a new generation of readers, producing work on the cutting edge of science that bristles with weird new ideas and often takes place against vistas of almost outrageously cosmic scope.

Baxter made his first sale to Interzone *in 1987, and since then he has become one of that magazine's most frequent contributors, as well as making sales to* Asimov's Science Fiction, Science Fiction Age, Analog, Zenith, New Worlds, *and elsewhere. He's one of the most prolific new writers in science fiction, and is rapidly becoming one of the most popular and acclaimed of them as well. In 2001, he appeared on the Final Hugo Ballot twice, and won both* Asimov's Readers Award *and* Analog's Analytical Laboratory Award, *one of the few writers ever to win both awards in the same year. Baxter's first novel,* Raft, *was released in 1991 to wide and enthusiastic response, and was rapidly followed by other well-received novels such as* Timelike Infinity, Anti-Ice, Flux, *and the H. G. Wells pastiche—a sequel to* The Time Machine—The Time Ships, *which won both the John W. Campbell Memorial Award and the Philip K. Dick Award. His other books include the novels,* Voyage, Titan, Moonseed, Mammoth, Book One: Silverhair, Manifold: Time, Manifold: Space, Evolution, Coalescent, Exultant, Transcendent, Emperor, Resplendent, *and two novels in collaboration with Arthur C. Clarke,* The Light of Other Days *and* Time's Eye, a Time Odyssey. *His short fiction has been col-*

lected in Vacuum Diagrams: Stories of the Xeelee Sequence, Traces, *and* Hunters of Pangaea, *and he has released a chapbook novella,* Mayflower II. *Coming up are a
flood of new novels, including* Conqueror, Navagator, First-
born, Weaver, Flood, *and* The H-bomb Girl.

*Baxter's Xeelee series is one of the most complex sequences
in science fiction history, a tapestry of dozens of stories and
many novels* (Raft, Timelike Infinity, Flux, Ring, Cilia-
of-Gold) *that spans millions of years of time as well as most
of the galaxy, and brings humans into contact (usually hostile
contact) with dozens of alien races, many of them initially more
powerful and advanced than humanity itself. Here, in a sce-
nario roughly halfway through the entire arc of the sequence, he
pictures the attempt of two Galactic Empires formerly locked in
conflict to uneasily coexist—with the stakes about as high as they
can possibly get.*

H is mother's screaming filled the lifedome. "He's gone. The
Ghosts have taken him. Lethe, Benj is gone!"

Shocked awake, Donn Wyman grabbed a robe and ran out
of his cabin.

His mother and father were in the plaza, in their sleep
clothes, clinging to each other. They were outside Benj's cabin.
The door was open. Donn could see at a glance that the room
was empty.

Only seconds after wakening, he had a sickening, immediate sense of what was wrong. The abduction from out of the
heart of his home was bewildering, as if part of reality had been
cut away, not just a human being, not just his brother.

"Now, Rima, don't take on." Samm Wyman was trying to
calm his wife. He was a careworn man, slight of build and with
his family's pale blue eyes. Donn knew that spreading calm was
his father's fundamental strategy in life.

But Rima was struggling in his arms. "He's gone! You can

see for yourself!" Her hair was wild, her face tattoos unanimated, just dead black scars on her cheeks.

"Yes, but you're jumping to conclusions, you always think the worst straightaway."

She pushed him away. "Oh, get off me, you fool. What else could it be but an abduction? If he'd gone out through the ports, the lifedome AI would know about it. So what good is being calm? Do you think you can just *wish* this away?"

Donn said uncertainly, "Mother—"

"Oh, Donn—help me look. Just in case he's somewhere in the dome, somewhere the AI hasn't spotted him."

Donn knew that was futile, but they had to look. "All right."

Rima snapped at her husband. "And you find out if he's anywhere else on the Reef. And call the Commissary. If the Coalition are going to meddle in our affairs, they may as well make themselves useful. They could start by finding out where every Ghost on the Reef was last night—and the Silvermen."

She stalked off and began throwing open doors around the rim of the plaza. The bots followed her, their aged servos whirring.

Samm eyed his elder son. "I already called Commissary Elah. Who knows? Maybe the Coalition goons will be some use for once. She's just taking out her anger on me. She'll take it out on you, too, before she's done. It's her way. Don't let it upset you."

"I won't, Dad. But this is bad, isn't it?"

"I'm afraid so, son. Go on, get searching."

Donn cut across the center of the plaza, the lifedome's central floor space. Much of it was given over to green, for the crew of this old ship, his mother's distant ancestors, had crossed the stars with a chunk of forest brought from Earth itself, a copse of mature trees, oak, alder, and lime, old enough to have wrapped thick roots around the struts of the lifedome's frame. But Donn, twenty-five years old, had never been to Earth, and to him the trees were just furniture.

Of course, there was no sign of Benj. Why would he have

hidden away among the trees? Benj, at twenty-one, liked his comforts. And even if he was here, the AI's surveillance systems would have known about it.

Something whirred past Donn's face, tiny, metallic. It was a robot insect. And a fine spray of water descended on him. He lifted his face and saw droplets condensing out of the air, an artificial rain born in the summit of the lifedome and falling all around him. Above the rain, the transparent dome showed a star field that had barely changed for centuries: the Association, a cluster of stars dominated by the Boss, a single monstrous star a million times as bright as Earth's sun, an unforgiving point of light. He was getting slowly wet, but he didn't mind; he found the sensation oddly comforting on this difficult morning.

"Beautiful, isn't it? The star field."

The smooth voice made him start. He turned.

Commissary Elah stood beside him. Her eyes were large and dark, her gaze fixed on his face, calculating, judgmental. Taller than Donn, she was dressed in a Commissary's floor-length black robe, a costume so drab it seemed to suck all the light out of the air. Her scalp was shaved, a starkness that emphasized the beauty of her well-defined chin and cheekbones, and her skin gleamed with droplets of the artificial rain. Donn had no idea how old she was.

"I didn't mean to startle you," she said.

Something about her made Donn pull his robe tighter around his body. "Commissary. It's good of you to have come out so quickly. My parents will be reassured—"

"I hope so. I've brought some specialist help. A woman called Eve Raoul—a Virtual, actually, but quite expert. This is what we're here for, the Commission for Historical Truth. To help." Her accent sounded odd to a Reefborn, slightly strangulated at the back of the throat—an accent from Earth. "The Coalition understands."

"I suppose it must," Donn said. "If it seeks to rule."

"Not to rule," said Elah gently. "To join all of scattered

mankind behind a common purpose. And by helping you sort out issues like this with the Ghosts—"

"Nobody knows for sure if the Ghosts are behind these abductions."

She eyed him. "But the Ghosts aren't denying it. Are you loyal to the Ghosts or your family, Donn Wyman?"

"I—" He didn't know what to say to that direct question; he didn't think in such terms. "Why must I choose?"

She reached out with a pale hand and stroked the trunk of an oak tree. "Remarkable, these plants. So strange. So strong!"

"They are trees. Don't you have any on Earth anymore?"

She shrugged. "Probably. In laboratories. Earth has other purposes now than to grow trees." She glanced around. "You know, I've visited the *Miriam Berg* several times. But I've never stood in this very spot, beneath these trees. Trade, your profession, isn't it?"

"I'm an interspecies factor, specializing in relations with the Ghost enclaves."

"It's all so deliciously archaic. And anti-Doctrinal, of course, your way of life, your ship's existence, its very name, all relics of a forbidden past!" She laughed. "But don't worry, we've no intention of turning you out summarily. All things in time." She pushed at the earth, the grass, with a bare foot. "We're on the ship's axis here, yes? Over the spine. Your mother's family came to the Reef in this ship, didn't they, a thousand years ago? I imagine there are access hatches. Is it possible to reach the drive pod from here?"

"That's nothing to do with you." Samm came bustling up. Beside Elah's cool composure, his father looked a crumpled mess, Donn thought, his hair sticking up like the grass under their feet, his face shining with the sweat of sleep.

"I apologize," Elah said easily. "You did invite me here."

With his arms outstretched, Samm escorted her away from the copse. "To help with looking for Benj. Not to go snooping around the *Miriam*." But as she walked with him, he backed down, nervous of offending the new agency from Earth that had taken over all their lives. "We're all distressed."

"I understand."

Donn lingered for another few seconds under the artificial rain. He wondered why his father should care about the Commissary, or any Coalition agent, snooping around this thousand-year-old heap of junk. Maybe he had trade goods tucked down there in the spine—given the Coalition's new tax codes, Donn thought that was quite likely—but if so, he couldn't have signaled it any more clearly. Not subtle, Donn's father, whatever other qualities he might have.

But as Donn stood there, the complexities of Reef politics faded, and the reality of his brother's loss crowded back into his head, the true story of the day. For months, the abductions had been an arbitrary plague. Nobody could rest, for at any moment, you could be taken, too, from the most secure place. What a horror it was. And now it had come here, to his own family. He wondered, in fact, how it was he felt so calm himself. Shock, perhaps.

He trailed after his father, and the Commissary. And in a lounge at the edge of the plaza, he found a Virtual woman trying to console his mother.

———

"Before I died, I spent most of my working life exploring the principles of remote translation systems."

The visitor sat beside Rima on a couch. Donn's mother's face was twisted with grief and anger. Bots hovered before them, bearing trays of drinks and pastries—breakfast; it was still early.

The visitor was slim, modestly dressed in a pale blue coverall. Her hair was gray, and she pulled at a stray lock of it absently. Donn had never seen anybody with gray hair before, though he knew it had once been the default shade for the aging. Evidently the visitor's projection was good enough to fool the serving bots, but Donn observed that her interfacing with the chair wasn't quite right, and a haze of tiny pixels shimmered around the underside of her legs.

Rima asked, irritated, impatient, "Remote translation systems?"

Commissary Elah said, "Teleportation, to you and me. Donn Wyman, meet Eve Raoul. The expert I told you about."

Eve stood. Donn clumsily offered this Virtual visitor a hand to shake. She bowed, apparently unoffended. "I'm sorry to meet you in such circumstances."

"Eve Raoul," Donn said, "do you have a connection to *the* Raoul, Jack Raoul?"

"He was my husband. I died before him." She gestured at her slim body. "It's thanks to him that this representation was reconstructed from my old Notebooks. He liked to have me around in person to counsel him about quantum mechanics and the like, in the course of his work. And in the work he did, his dealings with the Ghosts, there was a *lot* of that."

Elah said, "Eve is a specialist in the sort of technologies that seem to be deployed here–abduction through some sort of teleport device, apparently. And so we employ her to offer advice and counseling to relatives of abductees."

"Counseling," said Rima, skeptical. "Jack Raoul died eight years ago." She glared at Elah. "Or rather he was executed for his 'crimes.' He was pretty old by that time wasn't he?"

"Over two hundred years old," Eve said softly. "He left my Notebooks to the Commission, and to the Ghosts."

"He must have loved you," Donn blurted. Jack Raoul was well remembered here, a hero for the Reef's multispecies community, for his work in bringing about constructive working relationships between humans and Ghosts. Evidently, he was capable of great passion, too.

But Eve grimaced. "I was his legacy to an alien species. That tells you all you need to know about what it was like to be loved by Jack Raoul. However, here I am. And, since I know you're thinking it, it's more than a hundred and fifty years since my own death."

Rima snorted. "Then what use are you? How can these Notebooks of yours be up-to-date?"

"It's the best we have," Elah said sternly. "Rima, much human knowledge was lost during the Qax Occupation of Earth. That was a deliberate policy of the occupying power, in fact. One of our purposes in recontacting lost communities like this one."

"We weren't lost," said Donn.

Elah plowed on. "Our purpose is to reacquire such lost knowledge. And Eve and her Notebooks are a treasure. It's good of her to work with the Coalition, especially after the difficulties surrounding her husband's case."

Eve ignored this barrage of euphemism. "I have to tell you, though," she admitted, "that I may not be much help at all. Human technologists have never got very far with teleportation. How could a translation device work? Perhaps by scanning the position of every particle in an object, you might think. That information could be transferred somewhere else and a copy constructed of the original, exact down to the last electron."

Donn frowned. "But that couldn't work. The uncertainty principle—you can't specify a particle's momentum and position precisely."

"Correct," she said approvingly. "In quantum mechanics, such quantities as position are derived from probabilistic wave functions—mathematical descriptions that underlie all reality. *But* the principle says nothing about transferring exact data about the wave functions themselves. That was the approach I was working on, before I died."

Rima asked, "What about Ghost technology?"

"My husband, in the course of his career dealing with the Ghosts, came across one example of a teleport-like device. It was all to do with breaking up electrons: dividing indivisible particles."

They looked at her blankly.

Eve said, "Look—an electron's quantum wave function is spherical in its lowest energy state. But in its next highest energy state, the wave function has a dumbbell shape. Now, if that dumbbell could be stretched and pinched, could it be divided? If so, when the function collapses, it could be as if an electron leapt instantaneously from one bubble to another."

Rima was fighting her way through this fog of words. "Is that how the Ghosts took away my son?"

"No," Eve said regretfully. "I'm sorry. The sort of processes I've described would leave behind physical traces. Various exotic particles that your AI would record. We're investigating every case. I'm hopeful that when we do start to turn up physical traces of some kind—"

Samm said suddenly, "What about supersymmetry?"

Rima shook her head. *"What?"*

"Another corner of physics. Just an interest of mine. Have the Ghosts worked with that?"

"Not that we know of," said Eve.

Rima glared at her husband. "Don't waste time, you fool."

Donn felt he had to say, "Everybody keeps saying it's the Ghosts. We don't even know if it *is* the Ghosts behind this."

Rima said bitterly, "Oh, of course it's the wretched Ghosts. Everybody knows it." She glanced upward at the Boss, the gleaming star that cast shadows even here inside the lifedome. "I grew up thinking the Ghosts were all right. But things have changed. They're up to something. Everybody knows that. They say there's a new sort of Ghost up there, deeper in the Association. A Seer, who can see into past and future."

"Now, that's all rumor," Samm said. "Gossip. Troublemaking."

"No wonder they can take away our children, if *that's* true. Because if they can see into the future, they could sneak in here with one of those Silvermen of theirs."

"Oh, Rima," Samm said, distressed.

Eve said uncertainly, "Getting back to teleportation—"

"What use are you?" Rima snapped. "You don't know anything. You've said so."

Elah said smoothly, "She's here to assure you that the Commission is doing all we can."

Rima got to her feet and pointed. "And I suppose you brought *that* with you to reassure me."

They all turned.

A Silver Ghost hovered in the plaza, only paces away from them, a silver sphere, quite featureless, a mercury droplet as tall as a man. It shifted a little as it hovered just above the floor, as if its immense bulk could be pushed by the breezes of the air-conditioning.

"You took him," Rima said. "You took my son."

Samm tried to get hold of his wife. "Rima, be calm."

But she shook him away. "What have you done with him?" She ran at the Ghost, her fists flailing. Her fists just passed through its hull, scattering silvery pixels. The Ghost hovered impassively. Samm pulled Rima away. "Give him back," she begged. "Oh, give him back!"

Eve Raoul stood, obviously distressed, as if she longed to help. The Commissary simply watched, cold, observant. Donn was hot with anxiety and embarrassment.

The Ghost said: "I apologize for the intrusion. I am the Sink Ambassador."

Samm snapped, "The *what*?"

"The Heat Sink, Dad," Donn said, "which is the sky, to them. He's their Ambassador to the sky."

The Ambassador said, "Eve Raoul—it is good to see you again."

"I wish I could say the same," Eve said.

Samm, bewildered, tortured, looked from one to the other. "What do you want, Ghost?"

The Ghost rolled. "Donn Wyman, we need your help."

———

The Sink Ambassador said there was trouble in a bar called Minda's Savior, set in a generation starship near the heart of the

Reef's three-dimensional tangle of ships—a Silverman, in some kind of trouble.

Elah faced the Ghost Virtual. "Ambassador to the Heat Sink, you call yourself."

"Yes."

"You know Eve through Jack Raoul."

"I worked with Jack Raoul on many complex and demanding issues. I like to believe we were friends, Eve and I, and Jack and I."

Elah laughed at that, the idea that humans and Ghosts could be friends. "And now you consult Donn Wyman. He's just a factor, a trade negotiator."

Donn felt dismissed, vaguely insulted.

The Ambassador said, "Since the collapse of the old Raoul Accords, the legal interface between Ghost and human communities has been shredded. But humans like Donn, and Ghosts like myself, must work together over trade; the Ghost enclaves here could not survive without trade. And individual contacts made in such circumstances serve well in trying to resolve other issues as they arise."

"There was no need to call on a mere factor," Elah said. "I am a Commissary. I represent the Coalition, mankind's highest authority."

"Then it is a good thing that you happen to be here," the Ghost said, without a trace of inflection in its artificial voice.

"And it's all about a bar. A Ghost artifact in trouble in a bar," Elah said. She laughed. "How squalid. How absurd. Such a thing could never happen on Earth."

"Evidently," Eve murmured, "this is not Earth."

"This is stupid," Donn said. "It's got nothing to do with Benj."

"But we need you," the Ambassador said simply. "You personally."

"Go," Samm said. "There's nothing you can do at the *Miriam*, for now. If anything turns up . . ."

"Mom?"

Rima, her face buried in a handkerchief, waved him away.

So the four of them crowded into the bubblelike transparent hull of the *Suzy IV,* Samm Wyman's aging flitter: Donn, Elah, the Ghost, and Eve Raoul. Where the Virtuals brushed against the flitter's hull, they crumbed; Eve Raoul brushed stray pixels from her sleeve like flies.

You could get from any point to any other on the Reef by walking through the innards of the old ships, or by walkways and bridges thrown up over the centuries. Donn would have preferred to walk, to burn off some energy. But the *Suzy* would be quicker, and so here they were. Elah had insisted on coming along, as "trouble" of any sort was now the Commission's business, and so Eve had to come too—that or be shut down, Donn supposed, as Eve seemed tied to Elah, no doubt through some projection system lodged on her person.

So the flitter closed up around them, its systems humming, and rose from the Reef of ships like a stone thrown up into a bowl of stars.

Donn peered down as the Reef opened up beneath them. It was a logjam of ships, a roughly lenticular mass with ragged edges, entirely lacking in symmetry. The Boss was a fierce lantern at the zenith, so that the tangle of superstructures cast complex shadows. Many of the ships, like the *Miriam,* were of the ancient, durable GUTship design, a stalk topped and tailed by lifedome and GUTdrive. But there were more exotic designs, including the old generation starship at the hub of the complex, a frozen ocean of comet ice meant to propel its crew's descendants to a new world that had never been reached. Here and there in the long shadows of the Reef, you could see tangles of silver rope, ships without hulls or bridges or obvious drive units—ships that weren't of human design at all.

And today, ships of the Coalition's Navy hovered over the

crowded craft. They were Spline warships, living ships, balls of flesh studded with sensor mounts and weapons emplacements. They rolled like threatening moons, the green tetrahedral sigil of a free mankind tattooed onto their flanks.

Elah lifted her face to the light of the brilliant star that hung over all this. "I've been stationed here a year already, and I just can't get used to the sky. Strictly speaking, the Boss is cataloged as VI Cygni Number Twelve. Did you know that? Recently it's been flaring—there's some remarkable imagery; I can show you if you like. And this grouping of stars is called the Cygnus OB2 Association. It's all so different from what you'd see from Earth. That central monster casts shadows light-years long from clouds of interstellar dust, shadows distorted by the finitude of lightspeed—quite astonishing."

Donn was more interested in the cultural side of what she had to say. "Cygnus? What does that mean?"

Elah waved a hand, dismissive. "An old name from Earth. Pre-Occupation. Its meaning is lost."

Donn had never given much thought to Earth, a place remote in space and in history—or it had been, until the Coalition came. "Where is Earth, from here?"

Eve glanced around and pointed. "About five thousand nine hundred light-years away, thataway. Right around the Galaxy's spiral arm."

"Can you see the Association from Earth?"

"You'd be able to see the Boss with the naked eye if not for dust clouds in the way."

"Humans have traveled far from their origins," the Ghost said.

"You bet we have," Elah said with fervor. She pointed at right angles to Earthward. "We're filling up this spiral arm, and we're heading that way—toward the Galaxy Core. We've already pushed into the next spiral arm inward, the Sagittarius Arm."

The Ghost spoke, its artificial voice sonorous in the enclosed space. "And that, of course, is the source of all our trouble."

Donn knew it was right. Thanks to the explosive expansion of mankind, suddenly the Ghost communities scattered around the Association, including the enclaves in the Reef itself, had become alien islands stranded in human space.

The Reef as a whole had moved several times since its formation, embedded hyperdrive engines lifting the whole shebang across light-years, always moving further from Earth, off along the star lanes of the spiral arm. The Association had proven a good place to live, with plenty of worldlets and asteroids to mine for resources—even a few human colonies, refugees of one calamity or another, to trade with.

And here the Reefborn had forged tentative links with the Silver Ghosts, who were undergoing their own expansion out of the heart of the Galaxy. They welcomed small Ghost colonies into the Reef itself. You could say that the Reef culture was a composite of human and Ghost, an experiment in cohabitation.

For a time, even after the Coalition had made contact, the Reefborn had profited from trade between two interstellar empires. There had been a strange period when autonomous Ghost enclaves had been granted room to live under the new regime: Silver Ghosts, living under Coalition authority.

But times had changed, and the Coalition's embrace had become harsh.

Those elderly hyperdrive engines had all been confiscated or disabled, for a start, to be refitted into Navy ships. The Reef would never again go jaunting out of human ken into the alien dark. And the Ghosts had been taxed, marginalized, and suffered discrimination of all kinds.

With the crises over the Silvermen and the abductions, the Ghosts' position was becoming untenable. And perhaps, Donn thought, it was all coming to a head, with himself caught mysteriously in the middle of it.

The *Suzy* began its descent into the forest of infrastructure.

Minda's Savior: the bar announced its name in signs written in several human languages, and some nonhuman. Donn had once been shown how the name was inscribed in electromagnetic patterns invisible to human senses but vivid to a Ghost. There was even an image, painted rather than Virtual, of a young human girl accepting the gift of its very hide from a hovering Ghost. All this was based on a story, three centuries old, that the first contact between humans and Ghosts had involved a young girl who had been saved from freezing by a Ghost sacrificing its own life for hers. But the official Commission line was that the Minda story was just Ghost propaganda.

Inside, the Savior was basically a bar, selling intoxicating chemicals of various kinds diluted by the ice of a comet that had once orbited Sol. But there was also a kind of mud bath, salty and warm, meant to accommodate Ghost patrons. The light in this corner of the bar came not from the usual hovering light-globes but from glowing rope draped from the ceiling, Ghost technology.

There was no Ghost in the mud bath today, no Ghost in the bar save the Virtual projection of the Sink Ambassador. Only the Ambassador—and a Silverman, standing like a chromed statue in one corner, confronted by an angry human crowd.

They weren't actively doing anything to it, not touching or harming it in any way. Yet they surrounded it, sitting silently, defiantly drinking the Navy drink called Poole's Blood, walling in the Silverman with human flesh. Donn knew some of these people. Here was Bareth Grieve, one of the Reef's elders, a friend of his mother's and a member of the Reef's Grand Council. This morning Grieve and the rest barely acknowledged him. They were just a mob who had trapped a Silverman.

Elah was taller than most in the bar, as indeed was Eve. Donn had heard an insulting theory that Reefborn were becoming dwarfed, as populations stranded on islands often were, apparently. "What a spectacle," Elah said now, with utter contempt. "Makes you ashamed to be human."

The Ambassador murmured, "You can see why we have a problem. They've been like this for hours."

Eve said, "Something has been done to that Silverman. Look, Donn—can you see?"

At first glance the Silverman was typical of its sort: a kind of sketch of a human figure, head, torso, arms, and legs, but shorter than an average human—like a statue in Ghost-hide silver. It lacked detail, it had fingers but no toes, no fingernails, no navel, no genitalia, the face just a bland outline, all orifices sealed up save the eyes and mouth. It was as identical to the rest of its kind, just as every Ghost looked the same as every other. But this one had a sort of collar around its neck, of some heavy blue metal.

"*That* doesn't look like Ghost technology to me, that collar," Eve murmured. "That's human. They've done something to this thing. What, though?" She snapped her fingers, and a data slate appeared in her hands.

"It is an eerie construct, that Silverman," Elah said. "Look at it, all but faceless, expressionless, walking among us. . . . And if you were going to develop a weapon to penetrate a society like this, an assassin to work in a human environment of rooms and corridors, a human shape is exactly what you would give it. It's not surprising people are wary, especially in a politically underdeveloped society like this one."

Donn bridled at her casual insults. But the Silvermen *were* odd. They had only been appearing on the Reef since the arrival of the Coalition, while relationships between the Ghost and human communities on the Reef had steadily deteriorated. They wandered the Reef's corridors and haunted its bars and libraries, theaters and forums, even its churches. They simply *looked.* They stepped out of the way of humans. They would tolerate being touched, their silver flesh poked by curious children. They would speak if spoken to, answer questions if asked, but only of the most direct sort. But they volunteered nothing.

The Silvermen were a strange, eerie, uncomfortable presence. And they simply showed up, appearing as suddenly and as randomly as the human abductees disappeared. The Silvermen were antiabductees.

And they were clearly Ghost artifacts, for that silvery flesh was Ghost hide.

The Ambassador asked, "What are these people doing?"

"Maybe this is punishment," said Donn, "for the abductions. People want something to hit back at."

"They are not harming it."

"I wouldn't like being trapped like that. Pinned up against a wall, ignored."

"A human sort of harm, then. To learn such lessons is the Silverman's purpose. So I believe."

Donn stared at the Ghost. As far as he knew, this was the first time any Ghost had discussed a "purpose" behind the Silverman visitations.

Elah, naturally, had overheard, too. "It's here to learn, you say?"

"I speak at second hand," the Ambassador said. "You know that Ghost society is not like yours, not hierarchical. Our society is like our bodies, an embracing of diversity. But I believe that the faction behind the Silvermen intends them as an experiment to learn more of humanity."

"By sending these homunculi among us as spies," Elah said.

"Not that. They are all but mindless, intended as passive observers. They simply live a facsimile of a human life, for a period. The way each of us thinks is shaped by how we sense the universe, how we experience it and manipulate it; we are our bodies as well as our minds. We understand what you are doing," it said bluntly to Elah. "Your Coalition and the Expansion it is driving. We do not understand *why* you do this. Perhaps your restlessness is something to do with your ape anatomy, your manipulating hands, your heritage of the trees and the savannah."

Elah laughed. "You insult us without even trying, don't you? So do you think the experiment has worked?"

The Ghost admitted, "I don't believe we anticipated the hostility they have encountered."

Donn said, looking over at the Silverman. "It isn't human *enough*, perhaps."

Elah said, "In some corners of this Reef, people gang up on the Silvermen and dress them up in clothes! All to reduce that feeling of otherness about them. And in other corners, the Silvermen are insulted, abused by the families of the abducted. There's never been a physical attack before, however." She faced the Ambassador. "If you want us to help you, Ghost, you need to be honest with us. *How* are these homunculi being planted in the Reef? Is it through some teleportation mechanism? And is it the same mechanism that is used to abduct humans from the Reef?"

Again that long hesitation. "There is another faction—its motives are noble."

"Tell us, Ghost!"

"Yes," it said softly.

Donn blew out his cheeks. "I never heard it confirmed before, about the abductions."

Elah said stonily, "Are you disappointed?"

"Yes. Because it means that all the paranoids were right—all those who swallowed your anti-Ghost propaganda, Commissary."

"Don't push your luck, boy," she murmured.

"It does explain what they've done to that wretched Silverman over there," Eve said now. "I've been running some tests." She showed them a slate of results that meant little to Donn.

Elah nodded. "That collar they stuck on it is full of processors. It's a sentience booster." She smiled at Donn. "Do you see? This lynch mob has made the Silverman *smarter*. More self-aware."

Donn frowned. "Is that legal? And, *why*?"

"I don't think the law matters much here. And as to why–isn't it obvious? Yelling at those other dim homunculi was no longer enough to get rid of the rage. They made *this* creature smart enough to understand what it was suffering, what its perceived crime was. And who knows what they have planned for it once this long vigil is done? Can't you see the logic, Donn Wyman?"

At the sound of his name, the Silverman turned. It was the first movement it had made since Donn and the others had walked into the bar. "You are Donn Wyman?"

"Yes," said Donn uncertainly.

The Silverman walked straight toward Donn. It pushed through the barrier of drinkers, knocking a couple of men aside. Some of them got to their feet. "Don't you take another step, you Ghost monster."

But Elah raised her hand, a halting motion. The Reefborn had learned to recognize the authority of a Commissary.

The Silverman stood before Donn. It came up to his chest, like a boy dipped in silver. Even its eyeballs were silvered. "We need your help." Its voice was identical to the Ambassador's.

The Ambassador said, "This is why I asked you here, Donn Wyman. It has been asking for you, specifically. It's not very articulate, but it does seem to know what it wants."

"Sorry," said the homunculus.

"For what?"

"For this." The Silverman reached up and wrapped its arms around Donn's waist, a powerful, cold, unbreakable hug.

And the bar, the Commissary, the Ghost–all vanished.

———

No air.

His chest felt as if it would explode.

A raw sky, star-littered. Ice under his feet, hard, sucking the heat out through his thin boots. The Silverman's face before him, filling his vision, chromed eyes frosting over.

No air! He opened his mouth. Air gushed from his lungs, a shower of crystals. But when he tried to breathe in, there was nothing, *no air*. He was drowning in vacuum. His eyes filmed over. He could not blink. Pain stabbed in his ears.

Still the Silverman held him.

Machinery flashed, a blade, spinning in vacuum silence. The Silverman fell away.

Somebody stood before him. Short, slim, a girl perhaps, wrapped in a silver suit, her visor translucent. She held a weapon and a mass of silver cloth. She threw the cloth at him. It closed up around him, shutting out the stars.

Air flooded into his lungs. He gasped, and nearly fell. The silver material was squirming around his body, sealing itself up, forming sleeves and leggings. A panel before his face began to clear.

The woman's face hovered before him. "If you want to live, run." Her voice whispered in Donn's ears. She turned away.

He ran. But even as he staggered over the ice, utterly bewildered, the face of the girl stayed in his mind, delicate, beautiful, twisted in a snarl of anger.

His first few steps were like trying to walk in a deflating balloon. But gradually, step by step, it got easier, because the blanket itself was knitting itself up around him, the seams becoming finer around his limbs, the joints at his hips, knees, shoulders, elbows becoming more flexible. It was unlike any human engineering, silvered on the outside and oddly skinlike on the inside where it was in contact with his clothes, his flesh.

He knew what this was, what it must be. It was the hide of a Silver Ghost. And if he now possessed this hide, then surely there was a Ghost somewhere that lacked it.

He ran on, stumbling.

Wherever he was, gravity was high, a bit higher than the Earth standard maintained by the Reef's inertial fields. The sky above was black, littered with stars. Most of the light came from one brilliant star directly above his head, a bright pinpoint source. Surely that was the Boss; surely he was still in the Association. It seemed brighter than he remembered, and he thought he saw a splinter of light coming from it, some immense flare. Perhaps he had come closer to the Boss then, deeper into the Association. But other than that—

He tripped on something, a ledge sticking out of the ice, and fell flat. He lay there, bewildered, winded.

He lifted his head. Where the girl ran, vapor exploded upward, a sparkling fountain with every footfall. "Wait," he called. "Please."

She ignored him.

He had no choice. He dragged himself to his feet. His chest where he had hit the ground felt like one vast bruise.

He came to structures, just bits of stone wall sticking out above the ice. The remains of a city? There was nothing like a human geometry here, no right angles among these bits of straight line.

He ran through a patch of some softer frost, lying over the water ice, that gathered in the lee of the low walls. It sparkled around his footfalls, evidently vaporized by waste heat. When he looked back, he saw traces of green in the boot prints that faded as suddenly as they had come.

He came to a hole in the ground, a well, ragged and dark. The girl waited. "You've seen the flowers."

"What flowers?"

"Look at this." She lifted something up. It was like a human arm, small, like a child's, with a perfectly formed hand. Done in silver, it was like a bit of a broken statue.

"It's the arm of a Silverman," he said.

"Correct. The one that carried you over. The little bastard got away, but I hurt him. Watch this." She took a knife from her belt and stabbed the arm, slitting its silver skin from the base of the wrist up through the pit of the elbow to where it had been severed. Then she hauled at the skin, briskly peeling it off. What was exposed was bloody and steaming. Without the containing skin it fell apart into individual creatures, bloodred and wormlike, some of which wriggled feebly, still alive, even as they froze. The girl dropped all of this on the ground. A cloud of vapor rose up, quickly freezing back to ice and falling back.

And all around the bloody mess, green things blossomed, a kind of moss, what looked like shoots of grass, even a kind of flower that fired off seeds like a miniature cannon. But the heat was evanescent, and the living things quickly shriveled and died.

"They wait for a bit of heat. Billions of years if they have to. And when it comes, they take their chances. The story of all life, isn't it?"

"Who are you?"

"I don't have a name."

He did not recognize her accent. It was flat, toneless. "Everybody has a name. My name is Donn Wyman."

"I only have the number the fatballs gave me. I am Sample 5A43 Stroke 7J7 Stroke."

"We call her Five," came a male voice, perhaps somebody down in the pit. "Quit showing off, Five, and get down here."

Five grinned at Donn. "All right, Hama." She kicked apart the bloody mess on the ground and made for the hole, climbing down easily.

Donn saw that there were handholds cut into the water ice. He followed with more difficulty, not trusting the grip of his Ghost-hide gloves, which continued to mold themselves around his fingers. He came to a membrane, stretched across the well. The girl had just dropped through this, so he followed. The membrane opened up around him, clinging closely like the meniscus of some high-surface-tension fluid; it was a tight band passing up the length of his body.

Beneath the membrane, he reached the bottom of the well. He was in a kind of cellar, walled by rock—or maybe it was a natural feature, a cave. He had never visited a planet and knew nothing about rock formations. The walls were draped with silvery blankets, what looked like more Ghost hide. On some of them, tetrahedrons had been crudely scribbled, the sigil of free mankind. The light came from lengths of silvery, shining cable that had been draped over the walls, crudely nailed into place: Ghost technology. He saw low corridors cut into the rock leading off into the dark. Evidently this was a complex, down here under the ruins of an alien city.

And there were people here—not many, maybe a dozen. Some wore suits of Ghost hide, their hoods back. Others went naked. They sat in small groups, eating from silvered bowls, or they slept on ledges. One woman nursed an infant at her breast. They were all ages, from the infant up through adulthood to old age. Some glanced incuriously at Donn, standing there in his Ghost-hide suit; others didn't bother looking around at all.

The girl, Five, stood before him. She had pulled back the hood of her own suit. She rapped at his translucent visor with her fingernail. "It's safe to come out of there. We have warmth and air, thanks to the fatball hide panels."

"I don't know how."

"You just pull." She took hold of the hide over his cheeks, and hauled. His hood split open easily, sundering right down the middle of his visor. Warm, fuggy air washed over him; he smelled farts and sweat and piss, and a food smell, something like boiled cabbage. "Welcome to the rat hole," Five said.

With her help, he pulled the rest of his suit away. When he was done, standing there in the clothes he had worn in Minda's Savior, a man approached him. He was already naked, and Five was stripping down, too. The man was short, his head shaved, and his body was scrawny, his ribs showing. He was a typical earthworm, Donn thought.

"I am Hama Belk," he said. It was a Coalition accent. "You can see we go naked in here."

"I think I'll keep my clothes on, for now."

Five shrugged. "Suit yourself. We don't wear clothes because the fatballs don't bother with clothes for their Samples, so there's none to steal. Unless you feel like robbing a virgin Sample. That's known." Her face was as hard as her language.

She had short-cropped blond hair. She was slim, her body wiry and supple; it was hard to tell how old she was—no more than eighteen or nineteen, surely. She had obviously been badly damaged in her short life. Donn felt sorry for her—a ridiculous reaction in the circumstances.

He said, "Steal? Rob? Is that how you live?"

"This is Ghostworld. We are all escaped Samples." She gestured at the nursing mother. "Or the children of Samples. We came here with nothing. All we have, we steal from the fatballs."

"Including their hides."

Five snapped, "We have a way of things here, virgin. You were saved by a Ghost hide. Now you must save in turn. You must kill a fatball and strip it of its hide, when you get the chance. Carry it with you, and save another if you can."

He recoiled. "I *work* with Ghosts. Look, my name is Donn Wyman. I work as a factor on the Reef—that is, I develop trading relationships with the Ghosts. Perhaps I—"

"I don't care what you do, or did. None of that matters now, your old life. You've died and been reborn. Now you're just another Sample, like us. You don't even have a number, as I do, since you weren't processed by the Ghosts before you were liberated."

"Samples. Numbers." Donn saw it now. "This, wherever I am, is where you go when you're abducted."

"You've got it," Hama Belk said. "Just as the snatching is random, so is the depositing. Usually you end up in a processing chamber, surrounded by a thousand Ghosts. That's what happened to me before the rats busted me out. Others end up on the surface, exposed—evidently the transfer isn't a hundred percent reliable. There are places where the strays end up, and we wait for them, with blankets; that's how Five found you."

"How does it work, this transfer, the snatching?"

"Well, we don't know," Hama said. "Does it matter?"

"And those exposed on the surface?"

"They die, if they aren't found in a heartbeat by Ghost patrols, or by us rats."

"Rats?"

"Us," said Five. "Wild humans, living in the cracks. Though I personally have never seen a rat, I understand the concept."

"How come you haven't seen a rat? Never mind. Have you heard of Benj Wyman? My brother. He was abducted only hours before I–"

"No," Five said bluntly.

"Look," Donn said, "you can see there's been some kind of mix-up. I'm not an abductee, a Sample as you call them. I came here with a Silverman. You saw it. You cut its arm off! Maybe if you hadn't chased it off–if I could talk to it–"

Five laughed in his face. "Every virgin Sample says the same thing. 'I'm not supposed to be here. I'm special, I'm a mother or a father, I have this or that back home.' "

"How do I get back?"

She just laughed at him again. She walked away, and knelt down by the nursing mother.

All at once, the hardness of her manner, the shock of all his experiences today, hit Donn. He staggered, and stumbled back against the wall.

Hama grabbed his arm. "Here. Sit down. Look, there's a ledge." He handed Donn a silver bowl. "Try to eat some of this. It'll warm you up."

"It's just so sudden." He looked at Hama. "I hadn't even taken in my own brother's abduction. And now–"

"Well, you've plenty of time to get used to it. Take the broth." It contained a brownish sludge, like a thick soup.

"More Ghost technology." Donn dipped a cautious finger in the bowl and tasted the gloop. It was lukewarm and tasted faintly of mushrooms.

"Yes. We just scrape up the green shit from our footsteps outside and drop it in. This is how they feed the Samples. Here, your ears are bleeding." He handed Donn a scrap of cloth.

Donn dabbed at his ears; the cloth came away bloody. "I don't even know where I am."

Hama shrugged. "None of us do. We're obviously still in the Association. And this is obviously a rogue planet, far from any sun. But aside from that, we can't tell. After all, as Five said, nobody's ever been back to tell the tale. We just call it Ghostworld."

Donn nodded. "It seems like a typical Ghost colony world, from what I know of them."

"Yes. We were taught all about Ghosts in our training, on the way here in the Spline ships."

The Ghosts' world was once Earth-like: blue skies, a yellow sun. But as the Ghosts climbed to awareness their sun evaporated, killed by a companion pulsar. The oceans froze and life huddled inward; there was frantic evolutionary pressure to find ways to keep warm.

"That's the story," Hama said. "Though many of us in the Commission wonder if this is true, or just some kind of creation myth. Or propaganda. Certainly the thing we call a Silver Ghost is really a community of symbiotic creatures: an autarky, a miniature biosphere in its own right, all but independent of the universe outside. Even the skin that saved you is independently alive."

"Even when you take it from the Ghost, it lives on."

"I wouldn't be judgmental," Hama said evenly. "I myself was a clerk in the Commission for Historical Truth. Working on the reeducation of the Reef population. I come from Mercury, actually, a sister planet of Earth. I hadn't been on the Reef long, before the lottery of the Sampling picked me. But none of that matters now." He looked at his hands. "All I have here is myself and those around me. And I do what I must to stay alive."

"Why do they bring us here? Why the Samples?"

Hama eyed him. "You said you worked with Ghosts. You don't know? *I* think it's because they are trying to understand us, the Ghosts. They fear us, for right now the Third Expansion is overwhelming them. But you can't defeat what you don't understand."

"So they take us for study." Donn shook his head. "But these random abductions, of a child from a mother, a father from a daughter—my own brother was taken. The Ghosts couldn't antagonize us more if they tried."

"I guess that shows how little they understand us, yes?"

"And what about Five, the girl with no name?"

"Ah. She was taken as an infant, under two years old, I think. As she grew, she was surrounded only by Ghosts. The only human she ever saw was her own reflection in the hide of a Ghost. She grew up thinking that she was some kind of deformity, a mutant, disabled Ghost.

"Eventually, a rat pack broke into her cage. She thought they were as diseased as she was. I think they raped her. She was only thirteen, fourteen. What a welcome to humanity! Somehow, she came through that, and emerged as a functioning human being—I say functioning: all she knows is this, life as a rat, and all she wants to do is to kill Ghosts." He smiled. "She's inventive about it, though."

Donn watched Five with the mother. "I'll be wary."

"Yes, do. Don't get any foolish ideas of *saving* her. And there are worse. Rat packs that prey on humans, other Samples. Even at the moment of abduction."

Donn looked at him curiously. "And what do you want, Hama?"

"I came to the Association to save *you*, Donn, all of you living non-Doctrinally out here in the dark. If all I can do is live here as if in a guerrilla cell behind the lines, killing a few Ghosts before my short life is over—well, maybe that's enough. It is my duty to die. *A brief life burns brightly.*"

Donn said carefully, "I think I'm more afraid of you than of the feral girl over there."

Hama laughed.

Five came to stand over Hama and Donn. Naked, lithe, her body was a pale streak in the silvery light, her nipples hard, her public hair a blond tuft. "Rested, are you? We're mounting a raid. You're lucky, Donn Wyman. We've been planning this one for a while; you'll be there for the payoff."

Donn made to protest. "I only just got here. I need to find my brother—the Silverman—"

But she was already walking away.

Hama nudged him. "That wasn't a request. Come on, on your feet."

Donn struggled up, his chest still aching from his fall.

A party of a dozen adults suited up.

They clambered up through the airtight membrane into the spectral stillness of the landscape. Donn was shocked that the Boss had shifted in the sky, moving away from the zenith, and the shadows it cast were long. But Donn had never seen a sunset, or a dawn; this was a planet, not an artifice like the Reef.

They checked each other's suits and were handed weapons. Donn was astonished to be given a spear. Then, following Five's lead, they set off over the ice.

The weapons were mostly crude, things with spinning blades, or even cruder than that, daggers and swords, pikes and spears, lengths of barbed wire and ugly tangles of spikes and hooks. But there were a few more sophisticated instruments, a kind of projectile weapon like a bazooka, even what looked like a Qax-era gravity-wave handgun, much repaired, polished smooth by usage.

They carried these weapons, walking to war.

"I can't believe we're doing this," Donn said to nobody in particular. "We're like preindustrial savages."

"I know how you feel," said a woman walking beside him. "I was a food technician back on the Reef. I'm the nearest thing to a biologist this little crew has. But by day I'm a spear-carrier." Brisk, purposeful, she was perhaps forty; she might once have been plump, but now the skin of her cheeks and neck sagged, as if emptied. "My name's Kanda Fors, by the way."

"I am—"

"We all heard who you are." She smiled, a dogged sort of expression. "We like to act indifferent. I guess that's to do with Five's hold over us. But wait until she's asleep. We'll all be at you then, finding out what you know of home, our families. We only get news from Samples. And it's all one-way."

With her calm Reef accent, she was more like Donn's family than anybody else he had yet met here. "This is real, isn't it?" he said slowly. "I think maybe I'm working through some kind of shock." He looked at the spear he had been given. It was clearly improvised from some ripped-off bit of equipment, not much more than a steel rod with its tip laboriously sharpened. "I really am stuck here, at the wrong end of a one-way funnel to this shithole in the ice."

Hama Belk said, "It isn't so bad here. It's not just a scramble for survival, you know. We're still human. We can still have higher goals."

"Like what?"

"Like science," Kanda said. "There is life here, for instance."

"I saw it. In my footsteps."

"That's what survives." This rogue world had been detached from its parent star by a close stellar encounter perhaps, or a gravitational slingshot by a wandering Jovian. "Any civilization must have been smashed quickly. Quakes, tides, even before the oceans froze over, water ice setting hard as rock, and then the air froze out on top of that. But there is life here, still. You saw it in your footsteps. And," she said dreamily, "there is *other* life. A more exotic sort, blown in from the stars, cold-lovers, psychrophiles, colonizing this cold world."

"Psychrophiles?"

"Watch." She took the index finger of her left hand in her right and squeezed the fingertip of her glove. A seam broke, and ice crystals gushed out into the vacuum. She bent and pressed this breach to the frozen ground, just for a second. Then she pulled back her hand and sealed up the glove. "Ouch, that's enough. I can do without frostbite. Now, look."

Where she had touched, a pit opened up in the ground, the width of a fist, the lip pulling back as if recoiling. The little pit closed up again in a couple of seconds. But when Kanda stirred it with a fingertip, it was broken up, like dust. "See that? Ice, permafrost, even rock, broken up to powder."

"What's going on?"

Kanda grinned. "Cryo-panspermia bugs."

There were ways that even terrestrial life could survive at extremely low temperatures. There was always the odd scrap of water even in the coldest ice, in brine pockets perhaps, or in nanofilms, kept liquid through pressure contact. And even on this frozen world, there were nutrients, seeping up from the core, or drifting down from space, comet dust.

"At these temperatures, you can't be ambitious," Kanda said. "You don't aim to grow much, just repair a bit of cellular damage once every millennium or so. Chemistry can be a help. There is a gloopy, starchlike material called exopolymer that has a way of preventing the formation of ice crystals. To such creatures, though, even the Ghosts are refugees from a warmer regime, balls of liquid water, like lava monsters. There's a whole ecosphere here, Donn, that we know hardly anything about. I long to come back here someday and do some proper science. Fascinating."

"Fascinating," Donn repeated. "While we march to war like apes."

"But there is science in the fighting, too," Hama said, almost enthusiastically. "Most analysts think it will take millennia of war before the Ghosts are exterminated. There will be plenty of need for hand-to-hand combat—it's always true in any war. So the ways we learn to fight the Ghosts, here today, could be remembered forever."

"That's a lovely thought."

Kanda frowned. "Listen, Donn Wyman. You'd better take

our miserable little war seriously. We need the resources we steal from the Ghosts, or we'd die. Simple as that. So when Five tells you to fight, fight. We don't have a lot of spare capacity for passengers. Of course, she can hear every word we say."

Five turned. "Yes, though at least the Ghosts cannot hear your pointless babbling. Ever trained to fight a Ghost?"

"No." The very thought shocked Donn.

"The easiest way to bring him down is just to puncture his hide, and follow the trail of excrement and blood and heat until he dies, which might take a day or two. We'll show you how to skin a fatball later."

"You're a monster," Donn blurted.

"No. I'm alive." She smiled at him, her beauty dazzling.

After perhaps an hour's walking, only a few kilometers, they crested a frozen ridge. And here Five had them hunch down and approach more cautiously.

So Donn got his first glimpse of a Ghost city. Sprawled over a valley carved by some long-frozen river, it was a forest of globes and half globes draped in a gleaming netting. The colony lacked a clear center, and there was no simple geometry; it looked as if it had grown in place, and perhaps it had. A slim tower dominated, silvered like the rest, with a sharp electric-blue light pulsing at its summit.

Ghosts streamed everywhere, following their own enigmatic business, like silver blood flowing through the open carcass of their silver city. The Boss cast highlights from every hide, so the city gleamed, as if it had been scattered with diamonds.

Five grinned at Donn. "So what do you think of your prey, hunter?"

"I'm no hunter. I'm surprised we're so close to a city."

Hama shrugged. "We are all escapees from the Sample zoos in that city, or else we were teleported to the ice nearby."

Five said, "Actually, everywhere on this world is near a Ghost city. The planet is filthy with them, the fatballs, billions or trillions, swarming."

That electric-blue light winked mournfully. "What's the tower?"

"Well, we don't know," Hama said. "Best guess is, it's a Destroyer tower. The Commission knows of such things on other Ghost worlds."

"Destroyer?"

"In ancient times, the Ghosts' ancestors understood full well that it was the rogue pulsar that was destroying their sun. So they venerated it. They made it a god."

Kanda murmured, "Actually, it's fascinating. Humans have always worshipped gods who they believed created the world. The Ghosts worship the one that destroyed it."

"Quiet," hissed Five. "This talk is purposeless."

"Talking is what people do, child," said Kanda.

"We are not people. We are rats. We are here to fight, not to talk."

Donn looked down at the extraordinary, beautiful city in dismay. "Fight for what? Resources? Hides, equipment—"

"That," Five said, "and the destruction of the Seer."

Donn frowned. "What do you know of the Seer?"

"Not much more than you do on your Reef," Hama said.

Five said, "The Ghosts talked of it, when I was in their zoos, when they thought I could not understand. Those who dealt with me were far from the centers of power. Yet it exists."

"So what is it?"

"We don't know," said Hama. "But if the chance arises to destroy it, we should take it. The Green Army has learned that Ghost concentrations are hard to defeat, short of out-and-out genocide. It's like stabbing on a pool of mercury with a fork; it just fragments and runs away. They lack hierarchies, like human societies, which makes them impossible to decapitate. Assassinations are useless. But in this particular case you have this Seer, whatever it is, a source of power. So if we could get to that, we could indeed inflict a great defeat in this war."

"We're not at war," Donn said.

"Oh yes, we are."

Five whispered, "Let's move in." She waved them forward.

———

Donn approached the Ghost city, running at a crouch from one bit of cover to the next, watching the silvered backs of his companions running ahead—silvered as the city itself was silvered, for their suits were made of the same stuff.

The city itself loomed huge before them now, a sculpture park of silvered monuments that hovered off the ground, utterly still. Light rope trailed everywhere, linking one floating building to the next, and filling the whole with a silver-gray glow. And Donn heard music. The ground throbbed with a bass harmonization, as if he could hear the heartbeat of the frozen planet.

Five raised a hand to call a halt. They were at the head of a kind of thoroughfare that led into the heart of the city, reasonably clear, reasonably straight. The rats got to work, laying barbed wire and spiky obstacles across the smooth surface of the roadway.

Donn murmured to Kanda, "What are they doing?"

"Setting traps," she replied. "Ghosts don't follow human ideas of geography, you know that. But if they need to evacuate fast, they'll use thoroughfares like this. In fact, they come swarming along the ground when they're alarmed. Some primitive instinct, but useful for us. They'll hit the traps."

"What is going to make them evacuate?"

Five grinned at him. "We are. Come on."

Leaving half a dozen hunters behind at the barricade, the rest moved deeper into the city.

The crowded tangle of light ropes grew thicker over their heads. In the complexity, Donn saw denser concentrations—nurseries of Ghost subcomponents, perhaps, or control centers, or simply areas where Ghosts lived and played—little more than patches of silvery shadow in the tangle. It was characteristic

Ghost architecture, vibrant, complex, beautiful, alive, totally in-human.

And there were Ghosts all over. They drifted over and through the tangle, following pathways invisible to Donn, or they would cluster in little clusters, whirling in chains like necklaces, apparently for the fun of it.

In one place, Donn saw an orderly queue of Ghosts, almost like a line of human schoolchildren waiting for a punishment. They filed patiently into a floating dodecahedral box that opened to embrace each Ghost, closed around it, and opened again, empty, ready for the next.

There must have been thousands of Ghosts in the patient line, he saw. And as the dodecahedral chamber hovered, far from any building, it was hard to see where all the Ghosts it swallowed were going.

He pointed this out to Hama. "What's that?"

"I suppose there are two possible answers," Hama said. "It's either an extermination chamber. Or it's a teleport."

The thought excited Donn. "Like the Sampling, the abductions. So where are they going?"

"We only have rumors," Hama said cautiously. "Briefings from the Commission, gossip from the zoos. It may have something to do with the Seer."

"Or," Kanda said, "it may have to do with the instability of the star. The Boss—all that flaring."

"You're suggesting the Ghosts are trying to mend a failing star?"

"We know they think big," Hama said. "Anyhow, it makes no difference to us."

Donn stared at the chamber, avid. For if this was a teleport terminal, it might be a way off this dismal planet. But the dodecahedral chamber wasn't their destination.

The party came to a big transparent sphere, apparently pressurized. At the center of the sphere, a big ball of mud hung in the air, brown and viscous. It seemed to be heated from within; it was slowly boiling, with big sticky bubbles of vapor crowding its surface, and it was laced with purple and red smears. Tubes led off from the mud ball to the hull of the pod. Ghosts clustered there, sucking up the purple gunk from the mud.

Donn crouched with the others, awed. "The Ghosts are *feeding*."

"Yes," Kanda said. "This is how Ghosts live. Even on their home world, deep beneath their frozen oceans, a little primordial geothermal heat must leak out still, dragging minerals up from the depths. Life-forms feed. And the Ghosts feed on *them*."

So this mud ball was a kitchen—and no wonder the Ghosts liked a little sea-bottom ooze to play in at Minda's. "So what are we doing here?"

Kanda murmured, "It's not the kitchen itself that's the target. It's about the warmest place in the city. What we intend to do is release all that heat, dump it into the environment."

"Why?"

"We're going to give them indigestion," Five murmured. "Positions."

The hunters spread out. Their projectile weapons were aimed at the feeding pod and that antiquated handgun.

Five called, "Three, two, one."

Fire burst from the projectile weapons, and cherry-red starbreaker light ripped from the ancient handgun. The pod's wall was elastic; it burst like a soap bubble, and that big floating mud ball splashed to the ground amid a hail of ice droplets.

Steam flashed, instantly frosting. The feeding Ghosts fled in panic.

And as the mud's heat was dumped, the ground subsided, a pit dilating open, like an immense version of the fingertip dimple Kanda had made on the walk here.

Kanda said, "We've been seeding this whole area with cryo nests for weeks. If you hit the cryos with too much heat, they have ways of hitting back."

Away from the smashed pod, larger structures began to slip into the widening pit, or they floated away, gravitational anchors broken. The disruption spread rapidly as buildings far from the center were hauled over by the rope tangle. The hunters started to make the damage worse, slashing light cables with chain saws.

Ghosts spilled out of the tangle. They poured down the open throughway and flowed over the ground out of the city, just as Kanda had suggested. And they started to get caught in the traps the humans had set.

Five stood in the open. "We'll have fifteen, twenty minutes before they organize to get rid of us. Let's get this done." She raised her spear.

Donn watched Five slaughter one Ghost.

Its skin was already punctured where it was snagged on the wire, and bloody water and air fountained, crystalline, from the wounds. Now Five leapt on the Ghost, landing sprawled on its hide. Gripping with her legs, she coiled her back upward and struck down with a stabbing sword, as hard as she could. The blade was buried up to the hilt in the Ghost's carcass. But the hilt was attached by a rope to a stake driven into the hard ground, and as the Ghost thrashed, its own motions tore gouges into its flesh.

Five slid to the ground, then lunged in again. This time she used a tool like a long-handled hook to dig into the gaping wounds, and she dragged out a length of bloody rope, intestine perhaps. It coiled on the ground, steaming and freezing.

All around Donn, the humans labored at the trapped Ghosts with chain saws and axes and swords and daggers. Hama and Kanda worked as hard as the rest. One man thrust a kind of lance into the side of a Ghost. Donn couldn't see its purpose, the wound didn't seem deep, but it thrashed in agony. Kanda told him it was a refrigeration laser, cannibalized from a crashed Ghost ship, invisibly pouring out the Ghost's precious hoarded heat.

Above their heads, even as the slaughter went on, Ghosts

fled from the collapsing city, shimmering mercury droplets drifting away.

Five approached Donn. She held out the knife to him, handle first. "Here. Finish this one. Easy first kill, my treat."

Donn took a step forward, toward the Ghost she had eviscerated. He actually held out his hand, holding the knife. He knew this was the only way he was going to survive here.

But all the emotions, all the shock of this extraordinary day, focussed into this moment. He felt detached from the ice world, from the grinning girl before him, detached from it by more than the smear of frozen blood on his Ghost-hide visor.

He stepped back. "No," he said.

She glared at him. She took back the knife and cut through the Ghost's intestine with a savage swipe. Dark fluid poured out, congealing onto the ice, freezing immediately. The Ghost subsided, as if deflating. Five faced Donn. "I knew you were a weak one the minute I saw you."

"Then you were right."

"We only survive here by killing Ghosts. If you won't kill, you have no right to live."

"I understand that."

She held out her hand. "Your suit. Give it back to me. I'll find a better use for it."

He nodded. He had nothing else to say. He reached up and pinched his hood by the cheeks. One firm tug and–

"Wait."

A human being came walking out of the calamitous Ghost city–*walking without a pressure suit,* of Ghost skin or otherwise. It was Eve Raoul. And a Ghost rolled at her shoulder. It was the Sink Ambassador, Donn knew it must be.

The humans, Hama and Kanda and the rest, stood back from their butchery. They were crusted with frozen blood, weapons in their hands.

Trembling, exhausted, Donn felt *irritated.* It could all have been over in an instant. No more changes, no more transitions, no more choices. Death would have been easier, he felt, than facing whatever came next.

———

Around them, the Ghosts were starting to organize.

"We can still get out of here," Five said, "if we run. Now."

"No more running for me," Donn said. "Whatever happens."

"That's wise, Donn Wyman," said the Ambassador.

Eve Raoul stood at its side. She looked down at her feet, up to her ankles in frozen air. The Virtual protocol violations must be agonizing for her, Donn thought; it was *supposed* to hurt if you walked out into the vacuum without a suit. She turned to the Ambassador. "I did the job you wanted. I snagged their attention." Yes, Donn thought. As no Ghost, among a million Ghosts, ever could. "Let me go now. Please."

"Thank you, Eve Raoul."

Eve turned to Donn. "Listen to the Ambassador. Do what it says. It's more important than you can imagine." Her voice trailed off, and she broke up into a cloud of blocky pixels that dwindled and vanished.

Donn said, "How did you know I would be here?"

"You are not hard to track," the Ambassador said. "Your biochemical signature—none of you can hide. Not even you, Sample 5A43."

Five flinched. "You know where we are, our bunker?"

"Of course we do."

"Then why don't you hunt us down, kill us?"

"For what purpose? We brought you here to understand you, not kill you."

Hama said, a knife in his hand, "Perhaps seeing humans in the wild like this helps you understand a bit more, eh, Ambassador?"

Kanda said, "You do not stop us even when we come to slaughter you?"

The Ambassador lifted off the ground and hovered over the deflated corpses of its kind, impaled on the crude human traps. "We seem to have trouble anticipating such actions as this. We do not think the way you do. I suppose we lack imagination."

Donn said, "What do you want, Ambassador? Will you take me home?"

"Not yet." It was another voice. A Silverman came walking from the chaotic city—*the* Silverman, Donn saw, the one from Minda's Savior, with its human-tech neck band and one arm lopped off above the elbow. "We need your help."

" 'We?' Ambassador, since when have you and the Silvermen constituted a 'we'?"

"Since you made this one as smart as any Ghost. You Reefborn made him intelligent enough to suffer. But sentience always has unexpected consequences. In fact, he has been intelligent enough, and human enough, to be able to anticipate what humans will do next."

"Do?"

"When you learn what we have been up to. Donn Wyman, we need you to tell the humans. They would not listen to us. You, though, might be believed. We will show you. Come."

The Silverman turned and walked back toward the city. The Ambassador followed.

Donn saw that they were heading for the dodecahedral transfer station. "You want me to get into that thing?"

"Yes," said the Ambassador.

"Where will it take me?"

"To somewhere beyond your imagination."

"And what will I meet there?"

"The one known in your human rumors as the Seer."

Kanda laughed. "You lucky cuss. Go, man. Go!"

But still Donn hesitated. "I'll come with you if you let these others go. Back to their cave under the ice. And send them home. Don't harm them further."

The Ambassador didn't pause. "Done."

"Thank you," whispered Hama Belk.

Kanda grinned. "A brief life, Hama?"

"Not that brief, thanks."

Donn said, "One more thing, Ambassador."

The Ambassador rolled. "Jack Raoul would have admired your nerve."

"Find my brother. Benj Wyman. He's here somewhere, one of your 'Samples.' "

"Not mine. The faction who—"

Donn cut him off. "Find him. Send him home, too."

"Done."

"All right." Donn took a step toward the Ambassador.

"Wait." It was Five. "Take me with you, virgin. If you're to meet the Seer, I want to be there."

"Why? To kill it?"

"If it's necessary, you'll need somebody to do it. *You* won't, that's for sure."

Donn asked, "Ambassador?"

The Ambassador rolled. "Abandon your weapons, Sample 5A43."

"Five. My name is Five."

"Abandon your weapons."

Five was obviously reluctant. But she took her heavy projectile weapon and her quiver of arrows and her stabbing sword and handed them all to Hama.

Donn held out his hand to her. "Come, then. But no more of the 'virgin.' "

She clasped his hand; he could feel her strength through the double layer of Ghost fabric. They walked together, following the Silverman and the Ambassador, back into the devastated city.

———

The flow of Ghosts into the dodecahedral transport terminal had stopped, perhaps disrupted by the chaos the humans had caused. But Ghosts were still pouring out of the crumpled heart of the city, while more were flowing the other way, as a purposeful operation of recovery began. Donn found it hard not to flinch, as if all these suspended masses might come tumbling down on his head. The Ambassador assured them they would be safe.

Five's gloved hand grasped Donn's hard.

Donn asked, "So how are you feeling?"

"Like I'm two years old again," she said. "Stripped of everything I've built for myself. They've got me back, haven't they?"

"No," Donn said firmly. "You walked into this—your choice. And you'll be walking back out of it, too."

She thought about that. "You promise, virgin?"

"I promise." *And you were wrong, Hama,* he thought. *I did get to save her after all—or at least there's chance.* "So, Ambassador. This device—is this how you've been snatching people?"

"Shall we avoid such loaded words, Donn Wyman? We have been developing a new nonlocal transportation technology. It is the outcome of a wide-ranging program of physical research."

The Ghosts' origin, under a failing sun, had led them to believe they lived in a flawed universe. So they wished to understand its fine-tuning.

"*Why are we here?* You see, there is only a narrow range of the constants of physics within which life of *any* sort is possible. We study this question by pushing at the boundaries—by tinkering with the laws that sustain and contain us all. Thus we explore the boundaries of reality."

"While snatching children," Five said.

"Get to the point, Ambassador," Donn said.

"We have found a way to adjust the value of Planck's constant, which gives, in human physics, the scale of quantum uncertainty."

Donn frowned. "Jack Raoul was involved in a situation where Ghosts messed with Planck's constant. They reduced it."

"Yes. We were endeavoring to produce an AI of arbitrarily large capacity."

"It was a disaster."

"Well, yes. But in the end, a useful technology was derived—Ghost hide, as you call it."

Five was struggling to follow all this. "And is this what you've done here? You've decreased this Planck number again?"

"No. This time we have increased it, Five."

Donn saw it. "You've increased the uncertainty in the universe—or a bit of it." He thought fast. "A particle has a quantum function, which describes the probability you'll find it in any given location. But the probability is nonzero *everywhere,* throughout the universe. And if you increase Planck, then you increase all those probabilities."

"You're beginning to see it," the Ambassador said. "It is hard to imagine a more elegant mode of transport, in theory: you simply make it more likely that you are at your destination than your starting point."

Donn was stunned by this audacity. "*In theory.*"

"The engineering details are soluble."

Donn laughed. "Evidently. Or we wouldn't be standing here, would we?"

" 'Soluble.' 'Evidently.' " Five stared at Donn. "You're talking to this Ghost as if all this is *normal.* As if you're discussing a new kind of stabbing sword." She turned to the Ambassador. "*How* do you change the laws of physics?"

"Quagma," said Donn immediately.

He understood some of this. The principle of the GUT-drive, which powered ancient ships like his mother's own *Miriam Berg,* was related. Quagma was the state of matter that had emerged from the big bang, a magma of quarks—a quagma. And at such temperatures, the fundamental forces of physics unified into a single superforce. Quagma was bound together only by the superforce. And when quagma was allowed to cool and expand, the superforce decomposed into the four sub-forces. By controlling the decomposition, you could select the

ratios between those forces, ratios that governed the fundamental constants–including Planck's constant.

Humans knew the importance of quagma. Donn's father's
family had a legend of an earlier Wyman involved in a jaunt
nearly two hundred years ago, when humans had raced Ghosts
to retrieve a lode of this primordial treasure.

Donn said, "You scare us, with what you do, you Ghosts.
You always have and always will."

The Ghost rolled and bobbed. "Sometimes we scare ourselves, believe it or not. Shall we proceed?" And it swept boldly
into the open dodecahedral chamber. Doors dilated closed
around it, and when they opened, only a second later, the
Ghost had gone, a tonne of spinning flesh vanished.

Donn and Five were left alone, surrounded by anonymous
shoals of Ghosts. Donn grabbed Five's hand again. "Together?"

"Let's get on with it."

The chamber was a blank-walled box, silvered like all
Ghost architecture. When the doors closed behind them, they
were suspended in the dark, just for a heartbeat.

And when the doors opened, they were not in the dark anymore.

"Do not be afraid," said the Sink Ambassador.

The Ghost hovered before them, bathed in dazzling light. Behind it Donn saw the silent figure of the Silverman, the stump
of its severed arm a jarring asymmetry.

Five squeezed Donn's hand. "Virgin?"

"It's all right. I mean, if they were going to kill us, they'd
have done it by now. And stop calling me 'virgin.' Come on."
Deliberately, he stepped forward, into the light. Keeping tight
hold of his hand, Five followed.

Donn found himself standing on a silvered platform, three
or four meters across. The Ghost hovered before him. He
couldn't see any support for the platform, though gravity felt

about normal. They were entirely bathed in pure white light, above, below, all around, an abstraction of a sky. The light was bright, not quite dazzling. And as Donn's eyes adjusted, he gradually made out structure in the light: billows like clouds, all around, slowly evolving, vacuoles boiling.

When he glanced back, he saw that the dodecahedral transit chamber had vanished; somehow he wasn't surprised.

The Ambassador said, "Where do you think you are?"

"In the heart of a star," Five said. "Where else?"

"But not just any star."

"The Boss," Donn said. "But that's impossible. Isn't it, Ambassador?"

"How did you phrase it earlier? 'Evidently not. Or we wouldn't be standing here, would we?' "

The Silverman said, "I understand, Donn Wyman. I am human enough to fear falling. Don't be afraid. Step to the edge. Look down."

Five wouldn't move. She stood there, her hide suit still stained by Ghost blood, bathed in starlight. But Donn stepped to the rim of the floating disk.

And he looked down on a Ghost base in the heart of the star. It was a hollowed-out moon, a rock ball that must have been a thousand kilometers wide, riddled with passages and cavities.

The disk began to descend. The motion was smooth, but Five lunged forward and grabbed at Donn's arm.

The moon turned into a complex, machined landscape below them. Ghost ships and science platforms swept over the pocked landscape, tangles of shining net. And Ghosts themselves drifted up from the chambers and machine emplacements, bobbing like balloons, shining in the star's deep light. Behind the moon, there were threads of a more intense brightness, just at the limit of visibility, dead straight. All over the moon's surface, vast cylindrical structures gleamed. The Ambassador said these were intrasystem drives and hyperdrives, systems that had been used to fling this moon into the body of this star and to hold it here.

And there was quagma down there, the Ambassador said, little packets of the primordial stuff, buried in the pits of ancient planetesimal craters. *I knew it,* Donn thought.

"The work here is hard," the Ambassador said. "Often lethal. We have poured workers into this mine of light endlessly." And Donn thought of the stream of Ghosts he had seen filing patiently into the transportation booth on Ghostworld. "Few come back, despite all our precautions. But now the work is nearly done."

Five asked, "So how come we aren't all burned up? We're in the middle of a *star.*"

"Perhaps you can see those illuminated threads? Those are refrigeration lasers. By making ourselves hotter even than this star's core, we can dump our heat into it. Of course, what you are seeing is a representation, heavily processed. Starstuff is in fact very opaque."

Donn said, "You are messing with physics again, aren't you, Ambassador?" He thought back to the Coalition's recent observations of the Boss. "We've been observing flares. Are you trying to mend the star, to stop the flares? No, not that. Sink Ambassador, *are you destabilizing this star?*"

The Ambassador rolled. "How would Jack Raoul have put it? 'Guilty as charged.' What do you understand of stellar physics?"

Every star was in equilibrium, with the pressure of the radiation from its fusing core balancing the tendency of its outer layers to fall inward under gravity. A giant star like the Boss, crushed by its own tremendous weight, needed a *lot* of radiation to keep from imploding. So it ran through the hydrogen fuel it used to fuse quickly, and a detritus of helium ash collected in its core.

"But that 'ash' can fuse too," the Ambassador said. "The fusion process produces such elements as carbon, oxygen, silicon, each of which fuses in turn. The chain ends in iron, which cannot fuse, for if it did so it would *absorb* energy, not release it. And so an inner core of iron builds up at the heart of a star like this. A core bigger than most worlds, Donn Wyman!"

Five asked, "So how come it doesn't just collapse?"

"Its components are already crushed together as far as they will go. This is a property of atomic matter. Humans know it as the Pauli exclusion principle. Of course, in time, as the dead zone spreads through the heart of the star, the repulsion will finally be overcome. Electrons will be forced to merge with protons, producing neutrons—a neutron star will be born, smaller and denser than the iron core. And then there will be a collapse of the outer layers, a catastrophic one. But not yet, not for a long time; this star is stable."

"Or it *was,* before you came along," Donn said. "But now you're changing things, aren't you? Planck's constant again?"

"Jack Raoul would be proud of you, Donn. Like you, he was a good guesser."

"If you were to use your moon-machine to reduce Planck in the star's core—"

"Then Pauli repulsion would be reduced. The iron core would collapse prematurely."

The Ghost showed them a Virtual representation of what would happen next. The implosion would rapidly mutate into an explosion. Shock waves would form and rebound from the inner layers, and a vast pulse of neutrinos would power further expansion.

"The Boss will be blown apart," said Donn, wondering.

"Yes. A detonation over in seconds, after years of preparation. But the explosion will be asymmetrical, that layer heated by the neutrinos turbulent. This is the key to such explosions, and it is this turbulence we are hoping to control. For the asymmetry will blast the neutron star out of the debris of the Boss—it will leave with a significant velocity—while releasing a pulse of gravitational wave energy that we would hope to tap and—"

"A supernova," Five said. "That's what you're talking about, isn't it? You're going to turn the Boss into a supernova."

"We believe it will be the first *artificial* detonation of its kind in the evolution of the universe. A supernova used as a cannon to fire out a neutron star, directed as we please! History is watching us, Donn Wyman."

The Silverman comically raised its stump of an arm. "Magnificent!"

Donn paced around. "You're insane."

"Now you do sound like Jack Raoul," said the Ambassador.

"You will devastate worlds!"

"Actually, stars, too," said the Ambassador. "Nearby *stars* will be boiled away."

"And the Reef," Donn said grimly. "Surely, we're too close to survive."

Five said, "The Reef is ships joined up together, isn't it? I don't remember. You could just fly away."

"We don't have hyperdrive," Donn said. "Confiscated by the Coalition for their Navy ships. I don't imagine they will be handing them back." He turned on the Ambassador. "This is mass murder. Why are you doing this?"

"Because of the Seer." The new voice was a woman's: Eve Raoul's. Donn heard her words moments before a cloud of pixels popped into existence and coalesced into her thin form.

She stepped to the edge of the platform. "My. Quite a view. Quite a drop, too." She reached out absently, but none of them had a Virtual hand to offer her, and she stepped back.

"I wasn't expecting to see you again," Donn said.

"Well, I didn't expect to be revived again," she said with a trace of bitterness. "At least I'm not in any pain this time. I guess it's good to be useful."

"Useful how?"

The Ambassador said, "Eve is helping us understand an

entity of our own creation, an entity whose wishes have brought us all here today."

Donn's heart thumped. "You mean the Seer."

"Turn around, Five, Donn."

They turned. The Silverman was holding, in his one hand, a box, a tetrahedron ten centimeters or so to an edge. It seemed to have clear walls, and its interior was black and full of stars, stars that swarmed–that, at any rate, was Donn's first impression. Five and Donn both stepped closer to look. The "stars" were no more than dust motes, pushed to and fro by random currents in whatever air filled the box.

Donn said, "It's like a toy. What is it?"

"The Seer," Eve said.

The Ambassador said, "The control of the core of a giant star during a catastrophic explosion is ferociously difficult. Even modeling it was beyond our processing resources. So we devised a new generation of AI."

Five said, "This box of dust?"

"This box of dust," Eve said, "is about the most advanced AI we're aware of. For a machine like this, physically you need components that are small enough to be influenced by quantum effects, yet large enough to feel the effects of gravity. A swarm of smart microprobes–dust motes."

"A machine like what?"

"A quantum gravity AI."

"On the *Miriam,* we have quantum AIs," Donn said.

"Right," Eve said, nodding. "And that gives you an edge. A simple switch can only be in one state at a time–on or off. A quantum switch holds information about *all* possible states of the switch at any one time. And so you can use it to do parallel processing. Many inputs, many outputs. You get a speed advantage, and a significant one.

"But a *quantum gravity* machine goes one step further. You abandon causality altogether."

The blurring of position and velocity in quantum mechanics made traditional causality problematic. And in relativity, too, lightspeed limits ensured that causality was more an aspiration than an iron law.

Donn started to see. "And if you put quantum mechanics and relativity together–"

"In a quantum gravity computer, cause and effect are thoroughly mixed up. You don't even need to have input before output, causally. In practice, I think, the Seer is able to glimpse the outline of a solution to a given problem even before it has begun its calculation, and so can guide its processing efficiently to that outcome. In retrospect, its thinking feels like guesswork, an unlikely series of inductive leaps. But it's always right, and very, very fast."

"The Seer really can see the future," Five said, "just as the rumors say."

"But its visions are limited to the outcomes of computing algorithms a few microseconds ahead–or to the furthest future, millennia or more away."

Five glared at the Ambassador. "So why the tetrahedron, fatball? Why is this ultimate brain in a box the shape of the symbol of human freedom?"

"A tetrahedron was the most suitable shape for–"

"It's a totem, that's what I think. Some of the Samples believe Ghosts are starting to worship humans, because we're becoming so good at killing you. Hence the Silvermen, walking human statues. Hence the tetrahedral box."

The Ambassador said evenly, "We Ghosts do have a propensity for worshipping that which destroys us, it is true. But you are not yet a goddess, Sample 5A43."

Donn said sharply, "Enough. Eve, you said how the Seer's thinking *feels*. How can you know that?"

"Ah. Good question. Because, not for the first time, the Ghosts had trouble with an AI that ended up not performing *quite* as specified."

"Like the Silverman."

"Well, yes. And, not for the first time, I, or an avatar of myself, was asked to help interpret for it." She looked at Donn, her gray hair shining in the light of the stellar core. "It sees the future, Donn. And it is afraid."

———

Donn watched Eve. Her eyes were unfocused, and he thought her representation was degrading, her skin smoothing from lack of definition, a lock of her gray hair flickering. He wondered how it must be to *be* her, a representation every bit as sentient as he was, and yet having endured multiple lives already—and now locked into a consciousness like no other.

She said, "The Seer is sentient, born of dust into a baffling, acausal universe. But it is a Ghost artifact. And so it shares Ghost values, Ghost assumptions. The Ghosts survived the death of their world through symbiosis, dissimilar life-forms gathering together. The Ghosts have faith that the life-forms of this era of the universe, a transient age of light- and water-based chemistry, will similarly use cooperation and symbiosis to survive the transition to the new cold age to come when the last star dies."

Five shuddered. "How can you *think* like that?"

"This has happened already, in the universe's history," Eve said. "There are life-forms extant now, in this age of matter, that are survivors of earlier epochs, the age of radiation and of annihilation and of superforces and of—"

"Enough," Donn said. Her speech had become rapid, automated, as if she was hypnotized. "Go on, Eve."

"But when this age ends, when dark energy comes to predominate and the fabric of space-time is torn apart—when this happens, and the Seer can *see* it—there will be no Ghost left alive to witness it, and no symbiotic descendant of the Ghosts."

"Why not?"

"Because of *us*," said Five savagely. "Because of humans. *We win.* I don't need a quantum-gravity computer to tell me that!"

"You must understand," the Ambassador said. "The detonation of this sun—we do this because we, this Ghost enclave, have been cut off from our home range by the forces of your Coalition. Billions of individuals, a whole world, trapped behind the lines. We were desperate. We looked for a way to change the parameters–the rules of the game. That is our way of resolving problems. We were looking for a way out. Now we see we must do more than that; we must take the Seer and its dreadful counsel to our home ranges. We need time to consider what must be done."

"Such as what?" Five asked.

"Such as escape."

Escape to *where*? Donn wondered. Where could the Ghosts go to escape a rampant, Coalition-led mankind? Out of the Galaxy? Out of the *cosmos* altogether? He tried to focus on his own situation. "Then why have you brought us here? Why tell us this?"

"Because of me," said the Silverman. He stepped forward, still cradling the Seer. "You made me smart to punish me. But I am human enough to guess how you would feel about an exploding star."

The Ambassador said, "We did not mean to engineer this star as an act of war, only as a means of escape. We understand now that humans might not see it that way."

"You really don't get human psychology, do you?" Donn said.

"No," said the Silverman cheerfully. "Donn Wyman, you must warn your people. Make them believe, as we could not. Make them flee. And make them believe the Ghosts did not mean war."

"That's a tall order."

"You are our only hope," the Ghost said simply.

Donn felt empty. Could it be true that so much was pivoting on this moment? *Because if so,* he thought, *I am not strong enough to deal with it.*

"You don't have much time," said the Ambassador. It floated toward the lip of the platform.

Donn followed and looked down at the engineered moon. Ghosts swarmed, pinpricks of dazzling light against the worked regolith. "How long?"

"The mathematics is uncertain."

"There are human colonies scattered through the Association," Donn said. "Many of them have hyperdrive, I think. But the main human concentration is the Reef. And we no longer have hyperdrive."

"Ask your father," the Ambassador said.

"What?"

"I, too, approved of the Silverman's wish to contact you personally, Donn Wyman. Because I know that your family has resources. We will send you home now, Donn Wyman."

They pulled back and stood in a row, the Silverman with the tetrahedral box, the looming Ghost, and the Virtual of Eve, gradually disintegrating.

Eve raised her hand. "There is more," she said solemnly. "Human and Ghosts must both join the great confluence of mind in the far future, join with the rest. That is the only way the next transition can be survived *by either of us.*"

Donn was shocked by this latest bit of bad news. "And if humans destroy the Ghosts—"

"Then *neither* will survive. Remember," she said, her voice scratchy. "Remember—"

Five ran toward the Silverman, who stood stock-still, slow to react. She raised her fists and slammed them down on the Seer. Her hands passed through its substance, scattering pixels.

Donn pulled her away.

"Just an avatar," she said, breathless. "Worth a try. To strike such a blow . . . it would have been magnificent."

The Ghost and its companions were surrounded by a cloud of pixels now. The star's light flickered.

And Donn was home.

———

His mother ran up to him and grabbed him. "Oh, Lethe, Donn! I never thought I'd see you again!" He let her weep on his shoulder. "Benj is back, too," she whispered. "He's back!"

Donn saw Five, still in her bloodstained Ghost-hide suit,

looking even more scared and bewildered than in the center of the star. There was Samm, his father, grinning hugely, grabbing onto Benj as hard as his mother was to Donn. The Commissary, Elah, was here, too. She looked as shocked as any of them at Donn's sudden appearance, but she was looking up into the sky with some alarm and muttering into the air, evidently communicating with her Coalition colleagues.

Donn couldn't resist grinning at his brother. Benj was wearing a plain white bathrobe; all his hair had been shaved off. "Benj, what happened to you?"

"I've been a stark naked lab rat for a day. If it was you who got me out—"

"It was. You owe me."

"Damn."

There were twin concussions, soft explosions, and a breeze of displaced air. Hama Belk and Kanda Fors had coalesced, under the lifedome. Grubby, scrawny, they both staggered in the sudden change of gravity, and they clung to each other in shock. Then they realized where they were, and their clinging turned to a hug of joy.

Then Hama spotted Elah in her black Commissary's robe, and he went over to her immediately.

Donn gently disengaged his mother. "Mom—you have guests."

Rima turned. "Do I know you?"

Kanda, recovering her composure quickly, came forward. "Kanda Fors. Food tech, from the *Michael Poole*. We met a couple of times, I think . . . I've been lost for a number of years."

"It's a day of shocks for us all." Rima stepped forward, and the women clasped hands. Rima's face tattoos flared electric blue, and Donn was proud of her.

Amid more concussions, more of the ragged rats from Ghostworld started to appear, many naked, bewildered. One woman cradled a baby.

Donn took Five by the hand and led her to his mother. "Mom, this one's called Five. Long story. I think she'd appreci-

ate some help, her and her people. Some clothes, for a start."
But Five flinched back. "She's been living wild," Donn murmured. "It will take some time."

"We've all the time in the world. Come, child. And, Kanda,
you'll be wanting to tell your family you're back?"

"I feel nervous about it. Yes, of course."

"And you—Five, was it? What about your family?"

"I don't remember them."

"I'm sure we can trace them. Come on, we'll sort it out."

Donn approached his father. "Dad, I need to talk to you.
We're in trouble. The Boss—"

"I know. Look at this." He showed Donn an image, returned by faster-than-light inseparability links from a Coalition
drone observer close to the giant star. It was spitting, flaring,
ejecting knots of plasma large enough to swallow Earth's sun
whole. "It's becoming unstable."

"It's worse than that." As urgently as he could, he told his
father all he had witnessed, the Ghost experiments at the heart
of the Boss—the coming supernova. Samm listened gravely.

"You do believe me?"

"Of course I believe you."

"As do we," Elah said, walking over.

Hama followed in her wake. Though he was just as grimy
and underfed, he didn't seem to Donn to be the same person he
had been on the Ghostworld; he had immediately retreated
into his role, like a shadow of the Commissary.

"What you say," Elah went on, "ties in with the projections
we have been making of the star's instability."

Samm folded his arms. "You say you're here to protect us,
you of the Coalition. What are you going to do about this?"

"We have already put out a warning to the other human
colonies in the Association. Most of them have hyperdrive
ships; they will be able to flee in time. Other Coalition centers
are arranging refugee facilities."

"Blankets and hot water. Great. But what about us? You

know damn well the Reef contains the largest human population in the Association. You took away *our* hyperdrives!"

"In order to serve the greater needs of the Third Expansion."

"That star's going to expand before long, and cook us all. Going to give us back our technology, are you?"

"That isn't practical," Elah said simply. She listened absently. "Come," she said to Hama. "The flitters are lifting Coalition personnel from the Reef in fifteen minutes."

"And us?" Samm tried to grab her arm, but she shook him off. "What of us? You're leaving us to die!"

From nowhere, Elah produced a handgun, a starbreaker. "This conversation is over, regrettably." Backing up, she and Hama made for the door cut into the lifedome.

Samm made to follow, but Donn stopped him. "Dad, let me. Wait, Commissary." Cautiously, he approached Elah and Hama. In a few rushed words, he tried to tell them more of what the Ghost had told him within the star.

"The Ghosts don't want this to be seen as an act of war."

"Then they shouldn't detonate supernovas in human space," Elah said.

"They're only doing it to escape the cage we put them in."

"*They* put humans in cages. Your friend Five, Hama here."

"They fear we will drive them to extinction. That's what the Seer foresees. And if that's so, we may destroy ourselves as well."

Elah thought that over. "Better a Galaxy in ruins," she said, "than a Galaxy that is not ruled by *us*. Good luck, Donn Wyman." She backed to the door, and left. Hama looked back once, but it was as if he barely recognized Donn anymore, and he followed his superior.

Donn went back to his father. "I failed."

"Well, what did you expect? You aren't going to overturn an ideology like the Coalition's with a couple of sentences. But the Commission for Historical Truth records everything that transpires—*everything*. Maybe they will figure all this out one day, after a couple of thousand years' study in some library on Earth—maybe you planted a few seeds for the future. In the meantime, we've a supernova to deal with." Samm eyed his son. "So, did your new Ghost best buddy give you any advice?"

"It said I should ask you."

Samm sighed. "Smart of it. Okay, son. I guess it's time you learned a little family history." Carrying his data slate, he walked off toward the copse at the center of the dome, chlorophyll green leaves shining under the light of the burgeoning supernova.

Donn hurried after him. "Where are we going?"

"The engine room."

The kilometer-long elevator descent along the ship's spine was slow, frustrating.

Donn knew his way around the control room at the heart of the *Miriam*'s GUTdrive pod. He used to come down here as a kid, to play with his brother, and later, as a young man, to learn about the technological legacy of his mother's family. There wasn't much to see: a couple of seats and couches, a water dispenser, an emergency pressurized locker. The instruments were blank, antique data slates tiling the walls. All around this space, vast engines brooded, capable of harnessing the energies of cosmic inflation to drive the ship forward. But the engines hadn't been fired up in Donn's lifetime, not once.

Donn expected his father to boot up these control slates. He didn't. Instead he took the small portable slate he had carried down from the lifedome and pressed it against a wall. It lit up with a crowded panel of displays. "There you go," Samm said. "Two hundred years old, and it fires up like it was brand-new."

"What does?"

"This." He tapped the slate and showed Donn an external view of the *Miriam,* seen from below, its lifedome embedded in the rough plane of the Reef, its spine and engine compartment dangling like a lantern. Samm zoomed in on the hull of the engine compartment, where a black slab clung like a parasite.

Donn leaned forward and stared. "What is *that*?"

"The family secret." Samm eyed his son. "Look, Donn—you aren't the first Wyman to have run into the Sink Ambassador. Your grandfather a few times removed—his name was Joens Wyman—got involved in a kind of intergalactic race with the Ghosts. He was an entrepreneur. And he wanted to get his hands on—"

"A cache of quagma," Donn said. "You told me about this."

"The trouble was, the cache was somewhere over twelve billion light-years away—the figures are uncertain. Too far even for hyperdrive. But Joens Wyman didn't use hyperdrive. He used an experimental human technology. It was called a Susy drive."

"Susy? That's the flitter's name."

"The flitter, and a secret space drive. It was kind of risky. It's not like hyperdrive. Look, they taught you at school that the universe has more dimensions than the macroscopic, the three spatial, and one of time. Most of the extra dimensions are extremely small. When you hyperdrive, you sort of twist smoothly through ninety degrees into an extra dimension, and go skimming over the surface of the universe like a pebble over a pond. Simple. Whereas with supersymmetry, you're getting into the real guts of physics."

There were two types of particles: fermions, the building blocks of matter, like quarks and electrons, and force carriers, like photons. The principle of supersymmetry had it that each building block could be translated into a force carrier, and vice versa. "The supersymmetric twins, the s-particles, are inherently fascinating, if you're a physicist, which I'm not," said Samm. "But the magic comes when you do two supersymmetric transformations—say, electron to selectron and back again. You end up with an electron, of course—but an electron in a *different place*."

"And that's the Susy drive."

"Yep. A principle the Ghosts have never explored. Joens Wyman pumped his money into this thing, and got as far as a working prototype. But in those days, nobody would invest in human research and development; it was always easier and cheaper to buy alien tech off the shelf. Joens hoped to cut his losses by sending his Susy-drive ship in search of treasure nobody else could get to."

"The quagma. What happened?"

"Joens finished up with nothing but the Susy drive and the clothes he stood up in. He fled his creditors."

"He came here."

"Yes. Good place to hide, beyond Coalition law—anyhow, it was then. His son married into your mother's family, who owned the *Miriam.*"

"And he lodged the Susy drive on the hull of the ship."

"Yeah. So it's come down the generations. My father told me about it and gave me the data on this slate. I think Joens always thought this old monster might be useful as a last resort. Well, he was right."

Donn stared at his father. This was a side of him Donn hadn't seen before, this decisive adventurer. But maybe no son saw that in his father. "Dad, you're not serious. You're not planning to fire up this Susy drive, this two-hundred-year-old disaster."

"You have a better idea?"

"When was it last tested?"

"When do you think? Look, according to these displays, the field it generates will envelop the whole of the Reef. We'll get out of here, all of us. And then you and I will go down to Minda's Savior and drink free Poole's Blood for the rest of our lives."

"If it works. And if it doesn't work?"

"Then what have we lost?" He tapped the screen. It switched to the external image. Panels blew out from the black casing fixed to the base of the pod; a zoomed-in view showed them the jeweled guts of the Susy drive.

Then the data slate chimed an alarm. The Susy-drive display cleared, to reveal an image broadcast from the Coalition monitor drone—an image of an exploding star.

"Damn," said Samm. "I didn't imagine it would be so quick."

"Dad, look." The explosion was strongly asymmetrical, a flower of ugly light splashed across the slate. And there was a denser knot to one side of the supernova.

Samm tapped the screen, overlaying analyses of mass density and velocity vectors. "That's a neutron star. The core of the Boss? It's been spat out of there like an apple seed—thousands of kilometers a second." He brought up a Galactic display. "Look at that! It's been fired straight out of the Association toward the Sagittarius Arm."

"The Ghost home range." Green asterisks began to appear around the fleeing neutron star. "What's that?"

"Ghost technology . . . Ghost ships, popping up out of nowhere. Settling into orbit around that neutron star. And, wow, look at *that.*" A major green anomaly. "It has to have the mass of a planet."

"The Ghostworld."

"Looks like it. How are they bringing all this to the neutron star?"

Donn said, "Just by making it more *likely* that the planet should be in orbit around the neutron star than wherever it used to be."

"What?"

"To move an entire planet has to take a mess of energy. The gravity waves from the supernova? The Ambassador talked about tapping into that. They must be shielding the world from the supernova shock, too. They did it, Dad! Just as the Ambassador said they would. Oh, the Coalition ships can pursue them, but a runaway neutron star will smash through the Coalition lines as if they were made of rice paper."

Samm brought back the Susy display and began to scroll

through outputs. "Let's just hope this damn Susy drive lands us outside the Coalition's clutches, too."

"Dad—don't you *know*?"

"I told you. It's kind of unreliable. We ought to end up just a little above the Galactic plane, however. Okay, it's ready."

"As quickly as that?"

"Well, that supernova shock wave is going to take a while to get here—years, as we're light-years off from the Boss. But we can't expect rescue for years either, even if the Coalition is willing to try; the gravity waves from the detonation are going to churn up hyperspace for a long time. Best to get out of here now if we can—and if this doesn't work, we might have time to figure out something else. I've sent an alarm out through the Reef."

"Shouldn't we ask Mom first? It's her ship."

"She'd only say no. Hang on to that rail. Good luck, son!" He stabbed a finger at his data slate.

The Association stars turned to streaks and disappeared.

———

So, just as his father had tried to explain, Donn was leapfrogged through Susy-space. What he hadn't been told was what it would *feel* like.

Susy-space was another universe, laid over Donn's own. It had its own laws. He was transformed into a supersymmetric copy of himself—an s-ghost in Susy-space. And it was . . . different. Things were blurred. Susy-space cut through the distinction between Donn, here, and the stars, out there. Donn could *feel* the scale of the journey, as if the arch of the universe were part of his own being. Distance crushed him.

But at last it was done.

———

The Reef of ships popped out of Susy-space, sparkling with selectrons and neutralinos.

Samm and Donn stared at each other. "Let's not do *that* again," said Donn.

"Agreed." Samm tapped his data slate, to get an external view.

Darkness, broken only by the faintest smudges of gray light.

"Are they galaxies?" asked Donn.

"Oops," said Samm.

THE TEAR

Ian McDonald

British author Ian McDonald is an ambitious and daring writer with a wide range and an impressive amount of talent. His first story was published in 1982, and since then he has appeared with some frequency in Interzone, Asimov's Science Fiction, *and elsewhere. In 1989 he won the* Locus "Best First Novel" *Award for his novel* Desolation Road. *He won the Philip K. Dick Award in 1992 for his novel* King of Morning, Queen of Day. *His other books include the novels* Out on Blue Six, Hearts, Hands and Voices, Terminal Cafe, Sacrifice of Fools, Evolution's Shore, Kirinya, Ares Express, *and* Cyberabad; *and a chapbook novella,* Tendeleo's Story; *as well as two collections of his short fiction,* Empire Dreams *and* Speaking in Tongues. *His novel* River of Gods *was a finalist for both the Hugo Award and the Arthur C. Clarke Award in 2005, and a novella drawn from it, "The Little Goddess," was a finalist for the Hugo and the Nebula. His most recent book is another new novel that's receiving critical raves,* Brasyl. *Born in Manchester, England, in 1960, McDonald has spent most of his life in Northern Ireland, and now lives and works in Belfast.*

In the lyrical and dazzling story that follows, one filled with enough wild new ideas, evocative milieus, bizarre characters, and twists and turns of plot to fill many another author's four-book trilogy, he takes us to a quiet waterworld to follow a young boy setting out on a voyage of discovery that will take him to many unexpected destinations both across the greater universe beyond and in the hidden depths of his own soul, one that will embroil him in the deadly clash of Galactic Empires, and that will take him home the long way to find that enemies can be as close and familiar as friends.

PTEY, SAILING

O n the night that Ptey voyaged out to have his soul shattered, eight hundred stars set sail across the sky. It was
an evening at Great Winter's ending. The sunlit hours raced
toward High Summer, each day lavishly more full of light than
the one before. In this latitude, the sun hardly set at all after the
spring equinox, rolling along the horizon, fat and idle and
pleased with itself. Summer-born Ptey turned his face to the sun
as it dipped briefly beneath the horizon, closed his eyes, enjoyed its lingering warmth on his eyelids, in the angle of his
cheekbones, on his lips. To the Summer-born, any loss of the
light was a reminder of the terrible, sad months of winter and
the unbroken, encircling dark.

But we have the stars, his father said, a Winter-born. *We are
born looking out into the universe.*

Ptey's father commanded the little machines that ran the
catamaran, trimming sail, winding sheets, setting course by the
tumble of satellites; but the tiller he held himself. The equinoc-
tial gales had spun away to the west two weeks before and the
catboat ran fast and fresh on a sweet wind across the darkening
water. Twin hulls cut through the ripple-reflections of gas flares
from the Temejveri oil platforms. As the sun slipped beneath
the huge dark horizon and the warmth fell from the hollows of
Ptey's face, so his father turned his face to the sky. Tonight, he
wore his Steris Aspect. The ritual selves scared Ptey, so rarely
were they unfurled in Ctarisphay: births, namings, betrothals
and marriages, divorces and deaths. And of course, the Mani-
foldings. Familiar faces became distant and formal. Their language changed, their bodies seemed slower, heavier. They
became possessed by strange, special knowledges. Only Steris
possessed the language for the robots to sail the catamaran and,
despite the wheel of positioning satellites around tilted Tay, the
latitude and longitude of the Manifold House. The catamaran
itself was only run out from its boathouse, to strong songs
heavy with clashing harmonies, when a child from Ctarisphay

on the edge of adulthood sailed out beyond the outer mole and the fleet of oil platforms to have his or her personality unfolded into eight.

Only two months since, Cjatay had sailed out into the oily black of a late winter afternoon. Ptey was Summer-born, a Solstice boy; Cjatay a late Autumn. It was considered remarkable that they shared enough in common to be able to speak to each other, let alone become the howling boys of the neighborhood, the source of every broken window and borrowed boat. The best part of three seasons between them, but here was only two moons later, leaving behind the pulsing gas flares and maze of pipe work of the sheltering oil fields, heading into the great, gentle oceanic glow of the plankton blooms, steering by the stars, the occupied, haunted stars. The Manifolding was never a thing of moons and calendars, but of mothers' watchings and grandmothers' knowings and teachers' notings and fathers' murmurings, of subtly shifted razors and untimely lethargies, of deep-swinging voices and stained bedsheets.

On Etjay Quay, where the porcelain houses leaned over the landing, Ptey had thrown his friend's bag down into the boat. Cjatay's father had caught it and frowned. There were observances. Ways. Forms.

"See you," Ptey had said.

"See you." Then the wind caught in the catamaran's tall, curved sails, and carried it away from the rain-wet, shiny faces of the houses of Ctarisphay. Ptey had watched the boat until it was lost in the light dapple of the city's lamps on the winter-dark water. See Cjatay he would, after his six months on the Manifold House. But only partially. There would be Cjatays he had never known, never even met. Eight of them, and the Cjatay with whom he had stayed out all the brief Low Summer nights of the prith run on the fishing staithes, skinny as the piers' wooden legs silhouetted against the huge sun kissing the edge of the world, would be but a part, a dream of one of the new names and new personalities. Would he know him when he met him on the great floating university that was the Manifold House?

Would he know himself?

"Are they moving yet?" Steris called from the tiller. Ptey shielded his dark-accustomed eyes against the pervasive glow of the carbon-absorbing plankton blooms and peered into the sky. *Sail of Bright Anticipation* cut two lines of liquid black through the gently undulating sheet of biolight, fraying at the edges into fractal curls of luminescence as the sheets of microorganisms sought each other.

"Nothing yet."

But it would be soon, and it would be tremendous. Eight hundred stars setting out across the night. Through the changes and domestic rituals of his sudden Manifolding, Ptey had been aware of sky-watch parties being arranged, star-gazing groups setting up telescopes along the quays and in the campaniles, while day on day the story moved closer to the head of the news. Half the world–that half of the world not blinded by its extravagant axial tilt–would be looking to the sky. Watching Steris rig *Sail of Bright Anticipation,* Ptey had felt cheated, like a sick child confined to bed while festival raged across the boats lashed beneath his window. Now, as the swell of the deep dark of his world's girdling ocean lifted the twin prows of *Sail of Bright Anticipation,* on his web of shock-plastic mesh ahead of the mast, Ptey felt his excitement lift with it. A carpet of lights below, a sky of stars above: all his alone.

ˌ They were not stars. They were the eight hundred and twenty-six space habitats of the Anpreen Commonweal, spheres of nanocarbon ice and water five hundred kilometers in diameter that for twice Ptey's lifetime had adorned Bephis, the ringed gas giant, like a necklace of pearls hidden in a velvet bag, far from eye and mind. The negotiations fell into eras. The Panic; when the world of Tay became aware that the gravity waves pulsing through the huge ripple tank that was their ocean-bound planet were the bow-shocks of massive artifacts decelerating from near lightspeed. The Denial, when Tay's governments decided it was

Best Really to try to hide the fact that their solar system had been immigrated into by eight hundred and some space vehicles, each larger than Tay's petty moons, falling into neat and proper order around Bephis. The Soliciting, when it became obvious that Denial was futile—but on our terms, our terms. A fleet of space probes was dispatched to survey and attempt radio contact with the arrivals—as yet silent as ice. And, when they were not blasted from space or vaporized or collapsed into quantum black holes or any of the plethora of fanciful destructions imagined in the popular media, the Overture. The Sobering, when it was realized that these star-visitors existed primarily as swarms of free-swimming nanoassemblers in the free-fall spherical oceans of their eight hundred and some habitats, one mind with many forms; and, for the Anpreen, the surprise that these archaic hominiforms on this backwater planet were many selves within one body. One thing they shared and understood well. Water. It ran through their histories, it flowed around their ecologies, it mediated their molecules. After one hundred and twelve years of near-lightspeed flight, the Anpreen Commonweal was desperately short of water; their spherical oceans shriveled almost into zero gravity teardrops within the immense, nanotech-reinforced ice shells. Then began the era of Negotiation, the most prolonged of the phases of contact, and the most complex. It had taken three years to establish the philosophical foundations: the Anpreen, an ancient species of the great Clade, had long been a colonial mind, arranged in subtle hierarchies of self-knowledge and ability, and did not know whom to talk to, whom to ask for a decision, in a political system with as many governments and nations as there were islands and archipelagos scattered across the world ocean of the fourth planet from the sun.

Now the era of Negotiation had become the era of Open Trade. The Anpreen habitats spent their last drops of reaction mass to break orbit around Bephis and move the Commonweal in-system. Their destination was not Tay, but Tejaphay, Tay's sunward neighbor, a huge waterworld of unbroken ocean one hundred kilometers deep, crushing gravity, and endless storms.

A billion years before the seed ships probed the remote star system, the gravitational interplay of giant worlds had sent the least of their number spiraling sunward. Solar wind had stripped away its huge atmosphere and melted its mantle of water ice into a planetary ocean, deep and dark as nightmares. It was that wink of water in the system-scale interferometers of the Can-Bet-Merey people, half a million years before, that had inspired them to fill their night sky with solar sails as one hundred thousand slow seed ships rode out on flickering launch lasers toward the new system. An evangelically pro-life people were the Can-Bet-Merey, zealous for the Clade's implicit dogma that intelligence was the only force in the universe capable of defeating the physical death of space-time.

If the tens of thousand of biological packages they had rained into the world-ocean of Tejaphay had germinated life, Tay's probes had yet to discover it. The Can-Bet-Merey did strike roots in the afterthought, that little blue pearl next out from the sun, a tear spun from huge Tejaphay.

One hundred thousand years ago, the Can-Bet-Merey had entered the postbiological phase of intelligence and moved to that level that could no longer communicate with the biological life of Tay, or even the Anpreen.

"Can you see anything yet?" A call from the tiller. *Sail of Bright Anticipation* had left behind the carbon-soaked plankton bloom; the ocean was deep dark and boundless. Sky and sea blurred; stars became confused with the riding lights of ships close on the horizon.

"Is it time?" Ptey called back.

"Five minutes ago."

Ptey found a footing on the webbing and, one hand wrapped in the sheets, stood up to scan the huge sky. Every child of Tay, crazily tilted at forty-eight degrees to the ecliptic, grew up conscious that her planet was a ball rolling around the sun and that the stars were far, vast and slow, almost unchanging. But stars could change; Bephis, that soft smudge of light low in the southeast, blurred by the glow of eight hundred moon-sized space habitats, would soon be once again the hard point of light by which his ancestors had steered to their Mani-foldings.

"Give it time," Ptey shouted. Time. The Anpreen were al-ready voyaging; had switched on their drives and pulled out of orbit almost an hour before. The slow light of their embarka-tion had still not reached Tay. He saw the numbers spinning around in his head, accelerations, vectors, space and time all arranged around him like fluttering carnival banners. It had taken Ptey a long time to understand that not everyone could see numbers like him and reach out and make them do what they wanted.

"Well, I'll be watching the football," Cjatay had declared when Teacher Deu had declared a special class project in con-junction with the Noble Observatory of Pteu to celebrate the Anpreen migration. "We're all jumping up and down, Anpreen this, Anpreen that, but when it comes down to it, the aliens and we don't know what they really want; no one does."

"They're not aliens," Ptey had hissed back. "There *are* no aliens, don't you know that? We're all just part of the one big Clade."

Then Teacher Deu had shouted at them, Quiet you boys, and they had straightened themselves at their kneeling-desks, but Cjatay had hissed, "So if they're our cousins, why don't they give us their star-crosser drive?"

Such was the friendship between Ptey and Cjatay that they would argue over nodes of free-swimming nanotechnology or-biting a gas giant.

"Look! Oh look!"

Slowly, very slowly, Bephis was unraveling into a glowing smudge, like one of the swarms of nuchpas that hung above the waves like smoke on High Summer mornings. The fleet was moving. Eight hundred worlds. The numbers in his skull told Ptey that the Anpreen Commonweal was already at ten percent of lightspeed. He tried to work out the relativistic deformations of space-time but there were too many numbers flocking around him too fast. Instead, he watched Bephis unfurl into a galaxy, that cloud of stars slowly pull away from the bright mote of the gas giant. Crossing the ocean of night. Ptey glanced behind him. In the big dark, his father's face was hard to read, especially as Steris, who was sober and focused, and, Ptey had learned, not particularly bright. He seemed to be smiling.

It is a deep understanding, the realization that you are cleverer than your parents, Ptey thought. Behind that first smirking, satisfied sense of your own smartness comes a more profound understanding; that smart is only smart at some things, in some situations. Clever is conditional: Ptey could calculate the space-time distortion of eight hundred space habitats, plot a course across the dark, steepening sea by the stars in their courses, but he could never harness the winds or whistle the small commands to the machines, all the weather-clevernesses of Steris. That is how our world has shaped our intelligences. A self for every season.

The ravel of stars was unwinding, the Anpreen migration flowing into a ribbon of sparkles, a scarf of night beyond the veils of the aurora. Tomorrow night, it would adorn Tejaphay, that great blue guide star on the edge of the world that had become a glowing smudge, a thumbprint of the alien. Tomorrow night, Ptey would look at that blue eye in the sky from the minarets of the Manifold House. He knew that it had minarets; every child knew what the Manifold House and its sister houses all around the world looked like. Great hulks of gray wood gone silvery from salt and sun, built over upon through within alongside until they were floating cities. Cities of children. But the popular imaginations of Teacher Deu's grade eight class never painted them bright and loud with voices; they were dark, sooty labyrinths sailing under a perpetual cloud of black diesel smoke that poured from a thousand chimneys, taller even than the masts and towers. The images were sharp in Ptey's mind, but he could never see himself there, in those winding wooden staircases loud with the cries of sea birds, looking out from the high balconies across the glowing sea.

Then his breath caught. All his imaginings and failures to imagine were made true as lights disentangled themselves from the skein of stars of the Anpreen migration: red and green stars, the riding lights of the Manifold House. Now he could feel the thrum of its engines and generators through the water and the twin hulls. Ptey set his hand to the carbon nanofiber mast. It sang to deep harmonic. And just as the stars are always further than you think, so Ptey saw that the lights of the Manifold House were closer than he thought, that he was right under them, that *Sail of Bright Anticipation* was slipping through the outer buoys and nets, and that the towers and spires and minarets, rising in his vision, one by one, were obliterating the stars.

NEJBEN, SWIMMING

Beneath a sky of honey, Nejben stood hip deep in water warm as blood, deep as forgetting. This High Summer midnight, the sun was still clear from the horizon, and in its constant heat and light, the wood of the Manifold House's old, warped spires seemed to exhale a spicy musk, the distilled pheromone of centuries of teenage hormones and sexual angsts and identity crises. In cupped hands, Nejben scooped up the waters of the Chalybeate Pool and let them run, gold and thick, through his fingers. He savored the sensuality, observed the flash of sunlight through the falling water, noted the cool, deep plash as the pool received its own. A new Aspect, Nejben; old in observation and knowledge, for the body remained the same though a flock of selves came to roost in it, fresh in interpretation and experience.

When Nejben first emerged, shivering and anoxic, from the Chalybeate Pool, to be wrapped in silvery thermal sheets by the agisters, he had feared himself mad. A voice in his head that would not go away, that would not be shut up, that seemed to know him, know every part of him.

"It's perfectly normal," said agister Ashbey, a plump, serious woman with the blackest skin Nejben had ever seen. But he remembered that every Ritual Aspect was serious, and in the Manifold House the agisters were never in any other Aspect. None that the novices would ever see. "Perfectly natural. It takes time for your Prior, your childhood Aspect, to find its place and relinquish the control of the higher cognitive levels. Give it time. Talk to him. Reassure him. He will feel very lost, very alone, like he has lost everything that he ever knew. Except you, Nejben."

The time-free, sun-filled days in the sunny, smoggy yards and cloisters of the First Novitiate were full of whisperings; boys and girls like himself whispering good-bye to their childhoods. Nejben learned his Prior's dreads, that the self that had been called Ptey feared that the numbers, the patterns between them, the ability to reduce physical objects to mathematics and see in an instant their relationships and implications, would be utterly lost. He saw also that Nejben in himself scared Ptey: the easy physicality, the unselfconscious interest in his own body, the awareness of the hormones pumping like tidewater through his tubes and cells; the ever-present, ever-tickling nag of sex; everywhere, everywhen, everyone and -thing. Even as a child-self, even as shadow, Ptey knew that the first self to be birthed at the Manifold House was the pubescent self, the sexual self, but he felt this growing, aching youth to be more alien than the disembodied, mathematical Anpreen.

The tiers led down into the palp pool. In its depths, translucencies shifted. Nejben shivered in the warm High Summer midnight.

"Hey! Ptey!"

Names flocked around the Manifold House's towers like sun-gulls. New selves, new identities unfolded every hour of every day and yet old names clung. Agister Ashbey, jokey and astute, taught the social subtleties by which adults knew what Aspect and name to address and which Aspect and name of their own to wear in response. From the shade of the Poljeri

Cloister, Puzhay waved. Ptey had found girls frightening, but Nejben liked them, enjoyed their company and the little games of admiring insult and flirting mock-animosity he played with them. He reckoned he understood girls now. Puzhay was small, still boy-figured, her skin Winter-born pale, a Janni from Bedenderay, where at midwinter the atmosphere froze. She had a barbarous accent and continental manners, but Nejben found himself thinking often about her small, flat boy-breasts with their big, thumbable nipples. He had never thought when he came to the Manifold House that there would be people here from places other than Ctarisphay and its archipelago sisters. People—girls—from the big polar continent. Rude girls who cursed and openly called boys' names.

"Puzhay! What're you doing?"

"Going in."

"For the palps?"

"Nah. Just going in."

Nejben found and enjoyed a sudden, swift swelling of his dick as he watched Puzhay's breasts tauten as she raised her arms above her head and dived, awkward as a Bedenderay land-girl, into the water. Water hid it. Sun dapple kept it secret. Then he felt a shiver run over him and he dived down, deep down. He almost let the air rush out of him in a gasp as he felt the cool, cool water close around his body; then he saw Puzhay in her tight swim-shorts that made her ass look so strong and muscley turn in the water, tiny bubbles leaking from her nose, to grin and wave and beckon him down. Nejben swam down past the descending tiers of steps. Green opened before him, the bottomless emerald beyond the anti-skray nets where the Chalybeate pond was refreshed by the borderless sea. Between her pale red body and the deep green sea were the shimmering curtains of the palps.

They did not make them we did not bring them they were here forever. Ten thousand years of theology, biology, and xenology in that simple kinder-group rhyme. Nejben—all his people—had always known their special place; stranger to this world, spurted into the womb of the world-sea as the star-sperm, the seed of sentience. Twenty million drops of life-seed swam ashore and became humanity; the rest swam out to sea and met and smelled and loved the palps, older than forever. Now Nejben turned and twisted like an eel past funny, flirting, heartbreaking Puzhay, turning to show the merest glimpse of his own sperm-eel, down toward the palps. The curtain of living jelly rippled and dissolved into their separate lives. Slick, cold, quivering jelly slid across his sex-warm flesh. Nejben shivered, quivered; repelled yet aroused in a way that was other than sex. The water took on a prickle, a tickle, a tang of salt and fear and ancient, ancient lusts, deep as his first stiff dream. Against sense, against reason, against three million years of species wisdom, Nejben employed the tricks of agister Ashbey and opened his mouth. He inhaled. Once he gagged, twice he choked, then he felt the jellied eeling of the palps squirm down his throat: a choke, and into the lungs. He inhaled green salt water. And then, as the palps demurely unraveled their nanotube outer integuments and infiltrated them into his lungs, his bronchial tubes, his bloodstream, he *became.* Memories stirred, invoked by olfactory summonings, changed as a new voice, a new way of seeing, a new interpretation of those memories and experiences, formed. Nejben swam down, breathing memory-water, stroke by stroke unraveling. There was another down there, far below him, swimming up not through water but through the twelve years of his life. A new self.

Puzhay, against the light of a three o'clock sky. Framed in the arch of a cell window, knees pulled up to her chest. Small budding breasts; strong, boy jawline, fall and arc of hair shadow against lilac. She had laughed, throwing her head back. That first sight of her was cut into Nejben's memory, every line and trace, like the paper silhouettes the limners would cut of friends and families and enemies for Autumn Solstice. That first stirring of sex, that first intimation in the self of Ptey of this then-stranger, now-familiar Nejben.

As soon as he could, he had run. After he had found out where to put his bag, after he had worked out how to use the ancient, gurgling shit-eater, after agister Ashbey had closed the door with a smile and a blessing on the wooden cell—his wooden cell—that still smelled of fresh-cut timber after hundreds of years on the world-ocean of Tay. In the short season in which photosynthesis was possible, Bedenderay's forests grew fast and fierce, putting on meters in a single day. Small wonder the wood still smelled fresh and lively. After the midnight walk along the ceramic lanes and up the wooden staircases and through the damp-smelling cloisters, through the gently undulating quadrangles with the sky-train of the Anpreen migration bright overhead, holding on, as tradition demanded, to the bell hung by a chain from his agister's waist; after the form filling and the photographings and the registering and the this-is-your-ident-card this is your map I've tattooed onto the back of your hand trust it will guide you and I am your agister and we'll see you in the east Refectory for breakfast; after the climb up the slimy wooden stairs from *Sail of Bright Anticipation* on to the Manifold House's quay, the biolights green around him and the greater lamps of the great college's towers high before him; when he was alone in this alien new world where he would become eight alien new people: he ran.

Agister Ashbey was faithful; the tattoo, a clever print of smart molecules and nanodyes, was meshed into the Manifold House's network and guided him through the labyrinth of dormitories and cloisters and Boys' Pavilions and Girlhearths by the simple, aversive trick of stinging the opposite side of his map-hand to the direction in which he was to turn.

Cjatay. Sea-sundered friend. The only other one who knew him, knew him the moment they had met outside the school walls and recognized each other as different from the sailing freaks and fishing fools. Interested in geography, in love with numbers, with the wonder of the world and the worlds, as the city net declared, beyond. Boys who looked up at the sky.

As his burning hand led him left, right, up this spiral staircase under the lightening sky, such was Ptey's impetus that he never thought, would he know Cjatay? Cjatay had been in the Manifold House three months. Cjatay could be—*would* be—any number of Aspects now. Ptey had grown up with his father's overlapping circles of friends, each specific to a different Aspect, but he had assumed that it was a grown-up thing. That couldn't happen to him and Cjatay! Not them.

The cell was one of four that opened off a narrow oval at the head of a tulip-shaped minaret—the Third Moon of Spring Tower, the legend on the back of Ptey's hand read. Cells were assigned by birth-date and season. Head and heart full of nothing but seeing Cjatay, he pushed open the door—no door in the Manifold House was ever locked.

She was in the arched window, dangerously high above the shingled roofs and porcelain domes of the Vernal Equinox division. Beyond her, only the wandering stars of the Anpreen. Ptey had no name for the sudden rush of feelings that came when he saw Puzhay throw back her head and laugh at some so-serious comment of Cjatay's. Nejben did.

It was only at introductory breakfast in the East Refectory, where he met the other uncertain, awkward boys and girls of his intake, that Ptey saw past the dawn seduction of Puzhay to Cjatay, and saw him unchanged, exactly as he had been when he had stepped down from Etjay Quay into the catamaran and been taken out across the lagoon to the waste gas flares of Temejveri.

———

She was waiting crouched on the wooden steps where the water of the Chalybeate Pool lapped, knees pulled to her chest, goose flesh pimpling her forearms and calves in the cool of after-midnight. He knew this girl, knew her name, knew her history, knew the taste of a small, tentative kiss stolen among the crowds of teenagers pushing over Twelfth Canal Bridge. The memory was sharp and warm, but it was another's.

"Hi there."

He dragged himself out of the water onto the silvery wood, rolled away to hide his nakedness. In the cloister shadow, Ashbey waited with a sea-silk robe.

"Hi there." There was never any easy way to tell someone you were another person from the one they remembered. "I'm Serejen." The name had been there, down among the palps, slipped into him with their mind-altering neurotransmitters.

"Are you?"

"All right. Yes, I'm all right." A tickle in the throat made him cough, the cough amplified into a deep retch. Serejen choked up a lungful of mucus-stained palp jelly. In the early light, it thinned and ran, flowed down the steps to rejoin its shoal in the Chalybeate Pool. Agister Ashbey took a step forward. Serejen waved her away.

"What time is it?"

"Four thirty."

Almost five hours.

"Serejen." Puzhay looked coyly away. Around the Chalybeate Pool, other soul-swimmers were emerging, coughing up lungfuls of palp, shivering in their thermal robes, growing into new Aspects of themselves. "It's Cjatay. He needs to see you. Dead urgent."

Waiting Ashbey folded newborn Serejen in his own thermal gown, the intelligent plastics releasing their stored heat to his particular body temperature.

"Go to him," his agister said.

"I thought I was supposed to—"

"You've got the rest of your life to get to know Serejen. I think you should go."

Cjatay. A memory of fascination with starry skies, counting and numbering and betting games. The name and the face belonged to another Aspect, another life, but that old lust for numbers, for discovering the relationships between things, stirred a deep welling of joy. It was as rich and adult as the swelling of his dick he found in the bright mornings, or when he thought about Puzhay's breasts in his hands and the tattooed triangle of her sex. Different; no less intense.

The shutters were pulled close. The screen was the sole light in the room. Cjatay turned on hearing his lockless door open. He squinted into the gloom of the stair head, then cried excitedly,

"Look at this look at this!"

Pictures from the observation platforms sent to Tejaphay to monitor the doings of the Anpreen. A black-light plane of stars, the blinding blue curve of the water world stopped down to prevent screen-burn. The closer habitats showed a disk, otherwise it was moving lights. Patterns of speed and gravity.

"What am I looking at?"

"Look look, they're building a space elevator! I wondered how they were going to get the water from Tejaphay. Simple, duh! They're just going to vacuum it up! They've got some kind of processing unit in stationary orbit chewing up one of those asteroids they brought with them, but they're using one of their own habitats to anchor it."

"At twice stationary orbit," Serejen said. "So they're going to have to build down and up at the same time to keep the elevator in tension." He did not know where the words came from. They were on his lips and they were true.

"It must be some kind of nanocarbon compound," Cjatay said, peering at the screen for some hint, some elongation, some erection from the fuzzy blob of the construction asteroid. "Incredible tensile strength, yet very flexible. We have to get that; with all our oil, it could change everything about our technology. It could really make us a proper star-faring people." Then, as if hearing truly for the first time, Cjatay turned from the screen and peered again at the figure in the doorway. "Who are you?" His voice was high and soft and plaintive.

"I'm Serejen."

"You sound like Ptey."

"I was Ptey. I remember him."

Cjatay did a thing with his mouth, a twisting, chewing move-ment that Serejen recalled from moments of unhappiness and frus-tration. The time at his sister's name day party, when all the birth family was gathered and he had shown how it was almost certain that someone in the house on Drunken Chicken Lane had the same name day as little Sezjma. There had been a long, embar-rassed silence as Cjatay had burst into the adult chatter. Then laughter. And again, when Cjatay had worked out how long it would take to walk a light-year and Teacher Deu has asked the class, *Does anyone understand this?* For a moment, Serejen thought that the boy might cry. That would have been a terrible thing: un-seemly, humiliating. Then he saw the bag on the unkempt bed, the ritual white clothes thrust knotted and fighting into it.

"I think what Cjatay wants to say is that he's leaving the Manifold House," agister Ashbey said, in the voice that Serejen understood as the one adults used when they had uncomfort-able things to say. In that voice was a hidden word that Ashbey would not, that Serejen and Puzhay could not, and that Cjatay never would speak.

There was one in every town, every district. Kentlay had lived at the bottom of Drunken Chicken Lane, still at forty-something living with his birth parents. He had never married, though then-Ptey had heard that some did, and not just others like them. Normals. Multiples. Kentlay had been a figure that drew pity and respect alike; equally blessed and cursed, the Lonely were granted insights and gifts in compensation for their inability to manifold into the Eight Aspects. Kentlay had the touch for skin diseases, warts, and the sicknesses of birds. Ptey had been sent to see him for the charm of a dangling wart on his chin. The wart was gone within a week. Even then, Ptey had wondered if it had been through unnatural gifts or supersti-tious fear of the alien at the end of the wharf.

Cjatay. Lonely. The words were as impossible together as *green sun* or *bright winter*. It was never to be like this. Though the waters of the Chalybeate Pool would break them into many brilliant shards, though there would be other lives, other friends, even other wives and husbands, there would always be aspects of themselves that remembered trying to draw birds and fishes on the glowing band of the Mid Winter Galaxy that hung in the sky for weeks on end, or trying to calculate the mathematics of the High Summer silverlings that shoaled like silver needles in the Lagoon, how they kept together yet apart, how they were many but moved as one. *Boiling rain. Summer ice. A morning where the sun wouldn't rise. A friend who would always, only be one person.* Impossibilities. Cjatay could not be abnormal. Dark word. A vile word that hung on Cjatay like an oil-stained tarpaulin.

He sealed his bag and slung it over his shoulder.

"I'll give you a call when you get back."

"Yeah. Okay. That would be good." Words and needs and sayings flocked to him, but the end was so fast, so sudden, that all Serejen could do was stare at his feet so that he would not have to see Cjatay walk away. Puzhay was in tears. Cjatay's own agister, a tall, dark-skinned Summer-born, put his arm around Cjatay and took him to the stairs.

"Hey. Did you ever think?" Cjatay threw back the line from the top of the spiral stair. "Why are they here? The Anpreen." Even now, Serejen realized, Cjatay was hiding from the truth that he would be marked as different, as not fully human, for the rest of his life, hiding behind stars and ships and the mystery of the alien. "Why did they come here? They call it the Anpreen Migration, but where are they migrating *to*? And what are they migrating *from*? Anyone ever ask that? Ever think about that, eh?"

Then agister Ashbey closed the door on the high tower-top cell.

"We'll talk later."

Gulls screamed. Change in the weather coming. On the screen behind him, stars moved across the face of the great water.

Serejen could not bear to go down to the quay, but watched *Sail of Bright Anticipation* make sail from the cupola of the Bright Glance Netball Hall. The Manifold House was sailing through a plankton-bloom and he watched the ritual catamaran's hulls cut two lines of bioglow through the carpet of carbon-absorbing microlife. He stood and followed the sails until they were lost among the hulls of huge ceramic oil tankers pressed low to the orange smog-glow of Ctarisphay down under the horizon. Call each other. They would always forget to do that. They would slip out of each other's lives—Serejen's life now vastly more rich and populous as he moved across the social worlds of his various Aspects. In time, they would slip out of each other's thoughts and memories. So it was that Serejen Nejben ex-Ptey knew that he was not a child any longer. He could let things go.

After morning Shift class, Serejen went down to the Old Great Pool, the ancient flooded piazza that was the historic heart of the Manifold House, and used the techniques he had learned an hour before to effortlessly transfer from Serejen to Nejben. Then he went down into the waters and swam with Puzhay. She was teary and confused, but the summer-warmed water and the physical exercise brightened her. Under a sky lowering with the summer storm that the gulls had promised, they sought out the many secret flooded colonnades and courts where the big groups of friends did not go. There, under the first crackles of lightning and the hiss of rain, he kissed her and she slipped her hand into his swimsuit and cradled the comfortable swell of his cock.

SEREJEN, LOVING

Night, the aurora and sirens. Serejen shivered as police drones came in low over the Conservatorium roof. Through the high, arched windows, fires could still be seen burning on Yaskaray Prospect. The power had not yet been restored, the streets, the towering apartment blocks that lined them, were still dark. A

stalled tram sprawled across a set of points, flames flickering in
its rear carriage. The noise of the protest had moved off, but occasional shadows moved across the ice beneath the mesmerism
of the aurora; student rioters, police security robots. It was easy
to tell the robots by the sprays of ice crystals thrown up by their
needle-tip, mincing legs.

"Are you still at that window? Come away from there. If
they see you they might shoot you. Look, I've made tea."

"Who?"

"What?"

"Who might shoot me? The rioters or the police?"

"Like you'd care if you were dead."

But he came and sat at the table and took the bowl of thin,
salty Bedenderay maté.

"But sure I can't be killed."

Her name was Seriantep. She was an Anpreen Prebendary
ostensibly attached to the College of Theoretical Physics at the
Conservatorium of Jann. She looked like a tall, slim young
woman with the dark skin and blue-black hair of a Summer-
born Archipelagan, but that was just the form that the swarm
of Anpreen nanoprocessor motes had assumed. She hived.
Reris Orhum Fejannen Kekjay Prus Rejmer Serejen Nejben
wondered how close you had to get before her perfect skin
resolved into a blur of microscopic motes. He had had much
opportunity to make this observation. As well as being his
notional student—though what a functionally immortal hive-
citizen who had crossed one hundred and twenty light-years
could learn from a fresh twentysomething meat human was
moot—she was his occasional lover.

She drank the tea. Serejen watched the purse of her lips
around the delicate porcelain bowl decorated with the ubiqui-
tous Lord of the Fishes motif, even in high, dry continental
Jann. The small movement of her throat as she swallowed. He
knew a hundred such tiny, intimate movements, but even as
she cooed and giggled and gasped to the stimulations of the
Five Leaves, Five Fishes ritual, the involuntary actions of her

body had seemed like performances. Learned responses. Performances as he made observations. Actor and audience. That was the kind of lover he was as Serejen.

"So what is it really like to fuck a pile of nanomotes?" Puzhay had asked as they rolled around with wine in the cozy warm fleshiness of the Thirteenth Window Coupling Porch at the ancient, academic Ogrun Menholding. "I'd imagine it feels . . . fizzy." And she'd squeezed his cock, holding it hostage, *Watch what you say boy.*

"At least nanomotes never get morning breath," he'd said, and she'd given a little shriek of outrage and jerked his dick so that he yelped, and then they both laughed and then rolled over again and buried themselves deep into the winter-defying warmth of the piled quilts.

I should be with her now, he thought. The months-long winter nights beneath the aurora and the stars clouds of the great galaxy were theirs. After the Manifold House, he had gone with her to her Bedenderay and her home city of Jann. The City Conservatorium had the world's best theoretical physics department. It was nothing to do with small, boyish, funny Puzhay. They had formalized a partnering six months later. His parents had complained and shivered through all the celebrations in this cold and dark and barbarous city far from the soft elegance of island life. But ever after, winter—even on the coldest mornings when carbon dioxide frost crusted the steps of the Tea Lane Ladyhearth where Puzhay lived—was their season. He should call her, let her know he was still trapped but that at the first sign, the very first sign, he would come back. The cell net was still up. Even an e-mail. He couldn't. Seriantep didn't know. Seriantep wouldn't understand. She had not understood that one time when he tried to explain it in abstracts; that different Aspects could—should—have different relationships with different partners, love separately but equally. *That as Serejen, I love you, Anpreen Prebendary Seriantep, but as Nejben, I love Puzhay.* He could never say that. For an immortal, star-crossing hive of nanomotes, Seriantep was very single-minded.

Gunfire cracked in the crystal night, far and flat.

"I think it's dying down," Seriantep said.

"I'd give it a while yet."

So strange, so rude, this sudden flaring of anti-alien violence. In the dreadful dead of winter, too, when nothing should
rightfully fight and even the trees along Yaskaray Prospect drew
down to their heartwood and turned to ice. Despite the joy of
Puzhay, Serejen knew that he would always hate the Bedenderay winter. *You watch out now,* his mother had said when he
had announced his decision to go to Jann. *They all go dark-mad
there.* Accidie and suicide walked the frozen canals of the Winter City. No surprise then that madness should break out
against the Anpreen Prebendaries. Likewise inevitable that the
popular rage should be turned against the Conservatorium.
The university had always been seen as a place apart from the
rest of Jann, in summer aloof and lofty above the sweltering
streets, like an overgrand daughter; in winter a parasite on this
most marginal of economies. Now it was the unofficial alien
embassy in the northern hemisphere. There were more Anpreen in its long, small-windowed corridors than anywhere else
in the world.

There are no aliens, Serejen thought. *There is only the Clade.
We are all family. Cjatay had insisted that.* The ship had sailed
over the horizon, they hadn't called, they had drifted from each
other's lives. Cjatay's name occasionally impinged on Serejen's
awareness through radio interviews and opinion pieces. He had
developed a darkly paranoid conspiracy theory around the Anpreen Presence. Serejen, high above the frozen streets of Jann
in deeply abstract speculation about the physical reality of
mathematics, occasionally mused upon the question of at what
point the Migration had become a Presence. The Lonely often
obsessively took up narrow, focused interests. Now the street
was listening, acting. Great Winter always was a dark, paranoid
season. *Here's how to understand,* Serejen thought. *There are no
aliens after you've had sex with them.*

Helicopter blades rattled from the walls of the College of

Theoretical Physics and then retreated across the Central Canal. The silence in the warm, dimly lit little faculty cell was profound. At last, Serejen said, "I think we could go now."

On the street, cold stabbed even through the quilted layers of Serejen's greatcoat. He fastened the high collar across his throat and still he felt the breath crackle into ice around his lips. Seriantep stepped lightly between the half bricks and bottle shards in nothing more than the tunic and leggings she customarily wore around the college. Her motes gave her full control over her body, including its temperature.

"You should have put something on," Serejen said. "You're a bit obvious."

Past shuttered cafés and closed-up stores and the tall brick faces of the student Hearths. The burning tram on the Tunday Avenue junction blazed fitfully, its bitter smoke mingling with the eternal aromatic hydrocarbon smog exhaled by Jann's power plants. The trees that lined the avenue's centerstrip were folded down into tight fists, dreaming of summer. Their boot heels rang loud on the street tiles.

A darker shape upon the darkness moved in the narrow slit of an alley between two towering tenement blocks. Serejen froze, his heart jerked. A collar turned down, a face studying his—Obredajay from the Department of Field Physics.

"Safe home."

"Aye. And you."

The higher academics all held apartments within the Conservatorium and were safe within its walls; most of the research staff working late would sit it out until morning. Tea and news reports would see them through. Those out on the fickle streets had reasons to be there. Serejen had heard that Obredajay was head-over-heels infatuated with a new manfriend.

The dangers we court for little love.

On the intersection of Tunday Avenue and Yaskaray Wharf, a police robot stepped out of the impervious dark of the arches beneath General Gatoris Bridge. Pistons hissed it up to its full three meters; green light flicked across Serejen's retinas. Seriantep held up her hand, the motes of her palm displaying her immunity as a Prebendary of the Clade. The machine shrank down, seemingly dejected, if plastic and pumps could display such an emotion.

A solitary tea shop stood open on the corner of Silver Spider Entry and the Wharf, its windows misty with steam from the simmering urns. Security eyes turned and blinked at the two fleeing academics.

On Tannis Lane, they jumped them. There was no warning. A sudden surge of voices rebounding from the stone staircases and brick arches broke into a wave of figures lumbering around the turn of the alley, bulky and shouldering in their heavy winter quilts. Some held sticks, some held torn placards, some were empty-handed. They saw a man in a heavy winter coat, breath frosted on his mouth shield. They saw a woman almost naked, her breath easy, unclouded. They knew in an instant what she saw. The hubbub in the laneway became a roar.

Serejen and Seriantep were already in flight. Sensing rapid motion, the soles of Serejen's boots extended grips into the rime. As automatically, he felt the heart-numbing panic-rush ebb, felt himself lose his grip on his body and grow pale. Another was taking hold, his flight-or-fight Aspect; his cool, competent emergency service Fejannen.

He seized Seriantep's hand.

"With me. Run!"

Serejen-Fejannen saw the change of Aspect flicker across the tea-shop owner's face like weather as they barged through his door, breathless between his stables. Up to his counter with its looming, steaming urns of hot, hot water. This tea man wanted them out, wanted his livelihood safe.

"We need your help."

The tea man's eyes and nostrils widened at the charge of rioters that skidded and slipped around the corner into Silver Spider Entry. Then his hand hit the button under the counter and the shutters rolled down. The shop boomed, the shutters bowed to fists striking them. Rocks banged like gunfire from metal. Voices rose and joined together, louder because they were unseen.

"I've called the police," Seriantep said. "They'll be here without delay."

"No, they won't," Fejannen said. He pulled out a chair from the table closest the car and sat down, edgily eying the gray slats of the shutter. "Their job is to restore order and protect property. Providing personal protection to aliens is far down their list of priorities."

Seriantep took the chair opposite. She sat down wary as a settling bird.

"What's going on here? I don't understand. I'm very scared."

The café owner set two glasses of maté down on the table. He frowned, then his eyes opened in understanding. An alien at his table. He returned to the bar and leaned on it, staring at the shutters beyond which the voice of the mob circled.

"I thought you said you couldn't be killed."

"That's not what I'm scared of. I'm scared of you, Serejen."

"I'm not Serejen. I'm Fejannen."

"Who, what's Fejannen?"

"Me, when I'm scared, when I'm angry, when I need to be able to think clearly and coolly when a million things are happening at once, when I'm playing games or hunting or putting a big funding proposal together."

"You sound . . . different."

"I *am* different. How long have you been on our world?"

"You're hard. And cold. Serejen was never hard."

"I'm not Serejen."

A huge crash–the shutter bowed under a massive impact and the window behind it shattered.

"Right, that's it, I don't care what happens, you're going." The tea man leaped from behind his counter and strode toward Seriantep. Fejannen was there to meet him.

"This woman is a guest in your country and requires your protection."

"That's not a woman. That's a pile of ... insects. Things. Tiny things."

"Well, they look like mighty scared tiny things."

"I don't think so. Like you said, like they say on the news, they can't really die."

"They can hurt. *She* can hurt."

Eyes locked, then disengaged. The maté-man returned to his towering silos of herbal mash. The noise from the street settled into a stiff, waiting silence. Neither Fejannen nor Seriantep believed that it was true, that the mob had gone, despite the spearing cold out there. The lights flickered once, twice.

Seriantep said suddenly, vehemently, "I could take them."

The tea man looked up.

"Don't," Fejannen whispered.

"I could. I could get out under the door. It's just a re-forming."

The tea man's eyes were wide. A demon, a winter-grim in his prime location canal-side tea shop!

"You scare them enough as you are," Fejannen said.

"Why? We're only here to help, to learn from you."

"They think, what have you got to learn from *us*? They think that you're keeping secrets from us."

"Us?"

"Them. Don't scare them anymore. The police will come, eventually, or the Conservatorium proctors. Or they'll just get bored and go home. These things never really last."

"You're right." She slumped back into her seat. "This fucking world. . . . Oh, why did I come here?" Seriantep glanced up at the inconstant lumetubes, beyond to the distant diadem of her people's colonies, gravid on decades of water. It was a question, Fejannen knew, that Serejen had asked himself many times. A postgraduate scholar researching space-time topologies and the cosmological constant. A thousand-year-old posthuman innocently wearing the body of a twenty-year-old woman, playing the student. She could learn nothing from him. All the knowledge the Anpreen wanderers had gained in their

ten-thousand-year migration was incarnate in her motes. She
embodied all truth and she lied with every cell of her body. Anpreen secrets. No basis for a relationship, yet Serejen loved her,
as Serejen could love. But was it any more for her than a novelty; a tourist, a local boy, a brief summer loving?

Suddenly, vehemently, Seriantep leaned across the table to
take Fejannen's face between her hands.

"Come with me."

"Where? Who?"

"Who?" She shook her head in exasperation. "Ahh! Serejen. But it would be you as well, it has to be you. To my place,
to the Commonweal. I've wanted to ask you for so long. I'd
love you to see my worlds. Hundreds of worlds, like jewels,
dazzling in the sun. And inside, under the ice, the worlds within
worlds within worlds . . . I made the application for a travel
bursary months ago; I just couldn't ask."

"Why? What kept you from asking?" A small but significant
traffic of diplomats, scientists, and journalists flowed between
Tay and the Anpreen fleet around Tejaphay. The returnees enjoyed global celebrity status, their opinions and experiences
sought by think tanks and talk shows and news-site columns,
the details of the faces and lives sought by the press. Serejen
had never understood what it was the people expected from the
celebrity of others but was not so immured behind the fortress
walls of the Collegium, armored against the long siege of High
Winter, that he couldn't appreciate its personal benefits. The
lights seemed to brighten, the sense of the special hush outside,
that was not true silence but waiting, dimmed as Serejen re-
placed Fejannen. "Why didn't you ask?"

"Because I thought you might refuse."

"Refuse?" The few, the golden few. "Turn down the chance
to work in the Commonweal? Why would anyone do that?
What would I do that?"

Seriantep looked long at him, her head cocked slightly, al-
luringly, to one side, the kind of gesture an alien unused to a
human body might devise.

"You're Serejen again, aren't you?"

"I am that Aspect again, yes."

"Because I thought you might refuse because of *her*. That other woman. Puzhay."

Serejen blinked three times. From Seriantep's face, he knew that she expected some admission, some confession, some emotion. He could not understand what.

Seriantep said, "I know about her. We know things at the Anpreen Mission. We check whom we work with. We have to. We know not everyone welcomes us, and that more are suspicious of us. I know who she is and where she lives and what you do with her three times a week when you go to her. I know where you were intending to go tonight, if all this hadn't happened."

Three times again, Serejen blinked. Now he was hot, too hot in his winter quilt in this steamy, fragrant tea-shop.

"But that's a ridiculous question. *I* don't love Puzhay. *Nejben* does."

"Yes, but you *are* Nejben."

"How many times do I have to tell you?" Serejen bit back the anger. There were Aspects hovering on the edge of his consciousness like the hurricane-front angels of the Bazjendi Psalmody—selves inappropriate to Seriantep. Aspects that in their rage and storm might lose him this thing, so finely balanced now in this tea shop. "It's our way," he said weakly. "It's how we are."

"Yes, but"—Seriantep fought for words—"it's *you*, there, that body. You say it's different, you say it's someone else and not you, not Serejen, but how do I know that? How *can* I know that?"

You say that, with your body that you said could take many forms, any form, Serejen thought. Then Fejannen, shadowed but never more than a thought away in this besieged, surreal environment, heard a shift in the silence outside. The tea man glanced up. He had heard it, too. The difference between *waiting* and *anticipating*.

"Excuse me, I must change Aspects."

A knock on the shutter, glove-muffled. A voice spoke Fejannen's full name. A voice that Fejannen knew from his pervasive fear of the risk his academic Aspect was taking with Seriantep and that Serejen knew from those news reports and articles that broke through his vast visualizations of the topology of the universe and that Nejben knew from a tower-top cell and a video screen full of stars.

"Can I come in?"

Fejannen nodded to the tea man. He ran the shutter up high enough for the bulky figure in the long quilted coat and boots to duck under. Dreadful cold blew around Fejannen.

Cjatay bowed, removed his gloves, banging rime from the knuckles, and made the proper formalities to ascertain which Aspect he was speaking to.

"I have to apologize; I only recently learned that it was you who were caught here."

The voice, the intonations and inflections, the overprecisions and refinements—no time might have passed since Cjatay walked out of Manifold House. In a sense, no time *had* passed; Cjatay was caught, inviolable, unchangeable by anything other than time and experience. Lonely.

"The police will be here soon," Seriantep said.

"Yes, they will," Cjatay said mildly. He looked Seriantep up and down, as if studying a zoological specimen. "They have us well surrounded now. These things are almost never planned; what we gain in spontaneity of expression we lose in strategy. But when I realized it was you, Fejannen-Nejben, I saw a way that we could all emerge from this intact."

"Safe passage," Fejannen said.

"I will personally escort you out."

"And no harm at all to you, politically."

"I need to distance myself from what has happened tonight."

"But your fundamental fear of the visitors remains unchanged?"

"I don't change. You know that. I see it as a virtue. Some things are solid, some things endure. Not everything changes with the seasons. But fear, you said. That's clever. Do you remember, that last time I saw you, back in the Manifold House. Do you remember what I said?"

"Nejben remembers you asking, Where are they migrating to? And what are they migrating from?"

"In all your seminars and tutorials and conferences, in all those questions about the shape of the universe—oh, we have our intelligences, too, less broad than the Anpreen's, but subtler, we think—did you ever think to *ask* that question: Why have you come here?" Cjatay's chubby, still childish face was an accusation. "You are fucking her, I presume?"

In a breath, Fejannen had slipped from his seat into the Third Honorable Offense Stance. A hand on his shoulder; the tea-shop owner. No honor in it, not against a Lonely. Fejannen returned to his seat, sick with shuddering rage.

"Tell him," Cjatay said.

"It's very simple," Seriantep said. "We are refugees. The Anpreen Commonweal is the surviving remnant of the effective annihilation of our subspecies of Panhumanity. Our eight hundred habitats are such a minuscule percentage of our original race that, to all statistical purposes, we are extinct. Our habitats once englobed an entire sun. We're all that's left."

"How? Who?"

"Not so much *who,* as *when,*" Cjatay said gently. He flexed cold-blued fingers and pulled on his gloves.

"They're coming?"

"We fear so," Seriantep said. "We don't know. We were careful to leave no traces, to cover our tracks, so to speak, and we believe we have centuries of a head start on them. We are only here to refuel our habitats. Then we'll go hide ourselves in some great globular cluster."

"But why, *why* would anyone do this? We're all the same species. That's what you told us. The Clade, Panhumanity."

"Brothers disagree," Cjatay said. "Families fall out, families feud within themselves. No animosity like it."

"Is this true? How can this be true? Who knows about this?" Serejen strove with Fejannen for control and understanding. One of the first lessons the agisters of the Manifold House had taught was the etiquette of transition between conflicting Aspects. A war in the head, a conflict of selves. He could understand sibling strife on a cosmic scale. But a whole species?

"The governments," Cjatay said. To the tea man, "Open the shutter again. You'll be all right with us. I promise." To Serejen, "Politicians, some senior academics, and policy makers. And us. Not you. But we all agree, we don't want to scare anyone. So we question the Anpreen Prebendaries on our world, and question their presence in our system, and maybe sometimes it bubbles into xenophobic violence, but that's fine, that's the price, that's nothing compared to what would happen if we realized that our guests might be drawing the enemies that destroyed them to our homes. Come on. We'll go now."

The tea man lifted the shutter. Outside, the protestors stood politely aside as Cjatay led the refugees out onto the street. There was not a murmur as Seriantep, in her ridiculous, life-threatening house clothes, stepped across the cobbles. The great Winter Clock on the tower of Alajnedeng stood at twenty past five. The morning shift would soon be starting, the hot-shops firing their ovens and fry-pots.

A murmur in the crowd as Serejen took Seriantep's hand.

"Is it true?" he whispered.

"Yes," she said. "It is."

He looked up at the sky that would hold stars for another three endless months. The aurora coiled and spasmed over huddling Jann. Those stars were like crystal spearpoints. The universe was vast and cold and inimical to humanity, the greatest of Great Winters. He had never deluded himself that it would be otherwise. Power had been restored, yellow streetlights glinted from the helmets of riot control officers and the carapaces of counterinsurgency drones. Serejen squeezed Seriantep's hand.

"What you asked."

"When?"

"Then. Yes. I will. Yes."

TORBEN, MELTING

The Anpreen shatter-ship blazed star-bright as it turned its face to the sun. A splinter of smart-ice, it was as intricate as a snowflake, stronger than any construct of Taynish engineering. Torben hung in free fall in the observation dome at the center of the cross of solar vanes. The Anpreen, being undifferentiated from the motes seeded through the hull, had no need for such architectural fancies. Their senses were open to space; the fractal shell of the ship was one great retina. They had grown the blister—pure and perfectly transparent construction-ice—for the comfort and delight of their human guests.

The sole occupant of the dome, Torben was also the sole passenger on this whole alien, paradoxical ship. Another would have been good. Another could have shared the daily, almost hourly shocks of strange and new and wonder. His other Aspects had felt with Torben the breath-catch of awe, and even greater privilege, when he had looked from the orbital car of the space elevator—the Anpreen's gift to the peoples of Tay— and seen the shatter-ship turn out of occultation in a blaze of silver light as it came in to dock. They had felt his glow of intellectual vindication as he first swam clumsily into the stardome and discovered, with a shock, that the orbital transfer station was no more than a cluster of navigation lights almost lost in the star fields beyond. No sense of motion. His body had experienced no hint of acceleration. He had been correct. The Anpreen could adjust the topology of space-time. But there was no one but his several selves to tell it to. The Anpreen crew— Torben was not sure whether it was one or many, or if that distinction had any meaning—was remote and alien. On occasion, as he swam down the live-wood paneled corridors, monoflipper and web-mittens pushing thick, humid air, he had glimpsed a swirl of silver motes twisting and knotting like a captive waterspout. Always they had dispersed in his presence. But the ice beyond those wooden walls, pressing in around him, felt alive, crawling, aware.

Seriantep had gone ahead months before him.

"There's work I have to do."

There had been a party; there was always a party at the Anpreen Mission among the ever-green slopes of generous, volcanic Sulanj. Fellow academics, press and PR from Ctarisphay, politicians, family members, and the Anpreen Prebendaries, eerie in their uniform loveliness.

"You can do the research work on *Thirty-Third Tranquil Abode,* that's the idea," Seriantep had said. Beyond the paper lanterns hung in the trees and the glow of the carbon-sink lagoon, the lights of space-elevator cars rose up until they merged with the stars. She would ride that narrow way to orbit within days. Serejen wondered how he would next recognize her.

"You have to go." Puzhay stood in the balcony of the Tea Lane Ladyhearth, recently opened to allow spring warmth into rooms that had sweated and stifled and stunk all winter long. She looked out at the shooting, uncoiling fresh green of the trees along Uskuben Avenue. Nothing there you have not seen before, Nejben thought. Unless it is something that is the absence of me.

"It's not forever," Nejben said. "I'll be back in a year, maybe two years." *But not here,* he thought. He would not say it, but Puzhay knew it. As a returnee, the world's conservatoriums would be his. Bright cities, sun-warmed campuses far from the terrible cold on this polar continent, the winter that had driven them together.

All the good-byes, eightfold good-byes for each of his Aspects. And then he took sail for the ancient hospice of Bleyn, for sail was the only right way to come to those reefs of ceramic chapels that had clung to the Yesger atoll for three thousand hurricane seasons.

"I need . . . another," he whispered in the salt-breezy, chiming cloisters to Shaper Rejmen. "The curiosity of Serejen is too naive, the suspicion of Fejannen is too jagged, and the social niceties of Kekjay are too too eager to be liked."

"We can work this for you," the Shaper said. The next morning, he went down into the sweet, salt waters of the Othering Pots and let the programmed palps swarm over him, as he did for twenty mornings after. In the thunder-heavy gloaming of a late spring night storm, he awoke to find he was Torben. Clever, inquisitive, wary, socially adept, and conversationally witty Torben. Extreme need and exceptional circumstances permitted the creation of Nineths, but only, always, temporarily. Tradition as strong as an incest taboo demanded that the number of Aspects reflect the eight phases of Tay's manic seasons.

The Anpreen shatter-ship spun on its vertical axis and Torben Reris Orhum Fejannen Kekjay Prus Rejmer Serejen Nejben looked on in wonder. Down, up, forward: his orientation shifted with every breath of air in the observation dome. An eye, a monstrous eye. Superstition chilled him, childhood stories of the Dejved whose sole eye was the eye of the storm and whose body was the storm entire. Then he unfolded the metaphor. An antieye. Tejaphay was a shield of heartbreaking blue, streaked and whorled with perpetual storms. The Anpreen space habitat *Thirty-Third Tranquil Abode,* hard-docked these two years past to the anchor end of the space elevator, was a blind white pupil, an anti-pupil, an unseeing opacity. The shatter-ship was approaching from Tejaphay's axial plane; the mechanisms of the orbital pumping station were visible beyond the habitat's close horizon. The space elevator was a cobweb next to the habitat's three-hundred-kilometer bulk, less even than a thread compared to enormous Tejaphay, but as the whole assemblage turned into daylight, it woke sparkling, glittering as sun reflected from its billions of construction-ice scales. A fresh metaphor came to Torben: the sperm of the divine. *You're swimming the wrong way!* he laughed to himself, delighted at this infant Aspect's unsuspected tendency to express in metaphor what Serejen would have spoken in math, Kekjay in flattery, and Fejannen not at all. *No, it's our whole system it's fertilizing,* he thought.

The Anpreen ship drew closer, manipulating space-time on the centimeter scale. Surface details resolved from the ice glare. The hull of *Thirty-Third Tranquil Abode* was a chaotic mosaic of sensors, docks, manufacturing hubs, and still less comprehensible technology, all constructed from smart-ice. A white city. A flight of shatter-ships detached from docking arms like a flurry of early snow. Were some of those icy mesas defensive systems; did some of those ice canyons, as precisely cut as a skater's figures, conceal inconceivable weapons? Had the Anpreen ever paused to consider that to all cultures of Tay, white was the color of distrust, the white of snow in the long season of dark?

Days in free-gee had desensitized Torben sufficiently so that he was aware of the subtle pull of nanogravity in his belly. Against the sudden excitement and the accompanying vague fear of the unknown, he tried to calculate the gravity of *Thirty-Third Tranquil Abode,* changing every hour as it siphoned up water from Tejaphay. While he was still computing the figures, the shatter-ship performed another orientation flip and came in to dock at one of the radial elevator heads, soft as a kiss to a loved face.

On tenth days, they went to the falls, Korpa and Belej, Sajhay and Hannaj, Yetger and Torben. When he stepped out of the elevator that had taken him down through thirty kilometers of solid ice, Torben had imagined something like the faculty of Jann; wooden-screen cloisters and courts roofed with ancient painted ceilings, thronged with bright, smart, talkative students boiling with ideas and vision. He found Korpa and Belej, Sajhay, Hannaj, and Yetger all together in a huge, windy construct of cells and tunnels and abrupt balconies and netted-in ledges, like a giant wasp's nest suspended from the curved ceiling of the interior hollow.

"Continuum topology is a tad specialized, I'll admit that," Belej said. She was a string-thin quantum-foam specialist from Yeldes in the southern archipelago of Ninnt, gone even thinner and bonier in the attenuated gravity of *Thirty-Third Tranquil Abode*. "If it's action you're looking for, you should get over to *Twenty-Eighth*. They're sociologists."

Sajhay had taught him how to fly.

"There are a couple of differences from the transfer ship," he said as he showed Torben how to pull up the fish-tail mono-tights and how the plumbing vents worked. "It's lo-gee, but it's not *no*-gee, so you will eventually come down again. And it's easy to build up too much delta-vee. The walls are light but they're strong and you will hurt yourself. And the nets are there for a reason. Whatever you do, don't go through them. If you end up in that sea, it'll take you apart."

That sea haunted Torben's unsettled, nanogee dreams. The world-sea, the two-hundred-and-twenty-kilometer-diameter sphere of water, its slow, huge nanogee waves forever breaking into globes and tears the size of clouds. The seething, dissolving sea into which the Anpreen dissipated, many lives into one immense, diffuse body that whispered to him through the paper tunnels of the Sojourners' house. Not so strange, perhaps. Yet he constantly wondered what it would be like to fall in there, to swim against the tiny but nonnegligible gravity and plunge slowly, magnificently, into the boil of water-borne motes. In his imagination, there was never any pain, only the blissful, light-filled losing of self. So good to be free from the unquiet parliament of selves.

Eight is natural, eight is holy, the Bleyn Shaper Yesger had whispered from behind ornate cloister grilles. *Eight arms, eight seasons. Nine must always be unbalanced.*

Conscious of each other's too-close company, the guest scholars worked apart with their pupils. Seriantep met daily with Torben in a bulbous chapter house extruded from the mother nest. Tall hexagon-combed windows opened on the steeply downcurving horizons of *Thirty-Third Tranquil Abode,* stippled with the stalactite towers of those Anpreen who refused the lure of the sea. Seriantep flew daily from such a tower down around the curve of the world to alight on Torben's balcony. She wore the same body he had known so well in the Jann Conservatorium, with the addition of a pair of functional wings in her back. She was a vision, she was a marvel, a spiritual creature from the aeons-lost motherworld of the Clade: an *angel.* She was beauty, but since arriving in *Thirty-Third Tranquil Abode,* Torben had only had sex with her twice. It was not the merman-angel thing, though that was a consideration to metaphor-and-ludicrous-conscious Torben. He didn't love her as Serejen had. She noticed, she commented.

"You're not . . . the same."

Neither are you. What he *said* was, "I know. I couldn't be. Serejen couldn't have lived here. Torben can. Torben is the only one who can." *But for how long, before he splits into his component personalities?*

"Do you remember the way you . . . he . . . used to see numbers?"

"Of course I do. And before that, I remember how Ptey used to see numbers. He could look up into the night sky and tell you without counting, just by *knowing,* how many stars there were. He could see numbers. Serejen could make them *do* things. For me, Torben, the numbers haven't gone away, I just see them differently. I see them as clearly, as absolutely, but when I see the topospace transformations, I see them as words, as images and stories, as analogies. I can't explain it any better than that."

"I think, no matter how long I try, how long any of us try, we will never understand how your multiple personalities work. To us, you seem a race of partial people, each a genius, a savant, in some strange obsessive way."

Are you deliberately trying to punish me? Torben thought at the flicker-wing angel hovering before the ice-filled windows.

True, he was making colossal intuitive leaps in his twisted, abstruse discipline of space-time geometry. Not so abstruse: the Anpreen space drives, which Taynish physicists said broke the laws of physics, reached into the elevenspace substrate of the universe to locally stretch or compress the expansion of space-time—foreshortening ahead of the vehicle, inflating it behind. Thus the lack of any measurable acceleration, it was the entire continuum within and around the shatter-ship that had moved. Snowflakes and loxodromic curves had danced in Torben's imagination: he had it, he had it. The secret of the Anpreen: relativistic interstellar travel, was now open to the peoples of Tay.

The *other* secret of the Anpreen, that was.

For all his epiphanies above the spherical ocean, Torben knew that seminars had changed. The student had become the teacher, the master the pupil. *What is it you want from us?* Torben asked himself. *Truly want, truly need?*

"Don't know, don't care. All I know is, if I can find a commercial way to bubble quantum black holes out of elevenspace and tap the evaporation radiation, I'll have more money than God," said Yetger, a squat, physically uncoordinated Oprann islander who relished his countrymen's reputation for boorishness, though Torben found him an affable conversationalist and a refined thinker. "You coming to the Falls on Tennay?"

So they set off across the sky, a little flotilla of physicists with wine and sweet biscuits to dip in it. Those older and less sure of their bodies used little airscooter units. Torben flew. He enjoyed the exercise. The challenge of a totally alien language of movement intrigued him, the fish-tail flex of the flipper-suit. He liked what it was doing to his ass muscles.

The western windows of the Sojourners' house gave distant views of the Falls, but the sense of awe began twenty kilometers out when the thunder and shriek became audible over the constant rumble of sky traffic. The picnic party always flew high, close to the ceiling among the tower roots, so that long vistas would not spoil their pleasure. A dense forest of inverted trees, monster things grown kilometers tall in the nanogee, had been planted around the Falls, green and mist-watered by the spray. The scientists settled on one of the many platforms sculpted from the boulevard-wide branches. Torben gratefully peeled off his fin-tights, kicked his legs free, and spun to face the Falls.

What you saw, what awed you, depended on how you looked at it. Feet down to the world-sea, head up to the roof, it was a true fall, a cylinder of falling water two hundred meters across and forty kilometers long. Feet up, head down, it was even more terrifying, a titanic geyser. The water was pumped through from the receiving station at near supersonic speeds; where it met the ocean bead, the joined waters boiled and leaped kilometers high, broke into high looping curls and crests and globes, like the fantastical flarings of solar prominences. The roar was terrific. But for the noise-abatement properties of the nanoengineered leaves, it would have meant instant deafness. Torben could feel the tree branch, as massive as any buttress wall of Jann fortress-university, shudder beneath him.

Wine was opened and poured. The biscuits, atavistically hand-baked by Hannaj, one of whose Aspects was a master pastry chef, were dipped into it and savored. Sweet, the light sharpness of the wine and the salt mist of another world's stolen ocean tanged Torben's tongue.

There were rules to Tennays by the Falls. No work. No theory. No relationships. Five researchers made up a big enough group for family jealousy, small enough for cliquishness. Proper topics of conversation looked homeward; partnerships ended, children born, family successes and sicknesses, gossip, politics, and sports results.

"Oh. Here." Yetger sent a message flake spinning lazily through the air. The Sojourners' house exfoliated notes and messages from home onto slips of whisper-thin paper that peeled from the walls like eczema. The mechanism was poetic but inaccurate; intimate messages unfurled from unintended walls to turn and waft in the strange updrafts that ran through the nest's convoluted tunnels. It was the worst of forms to read another's message-scurf.

Torben unfolded the rustle of paper. He read it once, blinked, read it again. Then he folded precisely in eight and tucked it away in his top pocket.

"Bad news?" For a broad beast of a man, Yetger was acute to emotional subtleties. Torben swallowed.

"Nothing strange or startling."

Then he saw where Belej stared. Her gaze drew his, drew that of everyone in the picnic party. The Falls were failing. Moment by moment, they dwindled, from a deluge to a river, from a river to a stream to a jet, a hiding shrieking thread of water. On all the platforms on all the trees, Anpreen were rising into the air, hovering in swarms, as before their eyes the Falls sputtered and ceased. Drops of water, fat as storms, formed around the lip of the suddenly exposed nozzle to break and drift, quivering, down to the spherical sea. The silence was profound. Then the trees seemed to shower blossoms as the Anpreen took to the air in hosts and choirs, flocking and storming.

Numbers and images flashed in Torben's imagination. The fueling could not be complete, was weeks from being complete. The ocean would fill the entire interior hollow, the stalactite cities transforming into strange reef communities. Fear gripped him and he felt Fejannen struggle to free himself from the binding into Torben. *I need you here, friend,* Torben said to himself, and saw that the others had made the same calculations.

They flew back, a ragged flotilla strung across kilometers of airspace, battling through the ghostly aerial legions of Anpreen. The Sojourners' house was filled with fluttering, gusting message slips shed from the walls. Torben snatched one from the air and against all etiquette read it.

Sajhay are you all right what's happening? Come home, we are all worried about you. Love Mihenj.

The sudden voice of Suguntung, the Anpreen liaison, filled every cell of the nest, an order—polite, but an order—to come to the main viewing lounge, where an important announcement would be made. Torben had long suspected that Suguntung never left the Sojourners' house, merely deliquesced from hominiform into airborne motes, a phase transition.

Beyond the balcony nets, the sky seethed, an apocalypse of insect humanity and storm clouds black as squid ink rolling up around the edge of the world ocean.

"I have grave news," Suguntung said. He was a gray, sober creature, light and lithe and androgynous, without any salting of wit or humor. "At 12:18 Taynish Enclave time, we detected gravity waves passing through the system. These are consistent with a large numbers of bodies decelerating from relativistic flight."

Consternation. Voices shouting. Questions questions questions. Suguntung held up a hand and there was quiet.

"On answer to your questions, somewhere in the region of thirty-eight thousand objects. We estimate them at a range of seventy astronomical units beyond the edge of the Kuiper Belt, decelerating to ten percent lightspeed for system transition."

"Ninety-three hours until they reach us," Torben said. The numbers, the colored numbers, so beautiful, so distant.

"Yes," said Suguntung.

"Who are they?" Belej asked.

"I know," Torben said. "Your enemy."

"We believe so," Suguntung answered. "There are characteristic signatures in the gravity waves and the spectral analysis."

Uproar. By a trick of the motes, Suguntung could raise his voice to a roar that could shout down a crowd of angry physicists.

"The Anpreen Commonweal is making immediate preparations for departure. As a matter of priority, evacuation for all guests and visitors has been arranged and will commence immediately. A transfer ship is already waiting. We are evacuating the system not only for our own protection, but to safeguard you as well. We believe that the Enemy has no quarrel with you."

"Believe?" Yetger spat. "Forgive me if I'm less than completely reassured by that!"

"But you haven't got enough water," Torben said absently, amazed by the numbers and pictures swimming around in his head, as the message leaves of concern and hope and come-home-soon fluttered around. "How many habitats are fully fueled? Five hundred, five hundred and fifty? You haven't got enough, even this one is at eighty percent capacity. What's going to happen to them?"

"I don't give a fuck what happens to them!" Hannaj had always been the meekest and least assertive of men, brilliant but forever hamstrung by self-doubt. Now, threatened, naked in space, pierced through and through by the gravity waves of an unknowable power, his anger burned. "I want to know what's going to happen to *us.*"

"We are transferring the intelligences to the interstellar-capable habitats." Suguntung spoke to Torben alone.

"Transferring; you mean copying," Torben said. "And the originals that are left, what happens to them?"

Suguntung made no answer.

Yetger found Torben floating in the exact center of the viewing lounge, moving his tail just enough to maintain him against the microgee.

"Where's your stuff?"

"In my cell."

"The shatter-ship's leaving in an hour."

"I know."

"Well, maybe you should, you know–"

"I'm not going."

"You're *what?*"

"I'm not going, I'm staying here."

"Are you insane?"

"I've talked to Suguntung and Seriantep. It's fine. There are a couple of others on the other habitats."

"You have to come home. We'll need you when they come."

"Ninety hours and twenty-five minutes to save the world? I don't think so."

"It's home, man."

"It's not. Not since *this*." Torben flicked the folded note of his secret pocket, offered it to Yetger between clenched fingers.

"Oh."

"Yes."

"You're dead. We're all dead, you know that."

"Oh, I know. In the few minutes it takes me to reach wherever the Anpreen Migration goes next, you will have aged and died many times over. I know that, but it's not home. Not now."

Yetger ducked his head in sorrow that did not want to be seen, then in a passion hugged Torben hugely to him, kissed him hard.

"Good-bye. Maybe in the next one."

"No, I don't think so. One is all we get. And that's a good enough reason to go out there where none of our people have ever been before, I think."

"Maybe it is." Yetger laughed, the kind of laughter that is on the edge of tears. Then he spun and kicked off up through the ceiling door, his duffel of small possessions trailing from his ankle.

For an hour now, he had contemplated the sea and thought that he might just be getting the way of it, the fractal patterns of the ripples, the rhythms and the microstorms that blew up in squalls and waves that sent globes of water quivering into the air that, just as quickly, were subsumed back into the greater sea. He understood it as music, deeply harmonized. He wished one of his Aspects had a skill for an instrument. Only choirs, vast ensembles, could capture the music of the water bead.

"It's ready now."

All the while Torben had calculated the music of the sea, Seriantep had worked on the smart-paper substrate of the Sojourners' house. Now the poll was complete, a well in the floor of the lounge. *When I leave, will it revert?* Torben thought, the small, trivial wit that fights fear. *Will it go back to whatever it was before, or was it always only just Suguntung?* The slightest of gestures and Seriantep's wisp-dress fell from her. The floor ate it greedily. Naked and wingless now in this incarnation, she stepped backward into the water, never for an instant taking her eyes from Torben.

"Whenever you're ready," she said. "You won't be hurt."

She lay back into the receiving water. Her hair floated out around her, coiled and tangled as she came apart. There was nothing ghastly about it, no decay into meat and gut and vile bone, no grinning skelton fizzing apart in the water like sodium. A brightness, a turning to motes of light. The hair was the last to go. The pool seethed with motes. Torben stepped out of his clothes.

I'm moving on. It's for the best. Maybe not for you. For me. You see, I didn't think I'd mind, but I did. You gave it all up so easily, just like that, off into space. There is someone else. It's Cjatay. I heard what he was saying, and as time went by, as I didn't hear from you, it made sense. I know I'm reacting. I think I owe you that, at least. We're all right together. With him, you get everything, I find I can live with that. I think I like it. I'm sorry, Torben, but this is what I want.

The note sifted down through the air like a falling autumn leaf to join the hundreds of others that lay on the floor. Torben's feet kicked up as he stepped down into the water. He gasped at the electrical tingle, then laughed, and, with a great gasp, emptied his lungs and threw himself under the surface. The motes swarmed and began to take him apart. As the *Thirty-Third Tranquil Abode* broke orbit around Tejaphay, the abandoned space elevator coiling like a severed artery, the bottom of the Sojourners' house opened, and, like a tear, the mingled waters fell to the sea below.

JEDDEN, RUNNING

Eighty years Jedden had fallen, dead as a stone, silent as light. Every five years, a few subjective minutes so close to light-speed, he woke up his senses and sent a slush of photons down his wake to see if the hunter was still pursuing.

Redshifted to almost indecipherability, the photons told him, *Yes, still there, still gaining.* Then he shut down his senses, for even that brief wink, that impact of radiation blueshifted to gamma frequencies on the enemy engine field, betrayed him. It was decades since he had risked the scalarity drive. The distortions it left in space-time advertised his position over most of a quadrant. Burn quick, burn hot and fast, get to lightspeed if it meant reducing his reaction mass perilously close to the point where he would not have sufficient time ever to brake. Then go dark, run silent and swift, coasting along in high-time dilation where years passed in hours.

Between wakings, Jedden dreamed. He dreamed down into the billions of lives, the dozens of races and civilizations that the Anpreen had encountered in their long migration. The depth of their history had stunned Jedden, as if he were swimming and, looking down, discovered beneath him not the green water of the lagoon but the clear blue drop of the continental shelf. Before they englobed their sun with so many habitats that it became discernible only as a vast infrared glow, before even the wave of expansion that had brought them to that system, before even they became motile, when they wore mere bodies, they had been an extroverted, curious race, eager for the similarities and differences of other subspecies of Panhumanity. Records of the hundreds of societies they had contacted were stored in the spin states of the quantum-ice flake that comprised the soul of Jedden. Cultures, customs, ways of being human were simulated in such detail that, if he wished, Jedden could have spent eons living out their simulated lives. Even before they had reached the long-reprocessed moon of their home world, the Anpreen had encountered a light-sail probe of the

Ekkad, three hundred years out on a millennium-long survey of potential colony worlds. As they converted their asteroid belts into habitat rings, they had fought a savage war for control of the high country against the Okranda asteroid colonies that had dwelled there, hidden and unsuspected, for twenty thousand years. The doomed Okranda had, as a final, spiteful act, seared the Anpreen home world to the bedrock, but not before the Anpreen had absorbed and recorded the beautiful, insanely complex hierarchy of caste, classes, and societies that had evolved in the baroque cavities of the sculpted asteroids. Radio transmission had drawn them out of their Oort cloud across two hundred light-years to encounter the dazzling society of the Jad. From them, the Anpreen had learned the technology that enabled them to pload themselves into free-flying nanomotes and become a true Level Two civilization.

People and beasts, machines and woods, architectures and moralities, and stories beyond counting. Among the paraphernalia and marginalia of a hundred races, were the ones who had destroyed the Anpreen, who were now hunting Jedden down over all the long years, closing meter by meter.

So he spent hours and years immersed in the great annual eisteddfod of the Barrant-Hoj, where one of the early generation of seed ships (early in that it was the seed of the seed of the seed of the first flowering of mythical Earth) had been drawn into the embrace of a fat, slow hydrocarbon-rich gas giant and birthed a brilliant, brittle airborne culture, where blimp-cities rode the edge of storms wide enough to drown whole planets and the songs of the contestants—gas-bag-spider creatures huge as reefs, fragile as honeycomb—belled in infrasonic wavefronts kilometers between crests and changed entire climates. It took Barrant-Hoj two hominiform lifetimes to circle its sun—the Anpreen had chanced upon the song-spiel, preserved it, hauled it out of the prison of gas giant's gravity well, and given it to greater Clade.

Jedden blinked back into interstellar flight. He felt—he imagined—tears on his face as the harmonies reverberated within him. Cantos could last days, chorales entire weeks. Lost in music. A moment of revulsion at his body, this sharp, unyielding thing of ice and energies. The hunter's ramscoop fusion engine advertised its presence across a thousand cubic light-years. It was inelegant and initially slow, but, unlike Jedden's scalarity drive, was light and could live off the land. The hunter would be, like Jedden, a ghost of a soul impressed on a Bose-condensate quantum chip, a mote of sentience balanced on top of a giant drive unit. The hunter was closing, but was no closer than Jedden had calculated. Only miscalculation could kill you in interstellar war. The equations were hard but they were fair.

Two hundred and three years to the joke point. It would be close, maybe close enough for the enemy's greed to blind him. Miscalculation and self-deception, these were the killers in space. And luck. Two centuries. Time enough for a few moments' rest.

Among all the worlds was one he had never dared visit: the soft blue tear of Tay. There, in the superposed spin states, were all the lives he could have led. The lovers, the children, the friends and joys and mundanities. Puzhay was there, Cjatay, too. He could make of them anything he wanted: Puzhay faithful, Cjatay Manifold, no longer Lonely.

Lonely. He understood that now, eighty light-years out and decades to go before he could rest.

Extraordinary, how painless it had been. Even as the cells of Torben's body were invaded by the motes into which Seriantep had dissolved, even as they took him apart and rebuilt him, even as they read and copied his neural mappings, there was never a moment where fleshly Torben blinked out and nanotechnological Torben winked in. There was no pain. Never pain, only a sense of wonder, of potential racing away to infinity on every side, of a new birth—or, it seemed to him, an antibirth, a return to the primal, salted waters. As the globe of mingled motes dropped slow and quivering and full as a breast toward the world-ocean, Torben still thought of himself as Torben, as a man, an individual, as a body. Then they hit and burst and dissolved into the sea of seething motes, and voices and selves and memories and personalities rushed in on him from every side, clamoring, a sea-roar. Every life in every detail. Senses beyond his native five brought him impression upon impression upon impression. Here was intimacy beyond anything he had ever known with Seriantep. As he communed, he was communed with. He knew that the Anpreen government (now he understood the reason for the protracted and ungainly negotiations with Tay: the two representations had almost no points of communication) were unwrapping him to construct a deep map of Tay and its people—rather, the life and Aspects of one undersocialized physics researcher. Music. All was music. As he understood this, Anpreen Commonweal Habitat *Thirty-Third Tranquil Abode,* with its five hundred and eighty-two companions, crossed one hundred and nineteen light-years to the Milius 1183 star system.

One hundred and nineteen light-years, eight months subjective, in which Torben Reris Orhum Fejannen Kekjay Prus Rejmer Serejen Nejben ceased to exist. In the mote-swarm, time, like identity, could be anything you assigned it to be. To the self now known as Jedden, it seemed that he had spent twenty years of resubjectivized time in which he had grown to be a profound and original thinker in the Commonweal's physics community. Anpreen life had only enhanced his instinctive ability to see and apprehend number. His insights and contributions were startling and creative. Thus it had been a pure formality for him to request a splinter-ship to be spun off from *Thirty-Third Tranquil Abode* as the fleet entered the system and dropped from relativistic flight at the edge of the Oort cloud. A big fat splinter-ship with lots of fuel to explore spacetime topological distortions implicit in the orbital perturbations of inner Kuiper Belt cubewanos for a year, a decade, a century, and then come home.

So he missed the annihilation.

Miscalculation kills. Lack of circumspection kills. Blind assumption kills. The Enemy had planned their trap centuries ahead. The assault on the Tay system had been a diversion; the thirty-eight thousand drive signatures mostly decoys; propulsion units and guidance systems and little else scattered among a handful of true battleships dozens of kilometers long. Even as lumbering, barely mobile Anpreen habitats and Enemy attack drones burst across Tay's skies, so bright they even illuminated the sun-glow of High Summer, the main fleet was working around Milius 1183. A work of decades, year upon year of slow modifications, staggering energies, careful careful concealment and camouflage, as the Enemy sent their killing hammer out on its long slow loop.

Blind assumption. The Anpreen saw a small red sun at affordable range to the ill-equipped fleet. They saw there was water there, water; worlds of water to reequip the Commonweal and take it fast and far beyond the reach of the Enemy in the great star clouds that masked the galactic core. In their haste they failed to note that Milius 1183 was a binary system, a tired red dwarf star and a companion neutron star in photosphere-grazing eight-hour orbit. Much less then did they notice that the neutron star was missing.

The trap was perfect and complete. The Enemy had predicted perfectly. Their setup was flawless. The hunting fleet withdrew to the edges of system; all that remained were the relays and autonomous devices. Blindsided by sunglare, the Anpreen sensoria had only milliseconds of warning before the neutron star impacted Milius 1183 at eight percent lightspeed.

The nova would in time be visible over a light-century radius. Within its spectrum, careful astronomers might note the dark lines of hydrogen, oxygen, and smears of carbon. Habitats blew away in sprays of plasma. The handful of stragglers that survived battled to reconstruct their mobility and life-support systems. Shark-ships hidden half a century before in the rubble of asteroid belts and planetary ring systems woke from their long sleeps and went a-hunting.

Alone in his splinter-ship in the deep dark, Jedden, his thoughts outward to the fabric of space-time and at the same time inward to the beauty of number, the song within him, saw the system suddenly turn white with death light. He heard five hundred billion sentients die. All of them, all at once, all their voices and hearts. He heard Seriantep die, he heard those other Taynish die, those who had turned away from their home world in the hope of knowledge and experience beyond anything their world could offer. Every life he had ever touched, that had ever been part of him, that had shared number or song or intimacy beyond fleshly sex. He heard the death of the Anpreen migration. Then he was alone. Jedden went dark for fifty years. He contemplated the annihilation of the last of the Anpreen. He drew up escape plans. He waited. Fifty years was enough. He lit the scalarity drive. Space-time stretched. Behind him, he caught the radiation signature of a fusion drive igniting and the corresponding electromagnetic flicker of a scoopfield going up. Fifty years was not enough.

That would be his last miscalculation.

Twenty years to bend his course away from Tay. Another ten to set up the deception. *As you deceived us, so I will fool you,* Jedden thought as he tacked ever closer to lightspeed. *And with the same device, a neutron star.*

———

Jedden awoke from the sleep that was beyond dreams, a whisper away from death, that only disembodied intelligences can attain. The magnetic vortex of the hunter's scoopfield filled half the sky. Less than the diameter of a light-minute separated them. Within the next ten objective years, the Enemy ship would overtake and destroy Jedden. Not with physical weapons or even directed energy, but with information: skullware and dark phages that would dissolve him into nothingness or worse, isolate him from any external sense or contact, trapped in unending silent, nerveless darkness.

The moment, when it came, after ninety light-years, was too fine-grained for hominiform intelligence. Jedden's subroutines, the autonomic responses that controlled the ship that was his body, opened the scalarity drive and summoned the dark energy. Almost instantly, the Enemy responded to the course change, but that tiny relativistic shift, the failure of simultaneity, was Jedden's escape and life.

Among the memories frozen into the heart of the Bose-Einstein condensate were the star logs of the Cush Né, a fellow migrant race the Anpreen had encountered—by chance, as all such meets must be—in the big cold between stars. Their star maps charted a rogue star, a neutron dwarf ejected from its stellar system and wandering dark and silent, almost invisible, through deep space. Decades ago, when he felt the enemy ramfield go up and knew that he had not escaped, Jedden had made the choice and the calculations. Now he turned his flight, a prayer short of lightspeed, toward the wandering star.

Jedden had long ago abolished fear. Yet he experienced a strange psychosomatic sensation in that part of the splinter-ship that corresponded to his testicles. Balls tightening. The angle of insertion was so precise that Jedden had had to calculate the impact of stray hydroxyl radicals on his ablation field. One error would send him at relativistic speed head-on into a neutron star. But he did not doubt his ability, he did not fear, and now he understood what the sensation in his phantom testicles was. Excitement.

The neutron star was invisible, would always be invisible, but Jedden could feel its gravity in every part of his body, a quaking, quailing shudder, a music of a hundred harmonies as different parts of the smart-ice hit their resonant frequencies. A chorale in ice and adrenaline, he plunged around the neutron star. He could hope that the hunting ship would not survive the passage, but the Enemy, however voracious, was surely never so stupid as to run a scoop ship through a neutron star's terrifying magnetic terrain with the drive field up. That was not his strategy anyway. Jedden was playing the angles. Whipping tight around the intense gravity well, even a few seconds of slowness would amplify into light-years of distance, decades of lost time. Destruction would have felt like a cheat. Jedden wanted to win by geometry. By calculation, we live.

He allowed himself one tiny flicker of a communication laser. Yes. The Enemy was coming. Coming hard, coming fast, coming *wrong*. Tides tore at Jedden; every molecule of his smart-ice body croaked and moaned, but his own cry rang louder and he slingshotted around the neutron. *Yes!* Before him was empty space. The splinter-ship would never fall of its own accord into another gravity well. He lacked sufficient reaction mass to enter any Clade system. Perhaps the Enemy had calculated this in the moments before he, too, entered the neutron star's transit. An assumption. In space, assumptions kill. Deep in his quantum memories, Jedden knew what was out there. The slow way home.

FAST MAN, SLOWLY

Kites, banners, pennants, and streamers painted with the scales and heads of ritual snakes flew from the sun rigging on the Festival of Fast Children. At the last minute, the climate people had received budgetary permission to shift the prevailing winds lower. The Clave had argued that the Festival of Fast Children seemed to come around every month and a half, which it did, but the old and slow said, *Not to the children it doesn't.*

Fast Man turned off the dust road onto the farm track. The wooden gate was carved with the pop-eyed, O-mouthed hearth gods, the chubby, venal guardians of agricultural Yoe Canton. As he slowed to Parent Speed, the nodding heads of the meadow flowers lifted to a steady metronome tick. The wind-rippled grass became a restless choppy sea of currents and crosscurrents. Above him, the clouds raced down the face of the sun-rod that ran the length of the environment cylinder, and in the wide yard before the frowning eaves of the ancient earthen manor, the children, preparing for the ritual Beating of the Sun-lines, became plumes of dust.

For three days, he had walked up the eternal hill of the cylinder curve, through the tended red forests of Canton Ahaea. Fast Man liked to walk. He walked at Child Speed and they would loop around him on their bicycles and ped-cars and then pull away shouting, *You're not so fast, Fast Man!* He could have caught them, of course; he could have easily outpaced them. They knew that; they knew he could on a wish take the form of a bird, or a cloud, and fly away from them up to the ends of the world. Everyone in the Three Worlds knew Fast Man. He needed neither sleep nor food, but he enjoyed the taste of the highly seasoned, vegetable-based cuisine of the Middle Cantons and their light but fragrant beer, so he would call each night at a hostel or township pub. Then he would drop down into Parent Speed and talk with the locals. Children were fresh and bright and inquiring, but for proper conversation, you needed adults.

The chirping cries of the children rang around the grassy eaves of Toe Yau Manor. The community had gathered, among them the Toe Yau's youngest, a skipping five-year-old. In her own speed, that was. She was months old to her parents; her birth still a fresh and painful memory. The oldest, the one he had come about, was in his early teens. Noha and Jehau greeted Fast Man with water and bread.

"God save all here," Fast Man said as he blessed them. Little Nemaha flickered around him like summer evening bugs. He heard his dual-speech unit translate the greeting into Children Speech in a chip of sound. This was his talent and his fame; that his mind and words could work in two times at once. He was the generational ambassador to three worlds.

———

The three great cylinders of the Aeo Taea colony fleet were fifty Adult Years along in their journey to the star Sulpees 2157 in the Anpreen categorization. A sweet little golden star with a gas giant pressed up tight to it and, around that gas world, a sun-warmed, tear-blue planet. Their big, slow lathe-sculpted asteroids, two hundred kilometers long, forty across their flats, had appeared as three small contacts at the extreme edge of the Commonweal's sensory array. Too far from their flightpath to the Tay system and, truth be told, too insignificant. The galaxy was festering with little subspecies, many of them grossly ignorant that they were part of an immeasurably more vast and glorious Clade, all furiously engaged on their own grand little projects and empires. Races became significant when they could push lightspeed. Ethnologists had noted as a point of curiosity a peculiar time distortion to the signals, as if everything had been slowed to a tenth of normal speed. Astrogators had put it down to an unseen gravitational lensing effect and noted course and velocity of the lumbering junk as possible navigation hazards.

That idle curiosity, that moment of fastidiousness of a now-dead, now-vaporized Anpreen who might otherwise have dismissed it, had saved Jedden. There had always been more hope than certainty in the mad plan he had concocted as he watched the Anpreen civilization end in nova light. Hope as he opened up the dark energy that warped space-time in calculations made centuries before that would only bear fruit in centuries to come. Hope as he woke up, year upon year in the long flight to the stray neutron star, always attended by doubt. The slightest miscalculation could throw him off by light-years and centuries. He himself could not die, but his reaction mass was all too mortal. Falling forever between stars was worse than any death. He could have abolished that doubt with a thought, but so would the hope have been erased to become mere blind certainty.

Hoping and doubting, he flew out from the slingshot around the neutron star.

Because he could hope, he could weep; smart-ice tears when his long-range radars returned three slow-moving images less than five light-hours from the position he had computed.

As he turned the last of his reaction mass into dark energy to match his velocity with the Aeo Taea armada, a stray calculation crossed his consciousness. In all his redefinitions and reformations, he had never given up the ability to see numbers, to hear what they whispered to him. He was half a millennium away from the lives he had known on Tay.

For ten days, he broadcast his distress call. *Help, I am a refugee from a star war.* He knew that, in space, there was no rule of the sea, as there had been on Tay's world ocean, no Aspects at once generous, stern, and gallant that had been known as SeaSelves. The Aeo Taea could still kill him with negligence. But he could sweeten them with a bribe.

Like many of the country houses of Amoa ark, Toe Yau Manor featured a wooden belvedere, this one situated on a knoll two fields spinward from the old house. Airy and gracious, woven from genetweak willow plaits, it and its country cousins all across Amoa's Cantons had become a place for Adults, where they could mix with ones of their own speed, talk without the need for the hated speech converters around their necks, gripe and moan and generally gossip, and, through the central roof iris, spy through the telescope on their counterparts on the other side of the world. Telescope parties were the latest excuse for Parents to get together and complain about their children.

But this was their day—though it seemed like a week to them—the Festival of Fast Children, and this day Noha Toe Yau had his telescope trained not on his counterpart beyond the sun, but on the climbing teams fizzing around the sun-riggings, tens of kilometers above the ground, running out huge monoweave banners and fighting ferocious kite battles high where the air was thin.

"I tell you something, no child of mine would ever be let do so damn fool a thing," Noha Toe Yau grumbled. "I'll be surprised if any of them makes it to the Destination."

Fast Man smiled, for he knew that he had only been called

because Yemoa Toe Yau was doing something much more dangerous.

Jehau Toe Yau poured chocolate, thick and cooling and vaguely hallucinogenic.

"As long as he's back before Starship Day," she said. She frowned down at the wide green before the manor where the gathered Fast Children of the neighborhood in their robes and fancies were now hurtling around the long trestles of festival foods. They seemed to be engaged in a high-velocity food fight. "You know, I'm sure they're speeding the days up. Not much, just a little every day, but definitely speeding them up. Time goes nowhere these days."

Despite a surprisingly sophisticated matter-antimatter propulsion system, the Aeo Taea fleet was limited to no more than 10 percent of lightspeed, far below the threshold where time dilation became perceptible. The crossing to the Destination— Aeo Taea was a language naturally given to Portentous Capitalizations, Fast Man had discovered—could only be made by generation ship. The Aeo Taea had contrived to do it in just one generation. The strangely slow messages the Anpreen had picked up from the fleet were no fluke of space-time distortion. The voyagers' bodies, their brains, their perceptions and metabolisms, had been engineered in vitro to run at one-tenth hominiform normal. Canned off from the universe, the interior lighting, the gentle spin gravity, and the slow, wispy climate easily adjusted to a life lived at a snail's pace. Morning greetings lasted hours, that morning a world-week. Seasons endured for what would have been years in the outside universe, vast languorous autumns. The three hundred and fifty years of the crossing would pass in the span of an average working career. Amoa was a world of the middle-aged.

Then Fast Man arrived and changed everything.

"Did he give any idea where he was going?" Fast Man asked. It was always the boys. Girls worked it through, girls could see further.

Jehau pointed down. Fast Man sighed. Rebellion was limited in Amoa, where any direction you ran led you swiftly back to your own doorstep. The wires that rigged the long sun could take you high, kilometers above it all in your grand indignation. Everyone would watch you through their telescopes, up there high and huffing, until you got hungry and wet and bored and had to come down again. In Amoa, the young soul rebels went *out.*

Fast Man set down his chocolate glass and began the subtle exercise that reconfigured the motes of his malleable body. To the Toe Yaus, he seemed to effervesce slightly, a sparkle like fine silver talc or the dust from a moth's wings. Jehau's eyes widened. All the three worlds knew of Fast Man, who had brought the end of the Journey suddenly within sight, soothed generational squabbles, and found errant children—and so everyone thought they knew him personally. Truly, he was an alien.

"It would help considerably if they left some idea of where they were going," Fast Man said. "There's a lot of space out there. Oh well. I'd stand back a little, by the way." He stood up, opened his arms in a little piece of theater, and exploded into a swarm of motes. He towered to a buzzing cylinder that rose from the iris at the center of the belvedere. *See this through your telescopes on the other side of the world and gossip.* Then, in a thought, he speared into the earth and vanished.

———

In the end, the Fast Boy was pretty much where Fast Man reckoned he would be. He came speed-walking up through the salt-dead cityscape of the communications gear just above the convex flaring of the drive shield, and there he was, nova-bright in Fast Man's radar sight. A sweet, neat little cranny in the main dish gantry with a fine view over the construction site. Boys and building. His complaining to the Toe Yaus had been part of the curmudgeonly image he liked to project. Boys were predictable things.

"Are you not getting a bit cold up there?" Fast Man asked. Yemoa started at the voice crackling in his helmet phones. He looked around, helmet tilting from side to side as he tried to pick the interloper out of the limitless shadow of interstellar space. Fast Man increased his surface radiance. He knew well how he must seem; a glowing man, naked to space, toes firmly planted on the pumice-dusted hull and leaning slightly forward against the spin force. He would have terrified himself at that age, but awe worked for the Fast Children as amiable curmudgeon worked for their slow parents.

"Go away."

Fast Man's body-shine illuminated the secret roots. Yemoa Toe Yau was spindly even in the tight yellow and green pressure skin. He shuffled around to turn his back, a deadlier insult among the Aeo Taea than among the Aspects of Tay for all their diverse etiquettes. Fast Man tugged at the boy's safety lanyard. The webbing was unfrayed, the carabiner latch operable.

"Leave that alone."

"You don't want to put too much faith in those things. Cosmic rays can weaken the structure of the plastic: put any tension on them, and they snap just like that, just when you need them most. Yes sir, I've seen people just go sailing out there, right away out there."

The helmet, decorated with bright bird motifs, turned toward Fast Man.

"You're just saying that."

Fast Man swung himself up beside the runaway and settled into the little nest. Yemoa wiggled away as far as the cramped space would permit.

"I didn't say you could come up here."

"It's a free ship."

"It's not *your* ship."

"True," said Fast Man. He crossed his legs and dimmed down his self-shine until they could both look out over the floodlit curve of the star drive works. The scalarity drive itself was a small unit—small by Amoa's vistas; merely the size of a well-established country manor. The heavy engineering that overshadowed it, the towering silos and domes and pipeworks, was the transfer system that converted water and antiwater into dark energy. Above all, the lampships hovered in habitat-stationary orbits, five small suns. Fast Man did not doubt that the site hived with desperate energy and activity, but to his Child Speed perceptions, it was as still as a painting, the figures in their bird-bright skinsuits, the heavy engineers in their long-duration work armor, the many robots and vehicles and little jetting skipcraft all frozen in time, moving so slowly that no individual motion was visible, but when you looked back, everything had changed. A long time even for a Parent, Fast Man sat with Yemoa. Beyond the construction lights, the stars arced past. How must they seem to the adults, Fast Man thought, and in that thought pushed down into Parent Speed and felt a breathless, deeply internalized gasp of wonder as the stars accelerated into curving streaks. The construction site ramped up into action, the little assembly robots and skippers darting here and there on little puffs of reaction gas.

Ten years, ten grown-up years, since Fast Man had osmosed through the hull and coalesced out of a column of motes onto the soil of Ga'atu Colony, and still he did not know which world he belonged to, Parent or Fast Children. There had been no Fast Children then, no children at all. That was the contract. When the Destination was reached, that was the time for children, born the old way, the fast way, properly adjusted to their new world. Fast Man had changed all that with the price of his rescue: the promise that the Destination could be reached not in slow years, not even in a slow season, but in hours—real hours. With a proviso: that they detour—a matter of moments to a relativistic fleet—to Fast Man's old home-world of Tay.

The meetings were concluded, the deal was struck, the Aeo Taea fleet's tight tight energy budget would allow it, just. It would mean biofuels and muscle power for the travelers; all tech resources diverted to assembling the three dark energy scalarity units. But the journey would be over in a single sleep. Then the generous forests and woodlands that carpeted the gently rolling midriffs of the colony cylinders all flowered and released genetweak pollen. Everyone got a cold for three days, everyone got pregnant, and nine Parent months later, the first of the Fast Children was born.

"So where's your clip?"

At the sound of Yemoa's voice, Fast Man geared up into Child Speed. The work on the dazzling plain froze; the stars slowed to a crawl.

"I don't need one, do I?" Fast Man added, "I know exactly how big space is."

"Does it really use dark energy?"

"It does."

Yemoa pulled his knees up to him, stiff from his long vigil in the absolute cold. A splinter of memory pierced Fast Man: the fast-frozen canals of Jann, the months-long dark. He shivered. Whose life was that, whose memory?

"I read about dark energy. It's the force that makes the universe expand faster and faster, and everything in it, you, me, the distance between us. In the end, everything will accelerate away so fast from everything else that the universe will rip itself apart, right down to the quarks."

"That's one theory."

"Every particle will be so far from everything else that it will be in a universe of its own. It will *be* a universe of its own."

"Like I said, it's a theory. Yemoa, your parents—"

"You use this as a space drive."

"Your matter-antimatter system obeys the laws of thermodynamics, and that's the heat-death of the universe. We're all getter older and colder and more and more distant. Come on, you have to come in. You must be uncomfortable in that suit."

The Aeo Taea skinsuits looked like flimsy dance costumes to don in the empty cold of interstellar space, but their hides were clever works of molecular technology, recycling and re-

freshing and repairing. Still, Fast Man could not contemplate
the itch and reek of one after days of wear.

"You can't be here on Starship Day," Fast Man warned.
"Particle density is very low out here, but it's still enough to fry
you, at lightspeed."

"We'll be the Slow ones then," Yemoa said. "A few hours
will pass for us, but in the outside universe, it will be fifty
years."

"It's all relative," Fast Man said.

"And when we get there," Yemoa continued, "we'll unpack
the landers and we'll go down and it'll be the new world, the
big Des Tin Ay Shun, but our moms and dads, they'll stay up in
the Three Worlds. And we'll work, and we'll build that new
world, and we'll have our children, and they'll have children,
and maybe we'll see another generation after that, but in the
end, we'll die, and the Parents up there in the sky, they'll hardly
have aged at all."

Fast Man draped his hands over his knees.

"They love you, you know."

"I know. I know that. It's not that at all. Did you think that?
If you think that, you're stupid. What does everyone see in you
if you think stuff like that? It's just . . . what's the point?"

None, Fast Man thought. *And everything. You are as much point
as the universe needs, in your yellow and green skinsuit and mad-bird
helmet and fine rage.*

"You know," Fast Man said, "whatever you think about it,
it's worse for them. It's worse than anything I think you can
imagine. Everyone they love growing old in the wink of an eye,
dying, and they can't touch them, they can't help, they're
trapped up there. No, I think it's so very much worse for them."

"Yah," said Yemoa. He slapped his gloved hands on his thin
knees. "You know, it is freezing up here."

"Come on then." Fast Man stood up and offered a silver
hand. Yemoa took it. The stars curved overhead. Together, they
climbed down from the aerial and walked back down over the
curve of the world, back home.

OGA, TEARING

He stood on the arch of the old Jemejnay bridge over the dead canal. Acid winds blew past him, shrieking on the honed edges of the shattered porcelain houses. The black sky crawled with suppressed lightning. The canal was a desiccated vein, cracked dry; even the centuries of trash wedged in its cracked silts had rusted away, under the bite of the caustic wind, to scabs and scales of slag. The lagoon was a dish of pure salt shimmering with heat haze. In natural light, it would have been blinding but no sun ever challenged the clouds. In Oga's extended vision, the old campanile across the lagoon was a snapped tooth of crumbling masonry.

A flurry of boiling acid rain swept over Oga as he turned away from the burning vista, from the dead stone arch, onto Ejtay Quay. His motes sensed and changed mode on reflex, but not before a wash of pain burned through him. Feel it. It is punishment. It is good.

The houses were roofless, floorless; rotted snapped teeth of patinated ceramic: had been for eight hundred years. Drunken Chicken Street. Here Kentlay the Lonely had sat out in the sun and passed the time of day with his neighbors and visitors come for his gift. Here were the Dilmajs and the vile, cruel little son who had caught birds and pulled their feathers so that they could not fly from his needles and knives, street bully and fat boy. Mrs. Supris, a sea widow, a baker of cakes and sweets, a keeper of mournings and ocean leavings. All dead. Long dead, dead with their city, their world.

This must be a mock Ctarisphay, a stage, a set, a play city for some moral tale of a prodigal, an abandoner. A traitor. Memories turned to blasted, glowing stumps. A city of ruins. A world in ruins. There was no sea anymore. Only endless poisoned salt. This could not be true. Yet this was his house. The acid wind had not yet totally erased the carved squid that stood over the door. Oga reached up to touch it. It was hot, biting hot; everything was hot, baked to an infrared glow by runaway greenhouse effect. To Oga's carbon-shelled fingertips, it was a small stone prayer, a whisper caught in a shell. If the world had permitted tears, the old, eroded stone squid would have called Oga's. Here was the hall, here the private parlor, curved in on itself like a ceramic musical instrument. The stairs, the upper floors, everything organic had evaporated centuries ago, but he could still read the niches of the sleeping porches cast in the upper walls. How would it have been in the end days, when even the summer sky was black from burning oil? Slow, painful, as year upon year the summer temperatures rose and the plankton blooms, carefully engineered to absorb the carbon from Tay's oil riches, died and gave up their own sequestered carbon.

The winds keened through the dead city and out across the empty ocean. With a thought, Oga summoned the ship. Ion glow from the reentry shone through the clouds. Sonic booms rolled across the sterile lagoon and rang from the dead porcelain houses. The ship punched out of the cloud base and unfolded, a sheet of nanomotes that, to Oga's vision, called memories of the ancient Bazjendi angels stooping down the burning wind. The ship beat its wings over the shattered campanile, then dropped around Oga like a possession. Flesh melted, flesh ran and fused, systems meshed, selves merged. Newly incarnate, Oga kicked off from Ejtay Quay in a pillar of fusion fire. Light broke around the empty houses and plazas, sent shadows racing down the desiccated canals. The salt pan glared white, dwindling to the greater darkness as the light ascended. With a star at his feet, Oga punched up through the boiling acid clouds, up and out until, in his extended shipsight, he could see the infraglow of the planet's limb curve against space. A tear of blood. Accelerating, Oga broke orbit.

Oga. The name was a festival. Father-of-all-our-Mirths, in subtly inflected Aeo Taea. He was Fast Man no more, no longer a sojourner; he was Parent of a nation. The Clave had ordained three Parent Days of rejoicing as the Aeo Taea colony cylinders dropped out of scalarity drive at the edge of the system. For the children, it had been a month of party. Looking up from the flat end of the cylinder, Oga had felt the light from his native star on his skin, subtle and sensitive in a dozen spectra. He masked out the sun and looked for those sparks of reflected light that were worlds. There Saltpeer, and great Bephis: magnifying his vision, he could see its rings and many moons; there Tejaphay. It, too, wore a ring now; the shattered icy remnants of the Anpreen Commonweal. And there; there: Tay. Home. Something not right about it. Something missing in its light. Oga had ratcheted up his sight to the highest magnification he could achieve in this form.

There was no water in the spectrum. There was no pale blue dot.

The Clave of Aeo Taea Interstellar Cantons received the message some hours after the surface crews registered the departure of the Anpreen splinter-ship in a glare of fusion light: *I have to go home.*

From five AUs out, the story became brutally evident. Tay was a silver ball of unbroken cloud. Those clouds comprised carbon dioxide, carbonic, and sulfuric acid, and a memory of water vapor. The surface temperature read at two hundred and twenty degrees. Oga's ship-self possessed skills and techniques beyond his hominiform self; he could see the perpetual lightning storms cracking cloud to cloud, but never a drop of pure rain. He could see through those clouds; he could peel them away so that the charred, parched surface of the planet lay open to his sight. He could map the outlines of the continents and the continental shelves lifting from the dried ocean. The chains of archipelagos, once jewels around the belly of a beautiful dancer, were ribs, bones, stark mountain chains glowing furiously in the infradark.

As he fell sunward, Oga put the story together. The Enemy had struck Tay casually, almost as an afterthought. A lone warship, little larger than the ritual catamaran on which the boy called Ptey had sailed from this quay so many centuries before, had detached itself from the main fleet action and swept the planet with its particle weapons, a spray of directed fire that set the oil fields burning. Then it looped carelessly back out of the system, leaving a world to suffocate. They had left the space elevator intact. There must be a way out. This was judgment, not murder. Yet two billion people, two thirds of the planet's population, had died.

One third had lived. One third swarmed up the life-rope of the space elevator and looked out at space and wondered where they could go. Where they went, Oga went now. He could hear their voices, a low em-band chitter from the big blue of Tejaphay. His was a long, slow chasing loop. It would be the better part of a year before he arrived in parking orbit above Tejaphay. Time presented its own distractions and seductions. The quantum array that was his heart could as easily re-create Tay as any of scores of cultures it stored. The midday aurora would twist and glimmer again above the steep-gabled roofs of Jann. He would fish with Cjatay from the old, weather-silvered fishing stands for the spring run of prith. The Sulanj islands would simmer and bask under the midnight sun and Puzhay would again nuzzle against him and press her body close against the hammering cold outside the Tea Lane Ladyhearth walls. They all could live, they all would believe they lived, *he* could, by selective editing of his consciousness, believe they lived again. He could re-create dead Tay. But it was the game of a god, a god who could take off his omniscience and enter his own delusion, and so Oga chose to press his perception down into a time flow even slower than Parent Time and watch the interplay of gravity wells around the sun.

On the final weeks of approach, Oga returned to world time and opened his full sensory array on the big planet that hung tantalizingly before him. He had come here before, when the Anpreen Commonweal hung around Tejaphay like pearls, but then he had given the world beneath him no thought, being inside a world complete in itself, and his curiosity turned outward to the shape of the universe. Now he beheld Tejaphay and remembered awe. Three times the diameter of Tay, Tejaphay was the true water world now. Ocean covered it pole to pole, a

hundred kilometers deep. Immense weather systems mottled
the planet, white on blue. The surviving spine of the Anpreen
space elevator pierced the eye of a perpetual equatorial storm
system. Wave trains and swells ran unbroken from equator to
pole to smash in stupendous breakers against the polar ice caps.
Oga drew near in sea meditation. Deep ocean appalled him in
a way that centuries of time and space had not. That was distance. This was hostility. This was elementary fury that knew
nothing of humanity.

Yet life clung here. Life survived. From two light-minutes
out, Oga had heard a whisper of radio communication, from
the orbit station on the space elevator, also from the planet's
surface. Scanning sub-Antarctic waters, he caught the unmistakable tang of smart-ice. A closer look: what had on first glance
seemed to be bergs revealed a more complex structure: Spires,
buttresses, domes, and sprawling terraces. Ice cities, riding the
perpetual swell. Tay was not forgotten: these were the ancient
Manifold Houses reborn, grown to the scale of vast Tejaphay.
Closer again: the berg city under his scrutiny floated at the center of a much larger boomed circle. Oga's senses teemed with
life signs. This was a complete ecosystem, and ocean farm, and
Oga began to appreciate what these refugees had undertaken.
No glimpse of life had ever been found on Tejaphay. Water-
worlds, thawed from ice giants sent spiraling sunward by the
gravitational play of their larger planetary rivals, were sterile.
At the bottom of the hundred-kilometer-deep ocean was pressure ice, five thousand kilometers of pressure ice down to the
iron core. No minerals, no carbon ever percolated up through
that deep ice. Traces might arrive by cometary impact, but the
waters of Tejaphay were deep and pure. What the Taynish had,
the Taynish had brought. Even this ice city was grown from the
shattered remnants of the Anpreen Commonweal.

A hail from the elevator station, a simple language algorithm. Oga smiled to himself as he compared the vocabulary
files to his own memory of his native tongue. Half a millennium
had changed the pronunciation and many of the words of

Taynish, but not its inner subtleties, the rhythmic and contextual clues as to which Aspect was speaking.

"Attention unidentified ship, this is Tejaphay Orbital Tower approach control. Please identify yourself and your flight plan."

"This is the Oga of the Aeo Taea Interstellar Fleet." He toyed with replying in the archaic speech. Worse than a breach of etiquette, such a conceit might give away information he did not wish known. Yet. "I am a representative with authority to negotiate. We wish to enter into communications with your government regarding fueling rights in this system."

"Hello, Oga, this is Tejaphay Orbital Tower. By the Aeo Taea Interstellar Fleet, I assume you refer to these objects." A subchatter on the data channel identified the cylinders, coasting in-system. Oga confirmed.

"Hello, Oga, Tejaphay Tower. Do not, repeat, do not approach the Tower docking station. Attain this orbit and maintain until you have been contacted by Tower security. Please confirm your acceptance."

It was a reasonable request, and Oga's subtler senses picked up missile foramens unfolding in the shadows of the Orbital Station solar array. He was a runner, not a fighter; Tejaphay's defenses might be basic fusion warheads and would need sustained precision hits to split open the Aeo Taea colony cans, but they were more than a match for Oga without the fuel reserves for full scalarity drive.

"I confirm that."

As he looped up to the higher ground, Oga studied more closely the berg cities of Tejaphay, chips of ice in the monstrous ocean. It would be a brutal life down there under two gravities, every aspect of life subject to the melting ice and the enclosing circle of the biosphere boom. Everything beyond that was as lifeless as space. The horizon would be huge and far and empty. City ships might sail for lifetimes without meeting another polis. The Taynish were tough. They were a race of the extremes. Their birthworld and its severe seasonal shifts had called forth a social response that other cultures would regard as mental disease, as socialized schizophrenia. Those multiple Aspects—a self for every need—now served them on the hostile vastnesses of Tejaphay's world ocean. They would survive, they would thrive. Life endured. This was the great lesson of the Clade: that life was hope, the only hope of escaping the death of the universe.

"*Every particle will be so far from everything else that it will be in a universe of its own. It will be a universe of its own,* a teenage boy in a yellow spacesuit had said up on the hull of mighty *Amoa,* looking out on the space between the stars. Oga had not answered at that time. It would have scared the boy, and though he had discovered it himself on the long flight from Milius 1183, he did not properly understand it himself, and in that gap of comprehension, he, too, was afraid. *Yes,* he would have said. *And in that is our only hope.*

Long-range sensors chimed. A ship had emerged around the limb of the planet. Consciousness is too slow a tool for the pitiless mathematics of space. In the split second that the ship's course, design, and drive signature had registered on Oga's higher cognitions, his autonomic systems had plotted course and fuel reserves, and engaged the scalarity drive. At a thousand gees, he pulled away from Tejaphay. Manipulating space-time so close to the planet would send gravity waves rippling through it like a struck gong. Enormous slow tides would circle the globe; the space elevator would flex like a crackled whip. Nothing to be done. It was instinct alone and by instinct he lived, for here came the missiles. Twenty nanotoc warheads on hypergee drives, wiping out his entire rearward vision in a white glare of lightweight MaM engines, but not before he had felt on his skin sensors the unmistakable harmonies of an Enemy deep-space scoopfield going up.

The missiles had the legs, but Oga had the stamina. He had calculated it thus. The numbers still came to him. Looking back at the blue speck into which Tejaphay had dwindled, he saw the engine sparks of the missiles wink out one after the other. And now he could be sure that the strategy, devised in nanoseconds, would pay off. The warship was chasing him. He would lead it away from the Aeo Taea fleet. But this would be no long stern chase over the light-decades. He did not have the fuel for that, nor the inclination. Without fuel, without weapons, he knew he must end it. For that, he needed space.

It was the same ship. The drive field harmonics, the spectrum of the fusion flame, the timbre of the radar images that he so gently, kiss-soft, bounced off the pursuer's hull, even the configuration he had glimpsed as the ship rounded the planet and launched missiles. This was the same ship that had hunted him down all the years. Deep mysteries here. Time dilation would compress his planned course to subjective minutes and Oga needed time to find an answer.

The ship had known where he would go even as they bucked the stormy cape of the wandering neutron star. It had never even attempted to follow him; instead, it had always known that it must lay in a course that would whip it around to Tay. That meant that even as he escaped the holocaust at Milius 1183, it had known who he was, where he came from, had seen through the frozen layers of smart-ice to the Torben below. The ship had come from around the planet. It was an enemy ship, but not the Enemy. They would have boiled Tejaphay down to its iron heart. Long Oga contemplated these things as he looped out into the wilderness of the Oort cloud. Out there among the lonely ice, he reached a conclusion. He turned the ship over and burned the last of his reaction in a hypergee deceleration burn. The enemy ship responded immediately, but its ramjet drive was less powerful. It would be months, years even, before it could turn around to match orbits with him. He would be ready then. The edge of the field brushed Oga as he decelerated at fifteen hundred gravities and he used his external sensors to modulate a message on the huge web, a million kilometers across: *I surrender.*

———

Gigayears ago, before the star was born, the two comets had met and entered into their far, cold marriage. Beyond the dra-

mas and attractions of the dust cloud that coalesced into Tay
and Tejaphay and Bephis, all the twelve planets of the solar system, they maintained their fixed-grin gazes on each other,
locked in orbit around a mutual center of gravity where a permanent free-floating haze of ice crystals hovered, a fraction of a
Kelvin above absolute zero. Hidden among them, and as cold
and seemingly as dead, was the splintership. Oga shivered. The
cold was more than physical—on the limits of even his malleable form. Within their thermal casing, his motes moved as
slowly as Aeo Taea Parents. He felt old as this ice and as weary.
He looked up into the gap between ice worlds. The husband-
comet floated above his head like a halo. He could have leaped
to it in a thought.

Lights against the starlight twinkle of the floating ice storm.
A sudden occlusion. The Enemy was here. Oga waited, feeling
every targeting sensor trained on him.

No, you won't, will you? Because you have to know.

A shadow detached itself from the black ship, darkest on
dark, and looped around the comet. It would be a parliament
of self-assembling motes like himself. Oga had worked out
decades before that Enemy and Anpreen were one and the
same, sprung from the same nanotechnological seed when they
attained Class Two status. Theirs was a civil war. *In the Clade, all
war was civil war,* Oga thought. Panhumanity was all there was.
More like a family feud. Yes, those were the bloodiest fights of
all. No quarter and no forgiveness.

The man came walking around the small curve of the
comet, kicking up shards of ice crystals from his grip soles. Oga
recognized him. He was meant to. He had designed himself so
that he would be instantly recognizable, too. He bowed, in the
distances of the Oort cloud.

"Torben Reris Orhum Fejannen Kekjay Prus Rejmer Serejen Nejben, sir."

The briefest nod of a head, a gesture of hours in the slow-
motion hypercold.

"Torben. I'm not familiar with that name."

"Perhaps we should use the name most familiar to you. That would be Serejen, or perhaps Fejannen. I was in that Aspect when we last met. I would have hoped you still remembered the old etiquette."

"I find I remember too much these days. Forgetting is a choice since I was improved. And a chore. What do they call you now?"

"Oga."

"Oga it shall be, then."

"And what do they call *you* now?"

The man looked up into the icy gap between worldlets. *He has remembered himself well,* Oga thought. *The slight portliness, the child-chubby features, like a boy who never grew up. As he says, forgetting is a chore.*

"The same thing they always have: Cjatay."

"Tell me your story then, Cjatay. This was never your fight, or my fight."

"You left her."

"She left *me,* I recall, and, like you, I forget very little these days. I can see the note still; I could re-create it for you, but it would be a scandalous waste of energy and resources. She went to you."

"It was never me. It was the cause."

"Do you truly believe that?"

Cjatay gave a glacial shrug.

"We made independent contact with them when they came. The Council of governments was divided, all over the place, no coherent approach or strategy. 'Leave us alone. We're not part of this.' But there's no neutrality in these things. We had let them use our system's water. We had the space elevator they built for us, there was the price, there was the blood money. We knew it would never work—our hope was that we could convince them that some of us had always stood against the Anpreen. They torched Tay anyway, but they gave us a deal.

They'd let us survive as a species if some of us joined them on their crusade."

"They *are* the Anpreen."

"*Were* the Anpreen. I know. They took me to pieces. They made us into something else. Better, I think. All of us, there were twenty-four of us. Twenty-four, that was all the good people of Tay, in their eyes. Everyone who was worth saving."

"And Puzhay?"

"She died. She was caught in the Arphan conflagration. She went there from Jann to be with her parents. It always was an oil town. They melted it to slag."

"But you blame me."

"You are all that's left."

"I don't believe that. I think it was always personal. I think it was always revenge."

"You still exist."

"That's because you don't have all the answers yet."

"We know the kind of creatures we've become; what answers can I not know?"

Oga dipped his head, then looked up to the halo moon, so close he could almost touch it.

"Do you want me to show you what they fear so much?"

There was no need for the lift of the hand, the conjurer's gesture; the pieces of his ship-self that Oga had seeded so painstakingly through the wife-comet's structure were part of his extended body. *But I do make magic here,* he thought. He dropped his hand. The star-speckled sky turned white, hard painful white, as if the light of every star were arriving at once. *An Olbers sky,* Oga remembered from his days in the turrets and cloisters of Jann. And as the light grew intolerable, it ended. Blackness, embedding, huge and comforting. The dark of death. Then Oga's eyes grew familiar with the dark, and, though it was the plan and always had been the plan, he felt a plaint of awe as he saw ten thousand galaxies resolve out of the Olbers dazzle. And he knew that Cjatay saw the same.

"Where are we? What have you done?"

"We are somewhere in the region of two hundred and thirty million light-years outside our local group of galaxies, more precisely, on the periphery of the cosmological galactic super-cluster known as the Great Attractor. I made some refinements to the scalarity drive unit to operate in a one-dimensional array."

"Faster-than-light travel," Cjatay said, his upturned face silvered with the light of the ten thousand galaxies of the Great Attractor.

"No, you still don't see it," Oga said, and again turned the universe white. Now when he flicked out of hyperscalarity, the sky was dark and starless but for three vast streams of milky light that met in a triskelion hundreds of millions of light-years across.

"We are within the Bootes Supervoid," Oga said. "It is so vast that if our own galaxy were in the center of it, we would have thought ourselves alone and that our galaxy was the entire universe. Before us are the Lyman alpha-blobs, three conjoined galaxy filaments. These are the largest structures in the universe. On scales larger than this, structure becomes random and grainy. We become gray. These are the last grand vistas. This is the end of greatness."

"Of course, the expansion of space is not limited by light-speed," Cjatay said.

"Still you don't understand." A third time, Oga generated the dark energy from the ice beneath his feet and focused it into a narrow beam between the wife-comet and its unimaginably distant husband. *Two particles in contact will remain in quantum entanglement no matter how far they are removed,* Oga thought. *And is that true also for lives?* He dismissed the scalarity generator and brought them out in blackness. Complete, impenetrable, all-enfolding blackness, without a photon of light.

"Do you understand where I have brought you?"

"You've taken us beyond the visible horizon," Cjatay said.

"You've pushed space so far that the light from the rest of the universe has not had time to reach us. We are isolated from every other part of reality. In a philosophical sense, we are a universe in ourselves."

"That was what they feared? You feared?"

"That the scalarity drive had the potential to be turned into a weapon of unimaginable power? Oh yes. The ability to remove any enemy from reach, to banish them beyond the edge of the universe. To exile them from the universe itself, instantly and irrevocably."

"Yes, I can understand that, and that you did what you did altruistically. They were moral genocides. But our intention was never to use it as a weapon—if it had been, wouldn't we have used it on you?"

Silence in the darkness beyond dark.

"Explain then."

"I have one more demonstration."

The mathematics were critical now. The scalarity generator devoured cometary mass voraciously. If there were not enough left to allow him to return them home . . . Trust number, Oga. You always have. Beyond the edge of the universe, all you have is number. There was no sensation, no way of perceiving when he activated and deactivated the scalarity field, except by number. For an instant, Oga feared number had failed him, a first and fatal betrayal. Then light blazed down onto the dark ice. A single blinding star shone in the absolute blackness.

"What is that?"

"I pushed a single proton beyond the horizon of this horizon. I pushed it so far that space and time tore."

"So I'm looking at—"

"The light of creation. That is an entire universe, newborn. A new big bang. A young man once said to me, "Every particle will be so far from everything else that it will be in a universe of its own. It will *be* a universe of its own." An extended object like this comet, or bodies, is too gross, but in a single photon, quantum fluctuations will turn it into an entire universe-in-waiting."

The two men looked up a long time into the nascent light, the surface of the fireball seething with physical laws and forces boiling out. *Now you understand,* Oga thought. *It's not a weapon. It's the way out. The way past the death of the universe. Out there beyond the horizon, we can bud off new universes, and universes from those universes, forever. Intelligence has the last word. We won't die alone in the cold and the dark.* He felt the light of the infant universe on his face, then said, "I think we probably should be getting back. If my calculations are correct—and there is a significant margin of error—this fireball will shortly undergo a phase transition as dark energy separates out and undergoes catastrophic expansion. I don't think that the environs of an early universe would be a very good place for us to be."

He saw portly Cjatay smile.

"Take me home, then. I'm cold and I'm tired of being a god."

"Are we gods?"

Cjatay nodded at the microverse.

"I think so. No, I know I would want to be a man again."

Oga thought of his own selves and lives, his bodies and natures. Flesh indwelled by many personalities, then one personality—one aggregate of experience and memory—in bodies liquid, starship, nanotechnological. And he *was* tired, so terribly tired beyond the universe, centuries away from all that he had known and loved. All except this one, his enemy.

"Tejaphay is no place for children."

"Agreed. We could rebuild Tay."

"It would be a work of centuries."

"We could use the Aeo Taea Parents. They have plenty of time."

Now Cjatay laughed.

"I have to trust you now, don't I? I could have vaporized you back there, blown this place to atoms with my missiles. And now you create an entire universe."

"And the Enemy? They'll come again."

"You'll be ready for them, like you were ready for me. After all, I am still the enemy."

The surface of the bubble of universe seemed to be in more frenetic motion now. The light was dimming fast.

"Let's go then," Cjatay said.

"Yes," Oga said. "Let's go home."

OGA, RETURNING